Heart of Flesh

Namesake Chronicles: Book 4

By Rachel Marie Lang

Namesake Chronicles:

Heart of Stone

Hearts of Lead

Heart of Ashes

Heart of Flesh

Publisher: Rachel Lang Books
ISBN-13:978-1-999-1485-1-5

DEDICATION

To all who dream, fail, and dream again.

Jeremiah 19:11

"For I know the plans I have for you," declares the Lord, "plans to prosper you and not to harm you, plans to give you hope and a future."

List of characters

Captain Multifarious (Farious) – a high ranking Tarvin soldier
Captain Splendor – a high ranking Tarvin soldier
Courage (Rage) – a Tarvin soldier
Dire – a warrior from the city Estewryn in the Niben Weald, protector of Lady Roam
Dol – a Garatin woman, friend of Eam, mother of Mayhap and Fin
Dream (Eam) – a Garatin servant of Brier Ridge, handmaiden of Gime
Dynasty (Dyna) – betrothed of Theophany
Garden – a Garatin slave
Governor Endure – Tarvin governor of Garatin
Lady Loyal (Loy) – a lady of Tarva, betrothed of Rage
Lady Quell – a Tarvin lady, mother of Rage
Lady Regime (Gime) – a Tarvin lady, daughter of Lord Eloquence
Lady Roam – a princess from the Niben Weald
Lady Serene – a lady of the eastern courts of Fairthin, wisdom seeker
Lord Eloquence – a Tarvin, lord of Brier Ridge
Lord Tenacious (Acious) – a young Tarvin lord, son of Lord Eloquence
Manifest (Anifest) – Garatin rebel leader, Rebel Queen
Mayhap – a Garatin girl
Navigate (Avi) – a Garatin servant of Brier Ridge, mother of Eam
Rend – a Verlyance youth in the prince's company
Salvage (Sal) – Royal warrior of Verlyance, wife of Vig
Sir Fortress – a giant knight from Stonemark
The Ancient One – a mysterious being of unknown origin
The Foretold King – a Verlyance prophecy
Theophany (Theoph) – prince of Verlyance
The Prince of the Dawn and Dusk – the Niben prince of old
The Wise One – a Fairthin prophecy
Tylus – Sea god of Verlyance
Vigil (Vig) – Royal warrior of Verlyance, husband of Sal
Voy – a child who speaks for the Ancient One
Wilderness (Wilder) - a Garatin soldier in the Tarvin army

Prologue

The shouts and cries of soldiers sparring in the training courtyard echoed through the Tarvin barracks as midmorning sunlight streamed through small windows, intensifying the stench of sweat and the hazy smell of nearby stables. The sound of carts, horses, and other foot traffic from the streets outside filled the silence between the soldiers' voices.

A boy of eleven worked in the empty sleeping quarters, with a rag and a meticulous eye, he cleaned and polished a pile of battered and well used short swords. Glancing up, he craned his neck to see down the hall to the training courtyard; he was completely alone. Unable to resist any longer, he took up one of the blades and stood. Readjusting his grip a couple times on the hilt, he aimed an experimental swing through the air. Unsatisfied, he tried again, this time with more vigor; the blade sliced through the air, and he was rewarded with a pleasing whistle as the air parted around the blade's tip. Grinning, the boy checked down the hall once more.

Taking a stance that he had seen the soldiers do when training, the boy practiced swinging and stabbing. He imagined himself as a soldier on the battlefield, laying low his enemies and besting every opponent. Each new thrust he made held more power than the last. Becoming more excited and less calculated he ducked and spun, lunging out towards the door, blade extended.

"WATCH IT!"

The sword twisted out of the boy's hand and clattered to the stone floor. Three Tarvin soldiers had entered the room, the first of which the boy had nearly stabbed through the gut. Being quick on his feet, the soldier had deflected the blade with his thick leather vambrace.

"Back to your work boy!" he said angrily, cuffing the boy's head roughly.

The boy's face burned in embarrassment, and he stepped aside, allowing the soldiers to pass.

"I've had enough Garatins try to stab me today!" the first soldier declared, the other two snickered in amusement.

The boy's embarrassment turned to anger, "I'm not Garatin!" he insisted with venom, "I'm Tarvin!"

The soldiers laughed even more and flopped onto their bunks.

"Take it easy kid," a fourth soldier said from the door.

The boy turned to him, "I *am* Tarvin!" he repeated, "My father is a Tarvin soldier- and I will be too!" he shouted at the other three when their laughter grew in volume.

The fourth soldier grimaced; the boy could acquire the darkest tan this side of the Neenor, but it still wouldn't hide his blue eyes and shock of blond hair. The soldier thought of his own mixed blood; it was just luck that he hadn't inherited any of the distinctive features that marked this boy as Garatin. "You won't ever be a soldier with that attitude," he said flatly.

Hurt registered on the boy's young face and the soldier was moved to take pity on him. "Come here," he instructed, stepping closer, "There's a dagger on me; can you locate it without touching me?" he challenged.

Eager to prove himself, the boy's eyes raced up and down the soldier, "In your left vambrace!" he said, pointing to the soldier's forearm.

The soldier hid a pleased smile; the kid had found it sooner than he thought he would, "Good observation is a soldier's best weapon."

"If I can lift it without you noticing- can I keep it?" the boy asked boldly.

This time the soldier couldn't hold back his smile; the kid was gutsy!

"Watch it Endor- he'll be an expert pickpocket, Garatin's are born thieving," one of the others warned.

The boy turned on them angrily.

"Pay them no mind," Endor advised, ignoring his comrades, "Going into a fight angry will get you killed. This is the attitude I was talking about; anger and blind passion are fine enough weapons for the average foot soldier. You want to rise above them? Keep a clear mind." He picked up the short sword that had clattered to the floor earlier. It was a training blade for new recruits; dull and quite harmless. "Show me that thrust you were doing," he invited, handing the blade to the boy, hilt first.

The boy took the blade and gripped it tightly.

"Ease up on your grip there," Endor instructed, stepping alongside the boy, "Too tight and your weapon will snap out of your hand with the first blow, too loose? Same problem." He was pleased to see the boy's grip readjust.

"You're wasting your time with that one!" the other soldiers jeered.

The boy tensed. "Clear mind," Endor reminded quietly, "Now thrust and swing," he instructed and stepped back.

The boy took a calming breath, then went for it. Endor reached in quickly and delivered a playful jab to the boy's unguarded ribs. The boy grunted in surprise and spun to face him, his blade cutting carelessly through empty air. Endor dodged him effortlessly and started circling him, "As long as your opponent can make you angry- they can control you. Keep a clear mind and you'll always be one step ahead of them," he explained, "Try to land a blow," he invited, confident in his own evasion skills.

The boy watched him wearily before lunging at him wildly. Endor anticipated his movements a moment before they happened and deflected the blade with his vambrace just as his comrade had done, only this time the boy didn't lose the blade.

"Good!" Endor praised, choosing not to critique the boy's poor form and floppy movements, "Try again."

The boy took a moment to steady himself, then grinned confidently.

The corner of Endor's mouth tipped upward; he knew what the boy would do even before he moved.

The boy charged and thrust with his sword arm. With a subtle sidestep, Endor pinned the blade to his side, wrenching it from the boy's grip. "Overconfidence can kill you too-" his words ended abruptly when he found his own dagger held against his throat.

The boy stood, looking up at Endor, his grin had turned to an incorrigible smile.

"Well done!" Endor exclaimed, honestly impressed. He hadn't felt a thing!

The boy stepped back, eyes shining, the other three soldiers had grown silent and watched with slack jaws.

"That's the spirit!" Endor praised, "You have the heart of a soldier- I have no doubt!"

The boy blushed and held out the dagger, hilt first, all earlier anger eclipsed.

"Keep it! You've earned it kid," Endor said, tousling the boy's hair, "What's your namesake soldier?"

The boy beamed up at him, "Wilderness, sir!"

Chapter 1 Disgrace

The rowers picked up speed as the small royal war boat cut through the narrows into the harbor, a fleet of fourteen following them ashore. The stiff sea breeze that had been at their back shifted and blew into the faces of the sea weary warriors, carrying the noise of the harbor with it. Crowds had gathered on the docks and in the city streets, they had been alerted to the fleet's homecoming only a few minutes before and yet it seemed the whole island had come. The breeze brought the sound of their welcoming cry to the boats; hats were tossed in the air; triumphant horns were blown, and a choir of voices rose to drown out the others. They sang the Verlyance song of victory, it bolstered the rower's energy and they cut through the water swiftly.

Sal, royal warrior, turned away from the harbor to survey the rowers; they were the lucky ones. The sea battle against the pirates had not been at all what they had expected. They had won and destroyed the fleet of the twice cursed pirate king, the Sea Serpent, but victory had come at a high cost. They had left their island capital of Verlynn Nel three days ago with a fleet of twenty-two war boats; they now returned with only fifteen. The last exchange of blows had been before dawn that morning. Many had died and most were injured, but the Sea Serpent and his fleet had been utterly defeated and peace restored to the isles.

Sal flinched when one of the rowers, still in gore smeared armor, fumbled his oar and slipped clumsily onto the boat bottom, his limbs failing to break his fall. Sal rushed to him, left over adrenaline struggling to overpower her fatigue. Reaching the warrior, she slipped her hands under his arms to raise him back up, "On your feet, we're nearly home!"

The man gazed up at her, he was breathing raggedly, and his dark skin was slick with sweat. Sal's right hand slipped and came away dark red; he was bleeding badly from an untended wound.

"Vigil!" Sal called sharply to the other royal warrior. He abandoned his position at the stern by the prince's side and came without hesitation.

"He's wounded badly; we must get him ashore at once!" Sal instructed quickly but calmly as she stowed the warrior's oar and propped him up to be carried on Vigil's broad shoulders.

Blood from the past three days was still smeared across Vigil's wide brow, and sweat dripped from his nose, betraying his own exhaustion, "It's too late," he said grimly, gently holding the warrior's head.

Sal hesitated, masking her disappointment; she thought she had seen the last of death for that day. She closed the man's eyelids, ending his sightless gaze. Leaning over the prow of the boat she scooped a hand full of the salty brine and splashed it on the chest of the fallen warrior.

Vigil laid the man back down and whispered a final farewell, ending the warrior's death rite. Sal and Vigil shared a look, thinking of all the others they had lost. The crowd's victory song sounded suddenly hollow in their ears.

"It is good he died here," Sal spoke above the growing clamor. To die away from the sea was worse than death itself.

Vigil turned to another rower, "See that his body is taken to the sea grave," he instructed. Sal and Vigil stood and left the body, pushing their grief behind a warrior's demeanor. Soon the fleet would dock, and they would be expected to join the celebrations.

Sal made her way to the stern where the prince sat facing the sea, his slumped back to the island. He had not spoken since the battle was won. Sal breathed deeply through her nose; she had feared how the battle would affect the prince but did not foresee the loss of Courteous. He had died the night before; his body lost in the waves.

"My lord, we will dock soon," she said softly and knelt to be level with him.

Prince Theophany did not respond to Sal, his dark brown eyes were closed, and grime was smudged across his face in a careless attempt to wipe it off.

"Courteous would not have his death marred by self pity, my prince." Sal didn't realize how tactless her words sounded to someone who was unused to battle. "He died a noble death and--"

Prince Theophany cut off her words as he looked up, "The young fool always talked of a swift end," he said airily, his eyes dry, "I'm glad he got it."

Sal rocked back on her feet, uncertain how to respond.

Theophany smiled, but there was cynicism in it, "Come Salvage," he said addressing her by full namesake, "The people will think we returned in defeat with such long faces!" He stood and turned to the crowd as the war boat came alongside the dock.

The people roared in excitement and pride at the sight of him, he raised a hand- his left, while his right remained at his side, limp, the bandaged wound obviously causing discomfort; would anyone notice?

"Is he alright?" Vigil asked close to Sal's ear as she followed the prince, she tightened her lips in response and shook her head ever so slightly.

A royal litter, carried on the shoulders of strong slaves, waited for them, ready to bear the prince through the city. Sal and Vigil assumed positions on either side of the prince.

★ ★ ★ ★

Theophany couldn't believe the energy of the crowd as he left the docks. He expected to find mourning widows and heartbroken kin; didn't they know it was a bitter victory? Climbing into the litter, Theophany avoided eye contact, wishing the crowd would go away.

"CHAMPION OF VERLYANCE!" someone shouted from the crowd.

Theophany glanced over to see who the title was meant for. He was met with the shining faces of his own warriors as they embraced their kin.

"We owe him our lives!" one of them added earnestly, more and more eyes were turning toward the prince.

"THEOPHANY THE VICTORIOUS!" a man shouted, his eyes locking onto Theophanys.

If they only knew. The title was picked up by others and soon the harbor was ringing with it! Overwhelmed, the prince thumped his hand twice on the pole of his litter. "To the palace," he instructed.

Nearby, Salvage and Vigil worked to keep the people from pressing too close to the litter, while others tried to clear a path before them. The shouting continued, and word spread quickly; everyone hailed him as a hero.

Theoph shifted his wounded arm as the litter at last began to move forward, his wound was not a deep one, but even a scratch to his flesh could prove dangerous if it was found out by his people.

Sitting up straighter, Theophany rejected his fear and looked out over the crowd with as much pride as his damaged soul could muster. The crowd grew with each street they passed, more and more abandoned their work to join the joyous procession while the warriors led the people in cheering, repeating the prince's new title and spreading the story of their victory over the sea pirates.

In this way they traveled up the city streets, passing hovels and fish markets cluttered with baskets and nets. The crowd continued to grow in size and volume till Theophany's ears rang with the clamor. He did not mind though, the louder it grew the less he could linger on the horrors of the battle or the loss of Courteous.

The landscape changed as they climbed higher into the island. The hovels turned into multi leveled stone houses with luxuriant walled-in gardens and courtyards. Here Theophany and the warriors were adorned with flower necklaces, the fragrant flowers masking the stench of blood on their armor.

Soon the palace of Verlynn Nel came into full view, perched high and strong. The late morning sunlight glowed on its walls of living coral, while the golden spiers of the sea temple glittered behind it. Trumpets blasted from the palace and the gates were thrown open, warriors with the royal emblem marched out to welcome the homecoming prince.

Before crossing the threshold of the palace, Theophany braved a look back at the crowd; they adored him. They did not know the truth. The litter was carried through the gates, leaving the crowd behind, but the palace was hardly a safe refuge.

The palace of Verlynn Nel was not as large as the outside appeared to be. It housed a mere sixty people, including the royal house and the nobility. Many of the slaves who served in the palace lived elsewhere. The king's man slave waited for the prince inside the grand entrance. He was old and shrewd; his embroidered tunic spoke to his favoured position with the king, "My lord prince!" he greeted, bowing low.

Theophany stopped before him growing wary of what the slave would say next.

"The king requests your presence in the throne room," the slave said, as he rose.

Theophany abandoned any hope of changing from his battle garments before facing his father, and his thoughts returned to his forbidden wound. The slave's eyes darted to his arm; he knew exactly where to look. The king already knew.

"Very well," Theophany said, holding his head high and straightening his shoulders. A group of slaves, courtiers and noblemen passed by Theophany as he approached the throne room at an even pace, Sal and Vigil keeping a three-step distance behind him. Dreading what state he would find his father in, Theophany entered the throne room, Sal and Vigil stayed to guard the doors as they closed.

Large windows set high above allowed sunlight to flood the room and cast golden light onto the exquisitely crafted throne room of living coral. Every surface was carved with sharp detail but none more than the throne itself which sat upon a dais three steps up.

The king, Theophany's father, stood facing his throne with his back to his son. It was an obvious passive aggressive insult to whoever entered the room. His father clearly wished to arouse his son's anger before even beginning their discussion; Theophany was determined not to be manipulated though.

"I have destroyed the armies of the Sea Serpent," Theophany boasted as he came to stand at the foot of the steps leading up to the throne.

The king turned to look at his son, his eyes going straight to his wounded arm, "And yet you return in disgrace!" he hissed in anger.

"Disgrace!?" Theophany repeated in well prepared outraged, "The people line the streets and celebrate our country's mastery over the sea! You can still hear them now, hailing me victorious- you see disgrace in *this*!?"

The king descended the steps swiftly and seized Theophany's arm, to examine the bandage. Theophany pulled away before he could and glared at his father, daring him to say something.

"Yes, I see disgrace!" the king snapped, veins in his face popping out, "Do you deny that you deliberately put yourself in harm's way to save mere shield warriors!?"

Theophany felt his anger rise, "I will not have my actions in battle called into question!" he firmly stated, refraining from saying the name of the 'mere shield warrior' who had died despite his attempted intervention.

"You are the prophesied king!" his father reminded with venom, "Not some expendable spare son! Your place in battle is in the rear!" he emphasized with a forceful point, "Where you can observe, strategize, and retreat when necessary! The people believe you to be near immortal! And yet you throw yourself in the heat of battle, nearly killing yourself!"

His father turned away in anger. Theophany clenched his teeth, his pride smarting under his father's chastising.

"How many saw you bleed?" the king demanded to know sharply.

Theophany huffed in frustration, "I don't know father! It's a minor wound!"

"It is doubt in the minds of those who thought you invincible as the prophecy promised!" his father snapped, then his eyes moved past him to Vigil and Salvage.

Without turning to look, Theophany winced; Vigil had more faith in him than he did himself!

"Leave! You are dismissed," the king instructed, obviously anxious not to have any more of their words heard by others.

Vigil and Sal obeyed.

"Yes, I see disgrace," the king repeated, regaining self control, "You treat your own namesake as a mockery!" the king accused with scorn.

Theophany took a calming breath, "I can do no right in your eyes, can I? Defeating the scourge of our nation in glorious battle- is that not enough for you!?"

The king turned away in disgust and frustration. "And you would be the greatest king ever known," he muttered.

"Perhaps the prophecy was wrong," Theophany suggested quietly, his heart heavy with shame and regret.

The king stared at him, open mouthed. "Banish those doubts from your mind. They are the weak thoughts of mortal men," he said with a subdued tone, "You are destined to surpass even the greatest of our kings! You can not do that while bound to your humanity!"

"But I *am* only human!" Theophany felt his throat constrict; the battle with the pirates proved that quite clearly.

"Come," the king commanded and turned to exit the throne room by another door.

Fighting to control his emotions, Theophany made his feet follow his father, but he felt like his heart was left behind in ragged scraps. The king led him down passages and corridors before coming to the royal treasury; this chamber was made of stone instead of the crystal and was locked behind a small wooden door. Four warriors stood guard. The king withdrew a key and unlocked the door, Theophany followed him inside.

Verlyance was a small kingdom, with a small army, which was now even smaller. The island kingdom did not boast of large amounts of riches, nearly all the kingdom's wealth was held in the treasury room that was hardly large enough to accommodate eight men. Three large chests of gold sat locked tight, jewels and crowns were displayed on rich cloth and in the far wall were two alcoves, each one held a small box.

The king walked past the other riches and instead went to the alcoves. "In his twenty-first year, the sea god saw fit to honor your great grandfather and predict his future reign," the king spoke at last as he took one of the boxes and opened it. Inside were three sea stars the color of gold. "These precious talismans washed up on the royal beach as the sea god's gift. The sea priests discerned what they meant; the young prince would soon be the greatest king in all the seas."

This was history that Theophany knew well, but he listened mutely.

"Under your great-grandfather's reign, Verlyance prospered like never before." The king spoke with heavy emphasis, "He raised our first formidable fleet, and our people became feared and respected."

Theophany refused to meet his father's eyes, and instead studied the sea stars as if they were new to him.

"The sea is never wrong," the king stated with certainty and closed the box. He then raised the second box, "Then, in your eighteenth year; not three, but *five* sea stars washed up."

He opened the box and the golden talismans laid within, as bright gold as they were the first time Theophany had been shown them as a youth. It was a wonder to behold, prophecy aside; sea stars died when kept out of the water and turned white. But not these. They remained the same, as if mocking Theophany's failure to fulfill their promise of greatness.

The king put the trunk aside and took his son by the shoulders, "You are meant to surpass even your great grandfather. To do so, you must put aside your doubts and claim your inheritance. Arise above these mortal bound ways and you will transcend mere flesh. Let go of your desire to be one of them and become more than a king! Become a god in their eyes and your namesake will live till the end of time!"

Theophany bore his father's intense gaze without comment, the muscles in his face tightening.

His father made a sound of frustration. "Have the mutes bandage your arm," he instructed, "Tell no one else of your wound. Anyone found speaking of it, will be flogged; it never happened. Understood?"

Theophany nodded, disgusted with the secrecy. Anytime he had been wounded before the sea stars washed up in his eighteenth year, it was never an issue. But now, it seemed the sea would dry up and the world would end if anyone found out that he bled like everyone else!

* * * *

"Your offering is accepted," the priest said, as the gold coins fell into a small pool of standing water.

'They better!' Vigil thought cynically, he couldn't seem to rid himself of his cynicism after the battle.

The priest, with his flowing robes, bid him enter the inner chamber of the temple. Past the gapping archway of living coral, Vigil descended a flight of spiral steps that seemed to go on forever, the shadows growing and distorting shapes between torches. All was silent in the temple, it was something Vigil had grown to hate; silent, just like the gods.

The echo of water dripping and landing in a deep cavern pool announced he had reached the bottom. Here the stairs led into a wide chamber, the walls disappeared into darkness, while steps descended into a natural freshwater pool.

Vigil stood at the pool edge, soaking in the stillness, and hoping against hope that this time… the sea god Tylus would speak to him, the whisper of a single word would be enough.

Slowly he descended into the pool, fully dressed in his battle armor, the cold, fresh water enveloped him, washing away salt brine, and cleansing his soul. At least, that is what the temple priests claimed. He spent long minutes, soaking in the pool, meditating, straining his ears, searching his heart. Silence was his only answer.

When he could wait no longer, he climbed the stairs, dripping, his muscles aching from the abuse they had suffered in battle. At the top he was met by one of the other priests. Vigil bowed his head in respect, hoping he wouldn't be detained; he had no wish to speak to men who heard from the gods every day.

"Victory in battle," the priest said, he was one of the important ones.

Vigil nodded, "Indeed, I have offered my thanks to Tylus for our good fortune."

"And where is Salvage?" the priest's voice rose in pitch.

Vigil grimaced, "Not here." He tried to move past the insistent man.

"We have not seen her for weeks," the priest observed with accusation, "Not before your battle to ask for safety, nor even now to offer gratitude."

Vigil shrugged, "I suppose not." Mentally cursing Sal for putting him in this scenario. He moved past the priest towards the doors.

"We look forward to seeing her soon," the priest raised his voice so that Vigil would be sure to hear him.

'Yes, and her generous donations too!' the cynical thought nearly forced its way out of Vigil's mouth. "I will tell her as much," he assured and left, passing one of the other warriors on his way in.

'Will *his* gold buy him a message from Tylus?' Vigil wondered as he made his way past the palace and through the city to his home in the upper streets. The sun had begun its descent in the sky, but the heat of the day was still thick in the air, making Vigil's armor even more unbearable.

His thoughts became increasingly heavy the further he walked, and he nearly missed his house. It was a modest two-story stone abode, he could have had larger, but he never had much time to enjoy his estate to begin with.

A servant boy saw him coming and ran out to open the courtyard gate and lead him inside where a group of slaves silently removed Vigil's wet and worn armor. He stood still, pensive, his thoughts returning to fallen warriors, and how he would never train with them again. When the last of his armor was removed, Vigil went to the water room where he washed up, spending long minutes with his eyes fixed on some middle distance that only he could see.

It was an hour before he walked into his gardens, clean and refreshed, wearing simple garments, loose and airy. He walked along the garden path, and it seemed to him that his own garden did a better job at 'cleansing' his soul than the waters of the temple ever did.

He climbed a flight of steps up to a gazebo that stood high enough to view the sea over the surrounding rooftops. The structure had a pink hue to it and was made of crystal rock that they called 'living coral'. The strange crystal grew up from the ground wherever it pleased, forming new layers and formations through the years; it could be carved with a chisel and hammer to whatever shape you wished. Due to its ever-growing nature, it had to be maintained often, many a plant and building on the islands had found themselves slowly enveloped in the living coral. The largest crystal formation on the islands was that which the palace and temple were carved from.

Sitting on a bench with one leg tucked under her, in the shade of the gazebo, was Vigil's wife. Her back was straight, and her ebony locks of woven hair were carelessly tied back. Her lavender dress billowed and twisted in the wind as she gazed out to sea with eyes that could both laugh all by themselves and convince you to give up an argument. She was like a rock out in the sea, standing above the waves in defiance, never wavering, always certain and sharp like a blade edge.

"You risk the temple's wrath, wife," Vigil informed her without ceremony.

She smiled up at him boldly, her wide face and high cheekbones defying him as usual, "Let me worry about the temple's wrath; I can withstand it fine."

"Yes of course, I only worry that I could be singed standing next to you," he sarcastically complained and sat beside her.

She leaned her head on his shoulder, "And yet you remain by my side."

"No place better," Vigil sighed and kissed the top of her head.

They sat in each other's company, content.

"I gave my thanks to Tylus for our safe return," he shared softly.

"Did you receive a reply?" she asked, just as subdued.

"Have I ever?"

Sal was quiet, sharing in his frustration and sorrow.

"What of you?" Vigil asked, "Have you heard from your mysterious, nameless god?"

Sal didn't answer, it was answer enough though. Vigil stood up abruptly to brace his arms against the gazebo's low wall, the sea breeze cooling his face.

"I had another vision earlier," Sal confessed softly.

Vigil nodded, trying to be happy for his wife who seemed to have effortlessly stumbled across an unknown god who was more than eager to be close to her.

"What am I doing wrong?" he asked softly, "Am I being punished for my doubts?"

Sal rose and placed her battle-scarred arms around him, "I would give up my favor with the gods if it meant you could have peace."

Vigil knew she meant it, and he loved her even more. "I suppose your faith will have to be enough for both of us!" he said lightly, struggling to put aside his heavy thoughts.

"Don't give up Vig," she encouraged him with his shortened name, "Perhaps the silence you experience is just the height of battle before victory."

Vigil nodded, growing serious again, "I hope so, I do not know how much longer I can be strong for the prince."

Sal shifted, knowing of what he spoke.

"I see his self doubt increase with every day." When the sea had prophesied about the future of the young prince, Vig had believed that Theophany would at last be his guide to the gods. Now though, it seemed that the prince had as many doubts as Vig did himself. "We must be strong for him," he added softly, knowing how highly the prince valued his and Sal's faith in him.

Theophany looked up to see Lady Dynasty's maid servants clustered about the steps that led down to the royal beach. They hurried out of his way and bowed to him as he passed, beyond them, standing before the surf, was Lady Dynasty herself.

Although still early evening, the sun was setting, releasing the island from its stifling heat. Stars were coming to life in the dark purple sky and sea birds were returning to their nests. Nothing here spoke of the carnage and death that Theophany had been witness to before the sun had risen that morning. Theophany hurried down the last of the steps, making sure that his warriors remained behind.

Dynasty turned at his approach, her dark skin glowing and eyes shining at the sight of him. He bowed and she offered her hand.

"Theoph," she spoke his shortened name with an edge of frost that took him by surprise, "You kept me waiting, again."

He looked up from her hand and in the last glow of daylight saw the smile hiding on her full lips, he placed a hand on his heart to match her jesting. "Alas, the court would have proven more deadly than the pirates if I had tried to take leave of them early," he explained, and it was quite true, "The lords and ladies wanted to hear the battle retold at least thirty times, and they were still unsatisfied."

Dyna leaned away from him mischievously, "And just how exactly do you intend on asking for my forgiveness?"

Theoph lowered himself, not without difficulty, to one knee, "Will begging do?" he asked, finding it easy to be light of heart with his love.

Dyna laughed, "Hardly! I was hoping that you were detained for so long because you were arranging a certain ceremony?" she danced around the subject of their wedding, a child-like giddiness taking over.

Theoph rose to his feet and sighed, sorry to disappoint her, "I'm afraid not my love."

"He gave his word!" she insisted, "He said to you that if you defeated the Sea Serpent, we could be wed!"

"I'm sure the matter of our union is the last thing on my dear father's mind, right after being proud of me."

Dyna winced, doing her best to hide her disappointment. "You judge him too harshly," she scolded half-heartedly.

Theoph sighed again and looked at her, taking in every little detail of her face, "And you judge him too kindly. What did I do to deserve you?"

She smiled coyly, "Your folly is to assume that you *do* deserve me."

Theoph laughed, and stepped closer to her, but she stopped his kiss with a hand on his chest.

"We are not alone, my lord," she reminded ruefully.

Theoph sighed deeply and turned to the steps where her maid servants and his warriors were watching, unabashedly.

"I speak now to inform you," Theophany rose his voice boldly to address the small crowd, "that I and the Lady Dynasty will be running away to sea where we will perform our own wedding ceremony! Please inform my father!"

Dyna clung to him, giggling and begging him to stop. Theophany stifled his own chuckles at the shocked expressions on the servants and warriors alike.

The oldest of Dyna's maid servants, who had a stern face and fearsome eyebrows, marched down the steps, hitching her skirts high. She glowered at Theophany, and full of wrath, pointed a bold finger at him, "No you will *not*!" she declared and grabbed hold of Dyna, "Come along child! That's quite enough skylarking!"

"Now look at what you've done!" Dyna scolded Theoph between her giggles as she was nearly dragged away.

"This stays between us," Theophany informed his warriors who watched with barely contained amusement, they all nodded. Theoph trusted Dyna's 'keeper' to make sure his brash claim would not reach the ears of anyone else. He almost *did* wish his father would hear of his declaration though, perhaps then he would relent and give his blessing.

Just before she disappeared from view, Dynasty turned and caught Theophany's eye once more, her face dimpled the way it did right before her brightest smile.

'I should have told her about Courteous,' Theophany thought dully after Dyna had faded from sight. He always told her everything- why had he not told her of his dear friend's death? 'She'll find out soon enough,' he decided, bothered by how cold that sounded even to himself.

Theoph turned back to the sea, even thinking of Courteous as dead seemed wrong. He had been alive the day before; how could he be dead now? Theoph lowered himself to the sand, struggling with his own mind. He had heard that warriors often went mad after a battle, they said it was because they had passed too close to death. Maybe *he* had gone mad!

"Does a mad man know if he's gone mad?" he asked aloud, as much to think clearly as to hear his own voice.

"My lord?"

Theoph looked up in surprise, one of his warriors was standing there, a concerned look on his face. The sun's light had gone now, and the stars were awakening in the night sky. How long had he been sitting there pondering his madness?

"Nothing," Theophany assured the man, forcing confidence into his voice, "I will rest here on the beach for the night; dismiss as many warriors as you see fit. I hardly think we're at risk of attack."

The warrior hesitated; did he doubt Theoph as much as Theoph doubted himself? But sleeping on the royal beach was common for the prince, and soon all but two of the warriors had been dismissed. The two who were left, made themselves comfortable higher up on the beach, giving the prince plenty of distance.

"Grief is madness of the soul," Theoph spoke aloud again, certain the warriors couldn't hear him. The phrase was one Vigil had said to him once, this was the first time Theoph truly considered it though.

The sound of the rolling waves crashing on the sand seemed to stretch time out, the intensity rising and falling occasionally, but it was always there, a constant thing that Theoph had come to rely on as a fact of life. The sea would outlive them all; this had never been clearer than now, as Theoph thought of Courteous being cut down in what should have been his victory battle.

"Grief is for mortal men," he muttered, thinking of his earlier conversation with his father. If rising above his own humanity meant living beyond grief, perhaps… Theoph bowed his head and held it in trembling hands. Knowing that he could not talk about his internal conflict with anyone only made it worse. As his father had said, no one could know that he, the prophesied king, struggled with his heart like any mortal man.

Chapter 2 The Foretold King

Salvage knelt over a basin of water and scrubbed her hands methodically, but the stain wouldn't wash away. She grew more and more frantic, spilling water and rubbing skin raw. She glanced over her shoulder, her guilty conscience smarting with shame.

Her futile washing halted abruptly at the sound of a child crying, where was the child? Why wasn't someone tending to the distressed infant? Rising to her feet, her stained hands forgotten, Sal scanned her surroundings for the child. The crying continued and increased in volume. She abandoned her washing basin and rushed outside, a deep maternal instinct driving her forward.

She ran along the island, pulling grass thickets aside, and checking behind every rock- still the child's cry persisted. It was a wretched cry, hopeless in pitch. Sal's own eyes filled with tears; why couldn't she find the child!? She stumbled down a steep hill and found herself on a beach, the cry was swallowed by the roar of the sea and Sal's feet dragged to a stop in the sand, her eyes widening.

The sea was receding, the salty brine evaporating before her eyes and the bottom of the deep laid bare while all manner of sea creature died, choking on air. The world was ending.

"Salvage wake up!" Vigil called sharply.

Sal was awake in a moment, a habit born of battle, her vision forgotten as she sat up and took in her sleeping quarters draped in early morning light. There was no danger.

Sal flopped back with a terrific sigh, "Let a warrior rest in peace!" she complained.

"Arise Sal," Vig urged her again.

She propped herself up on an elbow, "What is it?"

"There are reports of golden sea stars washing up on the beaches!" Vig informed her as he pulled on a tunic.

Sal sat bolt upright, "For who!?" She mentally went through the upcoming royal heirs, but all Theophany's siblings were much too young to have the sea god honor them in this way.

"Wrong question," Vig said lacing up his tunic, he threw Sal her clothes, she caught them one handed and began dressing even before she left bed.

"How *many* sea stars?" Sal asked after a moment.

Vig paused to look her in the eye, a corner of his mouth betraying his amusement, "The reports say there are hundreds!" he said with mock grandeur.

Sal froze, "What!? That's impossible!"

Vig smiled and shrugged as he pulled double bandoliers of blades over his head.

Sal sat back down on the bed heavily, her own belt of weapons in her hands, she narrowed her brown eyes. "Is this a trick?" she questioned, knowing her husband's playful side all too well, "If this is for the time I filled your meal pouch with rocks-"

Vig laughed and tossed her shoes to her, "No my love! If this is a trick, then we are both fools!"

Sal grudgingly pulled on her boots and strapped her belt to her hips. "I'll have the head of whoever is responsible for intruding upon my sleep right after a battle!" she vowed as they grabbed a bite to eat along the way and rushed outside.

On the street they at once noticed a strange buzz of activity about the city, not the ordinary sort of fishermen going out to boats or preparing nets, but a frenzied energy. Something wondrous had occurred.

"Something is very wrong!" Vig muttered, and Sal grinned at how they had come to completely different conclusions.

They paused in the street when warriors bearing a royal litter came trotting from the palace, the litter's blue canopy flapped in the breeze and an escort of two warriors ran ahead: the king rode in the litter. Sal and Vig bowed low when they saw the king; he did not look pleased.

"What's going on!?" the king demanded to know as the litter came to a halt.

"I know not, my king, only that there are reports of hundreds of golden sea stars on the beaches," Vigil answered.

The king made a frustrated sound in his throat. "The palace is in an uproar!" he turned to one of his warriors, "Run ahead and get to the bottom of this!" The warrior took off down the hill at breakneck speed. "Where is Theoph?" the king questioned Vig and Sal.

Sal did not shrink back, "We know not, my king, he has not sent for us."

"He's not in the palace- find him and bring him to me," the king instructed, his agitated state increasing. He waved for the litter bearers to continue to the harbor.

Sal and Vig wasted no time. "He'll be on the royal beach," Vig guessed, and they started off, their feet pounding the paving stones as they ran lightly. Sal soon took the lead but stopped abruptly when she reached the top of the steps down to the beach, Vigil nearly ran into her.

Sal gaped down at what her eyes could only perceive as a beach covered in gold. The two stood, their breath heavy as they tried to understand what they saw in the early morning light. Vig reacted sooner than she, descending the steps two at a time, he raced through the sand towards the prince's sleeping form. Sal mentally shook herself and followed on her husband's heels.

"Arise warriors!" Vig shouted sharply as they neared the bottom and saw two warriors sleeping in the sand. The slumbering warriors jerked awake and jumped to their feet, fearing a reprimand. Both Sal and Vig passed by them without a second thought, the warriors turned, and their mouths dropped open at the dazzling shoreline.

Sal dropped to her knees at the prince's side and shook him awake, his stirring reassured her that he was unharmed. "Arise my prince!" she called urgently.

Vig went past them towards the pounding surf, he stooped and plucked a single golden sea star from the wet sand; there were hundreds of them, more tumbling onto the beach with every wave.

Theophany struggled to sit up, clearly confused, "Sal? What…" he paused when he beheld the beach.

"Something has happened," Sal explained uselessly, her own mind searching for answers.

Vig turned back to them, sea star in hand, his face screwed up in vulnerable confusion. "What does it mean?" he asked softly, looking to the prince.

Sal helped Theoph to his feet, his mouth going slack.

"Reports said they cover all the shorelines," Sal informed him subdued, no longer thinking it was funny. This was no trick, unless the sea god was mocking them!

"My father?" Theoph asked.

"He sent us to find you and bring you to him," Sal answered, she could see that her husband was terribly shook up by this strange omen. A memory of her vision nagged at the back of her mind, the idea of the world ending resurfaced.

* * * *

"Is it a mistake or a trick!?" the king demanded to know again, obviously frustrated with the temple priests.

Theophany remained silent, frowning, and thinking back to what his father had said the day before, 'The sea is never wrong.'

It was now late morning and the whole island was in confusion. The king had ordered that the sea stars be removed from the beaches as was normally done when such an event occurred, but this task proved to be harder to perform than ever. Nearly every warrior and slave were frantically clearing the beaches, filling baskets and carts with the sacred talismans, but still more sea stars washed up! There was no counting the sea stars, and rumors were flying wildly as to who they were meant for. The king had gone to the temple, with Theoph and other advisers in tow, all hoping the priests would have an answer for them.

"We know not, my king," the head priest answered, exchanging nervous glances with the other priests.

The king growled in frustration, "Is that the only thing anyone can say today!? You are the sea priests! The sea god Tylus speaks to you- so find an answer!"

"Be assured my king, we will not rest until we have divined an answer from Tylus," the head priest tried to calm the king.

Theoph winced, he knew it would not work.

The king stalked to a basket holding the golden sea stars, "I will not 'be assured' until I know what the meaning of *this* is!" he shouted and kicked the basket over, spilling the talismans over the temple floor.

Theoph flinched; his father's cold disrespect for the talismans disturbed everyone in attendance. He caught Vigil's eye; his friend was at a loss, grasping for truth in the madness of the day. Theoph felt a wave of guilt wash over him; if he was all he should be, he'd know the meaning of this strange message.

"Tylus will make his message clear when we are ready to hear it," the oldest priest announced with sage wisdom. There was silence as everyone exchanged nervous glances.

"See that you are ready to listen; I want an answer before sunrise tomorrow!" the king commanded, then turned away, his warriors quick on his heels.

Theoph watched the priests for a moment longer; they had no idea of what to do. The prince followed his father out of the temple and hurried to walk beside him.

"We tread the edge of a cliff," the king said under his breath, then turned to Theoph and stopped abruptly to pull him close. "The people will be looking to you for guidance," he whispered, "Whatever the priests decide will be meaningless if the people feel that you do not believe it!"

Theoph felt his throat constrict, all he could do was nod, the king tightened his grip on his arm then stormed away.

"Theophany!" Lady Dynasty called, her gown billowing in the breeze as she rushed to him.

Theoph half heartedly opened his arms to her.

"What has happened- do the priests know?" she asked breathlessly as she took hold of his hands.

"No, my love."

Dyna's face fell slightly, "Oh."

"I'm sorry, I should have an answer," Theoph apologized, feeling another wave of guilt.

Dyna shook her head, "No Theoph, do not blame yourself for not knowing! This must only be good news, perhaps Tylus is also rejoicing in your victory!"

Theoph tried to smile, "I hope you are right." He did not think she was though, his heart told him the sea stars couldn't possibly have anything to do with him.

Dyna dropped his hands and her eyes widened, "Theoph your *bleeding*!"

Theoph raised his arm to find that he had bled through his stealthy bandages; a red stain betrayed his battle wound.

"What happened!?" Dyna asked in alarm.

"A small wound from the battle; no one is to know of it," Theoph hushed his betrothed. "Just another one of my shortcomings. I must go," he said abruptly and walked away.

★ ★ ★ ★

Vigil and Salvage followed the prince through the palace at a respectful distance, all the while Vig's mind went over what the priests had said, his faith in them diminishing with every step. Soon Theophany stopped at an empty balcony and leaned against the railing.

"Salvage, will you take my apology to Lady Dynasty?" Theophany asked quietly.

Vig sensed Sal bristle. She opened her mouth, no doubt to respond sharply about how the prince could deliver his own apology.

Vig reached out and placed a hand on her arm, silently begging her to obey without a scene. She set her jaw and grit her teeth, *talk to him* she mouthed forcefully before turning on her heel and leaving.

Vig braced himself then approached the prince. "The priests will find an answer," he encouraged, even though he did not believe it.

Theoph swallowed hard, "*I* should have the answer."

Vig frowned and rested his arms against the railing beside the prince, "No one expects that of you."

"Because they know in their hearts that I do not have a connection with the gods; they know I am far from what the prophecy promised!" Theoph lamented.

Vig watched the prince with a sinking heart, what could he say to give him hope? "That is nonsense, the people hailed you victorious yesterday; they believe in you."

Theoph's face tightened, "Then I fear they have misplaced their faith. How can I lead them to the gods when I do not know the way myself?"

"You simply have not found your way yet."

"How can I? I fear I will be lost forever."

Vig felt his heart swell with inspiration, "Before greatness can be achieved, doubt must first be vanquished."

Theoph looked at him in surprise, "You really believe I will become the greatest king of Verlyance?"

The weight of knowing how his response could affect the prince made Vig hesitate, "I stake my life on it."

Theoph nodded, overcome with emotion, Vig dearly hoped that his statement proved to be more of an inspiration to the prince than a burden.

"Come, your arm must be seen to," Vig said at last when he felt that they both had regained control of their emotions.

* * * *

"The prince wished to extend his apology to you; he has behaved like a mongrel eel fish," Salvage said stiffly.

"Is that word for word what Theoph said?" Dynasty asked sceptically.

"I may have slightly altered his message."

Dyna smiled before her face fell, "Is he alright Sal?"

Sal searched the young woman's face carefully, not knowing what the prince had and had not told her. "It is a small wound, it will heal," she said at last.

Dyna sighed, "Do you know what the sea stars mean?"

Sal remained still; it was not exactly common knowledge that she had forsaken the religion of her people in favor of an unknown, nameless deity, "How can I? I am no priest."

"Theoph told me that you have visions from another god," Dyna confided quietly.

The corner of Sal's mouth twitched up; apparently the prince had told her plenty. "Yes, that is true."

"Have you had any visions of this?" Dyna asked, growing impatient.

The memory of her morning vision once again tugged at Sal's mind, the cry of a child ringing out, "I… no, my lady, I have not."

Dyna nodded, trying hard to hide her disappointment, "Do you think it is a good omen?" she asked, sounding vulnerable.

Sal let a reassuring smile spread across her face, "The golden sea star has always been a tiding of joy. And this I know, whatever the meaning of the stars, it will be no small thing."

The evening tide dragged out to sea, leaving behind a few stray golden sea stars. The sea creatures that had been sacred the day before had now become so commonplace that they were trampled underfoot and played with by children. The storerooms of the palace were filled haphazardly with baskets of the creatures and kept under guard, for no one knew what else to do. The whispers and rumors of what it all meant were shared afresh as doors were shut and lamps lit for the night. The sun bowed below the horizon much too slowly for those who awaited word from the priests, and the stars of the night seemed reluctant to appear, as if afraid of dimming in comparison to the brilliance of the sea stars.

When the last of the daylight faded, the priests set out from the temple towards the palace, dressed in ceremonial robes and chanting solemnly, as if they had not spent the entire day scrambling about to find an answer for the king. They entered the throne room, burning sticks of incense filled the room with their aroma and created a heavy atmosphere; a hush fell on those inside. Theophany glanced at his father's advisers and noted how they watched the priests with a mixture of fear and hope.

"What is the meaning of the message sent to us from Tylus?" the king asked formally.

The priests spread out as rehearsed, and the head priest spoke, his voice projecting easily, "In the time of your grandfather the omen of the golden sea star foretold a time of victory and mastery over our foes."

Theoph swallowed hard, and looked for Vigil and Salvage, they stood behind him, away from the gathered advisers.

"Then when our own dear prince came upon his eighteenth year, Tylus promised us of his coming greatness as king." The priest glanced Theoph's way.

"This I know well," the king interrupted, his patience growing thin, "What does Tylus foretell by the stars today?"

The eldest priest stepped forward and passed aside his burning stick of incense, "My king, these sea stars tell of an *even* greater king who has come into power. His greatness will cover all the lands and seas, even as the sea stars covered our island, and the deeds of this king will be just as uncountable. None will prevail against him when he sets out to conquer the lands, not even the greatest warrior with a mighty war fleet could stand against this king. Even the sea itself trembles in fear and awe; we would be wise to do likewise."

There was silence as the news sank into the minds of those present, like sand settling in the water after a wave.

"From where does this Foretold King hail?" the king asked, his tone subdued.

The head priest stepped back, and still another came forward, "Through much seeking and meditating in the cleansing pool, we have discerned that the Foretold King rules far to the north, beyond the edges of our maps."

"How can you know this?" Theoph spoke out, unable to keep quiet.

The priests hesitated.

"Well?" the king prompted.

"It became clear to us through much seeking-"

"And meditating in the cleansing pool!" Theoph interrupted, "Yes, I understand that- how do you know that the Foretold King is in the north?!"

The priest bowed to the prince, "There are many messages written on the sea stars for those who can read them," he said, and Theoph felt his pride smart.

One of the priests brought forth a golden sea star for the king and prince to examine, everyone else leaned in closer to see. The surface of the sea creature was textured and bumpy as expected.

"It depicts the night sky, my lords." The priest said quietly, "it shows the star constellation of the north."

Theoph looked closer, frowning until he saw the constellation himself; could it be a coincidence?

"It is the same on nearly every talisman, my lords," the priest boasted, and baskets of stars were brought forth to prove it; every sea creature had the same pattern on their underside.

"You said that *nearly* every sea star has this northern constellation," the king spoke, "What of the *other* sea stars? Do they have a different constellation?"

"No, my king, but they do have another message."

Another basket was brought forward, the king and Theoph examined these and found that each of them had the same pattern.

"A five-pointed star? What does it mean?" Theoph asked, his heart was beating fast now.

"We believe that it is not the shape of a star my prince, but that of a flower; the flower of Garatin."

No one spoke as the unfamiliar word faded to silence. The king glanced sharply at one of his advisers, a seafarer who knew the waters far beyond their islands. The adviser understood the king's meaning.

"I have heard tell of this country my king," he spoke, "It is indeed far to the north, over the mountains of the mainland. I have never dealt with any who can say they have traveled that far."

Theoph felt like he could breathe again, he turned and smiled in relief at Vig and Sal. Sal was the only one who returned the smile.

"This Foretold King is far removed from us then?" the king asked, clearly thinking hard.

"Indeed," the head priest agreed cautiously, "However my king, Tylus would not honor just any king. If the sea god has seen fit to tell us, then we would do well to use the information given to us."

Theoph's thoughts strayed from the conversation, his mind at ease. He reminded himself of his father's instructions to support whatever the priests said. 'And so, I will,' he thought with confidence, 'this is a time of destiny! Tylus has made a way for my love and I!'

The late morning sun had already heated up the island air, birds were retreating to shade and fishermen were returning from sea. The king's breezy chambers were cooled by slaves with fans, and nothing seemed out of place, except for a mighty table cluttered with maps and books.

"Father, I wish to speak with you," Theophany announced, feeling sure and rested even after his late night. All was right with his world.

"And I with you," the king replied briskly as he rearranged a pile of books.

Theoph hesitated; his father's tone made him wary.

"I have thought all night and been in counsel with the temple priests; it is clear to me that the omen of the sea stars can only be one of great fortune and should not be brushed aside."

Theoph re-centered himself; this was his chance, "I think the same."

"Then you know what you must do."

Theoph's blood pumped in his head and his hands felt clammy, he had not felt this way even in battle! "I ask for your blessing on my union with the Lady Dynasty."

The king did not respond.

Theoph wet his lips, hating himself for squirming before his father like a child, "Even Tylus has blessed us with the sea stars, what better time than now?" he pointed out, hoping against hope that at last his father would see things his way.

"Thousands of golden sea stars wash up, the temple priests say that the greatest king ever to live has come into power, and you take it as a blessing to wed!?" the king stared at him in disbelief. Theoph set his jaw. "You will seek out this king, that is what you must do!" his father stated with finality.

Theoph blinked, "What?"

"This Foretold King will rise above all the lands and bring about a new age, if the priests are to be believed," the king muttered. "Verlyance *will* be a part of it! It is a choice between joining the victor before the war is waged or being trampled beneath his conquest when he comes!"

Theoph's mind reeled, "But this king is far to the north; beyond our maps!"

"Did you not listen?" his father snapped, "did you not see the sea stars!? Only a fool would stand idle when such things are afoot! Now is the time to act!"

Theoph gaped; this could not be happening! "I won't go!" he declared defiantly, "I will stay here and wed Dynasty; my place is here! Send a warrior on this quest if you must- but I will not go!"

The king's face hardened, "I will give no blessing to your union unless you do as I say."

Theoph took a step back in surprise, "You gave your word that I would have your blessing after I returned from the sea battle!"

"Hear me well Theophany; I will give no blessing to your union till you have sought out the Foretold King and secured an alliance."

Theoph's chest heaved up and down. The eyes of father and son locked, both willing the other to concede.

Theoph turned on his heel and stalked from the chambers.

"I will begin the preparations for your journey," the king said before he was quite gone.

Theoph clenched his teeth until they ached, his frustration felt like a geyser bursting out over him. Turning a corner, he nearly ran a servant boy over, the boy stumbled out of the way and apologized, but Theoph was already halfway down the hall.

'I need to talk to Courteous- he would understand!' Theoph thought with barely restrained rage. But he could never share in Theoph's frustrations, or comfort him in sorrow, or even laugh at his misfortune; Courteous was dead. The realization hit Theoph hard enough that his feet faltered and stalled, his footfalls echoing into silence.

Sorrow and grief were often described as thieves in the night, but Theoph felt more like he had been ambushed and left for dead. Tears that he did not even know were there, spilled out and a sob escaped his throat, broken and breathless. Why couldn't Courteous have just…

Grief is for mortal men. Theoph raked his arm across his face to erase his tears and shoved his overwhelming emotions back behind the door in his mind that he knew was denial.

He would go to Dynasty. She always knew how to comfort him. Theoph went first to her chambers and learned that she had gone to the great hall. He was glad of the extra time to compose himself as he made his way to her.

Dyna sat with other maidens and worked together on a large tapestry of a sea serpent. They all looked up when Theoph entered. Dyna recognized his expression at once and rose to her feet, abandoning her work; she met him halfway across the hall. Not caring who watched, Theoph threw his arms around her and held her close, cursing his father for demanding that he leave her for even a day!

"My love, what is it?" Dyna whispered, holding him tight.

Theoph looked up to see everyone watching with wide eyes, "Get out- all of you!" he ordered sharply. The maidens and their servants rushed to obey with muffled movements, casting curious glances at the two embraced lovers.

Dyna pulled back, "What is it, Theoph?"

"I asked for my fathers blessing on our union," he admitted, his voice thick with emotion, whether it was sorrow or anger he could not tell.

Dyna's face fell in dismay.

"He forbid us!"

Dyna blinked in surprise. He had failed her.

"He demands that I go on a quest to make an alliance with this Foretold King before he will give us his blessing!" he explained.

Dyna hid her dismay with effort, "A quest?"

"Yes, to the country of Garatin- wherever that is!"

"*Then* he will give his blessing?" Dyna pointed out, her face brightening, "Theoph he has not forbidden us- you have but to do this one quest!"

"I will be gone for months!" Theoph raged, stepping back, "He thinks he can manipulate me like a fool! I won't do it; we can wed without his blessing!"

Dyna looked like she had been slapped, "Go against the king?"

"I am the prince, Theophany the Victorious- we don't need his blessing!" Theoph stated impulsively.

Dyna stepped back; she was angry! "Then what Theophany? You would curse me to live in disgrace; I would never be recognized as your wife.

Our children would be illegitimate and shunned by the court, shamed, and dismissed! Is that what you would do to us!?"

Theoph took a breath to steady himself. "No, my love," he tried to soothe.

Dyna stepped back up to him and held his face with both hands, "Theophany, to go against the king would be madness. We have no choice in this," she reasoned softly, her eyes pleading him to change his mind.

"What if he doesn't honor his word- again?" Theoph argued.

Dyna looked down and smoothed his tunic, "Force him to give his word before the court! You could announce your intention when you leave, in front of everyone, he would have to promise to give his blessing on your return! Then I will prepare our wedding while you are away."

"I don't know how long I'll be gone for!" he pointed out, his resolve waning.

Dyna smiled, "It will be a very grand wedding then."

Theoph sighed, not convinced.

She placed a hand on his face again, "Do as your father wishes; go on this quest and return to me."

"It is a fool's quest!" he argued.

"You will seek out a great king- he could help you!" she pointed out.

Theoph frowned.

"Theoph, I know you have struggled with your destiny. Perhaps this king can guide you- teach you. This need not be a misfortune."

Theoph took a few short breaths, "You believe in my prophecy?"

Dyna smiled confidently, "Of course I do, you are Theophany, you are destined for greatness!"

Theoph pulled her close in another embrace, his frustration ebbing away to quiet resignation.

"Will Salvage and Vigil go with you?" she asked.

"Undoubtedly."

"Good, I made them vow long ago they would always return you to me alive and well. To break their vow would mean to never see me again- and who could live with that punishment?" she joked softly.

Theoph sighed into her hair, "Understand this, I do not go on this quest in my father's namesake. I do it in yours."

Chapter 3 Northward

Salvage struggled to row the small boat against the fierce wind, her arms aching and her movements frustratingly slow. The hauntingly familiar cry of a child halted her. She searched the waves for another vessel, but she was alone on the sea.

Sal's eye's fell to the bottom of the boat, Prince Theophany lay there, curled up, bruises and deep bloody cuts marred his face and limbs. Sal knelt by him and called his namesake; he did not stir. Still the child cried out.

The vision began to fade and the sounds of early morning Verlyance rose in volume. Light filtered in through Sal's closed eyelids and she became aware of herself and her surroundings. She opened her eyes slowly, the events of her vision standing out in her mind like spears driven into a battlefield. She sat up and swung her legs over the side of her bed, beside her Vigil began to stir.

What did her dream mean? Was it a vision from her nameless god? Sal frowned, the child's cry sounded again in her memory, and she placed a trepidatious hand on her abdomen; was it… *her* child? That was impossible.

She pushed the troubling yet hopeful thoughts aside and focused on the day before her. There was much to do, before long they would be traveling with the prince northward in search of the Foretold King. The prospect both excited and frightened her. To go further north than anyone else had gone before appealed to her pride, but there would be many perils. Before this, there had never been a need to travel far from Verlyance, their people had never done it! And the task to plan for the journey was in part hers. Sal and her husband rose and began readying themselves for the day ahead of them.

"We'll have to make a decision soon," Vig said suddenly as he sat on the bed and laced up his tunic.

Sal smirked, "I agree; I think a tree in the back garden would be lovely."

"Well sure, but don't you think it might ruin the view?" he shot back without missing a beat.

Sal buckled a belt around her hips, "How about the front garden then?"

Vig smiled ruefully at his wife, "I meant a decision about who to bring on the quest."

"Um, I suppose the tree can wait."

"I was thinking Atten would be a handy warrior to have along," Vig redirected their banter and stood to his feet.

Sal glared at him in annoyance. "No," she proclaimed and held up one of his throwing knives, hilt pointed at Vig.

Vig frowned as she readied herself. Sal threw the knife at his right shoulder, he plucked it out of the air before it made contact. The hilt fitting into a scarred hand that proved he had not always been so skilled at the trick.

"Why?" he asked, placing the knife into a sheath on his belt.

"Because I don't like him," Sal explained shortly and held up his second knife. This time Vig shifted slightly out of the way allowing the blade to pass over his shoulder and thud into the wall behind him.

"Alright, you know I won't argue with you when you're armed," he conceded easily and turned to retrieve his knife.

"You're getting sloppy."

Vig turned back to her and smiled cheekily, "And yet I still have all my fingers!"

Sal grew serious, "I just need to know I can rely on whoever comes with us. We'll be going into the utterly unknown, whoever goes with us must be able to think on their feet in an ambush and keep their head during negotiations. Atten is simply not the right warrior."

Vig nodded his understanding, "I suppose that means I also will have to stay behind!"

Sal smirked again, "Nonsense, you may not be all that bright, but who else could entertain me each evening with love songs?"

"I'll just leave my weapons here and bring my lute then," he joked ruefully.

"And of course, if worse should come to worse, you can always use the lute as a club."

The two continued in this way through a hearty meal then set about their day. Vigil went to the palace and the training grounds while Sal made her way through the city streets to the harbor. There, in a hovel by the beach she found the boat master at work. He was a man in his mid fifties with missing teeth and strong hands. Every boat on the island, had at some point, been under his tool. Since wood was limited on the island, the construction of a new boat was a serious thing and not undertaken by just any fisherman.

Sal found the boat master standing over one of the war boats from the battle with the sea pirates, his grandchild worked away at repairing cracks and other damage to the hull.

"Hail boat master," Sal greeted.

The man looked up and gave a toothless grin, "I knew you would be coming to see me today."

Sal smirked, "Why is that?"

He gave her a sly look, "Because the prince is going on a sea voyage."

"Has word got out so soon?"

He looked unimpressed, "Whenever there is talk of a journey over the water; I know about it."

Sal smirked again, she stooped and plucked a golden sea star from the sand, the sacred talisman must have been missed the day before. "We're not sure how many boats we'll need yet, how many are there now?"

The boat master's face grew dark, "If you hadn't lost so many in the battle- there would be plenty! Now there are only thirteen war boats fit for a voyage."

"Have you begun making more?"

"That takes time, unless the prince will wait a few months, he will only have thirteen war boats at his disposal, possibly fourteen."

The cry of a child interrupted them. Sal spun about, searching, the boat master did not notice. A woman could be heard calming the child and Sal felt momentarily defensive, she pushed the feeling aside. "Alright, thank you boat master," Sal ended the conversation, still distracted.

★ ★ ★ ★

"What about Atten?" Prince Theophany asked as Vigil walked with him around the training grounds. All the best warriors had been gathered about the grounds and were sparring and doing target practice. Each one was keenly aware of the prince and Vig inspecting them, looking for who to bring on the quest.

Vig shook his head, "Sal said no."

Theoph only nodded.

"Ursue would be a good choice," Vig directed, nodding to a stocky woman wrestling another warrior.

Theoph nodded again.

"Ti is strong and determined, I'd trust him to carry me across the island," Vig added, nearly talking to himself.

Theoph nodded and Vig wondered if he was thinking of Courteous; he would have been an obvious first choice for the quest, level-headed, easy going… reliable.

Activity halted slightly among the warriors, then they put even more effort into their training. Vig turned to find that the king had entered the courtyard, his entourage of warriors and slaves following him. Vig bowed.

"Have you selected your warriors yet?" the king asked his son as he approached.

Theoph tried to hide a sigh of boredom, "Nearly, we have yet to decide on the number of our company."

The king surveyed the training warriors, "Well, I have one less man for you to find."

"Who is that?" Theoph asked and Vig listened closely, he was probably more interested than the prince.

"The gods made way for you long ago and sent a slave many years past," the king explained, "He is from Garatin, the very country the Foretold King rules! Not only can he speak the tongue of that country, but he will be able to act as a guide."

Vig raised his eyebrows, that was good news. The king turned and waved a slave forward and everyone in the yard hesitated again. The slave was unusual. He was an old man with wild, wispy white hair and beard. But it was his skin that gave everyone pause; although he was tanned like worn leather, compared to everyone else on the island, he was as pale as grass growing under a pot. The man's blue eyes stood out shockingly in the crowd of dark faces and warm brown eyes. Vig had glimpsed the slave before on occasion, the old one had been around for a long time, regarded as a strange foreigner and vaguely mistrusted.

The old man bowed to the prince and king, "How may I serve you, my lords?"

Theoph nodded to the old man, "You speak the languages of the north?"

The man paused, like he had not expected the question, "It has been a long time my prince," he looked at the king uncertainly, "But yes, I can speak a few tongues of the north."

Vig looked him up and down; he was old. Could he walk to the harbor let alone travel beyond the maps?!

"Well, the one that matters most is the tongue of Garatin," Theoph commented.

"Indeed," the king turned away, dismissing the slave, "Show me who you're considering bringing on the quest." He instructed his son and Theoph reluctantly walked with him through the warriors.

Vigil remained behind, watching the old man. He swayed unsteadily on his thin legs, his pale blue eyes blinking rapidly.

"Are you ill, old one?" Vig asked kindly, finding him both fascinating and disturbing to look at.

The old man moved his jaw like trying to form words, "Will *I* go to Garatin?"

Vig smirked, "Only if you can last that long." He wondered if the man would need to sit down.

The old man sighed and nodded his head, his white beard brushing his hollow chest, "Aye," he breathed, "I can last however long the road is, so long as it takes me home again."

Vigil was moved, "How long since you came here?"

"I was a child when I was taken, it has been many moons since last I saw my country," he said, tears brimming in his eyes.

"What's your namesake old one?" Vig asked gently.

"Garden, my lord," he smiled and clasped his bony hands, "I have been a garden in drought for a long time, but the rain has come at last; I will go home!"

Vig couldn't help but smile at the man's mirth, "And I am Vigil," he introduced himself, clasping the old one's forearm, "I will see that you return home, even if I must carry you myself!"

"I feel as though I could carry *you*!" Garden bragged gleefully.

Vig laughed, "I'll walk, if it's all the same with you."

The old man's smile continued to linger in Vigil's mind as preparations were completed for the quest in the following days. A total of thirty-eight warriors were selected to escort the prince over the waves to the northern mainland. Half of them would journey back to Verlyance, while a few would remain on the mainland, so that the prince could return when the quest was done. The other half of the company would journey with the prince into the north. Counting the prince, the slave Garden, Vigil and Salvage, their company would be twenty-four strong. Vig wondered if it would be strong enough.

Each night Vig and Sal stayed up long hours discussing their plans, wondering what kind of provisions they would need to bring. Fresh water was a concern for the journey over the waves, another worry that kept Vig awake in the night was what kind of threats would they meet along the way? Would twenty-two warriors be enough to keep the prince safe? Vig did not count Garden among the warriors.

"We will be at a disadvantage, on land we do not know, in weather we can not predict and among strangers we can not trust," Vig spoke his fears to Sal on the eve of their departure.

"Love, you know that whenever you are frightened you can hold my hand," Sal invited with a smirk, as slaves prepared her hair for travel.

Vig sighed as he fidgeted with his throwing knives, tossing them up and catching them again. "I can't help but feel like we're about to make a mistake," he muttered.

Sal sent her slaves away and watched him for a moment, "Would you be at peace if you knew our quest was smiled upon by the gods?"

Vig paused and returned her gaze, "Is it?"

"I only know what my visions reveal to me."

"What do they reveal now?"

Sal hesitated and placed a hand to her abdomen, Vig frowned.

"I feel that our quest is… watched, guarded over," she said, her eyes drifting away. Vigil again envied her. What would he give to commune with a god?

"That'll be good enough for me then," Vig decided. Yet he knew that come morning, he would still go to the temple, he would still listen for Tylus.

"Let's hope it's enough for Theophany too," Sal murmured.

★ ★ ★ ★

Theophany knelt before the throne, Salvage and Vigil flanking him, while the other members of their company knelt behind them. All wore their travel garments with their weapons at their sides, and all except Sal were damp from the temple pool where they had prayed for good fortune.

The early morning sun had yet to rise high enough to fully light the throne room and the dusky light set a somber tone over the proceedings. The king sat on the raised throne with his advisors gathered about him, Theoph did not dare raise his eyes to his father and instead studied his boots, the detail of them offering distraction from the imminent quest. The sea priests went to and fro among the warriors, mumbling blessings of good fortune and swift wind to aid them in their quest.

Theoph closed his eyes and forced himself back to the present. A weight on his belt reminded him of the jewels that his father had entrusted to him as a gift for the Foretold King. There were more riches packed for the quest, but the satchel on Theoph's belt held the finest Verlynn Nel had to offer. The mutterings of the priests grew louder as one drew nearer to Theoph, but his mind was far from the gods. He dared a glance upwards and caught Dynasty's eye; she nodded to encourage him, but his heart still hesitated.

At last, the priests finished, and the company stood as one, the creak of their leather and their weapons readjusting was the only sound.

The king stood slowly, then descended the steps till Theoph had no choice but to meet his gaze. His father spoke quietly, his words meant only for Theoph, "Return with the alliance of the Foretold King and begin the fulfilment of your own destiny."

Theoph swallowed hard, he had hoped that his departure would not be marred by his father finding one last fault in him.

The king straightened slightly and raised his voice to address the whole gathering, "Go now, Theophany the Victorious, with the spirit of Tylus to strengthen you and the prayers of all Verlyance to guide you to a true current that will lead you to the Foretold King."

Theoph's heart swelled unexpectedly when his father used the title the people had given him, the feeling gave him courage to speak, "And upon the completion of this quest I will return to these shores, wed Lady Dynasty and begin a new era as Tylus has foreseen!"

The gathered crowd and warriors cheered, but Theoph and Dynasty held their breath while the king remained motionless.

"So be it," the king agreed.

Theoph felt a great weight lift from him like the quest was already complete. He met Dynasty's beaming face and felt as though an eternity would pass before he could hold her again. A great procession escorted Theoph and his company through the city to the harbor. The cheers of the city woke sea birds and carried on the breeze for miles.

Before Theophany could savor his last moments on the island, the fleet of six boats left the shore and cut into the waves eagerly. The voices of the island grew distant alarmingly fast and soon they were out in the open sea with the wind at their backs pushing them further into the north and closer to the Foretold King.

Chapter 4 A Blessing and a Curse

The evening sun approached the horizon, casting waves into golden ripples while the wind forced the water into swells around vibrant coral reefs. Sea birds called to each other over the shore of Wyren Fole as the six war boats came fast into the sandy bay, relieved they had reached the island before nightfall.

"Look sharp everyone, don't make me look bad in front of the locals," Vigil said as he steered the lead boat through the rocks. Stone huts were nestled into the low hills of the island and a few locals cleaning their nets on the beach looked up in awe.

Salvage stood up and waved her arm. "Verlyance!" she called out to let them know they were not an invading force. The island of Wyren Fole was part of Verlyance, but being eight days from Verlynn Nel, was too far removed to be kept up to date on events. The island boasted a small fishing community and was the most northern reach of Verlyance, beyond it was only small isles, open sea and then, lost in the horizon, the mainland.

The fishermen on the beach waved in response to Sal, and children ran up to the huts where women folk stepped out to stare, while those on the beach waded out into the water to meet the boats.

"Prepare for Prince Theophany the Victorious!" Sal announced as they drew near, the locals exchanged bewildered looks but otherwise did not know what to do. Sal and several others jumped from the boats as they came into shallower water and began dragging them ashore, the locals joined and soon all the boats were pulled onto the beach.

One of the island men bowed to Sal, "I am Voi, welcome and rest to your company." His accent was strange and pronounced to Sal's ears and she smiled.

"Well met. The prince will be staying one night on Wyren Fole's shores and will continue his voyage north in the morning," she explained. Noticing a child nearby watching with wide eyes, Sal waved, and the child ducked their head shyly.

Vig helped Theoph ashore, and the prince approached, Voi glanced at Sal before bowing low.

"Good to be ashore," Theoph commented, trying to sound happy to be there. It was the most he had said since setting out.

Sal only hoped that he would shake out of his distant state before they met any kind of trouble on their quest. His distracted behaviour was exactly the kind of thing that killed good people.

* * * *

The youth groaned in frustration as the older warrior once again landed a blow on his shoulder armor.

"Be light footed, Rend, you need to be able to move out of range quickly," Vigil instructed, from where he observed the short sword match. The locals had been most hospitable to the company and after their first hot meal in over a week, they had settled down on a hillside. Vig sat with Theoph in the grass and watched as one of the older warriors challenged a youth of their company to a match. Vig had yet to decide which of the warriors would return to Verlyance and who would journey on northward with them, the match gave him the chance to decide about the youth. He was just a boy.

"You can't afford to be rooted to one spot," Vig continued.

The youth, Rend, frowned, "You said to ground myself and keep my weight equally distributed!"

"Being grounded and rooted to one spot are not the same," Salvage joined the conversation as she came into the torch light to stand beside Vig and the prince.

The warriors began another match.

"Seems unnecessary to bring the boy with us," Theoph commented quietly, drawing surprised glances from both Sal and Vig.

"He's a fast learner!" Sal pointed out.

Vig withheld his opinion, frowning.

"And what better teacher is there than experience?" Sal continued, "Besides, he's excited to join such a noble quest, who are we to deny him?"

"*Is* this quest so noble?" Theoph asked, his tone serious.

"Of course, it is," Vig assured with confidence he did not quite feel, "Tylus himself *sent* us!" It was hard to see the prince's face in the fire light, but he looked less than convinced.

"And then there is always Sal's vaguely helpful visions to rely on!" Vig pointed out and slapped Sal's shin, "If this quest were not so noble, then why would she be given visions of it?"

Sal smiled and shook off his hand.

"You have been given visions of our quest?" Theophany asked, trying to sound casual.

Sal hesitated, and Vig winced. "My husband speaks out of turn, but I am sure I will soon be given visions to aid us."

Theoph nodded and said no more.

Vig took a deep breath, longing to ease the discomfort of the moment, "Well, I hope the warriors do learn quickly, I'd hate for them to embarrass me in front of the armies of the Foretold King."

Sal laughed, "You don't need someone else to embarrass you my love, you are skilled enough to manage that on your own."

"Do you think the Foretold King will be amassing an army, or will he already have one?" Theoph pondered darkly, ignoring the lighthearted banter.

"I don't know," Vig admitted helplessly.

"Perhaps he has already started his conquest and we will meet him on the battlefield," Garden suggested with false cheerfulness.

Vig had not even noticed that the old man was nearby, but when he turned, he saw Gardens pale face and white hair glowing in the torchlight.

"If this king is as great as we think, is it not likely that he will scoff at our gifts? Why would he want us as allies?" Theoph pondered.

The four were silent at the sobering thought.

"I could sing a song as a peace offering," Vig suggested sarcastically.

"That should scare the whole army off for good!" Theoph surprised them by joining in the joke.

Sal laughed heartily and Vigil was pleased to see Theoph crack a smile, even Garden's grin could be seen behind his beard.

'Everything will be alright' Vig decided as he feigned offence, 'as long as I can keep their spirits up.'

"Or' the waves and or' the brine till my lady I shall find. Her hair like the night and eyes like the stars, into their depths I shall dare, yet beware the secrets they guard," Vigil's rich baritone voice drifted up and hung in the heavy fog. He reclined in the bottom of the boat, eyes closed, head resting on a pack and his fingers plucking out a lighthearted tune on his lute.

They had left the island of Wyren Fole nine days past and on the morn of their seventeenth day of their quest they found themselves lost in a heavy fog. Having no breeze to fill them, their triangle shaped sails were useless and had been lowered. To keep from drifting apart they linked the boats with ropes and sat still for hours without a breath of wind to stir the fog; an air of anxiety grew as they waited.

"An' we shall wed, and we shall dine in a land so divine-" Vigil's song ended in a grunt when Sal kicked him.

"Just *who is* this lady?" she asked frostily as she lounged against the boat side. A fellow warrior nearby tried to hide a smirk.

Vigil scowled at his wife playfully, "Just an ill-tempered woman with a hearty kick."

Sal shook her head and shifted to look over at the other boats- one was drifting off into the fog and she gave the connecting rope a tug to draw them closer again. She glanced behind her at Theophany; he stared off into the fog, uninterested in the conversation. Sal wondered if the lyrics of Vigil's song were a little too relatable for him.

"Sing something else before I throw you overboard," Sal advised as she resettled, trying hard to subdue her anxiety over their lack of progress in the fog; how long would they be stuck? If they tried moving, would they come out of the fog, or become even more lost?

"Sing about the first warrior of Verlynn Nel," someone from the closest boat asked; it was an old favourite.

Vigil took a deep breath, but his first note died, and his eyes fixed on a point beyond Sal's shoulder.

Sal turned and frowned, "What is it?" she could see nothing but the thick fog.

"There," Vig said, sitting up and pointing; the fog near the water swelled and cleared like something large disturbed it. "It's something in the water." He said setting his instrument aside and drawing his short sword.

"Be still," Sal urged, "We will not come to harm."

Vig ignored her. "Attend to me!" he called as he stood to his feet, his expert balance hardly disturbed the boat.

In the surrounding boats the warriors collected their weapons and fixed their eyes on the disturbance in the fog; whatever it was, it was coming closer.

Sal reluctantly readied her spear. "Stay down Theoph," she advised in a low tone.

The prince obeyed without question. For a moment there was near silence as they waited. There was a collected intake of breath when a series of spike-like hooks rose from the water nearby. Sal knew uncertainty at that moment.

A burst of air erupted between the boats and the water rushed out of the way of a great head as it rose among the boats. The creature had thick leathery skin with dark green patches broken up by white lines as if it wore plates of armor. The head was rounded with a pointed beaklike maw and was as large as a stone hut. Two great dark eyes gazed down at them with silent dignity as the head extended high over the waves. The spikes rose higher as well and a large surface appeared, like a small island. The wide flat arms of the creature moved under the water, sending swells outward, rocking the boats. It was a giant sea turtle!! Water dripped from the head as it gazed down and met Sal's eyes, then its gaze shifted to Theoph.

"No one move," Vigil ordered gently.

Sal glanced down at the prince and a flashback of her vision ripped at her consciousness. Theoph shifted uneasily as the creature blinked down at them.

"Steady," Sal whispered, gripping her spear with sweaty hands.

The creature sucked air through its nose and its dark green patches along its stout neck and shell shimmered and turned white, making barnacles and other growth stand out in stark contrast. The creature opened its mouth and a deep rumble seemed to emanate from its body rather than its mouth. It lowered its head back into the water, but instead of submerging completely, its shell with all its spikes and hooks remained on the surface. No one dared relax or even breathe in relief.

They could see the white body float for a moment amongst them, then it pushed its fins backwards and was propelled through the boats at an alarming speed.

"Watch it!" Sal called sharply as the great jagged shell passed between their boat and another, catching the connecting rope. The turtle picked up speed and the two boats shot forward; Sal nearly fell over the side into the water.

"Cut the rope!" Sal ordered, an image of being dragged to the depths played in her head. The two connected boats were drawn closer together and collided, catching one warriors' hand between them, he cried out in pain. Sal forced herself to her feet, her eyes wide but all she could see was the sea creature's shell plowing a path ahead of them through the fog. She glanced over her shoulder; the other boats were being dragged behind in a row.

Sal moved forward, thrown off balance each time the two boats bashed against each other, ahead of her one of the warriors was in the prow with their knife, sawing through the thick rope.

Sal lost her footing and fell into Vigil's arms. "This will make for an interesting song," Vig commented casually. Sal rolled her eyes and shoved past him, still holding her spear.

In the second boat another warrior worked at cutting the rope attached to their prow. Sal kept her eyes fixed ahead of them. Seconds apart, the two ropes were cut, and the boats glided forward on the momentum. Sal refused to be relieved; the creature could still come back for them.

The other boats glided up around them, "Be ready should the creature return!" Vigil warned.

"Look!" Theoph exclaimed, pointing ahead.

Sal turned; spear ready. The fog ahead of them was clearing like a window had been opened in a smoky room. The creature's shell could be seen rise for a moment, then submerge completely, it's white shape disappearing under the waves. The late morning sun seemed to be waiting for them in the clear air, and to the north, far ahead of them on the horizon, was the distant, purple, and gray, lumpy shape of land.

"The creature led us through the fog!" Sal breathed in astonishment.

Vig laughed, clearly, he didn't agree with Sal's conclusion; but it seemed plain to her!

"Keep a sharp eye out for the creature, untie the rest of the ropes and set your prow for the mainland!" Vig ordered.

Sal made her way to the back of the boat and took up her oar.

"What do you make of this!?" Theoph asked from behind her.

"Just that my prince; a blessing for our journey!"

"From Tylus?" Theoph asked, gazing back at the wall of fog.

"Or from another," Sal shrugged, assured now more than ever; whatever dangers they met, she had no reason to fear, their quest was guarded over.

* * * *

Salvage awoke with a start. She sat up, her hands grasping for her weapons out of reflex. The camp was awaking after their first night on the mainland, and all was as it should be. The waves of the sea pounded the jagged rocky shore, and the wind stirred the long wispy leaves of gnarled trees further inland. Sea birds called to each other as they flew out over the foggy surf. Sal tried to calm her breathing so that she could listen; but try as she might, there was no cry of a child.

"Are you alright?" Vigil asked as he sorted their equipment nearby.

Sal took a deep breath, "Just another dream."

Vig paused, "A vision?"

Sal watched him for a moment; he was always so eager to know what her nameless god had revealed to her. Like struggling to carry water in his hands, the gods seemed to be eluding him. "I don't know, perhaps."

"What did you see?"

"It wasn't clear," she said at length, thinking about the child. If Vig knew of her suspicion that she was with child, he would want to send her back to Verlyance with the returning warriors. She would not allow that. Her place was by his side, protecting the prince. She sat up straighter, her deception forgotten when she remembered the other part of her vision. "West!" she exclaimed, "We are to go west along the shore!"

Vig brightened, "Are you certain?"

Sal got up and looked westward, in her vision she had been urged west by the child's cry- Vig did not need to know that part. "Very. Where is the prince?" she asked, looking over the company as they fussed over breakfast and broke camp.

Vig nodded higher up on the rocks. "His majesty didn't sleep well; be gentle, love," he advised.

Theophany sat atop a boulder a stone throw from the camp, he was gazing out into the foggy sea with his back to the mainland and all its unknown adventures. Sal climbed up to him and stood at the boulders edge, looking up to him. She wondered if he was thinking of Courteous.

"My prince? I have been given a vision of where we are to go."

Theophany had been trying to connect with Tylus, hoping that somehow, he would achieve that which he had never been able to do before. He kept his gaze on the surf.

"Yes?" he asked, trying his best not to sound eager; a great king did not *need* to depend on others.

"My vision directs us west along the coast, I am certain of it," Sal explained, her voice suddenly subdued.

Theoph could not help it, he glanced down at her; she was watching him closely.

"Are you alright?" she asked.

Theoph raised his eyes again and straightened his back, "Yes of course." Did she think he was weak? "This vision came from your nameless god?"

She nodded.

He struggled for a moment; was it right to rely on visions from an unknown god when he could not receive guidance from Tylus? "West it is then," he declared and rose from his perch but could not withhold a sigh.

The company soon prepared breakfast, and it was revealed to the company that they would head west along the coast. The decision surprised some, as it had been discussed that their destination lay northward beyond the mountains, and some did not see the sense in wasting time traveling west, but these doubts were not shared freely amongst everyone.

Breakfast lasted longer than necessary, as everyone knew that when it was over, the company would be parting ways. Before everyone was quite done, Vigil began to announce who would be returning to Verlyance, and who would be accompanying the prince northward. There was some disappointment over the issue from a few, but none spoke out against the final decision. Theoph was surprised when Vig announced that Rend, the youth of the company, would go northward with them. The decision pleased the lad, as well as Salvage.

By late morning, the company that would go northward, set out along the shore, while the others stayed behind. Theoph could not help but wonder how long it would be till he saw them next. How far would they have to go before they found the Foretold King?

As they walked along the rocky shore, the view inland became clearer. "Vigil, what do you make of that?" Theoph asked as they stopped by a freshwater stream that flowed into the sea.

Vig turned to look; it seemed to turn to hill country further inland, but where the sky should be above the hills was a strange color.

Theoph gasped when he realized what it was, he was seeing, "Look higher!" he exclaimed, for what they were looking at was only the foothills, a layer of clouds topped these and above the clouds, far in the distance, were the mighty slopes of mountains that rose higher than Theoph thought possible! Everyone was now looking upwards.

Vig gave a low whistle, "So those are mountains!"

"How will we get through them?" Rend asked, gaping.

"We'll find a road further west," Salvage assured.

"Aye, I remember traveling on a road of sorts," Garden offered, "I can not say where we would find it though."

"How many mountains do you think there are?" Theoph asked, looking up and down the coast.

Garden answered humbly, "Many, my prince. It will take weeks to reach the northern side."

"Right then, shouldn't be much trouble!" Vig quipped sardonically.

The company traveled along the rocky shoreline for the better part of the day, with the sea on their left and the lofty mountain range on their right. As they went, the tree line became thicker and closer to the shore and the group marveled at how large, and straight the great trees were. They were quite unlike the foliage they were used to. When midday found them, the clouds cleared and more of the mountains were revealed; no one spoke anymore of how they were to cross them. Salvage put her mind to rest by thinking of a road through the mountains that they would find to the west, she imagined a wide, flat road, with plenty of signs pointing the way to their destination.

When the sun began her descent in the west and shone full on the company's faces, Sal noted that Garden was falling behind, his breath having grown labored. Sal quickened her pace to catch up with Vigil, who had gone up ahead and climbed a large outcropping.

"I think we should call a rest," Sal directed her voice upward when she came to the foot of the outcropping, "I fear the elder of our company is losing his strength."

Vig looked back, "That's alright, I told Garden I would carry him if need-be, and I'd say we haven't far to go." He returned his gaze west beyond the rocky outcropping.

Curious, Sal climbed the rocks and beheld a bay that carved into the land, where the mouth of a great mountain river joined the sea. On their side of the river lay a town of weathered wood logs and great stones. In the bay a handful of fishing boats rested in the late afternoon sun. Smoke from chimneys curled up and sat above the town, promising comfort, and rest.

"Did you see this in your vision?" Vig asked.

Sal shook her head but had a feeling it was the reason they had been sent west.

"Vigil, what see you?" Theophany called as the rest of the company drew near.

"A town, sire, we'll reach it before nightfall," Vig answered.

"They'll be able to tell us where to find a road through the mountains," Sal said happily to Vig.

"If they aren't hostile," Vig warned.

"I'm sure we'll be fine."

"My love, I admire your certainty," he said delicately, "but caution has always served a warrior well."

Sal smirked ruefully, "Very well, you think it's unwise to enter the town?"

"I wouldn't mind an assurance that they are friendly before deciding." He gave her a wink. Together they climbed back down to discuss the matter with the prince.

"Do we go forward?" Theoph asked.

"They could prove to be unfriendly to strangers, sire," Sal answered, receiving a grateful look from Vigil.

"Especially a foreign prince with a company of warriors," Vig added.

"They may have heard of the Foretold King," Theoph pointed out, "And if we are to know where to find a road that will take us north, we may have no choice but to enter the town."

Sal raised a challenging brow to her husband.

"I agree that to bypass the town we risk missing information that will aid us on our journey," Vig spoke, the frown on his dark face testifying how thoroughly he was considering their options.

Sal rolled her lips in, perhaps she *was* being too rash about this. Vig's level head was the better choice for considering all the options.

"Would it be best to send one or two into the town to discern what we need to know, and keep the rest of our company a secret?" Theoph asked while the others of the company stood about them.

Vig took a moment to think, "I advise against it my prince. If they prove to be unfriendly then we will have given them a hostage. On the other hand, if they are friendly but find we have deceived them and hidden a band of warriors, they may turn on us. It would be best to go in our full force, peacefully and without deception."

Theoph nodded, "Very well then. We continue on."

Sal tried not to be smug about the decision, but Vig caught her smile and shook his head ruefully. Soon the company regathered themselves and climbed the outcropping, before long they came upon a dirt road that led up to a wooden bridge that crossed the river. Before they had time to reconsider, they had reached the outskirts of the town.

Sal then arranged the warriors in a nonthreatening way that also situated the prince safely in the middle. She ordered them to not draw arms unless she or Vigil did so, but to keep a sharp eye on their surroundings. She did not believe it was necessary though.

Soon they began meeting the townsfolk, they looked similar to those on the Verlyance Isles, but their houses were so different from what Sal and the others were used to that they couldn't help but stare. Instead of huts with stone or living coral foundations and airy windows, nearly every building was made from great logs. Chickens wandered the streets, and fishing nets were stretched out over fences. One of the townsfolk they met looked them up and down, then turned and ran further into the town.

Sal guessed where he was heading and raised her eyes to a beautiful building in the center of town; it may even be considered a small castle.

"Steady now," Vig reminded the company as they moved forward at a leisurely pace. Now they had truly entered the town, and people were pausing in their work and staring at the strange company.

Sal's sixth sense prickled, and she glanced over her shoulder, sudden unease assailing her. Had she been wrong? They entered the town square, keeping their tight formation, before them rose the small castle. A crowd had now gathered to gape and watch.

"Keep sharp," Vig warned, "Here comes someone important looking."

A group of warriors matching their own in number, came to meet them, at their center was an elderly man with a gray beard, from the clothes he wore Sal guessed that he was the king, or more likely the lord of the town.

"Hail good folk," the old man said, his manner of speech was similar but had an accent that sounded strange to Sal's ears. "I am Orchard, lord of Fisher's Hamlet. I meet you in good faith."

Sal smiled, shooting her husband a triumphant look.

"Well met Lord Orchard," Vigil responded, ignoring her, "Theophany the Victorious, prince of Verlynn Nel of the Verlyance Isles, meets you also in good faith."

Theoph stepped forward, and Sal noted how he seemed to hold himself with greater pride than she had seen before, as if he was intent on proving something.

"Let us be friends Lord Orchard, my father the king of Verlyance sends his greeting through me. We have come on a quest from the sea god

Tylus; we seek a great king. He is the Foretold King, a mighty warrior and leader that has come into power in recent days." He paused, Lord Orchard looked bored as if he had heard the speech before, "You… have not heard of such a person?"

Lord Orchard cleared his throat, "Indeed we have not. There are no kings in these lands."

Sal could tangibly feel Theoph's disappointment.

"Our quest then takes us further north," Theoph said in a subdued tone. Sal knew he was thinking of Dyna. "Is there a road through the mountains?"

Lord Orchard answered quickly, "Indeed there are many passes through the Honorfell Mountains; Sentinel's Pass will take you northward through them, it lays inland from the hamlet. But I can not offer you a guide." He hesitated, "It is a long treacherous road; I will not risk any of my people."

There was a pause and both companies moved uncomfortably.

Sal turned her head, feeling again that something was not right. Her eyes caught onto an onlooker who stood on the outskirts. It was a child, of seven or so. The child had very dark skin and their hair stood up in a wild fashion. The child watched intently with a solemn face. Something about it stuck fast in Sal's mind, like an echo from a memory long lost.

"You and your company are welcome to camp on the northern outskirts of town with the other travellers," Lord Orchard offered after a moment of silence.

"*Other* travellers?" Vig asked with a frown.

"Indeed, you are not the first to come here with a divine quest." With that Lord Orchard turned and left. Sal found it all rather abrupt and wondered how many 'others' there had been.

"Not very welcoming," Vig grumbled to Sal as they all turned to the road that would take them to the northern outskirts.

Before they had quite left the streets of Fishers Hamlet, Sal caught sight of the child she had seen earlier, they were following along, watching with an intent gaze. Sal paused for a moment, and the child smiled knowingly, then turned and ran away.

"What is it?" Vig asked.

Sal shook her head, "I don't know. Something's… strange here."

Soon they had left the houses behind, and the front of their company halted overlooking the river that flowed from the Honorfell Mountain range. Sal, Vig and the prince made their way through the company and saw the reason for the halt; before them stretched out on the flat banks of the river, was a camp with strange men and women, in the center was a tent of dark blue. A banner blew in the wind at the top of the tent, it bore a strange signina.

"The other travellers?" Theoph guessed.

"I wonder what the gods have them seeking," Vigil mused.

Along the riverbanks, leading north into the wooded foothills was the path that led up into the mountains, towards Sentinel's Pass. It was well into dusk when the company had finished setting up camp. Conversation was subdued, for everyone was avoiding the topic of crossing the mountains. The reality that they would have to leave behind the sea had now dawned on them, and it was a sobering realization indeed.

"What happens to us if we die away from the sea?"

Sal heard Rend ask another warrior as they sat about a cook fire.

The warrior took a moment to respond, "We are separated from Tylus for all eternity, banished to a dry land, devoid of water. Cursed to thirst and wonder till the sea's dry up," he ended with false cheerfulness and clapped a hand on Rend's shoulder, "Try not to die, alright?"

Sal smiled grimly to herself; she would not share that fate when death claimed her. In the same way that she had forsaken Tylus, so she would be forsaken by the sea god. She was not bothered by this, only that Vigil's fate would be different from hers.

"Hail and good fortune to you," a servant from the other travellers greeted as he came into their camp.

Vigil moved to block his way to the prince, his face unmoving.

"Well met," Theoph returned the greeting.

"My mistress, Lady Serene of the eastern courts of Fairthin invites you to break your days fast with her, and bids that you be welcome in her presence." The servant delivered the formal invitation with aplomb, and it took Sal and the others a few moments to interpret his strange way of speech.

Although he looked much like the people of Fisher's Hamlet, he spoke with yet another accent.

Theoph looked to Sal, she shrugged; she saw no harm. Theoph looked to Vig next, he hesitated, then nodded grimly.

"The invitation is most gracious," Theoph responded, "I am Theophany-"

Vig interrupted, "The Victorious, prince of the Verlyance Isles and honored champion of Verlynn Nel."

Sal smirked at Vigil's over the top introduction.

The servant nodded and indicated that they should follow. Vigil picked up his weapon and led the way, while Sal beckoned two other warriors to come with them.

Theophany was ushered into the tent and blinked in the well-lit interior. Before him was an arrangement of pillows around a splendid spread of brass platters and goblets. A steaming feast was set out, complete with different meat dishes, fruit, and a soup.

An elegant woman rose to greet them, her skin was a rich brown, and her white wiry hair was held back in a net. She wore a gown the color of a sunset, it had long sleeves and a high lace collar. Her face was long and gaunt with age, yet she held herself with dignity and poise. She held in her hand a short staff of carved wood, on its head was a silver ball, it shone with luster in the firelight.

"Theophany the Victorious, prince of the Verlyance Isles and honored champion of Verlynn Nel," the servant announced, then bowed and backed away.

Theoph bowed his head, unsure of what was proper, "Lady Serene, your invitation is most gracious."

She bowed her own head, "Who is the more gracious? The one to extend the invitation, or the one to accept it?" her strict face broke slightly in a tight smile, "I was unaware that I would be graced with the presence of a prince on my travels, please excuse these humble surroundings," she gestured around her.

Theoph felt foolish; this woman appeared to travel with more wealth than the palace of Verlynn Nel!

"Humble accommodations are to be expected while traveling." Theoph pointed out, wondering how his father would have responded.

"Indeed. Please join me, your maiden is welcome too," she said, eyeing Salvage dubiously.

This comment caught Theoph off guard, he glanced at Sal and saw that both she and Vigil were dumbfounded.

"These are my… most loyal warriors, Salvage and Vigil," Theoph said, uncertainly.

Lady Serene blinked once, Theoph supposed it was surprise that flitted across her face, "Yes, of course," she recovered quickly, "Bring food for the guards of our guest." She again eyed Salvage, like she wasn't sure what to do with her.

It dawned on Theoph then that Lady Serene's company, while having maidservants, did not have any women garbed as warriors. Theoph tucked away the observation for another time, and sat down on the pillows, they were soft and made from something shiny that Theoph had never seen before.

Lady Serene lowered herself to the pillows with apparent ease, "You hail from the Verlyance Isles you say, where is that? I have heard of no such place."

"Nor I of your country," Theoph helped himself to the food before him and noted that Sal and Vig had taken up a stance behind him. "The fair islands of Verlyance are many weeks to the south across the sea."

Lady Serene nodded, "I did not realize there were any rulers to be found on the seas, my ignorance has been enlightened. While my fair home is far to the west. Unlike your most prestigious self, I lay no claim to royalty. Merely the daughter of a lord in the eastern courts of Fairthin."

Theoph again took stock of the rich surroundings and felt a moment of uncertainty; he had always known Verlyance was a small and humble kingdom, he just had not realized how true that was! He reminded himself of the satchel on his belt and the precious treasures within. It was a king's ransom by any standards surely! He told himself this to boost his confidence, it worked only slightly.

"The lord of the Fishers Hamlet spoke of travellers on a quest like ours," Theoph steered the conversation, "I confess that I was intrigued."

Lady Serene raised her eyebrows, "Indeed, as I am intrigued, it seems we both would ask the same question of each other. I will save us the trouble and ask it only once; what is the nature and goal of the quest you are on?"

Her strange and lengthy way of speaking bemused Theoph, and he was not sure if she was entirely serious. "My company and I set out some weeks past on a quest most wondrous. A mighty omen was sent to us from the sea god Tylus; thousands of golden sea stars washed up on our shores many nights past."

Lady Serene returned his gaze blankly, as if his statement meant nothing.

Theoph cleared his throat and glanced at Sal and Vig, "Golden Sea stars are a treasured talisman from the god of our people," Theoph explained, feeling foolish- didn't she know? "They foretell of a great king coming into power, and in this instance, a king like no other, he will conquer all the lands and bring them all under his standard. Tylus has sent us out to seek this Foretold King and make an alliance with him."

Lady Serene set aside her drink and closed her eyes, Theoph could not guess what she would do next.

She smiled, even laughed slightly, "When I told you that I did not expect to meet a prince on my travels, I lied. I did not want to raise my hopes in vain. For you see, I too am on a wondrous quest."

Theoph blinked in surprise and heard both Sal and Vig move slightly behind him. "You seek the Foretold King?"

Lady Serene actually scoffed, "Certainly not. Allow me to share my tale with you. From an early age I sought after that which all may grow rich from, yet that which few seek, wisdom. I began collecting ancient books and tomes from days long lost to us, many saw folly in my actions; but I am now revered in my land as the wisest counsellor."

Theoph's mind drifted unintentionally, and his thoughts were captured by a memory of Dyna reading aloud to him an old folktale.

"Do you grow tired?" Lady Serene's sharp voice focused his mind quickly.

"Forgive me- please continue," Theoph urged, knowing that Sal was rolling her eyes.

Lady Serene gave him a look to wither fresh flowers, "It came to my attention, many years past, of a prophecy. The script was vague, but it spoke of the coming of one who would contain the wisdom of all the ages; the prophecy named them, the Wise One. I have spent the last years of my life searching for more on the Wise One, I searched and collected books from every land far and near, a task that has cost me much, and required that I learn the tongue of different lands. Woven into each one, sometimes deep into the history of some countries, there are legends, prophecies, and songs of the Wise One. I have done little else than study these words of old, and at last I discovered the treasure of my life's labor." She paused to breathe deep, as if reliving the moment again, "The Wise One has come. Many nights I dared to hope that I might see the days of the Wise One, and now, before I breathe my last, I shall."

Theoph raised his goblet. "A toast to your quest; may you find that which you seek," he offered, hoping that her tale was nearly done.

She smiled knowingly, "Your words are fitting, for it is your presence that confirms I am on the right path."

Theoph froze, his goblet hovering halfway to his lips, "*My* presence?"

"Indeed, many of the old songs and legends promised that she who would seek the Wise One would know her path is true when once she joined the company of a prince on a quest set to him by the gods." Her words hung heavy in the air.

"Truly!?" Theoph was baffled, surely the woman was half mad!

"I have dedicated my life to this quest," she answered sternly, "I know that of which I speak."

Theoph glanced back at Sal; if anyone could make sense of this, she could!

Sal hesitated before speaking, "My lady, are you certain that my lord the prince is the omen of your quest?"

Lady Serene raised her own goblet, "My dear child, I am very certain. All that remains now, is whether or not you will accept my company on your travels."

"We are set to venture north through Sentinel's Pass and into the lands beyond," Theoph pointed out, remembering the warnings of danger.

But Lady Serene did not even flinch, "A treacherous path to be sure, I would be glad of the extra security of your company."

"My lady you do understand that we seek the Foretold King- how will you find the one you seek if you come with us?"

"Solutions present themselves to those who work hard," Lady Serene said it like an old proverb, "Perhaps your Foretold King is seeking out the counsel of the Wise One. Now, what is your answer?"

Theoph was speechless for a moment, "Very well then! We shall travel north together!" he decided and raised his goblet in agreement.

Lady Serene smiled and nodded her head like he was a student she had been training. "It is said in my lands that 'a treasure is readily found when searched for by earnest hearts.' May both our hearts be earnest, and our journey's fruitful."

The stones crunched under Salvage's boots as she walked along the shore of the river. There was an incline ahead that the river curved away from, and beyond it came the reassuring sound of surf pounding the shore. Outlined by the starry sky, stood the prince and Vigil. The night was growing old, yet there was too much excitement in the air to sleep after the prince and Lady Serene's dinner; there were many things to prepare for their journey inland.

"I advise against saying anything to them." Vigil's voice was carried to Sal on the breeze as she approached them. "They know the risks ahead of us, if this brings them peace, then nothing you can say would help."

Sal reached them and saw what they were talking about; below on the shore were their warriors, kneeling and standing in the water, some up to their necks. Sal saw one stoop to collect sea water in a small leather flask. They were taking as much of the sea with them as they could, in the hopes that if they should die far inland, that the small amount of salt water they brought with them would be enough to see their soul safely back to Tylus.

It brought a deep sorrow to Sal's heart; they, unlike her, had to leave their god behind. As though his thoughts were similar to hers, Vig raised a hand to his neck and subconsciously touched something beneath his tunic; he carried his own flask of salt water.

A silence stretched between the three of them as they watched.

"Would you like me to fetch you some salt water, sire?" Sal asked the prince respectfully.

"Fear of death is for mortal men," Theoph muttered, "I am the prophesied king; it would dishearten the men if they knew that I feared my own demise."

Sal frowned.

They were startled by the sound of a footfall behind them. The child that Sal had seen in the town stood behind them with great big, solemn eyes; brilliantly blue. The contrast between the child's eyes and dark face was startling, and aside from Garden's eerie features, Sal had never seen the like before.

"Hello, are you lost?" Vig asked, scanning the area for others, but the child was alone.

"The Ancient One would speak with you," the child informed them.

Sal's mouth opened slightly, and a shiver ran across her skin.

"Who?" Vig asked, unaware of what Sal could sense.

"My master; the Ancient One. Will you come?"

"What does he want with us?" Theoph asked, baffled.

The child turned their blue eyes on the prince, "You seek the Foretold King, the Ancient One would have you find him."

Sal felt breathless; something beyond what she could see was happening. She could hear the child's cry from her visions.

"Very well, take us to your master," Theoph decided.

Vig straightened his weapon belt and followed behind as the child turned inland.

Sal fought to keep her wits about her, she felt as though she had slipped into another vision. In the back of her mind, she questioned why she felt that way, but as Vig always said, she let her heart get away with her too often.

The child led them along in the starlight, sure footed and never once looked back. They passed by their camp and continued into the tree line, climbing a rocky incline. White stones marked their path, and soon the sound of the sea was left behind. At last, they turned a corner in the path and beheld a small hut, glowing with candlelight.

White linen was hung in the doorway and windows, shifting in the gentle breeze, while the soft glow of candles revealed silhouettes within.

Vigil went on ahead of them and circled the hut, making sure nothing was afoot. The child waited till he returned then slipped past the cloth door, Sal followed first.

The hut had rough interior walls, and a dirt floor covered by a woven reed rug. An old woman with wild hair to match the child's, sat in the center of the rug. Her eyes were deep brown, and her skin was worn, brown and wrinkled. A basket of seeds sat in her lap, and her skinny hands worked methodically to shell them. There was little else in the room except for a large thin object concealed under more white linen.

Theoph sat down facing the woman and waited. Without a word the child sat down beside the woman and beckoned for Vig and Sal to do the same.

"What do you want with us?" Theoph asked quietly.

"Bring water for our guests," the child instructed the woman.

Sal blinked in surprise when the woman got up, took her basket, and left.

"I am Voy; I speak for the Ancient One," the child said with authority.

They all turned their eyes on the child, uncertain what to expect next.

"The Ancient One speaks through whoever will listen when they are called to."

"Who *is* the Ancient One?" Theoph asked slowly.

"The believer knows," Voy said, looking directly at Sal.

Sal was taken aback, "I do?"

"You have heard the call of the Ancient One in your visions."

"My visions are from the Ancient One?!" Sal felt Vigil's eyes on her.

"The Ancient One calls to many, yet few are those who listen, even fewer are those who hear."

"You said your master wants us to find the Foretold King, can you tell us where to find him?" Theoph asked, Sal could tell his patience was growing short.

"My message to you is threefold. First to the believer, your visions are truths directly from the Ancient One, think on them often, yet beware, to reach you they must travel through the human veil that is your mind. The truth will often become distorted and confused, do not be eager to grasp that which you most want to be true. Secondly, to the seeker," the child looked at Vig, "Your heart is both earnest and sceptical, it serves you well. You understand the lies for what they are, and it has driven you to seek out the truth. Do not give up; the Ancient One is revealed to those who seek earnestly. And lastly, to the vessel," the child's eyes rested on Theoph, "You seek that which can not be found but the path you take will lead you to a greater treasure still. Heed the words of the believer and trust those of the seeker. Be warned that you will never find the Foretold King so long as your heart is plagued, and your eyes closed."

"What do you mean? Speak plainly!" Theoph demanded.

"Even the plainest words are riddles to those who are not ready to understand."

"Please, tell us where to find the Foretold King," Sal urged.

"A reward given that is not earned is never truly appreciated. Many will seek the Foretold King, and many will never find him. A broken vessel can not carry anything of worth; it must be remade. It is the same with you," Voy pointed at Theoph.

"What is wrong with the prince- please tell us!" Sal begged, sensing that they were straying from safety.

Voy beckoned and the old woman came back inside. She picked up the large object with care, set it down beside the child and removed the cloth; it was a looking glass.

For a moment Sal looked into her own eyes.

"Some will not believe until they have seen. Others will not see, until they believe," the child went on.

"What sorcery is this?" Theoph asked in a shaken voice, his eyes were fixed on the mirror. Sal followed his gaze and froze in shock. The prince's reflection was distorted and disfigured, his flesh missing, bones showing, and his clothes riddled with holes. Sal and Vig's reflections sat on either side, perfectly normal and whole.

"I have spoken no falsehood; the mirror reveals the state of your soul; it is plagued by a heart stain. You are the vessel that is broken."

"What have you done?!" Vig asked, astonished, and confused, his eyes going between the looking glass and the prince.

"I have revealed the truth. The heart stain is of the prince's own actions, and he will face the consequences."

"Lift this curse at once!" Theoph demanded, rising to his feet angrily, Sal and Vig followed him.

"I can not."

"Liar!" Theoph shouted angrily, his arm flinging out and striking the looking glass, it tipped over and fell, shattering on the dirt floor. The child met his stormy gaze unflinchingly. Theoph sucked air in through his teeth, then he turned and stormed out.

Sal glanced at Vig, then followed the prince. "Sire!" she called as Theoph found the white stone path and began the descent, she hurried to catch up.

"Was this your doing!?" Theoph turned on her, his body trembling in anger.

Sal caught her breath and stepped back, "Sire…" she breathed in disbelief, she had never seen him like this, not even when Courteous died.

"Your god; your curse!" he accused boldly.

"My loyalty is yours, as it always will be," she answered carefully, "I know nothing more of this than you."

Theoph breathed heavily, searching her face, "I want nothing to do with your god. I have no use for the gods of mortal men." He turned on his heel and hurried down the path.

Back in the hut, Vigil pulled aside the cloth door and hesitated as he saw Theoph, and Sal disappear into the night. His heart was beating wildly, and his thoughts were like sea foam tossed in a storm. He had wasted so much time begging Tylus to answer, or even acknowledge him, and here was Sal's nameless god, named at last, speaking aloud.

He turned back to the child, "How can I help him?" he asked.

Voy smiled, an honest one, like something good had at last happened. The child picked up a shard of the looking glass and handed it to Vig, "Seek the truth."

Vig looked down at his reflection for a moment, remembering the grotesque one of the prince. The first thing to seek was the nature of a heart stain.

Chapter 5 Out of place

The evening crowds of Garatin City were thick in the streets as workers made their way home, kitchen maids ran errands and stableboys prepared horses for their masters. Tarvin guards riding spirited mounts, cleared the street for a carriage bearing the emblem of Brier Ridge Castle, while the Tarvin lord and his son rode with them. They were dressed richly for a banquet thrown by the Tarvin governor, Endure, of whom they were eager to impress and please. Inside the carriage was the lord's daughter, Regime, it was to be her first banquet amongst the court that night, and she fidgeted with nervous energy. Across from her, sat her handmaiden, a Garatin girl by the namesake of Dream.

Regime carefully arranged her long raven hair over her shoulder, pleased with how the setting sun gleamed on its curls. Her dress was navy blue with open sleeves of deep mauve, matching flowers had been pinned into her hair, each one approved for perfection by Gime herself.

"I want you to watch him all night, tell me who he speaks with, who he dances with and if he ever watches me," Gime instructed, "But don't be caught watching him!" she warned sharply.

Dream nodded, focusing intently on what her mistress was saying, but the growing rumble of the crowd outside nagged for her attention.

Gime looked her up and down, "Keep well away from me through the evening, I don't care what my father said, having no escort is better than having a Garatin girl hanging about." She turned her eyes away like Dream's appearance pained her, "I will not have my first appearance in court talked about because of you."

Dream swallowed hard, she wished she had been left behind. Regime was extra cutting with her words that evening, leaving a raw lump in Eam's throat.

"Oh, and keep an eye on who Tenacious keeps company with," Gime spoke of her older brother with a mischievous gleam in her dark eyes.

Eam's attention was at last claimed by the intensifying noise outside the carriage, Gime noticed too, and leaned a hand on the door to look out the window.

The door swung open and Gime pitched forward, angry shouts and cries filled the carriage and the dusty cobble stones of the street blurred past as the carriage picked up speed suddenly.

Eam jumped forward and caught Gime's arm and pulled her back to safety. Her mistress squealed and flopped back into her seat. Eam reached out to shut the door and was face to face with a stranger, he was a Garatin. He reached for her with one hand, in the other he wielded a knife. Eam fell back, slipping from his grasp, she landed a kick to his chest, behind her Gime released an ear-splitting scream and the carriage pitched to a halt.

The assailant clung to the carriage door and reached for Eam's foot. She kicked again, pulling free, even as she heard the coachmen and other guards dealing with what must be more of the rabble attacking the carriage. The assailant was suddenly pulled from the doorway and thrown down to the street by a young man in the armor of a Tarvin soldier. The assailant swiped at the soldier's feet with his knife, the soldier jumped nimbly, his movements faster than Eam could follow. The knife soon clattered to the cobblestones.

The carriage guards swarmed in and restrained the disarmed attacker. The soldier turned, his pale Garatin face surprised Eam and made her stare when she did not intend to. His light brown hair hung about his sharp jawline and his gray eyes grabbed hold of her own.

"Are you harmed, my lady?" he asked, leaning into the carriage and offering his hand.

'Lady!?' no one addressed her as a *lady*! She took his hand and sat up, flicking her dress hem back over her feet. "No, I'm alright," she managed, certain that Gime would scold her soundly for allowing the soldier to assume *she* was the lady. But a quick glance over her shoulder revealed that Regime had fainted.

Regime's father appeared at the door and pushed the soldier aside, "Regime!?" he called urgently, ignoring Eam as she scrambled out of his way. She caught the soldier's gaze for a moment longer, he nodded as if to confirm that she was indeed all right. She managed to answer with a nod of her own before her view was obstructed.

Dream was pushed to the edge and forgotten about as the older women of the court fussed over Regime, asking a thousand questions, hardly pausing for answers. Gime soaked in the attention, embellishing the story of the carriage attack till it sounded like they had wandered into a battlefield instead of running afoul of a few rioters.

Eam backed away, mentally rehearsing what she would tell her own mother when the night was over. She could already hear her mother mutter about how the riots were getting worse and how nothing was being done about it. Music and the hum of a crowd's soft conversation drifted in from the banquet hall while the women fussed over Gime in the entrance. Eam tried to get a better view of the hall, hoping to find a corner where she could go unnoticed.

Lord Eloquence, Regime's father, approached the gaggle of women and they shied away from him as he faced his daughter. Gime pouted at her father, trying to gain special treatment, but Lord Eloquence would have none of it and he impatiently escorted Gime into the hall. Before following them, Gime's older brother lingered among the women for a moment, his charming smile bringing forth their shy laughter. From the far edge of the room, Eam observed as though invisible.

When everyone had entered the banquet hall, Eam slipped in after them, hugging the walls, she kept up with Regime while Lord Eloquence began formal introductions to lords and dukes. Gime fluttered her eyelashes and smiled coyly, obviously recovered from her 'near brush with death.'

'He wouldn't have harmed her' Eam reasoned to calm her own nerves. No one in their right mind would harm the daughter of a Tarvin lord- not if he wanted to live long, the man was probably lucky to only be punished with twenty years in a cell as it was! Eam on the other hand, was just a Garatin handmaiden, she could have been run through and left bleeding in the street, and no one would have cared all that much. Eam's thoughts ran headfirst into the Garatin soldier in Tarvin armor; *he* seemed like he would have cared.

Dream's attention was refocused as Governor Endure raised his voice to address the crowd, "Welcome my guests!" he lifted his goblet to the room, he was an old man with dignified eyes and a serious face. "Raise your glass to a young soldier who this very hour, saved Lord Eloquence's dear daughter from Garatin rebels, though some have doubted his devotion, this young soldier has proven time and again his loyalty to Tarva!" he beckoned forth a young man.

Eam stepped forward to get a better look at her rescuer. The toast was raised, and Eam noticed there were many who upon seeing the soldier's fair skin, refused to raise their glass, if the soldier noticed, he did not show it. After the governor had drunk, he clapped a hand on the soldier's shoulder, and spoke a few words to him, Lord Eloquence did likewise. Soon the banqueters returned to their conversations, anxious to move away from the unpleasant topic of Garatin's in Tarvin armor.

Eam's face heated up when the young soldier's eyes found hers, she looked away quickly, dearly hoping that her face had not gone red; did he recognize her?

Soon the area between the banquet tables was cleared for a dance and circles of eight people were formed. The musicians began a lighthearted tune and those who were not dancing stepped aside. Eam watched Regime wait expectantly for a dance partner, but she was left standing alone, overlooked in favour of other maidens. Eam winced in empathy.

"I apologise about earlier," a kind voice spoke at her side.

Eam moved out of the way, assuming the voice addressed someone else. Out of the corner of her eye she saw the Garatin soldier, waiting for her response. She opened her mouth but could think of nothing to say.

His gray eyes betrayed no humor in her discomfort. "I trust you are unharmed," he shifted his feet and did not meet her gaze directly.

He was nervous; this gave Eam new confidence, "Yes of course, I am quite alright. I am just relieved that my mistress did not come to harm."

"She almost seemed restful."

Eam was taken aback for a moment; was he serious? She remembered Gime slumped on the carriage seat, passed out from fright.

The soldier's right eyebrow raised ever so slightly.

Eam tried to hold back a smile, "I suppose she was."

He bowed his head slightly, "I am Wilderness." He held out a tentative hand for hers.

"Dream," she answered, and placed her hand in his, aware of her heart fluttering in her chest.

He bowed over her hand in a formal greeting, Eam took the chance to look him up and down quickly. "You are a soldier?" her curiosity taking over; she didn't know Garatin's could be Tarvin soldiers!

He straightened and released her hand. "That's right," there was a hint of defensiveness in his tone, "I was tasked with controlling the crowd, something I did rather poorly, I'm afraid."

"Governor Endure seemed pleased enough," Eam pointed out.

"All the same, I should have been more vigilant," his tone had turned shameful, "and prevented the rioters from ever reaching your carriage."

Eam wondered if he was always this hard on himself and wished that he would go back to jesting. "I suppose you have much to pay attention to," she hesitated, wondering how well he would take a jest from her, "Putting one foot in front of the other can be a trifle difficult."

The smallest of rueful smiles formed on his face, "Well said. Although I admit that I *am* glad my attention lapsed, for if I had stopped the rebel from reaching your carriage, I might never have met you."

Eam pretended to be shocked, "The governor would be dismayed to hear that one of his soldiers was *glad* he made a mistake!"

"If he were to find out I would simply have to defend myself by listing all that I must pay attention to."

"Like walking?" Eam teased, surprised to find herself so at ease with his company.

Wilderness shrugged and held his hands behind his back. "A soldier must know many things about his environment," he bragged humbly.

Eam raised her eyebrows, "Indeed? like what, may I ask?"

"Take this banquet for example, I should be aware of how many people there are, how many of them have weapons, who of them might become a threat... There are about thirteen who I would find difficult to subdue if they became a threat," he reported, frankly.

Eam followed his gaze about the room, all she saw were lords and their ladies, dancing and enjoying the music, none of whom paid them any mind. She was not sure if Wilderness was being serious or not.

"I must also know how many exits there are," he ended.

"That's simple enough," Eam declared, "There are four." She smiled, pleased with herself.

He smirked, "Twelve, actually."

Eam blinked in surprise, searching the hall for other doors that she had missed, "Twelve!?"

He nodded, "Counting all the doors, and windows there are ten possible escape routes."

"And the other two?" She felt sure he was jesting again.

"A fireplace may seem unlikely, but they can be climbed out of if need be."

Eam laughed this time, "And the last exit is someone's pocket?"

He frowned playfully, "I would never fit. No, the last is the secret passage."

"Where?" she asked sceptically.

"If I told you, it would hardly be a secret," he pointed out stubbornly.

Eam tilted her head back, "There is no secret passageway, is there?"

"By the Neenor; there *is*!" he insisted.

Eam looked away, keeping her sceptical expression, "If you insist."

"It's under the dais," Wilderness assured her, "around to the side there is a little door, it leads to a passageway that lets out in the servant quarters. I was once a guard here, I had to know everything about this castle."

Eam smirked, "Is it also a requirement of soldiers that they must give away secrets so easily?"

He froze for a moment, then a slight blush rose in his pale face, "Only when they're trying to impress a beautiful maiden." The words seemed to be forced from his lips in a rush.

She gaped at him for a moment, trying to decide if he was in jest or not. He looked down and scoffed his boot on the floor.

"Eam," Lord Eloquence called sharply, he stood nearby waving for her impatiently.

"I must go," Eam explained, slipping past Wilderness. He bowed his head meekly, avoiding looking at either her or Lord Eloquence.

Eam turned her back on him, hardly believing the conversation had happened at all. Ahead of her the governor and Lord Eloquence stood with another Tarven that Eam did not know.

"Where is the guest of honor?" the third man asked impatiently in a low tone.

Lord Eloquence frowned. "There have been heavy rains, the river could be swollen, delaying his arrival," he suggested.

"He will come, the champion of the Five Isles would hardly be washed downriver," the governor assured.

"Nevertheless, I will take charge of the maiden as was agreed," Lord Eloquence waved for Eam to step forward. It was then that she noticed a young Tarvin maiden waiting nearby. She stood with head bowed and face downcast.

"I would have my daughter look after her, but as you know, she has had a nasty shock earlier. Her handmaiden will look after her," Eloquence explained.

"Very well, I present Lady Loyal, of the Tarvin courts," the third man said, waving the maiden over to Eloquence like passing off a parcel. The Tarvin maiden stepped forward, her eyes never leaving the floor.

Eloquence bowed over her hand. "Sit and rest till your betrothed arrives, my lady," he instructed, and passed her off to Eam, "See that her appearance isn't spoiled," he added.

Eam nodded, swallowing her dislike of the situation; no wonder the maiden was downcast, she had been prepared like a flower arrangement for a stranger.

"I am Dream my lady; you may call me Eam. You can sit at the banquet table for a time and rest," Eam suggested as she led her away.

Loyal did not respond, and only kept her eyes down, like afraid of meeting anyone's gaze. She was a very lovely maiden, Eam envied her; she was a classic Tarvin beauty with long raven hair and delicate features. She wore jewels on her neck, in her hair and even sewn into her dress, her dowry. A final plea from the bride's family to her new husband, to treat her well. Eam wondered what this maiden's future held. She led her to a seat near the dais, as was fitting for the betrothed of the guest of honor. Eam made sure her goblet was full and had all she needed, then she stepped back to wait by the wall for further instructions.

Loyal grabbed her hand, keeping her by her side, "Please sit with me," she spoke for the first time, unshed tears in her brown eyes.

"Of course, my lady," Eam assured softly and sank down on the bench beside her, wary of someone scolding her for sitting there, but no one took notice of them.

"Is…" Eam hesitated, "Are you all right, my lady?"

Loyal, looked at her from the corner of her eye. "I miss my home," she whispered.

"Where are you from?"

"Tarva," Loyal said, "I left almost two months ago."

Eam blinked in surprise; the guest of honor must be an especially important man to have a bride brought all the way from Tarva! "You are here alone?"

Loyal nodded, "To meet the man I am to marry."

Eam fell silent, and she thought of her own future, luckily, being a servant, she had a good chance of knowing the man she would marry, she may even have a say in who it would be. Not all were as fortunate.

Loyal's eyes wandered the room, and her breath became shallow. "I can not stay here! Will you help me?" she whispered breathlessly- desperately.

Eam felt frozen, "How?"

"A ship leaves for Tarva next week, and there is a caravan on the road west of here going towards the sea. They will leave in the morning; but they promised I could travel with them. I have only to escape the city!" her eyes darted towards the hall entrance where Lord Eloquence could be seen. "This is the first time that I haven't been heavily watched- Eam, please," the tears were welling in her eyes now, "Help me."

Eam felt like the walls were closing in on her, the noise of the banquet was either too loud or not there at all. What would her mother say? If she were discovered, her punishment would be severe. But…

"I can get you out of the castle," she offered, hardly believing her own words. Her heart was pounding faster than when the rebel had attacked her. "I know of a secret passage; the guards will never know where you went!" She glanced to the dais where Wilderness had insisted there was a door, she dearly hoped he had been telling the truth.

"Now- it must be now," Loyal urged, "If my betrothed comes, I'll never be able to get away!"

Eam glanced about the room to make sure they weren't being watched. "This way, towards the dais, don't rush though! There should be a door…" Eam led the way, fear rising; what if there was no door?

Around to one side the dais, the girls inched, and there, set into the stone, was a little wooden door with an iron latch. Loyal clasped Eam's hand- her skin was like ice! With one last look around, Eam reached down and tried the latch; it opened easily, and the door swung inward.

"Quickly!" Eam urged, pushing Loyal through first, then slipping in behind her, she shut the door as quick as she could and they stood in the darkness, listening to the muffled music and laughter over their own breath. Eam's eyes adjusted to the darkness, and she felt along the wall, the passage was narrow and the floor slightly uneven. Ahead there came a faint light, it was enough, and Eam tugged on Loyal's hand, "This way."

"Thank you Eam- I will never forget this!" Loyal whispered, relief and anxious hope filling her voice.

Wilderness stood still in the torchlight and forced his breath to still so that he could listen. A faint shuffling of feet echoed from the passage on his right; they had not slipped past yet. He tried to relax and ran through the situation in his mind. Should he have told someone else? When he saw the maidens disappear into the secret passage, his first thought was to catch them, not inform others. He wondered briefly if he was trying to protect Eam.

'She could be delivering the lady to kidnappers!' he tried to tell his runaway heart, 'Don't be distracted by a pretty face, keep a clear mind.' He struggled to do so.

The voices of the two women crept down the passage to his ears and he readied himself for whatever would happen. Changing his mind last minute, he shifted into the shadows.

Dream appeared first, wide-eyed, Lady Loyal coming up behind her, clinging to her hand.

"Which way?" Loyal asked in dismay when they saw the two passages before them.

"That depends on where you're going," Wilder spoke and stepped into the light, he leaned against the wall, to try and put them at ease; he did not want to chase them in the narrow passage.

Dream stepped back and sucked in her breath, her eyes widening even more. She kept the Tarvin maiden behind her.

"If you're headed back to the banquet, it's the way you came," he added, searching Eam's face; what was she up to?

"Please don't punish her!" Loyal begged, stepping out in front, "She was only following my orders."

Wilder was surprised by this, and he studied them for a moment, "And what *are* you doing, my lady?"

Loyal hesitated.

"My lady was feeling overwhelmed," Eam volunteered humbly, "I only wanted to help."

Wilder waited, unconvinced.

"Is it so hard to believe that a lady should be nervous to meet her betrothed for the first time?" Loyal asked, drawing herself up, no doubt realizing that he was only a foot soldier.

Wilder set his jaw, "May I escort you back, my lady?"

Loyal let a small breath escape her, "Very well."

Taking her arm gently above the elbow, Wilder directed her the way he had come- it would be hard to explain things if they all appeared from the door under the dais! Eam followed silently, and Wilder could not help but wonder if she would be punished. Soon they reached the edge of the banquet hall. Luckily, there was no one nearby to see them re-enter. Beyond them the dancing had paused, and attention had been centered on one man, a young Tarvin soldier,

Dismay took over Loyal's features for a moment before she swept them away and replaced them with a stoic, blank expression. "I will not need an escort from here," she waited unflinching for Wilder to release her, then she glided into the hall with head held high.

Dream tried to slip past but Wilder raised his arm to halt her. "She was running away," he guessed in a low tone.

Eam searched his face for a moment. "If she was, I would find no fault in it., she answered with a surprising tone of defiance. She was angry with him. She walked past him, and he was left alone to wonder if he had done the right thing.

"Keep a clear mind," he muttered to himself, refusing to let his eyes linger on Eam. He watched as Loyal approached her guardian, the men around her all bowed respectfully, and her guardian formally presented her to the guest of honor. Wilder narrowed his eyes as the young soldier looked her over with a proud expression; he had an instant disliking of the man.

* * * *

"By this time, the Earl of Sea Stone had emptied his holdings and fled to the east side of the island, leaving his keep empty and unguarded. A group of rebels, thirty strong, broke in and made the keep their base, barricading themselves in. Cut off from the rest of the knights with no hope of reinforcements, Sir Voi led his men in an attempt to storm the keep at dawn, they were slaughtered, and Sir Voi was cut down with two arrows in his neck," the speaker paused for dramatic emphasis.

The group of soldiers who had gathered about in the barracks listened eagerly to the story, while Wilderness sat on the corner of his cot, applying oil to the blade of his dagger.

"The company was reduced to fourteen men, three of them could no longer walk, and they all scattered after the failed attack."

The storyteller was interrupted by another soldier, "I heard Courage was captured in the attack and that he fought his way out, taking with him a captive." The others hushed him and urged the original storyteller to continue.

Wilder smirked in scorn; the story became more gloriously impossible each time he heard it! It was late in the morning after the banquet, and after their morning training the soldiers had gathered in the barracks to hear the tale of Courage's deeds in full. They had yet to see the guest of honor from last night's banquet, and Wilder dearly hoped that his comrades would be disappointed when the man finally showed himself.

"Courage searched the island and found the remains of his comrades," the storyteller continued. "They had to hide from roaming rebel bands, all the while Courage nursed his own wounds from the earlier attack. Knowing that their lives depended on it, Courage climbed the tallest tree he could find, and discovered another company of rebels, fifty strong, approaching from the north. They would reach the keep an hour after sundown. That's when he devised his plan."

Wilder rolled his eyes.

"He had some men sneak up to the wall of the keep and hang the flag of Tarva on it's ramparts, all the while the rebels inside were none the wiser. Next, he posted men near the keep, hidden in the trees, while others waited by the road. Some time before the rebels arrived, Courage sounded a great bell, like the harbor sounded when a ship docked, thus, to make those in the keep believe that an enemy ship had arrived. Next Courage and the others waited till nightfall. When the approaching band of rebels came within sight, Courage's men shouted out as though part of their company and exclaimed that the keep was still in the hands of the Tarvins! At this same time, the men posted near the keep shouted out in warning that Tarvin troops had arrived to retake the keep!

"The two groups of rebels were set into a frenzy and the band on the road rushed forward to attack the keep, while those inside defended as best they could, but the gates were broken in and Courage and his men rushed in with the rebels. In the confusion and rage of battle, Courage rallied his men and routed the rebels, killing forty with his own sword while his men killed another sixty! They took the rest of the rebels captive and made safe the keep of Sea Stone, thus turning the tide of the Five Isle war!"

The others grinned and applauded the storyteller.

"Hogwash and fool's bait!" Wilder exclaimed, unable to hold his tongue a moment more.

The others turned to him in silence, and he bore their dark Tarvin gazes without flinching.

"I beg your pardon?" the storyteller questioned quietly.

"Earlier you said that there were thirty rebels inside the keep and another fifty on the road, making eighty in all- so how could they have killed a hundred rebels and taken yet more captive?!" Wilder's body tensed and his face reddened with passion.

The soldiers glanced back at the storyteller, who blinked indignantly. "I must have misspoken," he said at last.

Wilder scoffed again, "You would have us believe Courage came riding in on the dragon of Tarva itself, wielding the fabled swords of Alabaster!"

The storyteller leaned back and looked down on Wilder with disdain, "What would you know of battle?"

Wilder gritted his teeth in contempt, "I know more than you."

"Certainly!" a new voice interrupted, they all turned and there was the infamous soldier himself! Courage stood in the barracks doorway, his arms crossed and an arrogant smile on his dark face. "If you had been present on the isles with me, I have no doubt that you would have cleared up the issue with ease, my friend!"

Wilder narrowed his eyes.

"Being one of their kind, you no doubt would have appealed to their cowardness and organized a surrender."

Wilder stood abruptly to his feet, embedding his dagger in his bed post, "Match your words with action soldier, and test my 'cowardness' for yourself!"

The other soldiers stirred in excitement.

Courage smirked like Wilder was a child, "Come now, there's no need for this."

Wilder tried hard to calm his racing heart, 'keep a clear mind!' he reminded himself desperately.

"Soldiers shouldn't fight amongst themselves," Courage moved to stand before Wilder, "Besides, I wouldn't want you to be harmed; a man's pride is not easily healed." He dared to lay a hand on Wilder's shoulder.

Wilder seized his hand and spun, heaving Courage over his back, sending him crashing into a cot. The other soldiers all jumped to their feet, shouting and jeering. Courage leapt to his feet, the look of shock on his face was like a fresh breeze to Wilder. Courage's face changed to that of anger, and he charged at Wilder, barreling into him. The two fell and Wilder's head bounced off the floorboards, next Courage's fist pounded against his cheek, bursts of light and color played before Wilder's stunned eyes.

Ignoring the pain, Wilder landed a jab to Courage's ribs. Gaining an opening, Wilder pushed with his feet against a cot leg and sent himself sliding out from under Courage. He rolled backwards, feet over head, into a crouching position.

Courage matched his stance, but before Wilder could plan his next move, he was pushed from behind, and sent stumbling towards Courage, who met him with another blow to his face. Wilder shook off the dizziness and turned to swing a punch of his own, he caught Courage on the side of his head. Courage wheeled away and checked his head to find a cut, he looked back at Wilder like an enraged marsh wolf.

Wilder prepared himself for another attack, but Courage did not move. Their comrades stirred and stepped in, glancing at each other. Wilder's hatred of Courage increased; he would let others finish his fight!

"Leave him!" Courage instructed and walked towards Wilder, his fits clenched. Wilder waited till he swung his arm, then ducked, ramming into Courage, and driving him backwards. They ended up on the floor, scrambling till Courage broke free. They both jumped to their feet to meet one another, chests heaving.

The sound of a slow clap gave them pause and the other soldiers jumped to attention, their eyes on the doorway.

Panting and still on alert, Wilder and Courage turned to find an older soldier, wearing the garb of an officer, standing in the door, a mildly bored expression on his Tarvin face. He clapped twice more, deliberately slow, then reached for a walking cane leaned against the door.

Wilder relaxed slightly, watching carefully to see that Courage did the same.

"Excellent display of fighting prowess," the man said, his expression only hinting at disdain, "I'll speak with both of you now. The rest of you lot, clean up and gather in the yard with the rest of the barracks for an announcement." He did not wait to see his orders followed.

Wilder sniffed and found that his face was bloody; how had he been so distracted that he had not noticed? He scolded himself for his shameful attempt at keeping a clear mind.

Straightening his tunic, Courage followed their superior with head held high. Wilder's sense of unjustness writhed within him; he would receive a harsh reprimand and be ordered to beg forgiveness of the 'clearly' innocent Tarvin. It had happened before.

They were led to the officer quarters and into a small room with a large desk, and a ceremonial suit of armor in a corner; it was the captain's office.

"As you may have heard, Captain Ragged has been reassigned, I am Multifarious, knight of Tarva; his replacement." The new captain made his way behind the desk and sat down stiffly; his right leg causing him discomfort.

Wilder and Courage pounded their right fists over their hearts in a Tarvin salute.

"You may address me as Captain Farious," the captain said and brushed away dust from the desk surface, "I am no stranger to the garrison stationed here in Garason and have served many years in the king's army." He eyed them both, as if looking for something.

Wilder shifted uncomfortably, his face was beginning to throb.

"When I heard of the victory in the Five Isles and how a young soldier was largely responsible for it, I knew he would become a great asset." Captain Farious leaned back and fixed his gaze on Courage.

Wilder grit his teeth and fixed his eyes on the back wall.

"And then there is Wilderness," the captain turned his attention to him, "The stableboy turned soldier; I've been told twice that you have exceeded expectations and advanced through the training with ease. I know I'll be further impressed by you."

Wilder's lips parted in uncertainty, his heart picking up an extra beat; this was new.

"With soldiers the likes of you two in the same barracks, I foresee greatness in the future of this city and the name of Tarva," he paused and shifted his jaw.

Wilder shifted his feet and glanced at Courage out of the corner of his eye.

"Working alongside one another, I predict that the possibilities are endless… what say you?" Captain Farious seemed to dare them to disagree.

Wilder set his jaw, running through in his head how he could make this work.

"He is Garatin," Courage spoke the word like a curse, "What greatness can be achieved by his hands?"

"The Tarvin blood in me more than makes up for my mixed heritage!" Wilder snapped in heated defence.

"Peace," Captain Farious demanded calmly, and Wilder forced himself to turn away from Courage's smirking face.

Captain Farious watched them for a moment. "What's under that helmet?" he asked suddenly, gesturing to the suit of armor.

Wilder was too enraged to speak.

Courage glanced at the armor before returning his gaze to the captain. "A Tarvin soldier," he answered confidently.

"Wrong," Captain Farious informed sharply.

Courage shifted in annoyance.

The effort of thinking about it calmed Wilder's mind enough to answer, "A clear mind."

"Closer, but still wrong." Captain Farious stood with effort and approached the suite of armor; he removed the helmet revealing a simple wooden frame beneath. Placing the helmet on his desk he faced the two men once more, "The answer is *it doesn't matter.* Whoever it is, they are a soldier, clear and simple, serving their king for the glory of Tarva. Who they may be, where they came from or who their people are; is of no consequence." He let his words settle in the tense room.

Wilder breathed deep, a weightlifting from his chest; this captain was unlike all others.

"Now, I expect great things from both of you- do you think I mean brawling on the floor again?"

Neither Courage nor Wilder dared answer.

"Join the others in the yard, I will make the announcement of the change in captain. You are dismissed."

★ ★ ★ ★

Loyal sat up in bed and shivered; no one had told her how much colder Garatin was from Tarva. She watched as the maid set a tray of food on a table then crossed the room to pull back thick drapes; the late morning sun streamed in brightly, Loy looked away. She realized that her face was wet;

she had been crying in her sleep again. The maid began to set out Loyal's breakfast, she was an older Tarvin woman.

"Where is Dream?" Loy asked, wiping her face. Eam had told her the night before that she would likely be looking after her in the mornings, after seeing to Lady Regime.

The maid paused, her eyes darting briefly to the window, "Lady Regime is having the girl punished."

Loy sat up straighter, "What for?"

The maid pressed her lips together and shook her head slightly, "If that's all, my lady, I'll return shortly to help you dress." She left the room.

Loy's thoughts ran about in her mind; had Eam's involvement in her attempted escape been found out? How was that possible, unless… the soldier Wilderness had told someone?

A sound from outside captured Loy's attention, she slipped from the bed and crossed to the window, her breakfast forgotten. Three stories below the castle garden spread out, it was a bright morning, and sounds from the street beyond the outer wall drifted up to Loy's ears. The sound came again; it was from inside the castle walls. Loyal leaned out the window and listened; it was the sound of someone being flogged.

Rushing to her chamber door, Loyal grabbed an outer dress and pulled it on over her night gown as she fled into the hall, she did not waste time doing up the lacing. Guessing her way through halls Loy soon became hopelessly lost. Ringing her hands in anxiety, she hesitated between two stairways. A young maid came up one stair and stopped in surprise.

"Where are Dream's quarters?" Loy asked breathlessly.

The girl stared at her, obviously uncertain what to do.

"Dream, the serving maid, bring me to her- at once!" Loy demanded, her fear growing.

The girl bowed, "This way, my lady!" she turned, Loy followed, urging her to go faster. Down a few steps and through a door, Loy found herself in the servant quarters, busy with activity. The chilly morning air came in from open doors that lead out into a small courtyard.

Lady Regime stormed in from the courtyard. She was dressed much the same as Loy, her hair in a tangle and a strange expression of disdain and satisfaction on her pretty face. She didn't stop to greet Loy. Outside was another maid servant holding a flexible rod, she too passed by Loy without a word.

Loy ventured forward, in the courtyard kneeling with her back to Loy, was Dream. Her copper hair pulled aside, and her outer dress unfastened at the back, exposing a white woollen shift. It was torn in two places, and red streaks lined her back. She quivered with silent sobs. Another woman knelt by Eam, she was older, and her face was drawn tight.

"Come on, get up." the older woman encouraged quietly.

Loyal stepped forward, "Eam?"

The older woman looked up, recognition crossing her face, "My lady, you should not be here."

Eam turned her head slightly, surprised.

"Are you alright, Eam?" Loy ignored the woman and dared step closer.

Eam nodded, bowing her head to hide her tearful face.

"This is my fault- I'm so sorry!" Loy took Eam's arm to help her stand.

Eam shook her head, but the other woman pulled her upright. "Come inside now," she instructed.

"Let me help," Loy begged.

The older woman hesitated a moment before grudgingly accepting Loy's help, as they went, she introduced herself in clipped tones as Eam's mother, Avi. Loyal did her best not to stare as they entered Eam's chambers. It was simple and bare. None of the comforts that Loy was used to could be found, only sturdy, functional objects. A single flowerpot on a windowsill was the only decoration. Avi directed her daughter to sit, then left swiftly to fetch water and dressing for Eam's back.

"Eam, I'm so sorry!" Loy repeated, holding her hand.

"Lady Regime knows nothing of last night," Eam assured in a whisper, no doubt wary of being overheard, "She was merely cross with me this morning." She looked up at Loy, tears still wet on her face. "You did not need to come," she pointed out.

Loy knelt to be level with her, "I told you; I'll never forget what you tried to do for me. I will not have you come to harm because of it."

Eam tried to smile. "Thank you," she whispered.

Avi returned, a bucket of water in one hand. "Please my lady, this is no place for you," she urged again, "Let one of the maids take you back to your chambers."

Loy let her hand slip from Eam's and stepped away. "Very well," she conceded, anxious that her actions should not put them in harm's way. She wondered how she would ever face Lady Regime knowing what she had done to her friend!

Chapter 6 The Tower

Vigil eased himself down onto a rock, propping his aching feet up, he sighed in relief. The company did much the same, welcoming the overdo rest. Around him dusk was settling down into the mountain valley as the sun bowed out of another long day. They had set out from Fishers Hamlet three days before, following the river up into the foothills, their spirits had lifted upon finding the road wide and easy to traverse. But their second day found them leaving the hills behind and climbing into the Honorfell Mountains, where the path became increasingly more treacherous.

Alongside them, the river grew deeper and narrower, dropping down into a gorge with slick rock walls, it thundered its way to the sea, sending up clouds of mist and spray. It was on their third day that the path left the riverside and led the footsore travelers high up the gorge walls on narrow ledges. Large boulders and loose shale hindered their way at every turn, but after the day's grueling climb they had nearly reached the top of the gorge where the land flattened out enough for large trees and thick foliage to grow.

Exhausted yet hopeful for the morning, the company had chosen to make camp on the path where the ledge widened out over the gorge, far below the river roared unceasingly, but after their climb, Vig was certain no one would be kept awake by the noise.

"What are they doing?" Lady Serene asked with mixed tones of scorn, bewilderment, and curiosity. She sat nearby, watching as a group of Verlyance warriors ventured ahead and began to scale the cliff side to a higher ledge.

"Hoping for a view of the sea," Vigil explained as he removed his pack.

"Homesick already?" Lady Serene adjusted herself on the rock, her hands resting on her staff.

Vig sighed again. "No, just eager to offer more prayers that Tylus will not forget them. They're afraid," he ended in a subdued manner.

Lady Serene eyed him, "Not you though?"

Vig smiled, "The gods can't remember a man they never acknowledged in the first place!"

Lady Serene nodded as though it was a familiar problem. "And him?" she inquired, directing a pointed look at Prince Theophany.

The prince had made himself comfortable away from the others and was gazing down into the gorge.

Vig hesitated, "My lord the Prince Theophany is the prophesied king. He is the link between my people and the gods."

Lady Serene raised a single brow, "He communicates directly with your gods?"

Vig shifted uncomfortably, grateful the river's roar masked their conversation from the prince, "He… has yet to claim his birthright."

Lady Serene stared at Vig for a long moment. "Hum!" she grunted and looked away.

"What of your gods?" Vig asked to change the subject; he had yet to see the elderly woman pray on their journey.

Lady Serene's smile widened, "Wisdom is the only god worth pursuing, and I have devoted my life to it."

Vig nodded, bemused. "And does your wisdom predict how many boots I'll wear through before reaching the end of these mountains?" he asked, not realizing how his jest belittled her faith.

She smirked, "No, however even a fool could see the solution to such a problem is *riding* instead of walking."

Vig shot a glare at the strange hooved beasts that Lady Serene had obtained in Fishers Hamlet. Under her advisement, Theophany had also bought a few of the beasts to carry supplies, but no amount of persuasion would convince him or any of the other Verlyance warriors to *ride* one of the hairy creatures! The idea of climbing up on top of a strange animal and trusting it to carry them was completely foreign.

"The gillup are bred for mountain travel and are surer footed than you could ever be," Lady Serene pointed out.

Vig eyed the creatures; they were strange to the eyes of someone who had never seen a hooved animal before. They had four skinny legs, and their backs came up to his chest height, while their thick necks curved into a long narrow face. They had large black eyes, and the points of small fangs rested on their lower lips. Each gillup had large horns the color of a clear sky, they curved back along its neck, allowing a rider to hold on to them. The creatures were covered in long, coarse, blue gray hair. They were allowed to wander free each evening and climbed up and down the cliff face with ease, never seeming to lose their footing, and they could jump great distances.

"Why won't you and your people even consider riding one?" Lady Serene pressed.

Vig screwed up his face in discomfort at the thought. "It's not natural," he complained and shivered with exaggerated movements.

Lady Serene shook her head but allowed the subject to be dropped.

Nearby Garden squatted by the beginnings of a cook fire, out of all of them, *he* should be the one to ride a gillup! The old man had made a heroic effort to keep pace with the company, his determination putting some to shame, but each day seemed to add a year onto him.

Lady Serene observed the old man thoughtfully, "Can he read?" she asked suddenly.

Vig raised his eyebrows, he did not know, "Garden," he beckoned.

The old man looked up, "Yes?" he asked, coming to them.

"Can you read?" Vigil asked.

Garden looked between the two of them with watery eyes, then nodded twice.

"What languages?" Lady Serene asked, her interest growing.

Garden looked uncertain for a moment, "The Common tongue mainly… um, my own mother tongue, and a bit from a few others."

"Excellent! Here, sit here," Lady Serene instructed enthusiastically, "You, bring me my satchel," she ordered one of her servants.

As the servant obeyed, Garden hesitantly sat with Vig, eyeing Lady Serene nervously. The satchel was a strange thing to Vigil's eyes. It was the size of a large book, carved out of wood and kept shut with silver clasps. A leather strap had been nailed to the sides so that it could be worn over one's shoulder.

Lady Serene handled it with reverence; opening it she carefully withdrew a large leather-bound book. "This is my life's work," she explained with pride as she opened the book and flipped through its thick pages with long bony fingers. "Alas, it's final pages shall remain blank, for my demise will surely come before I could ever finish it."

Vig raised his eyebrows; a little over half of the book was filled with beautiful handwriting, neat and styled, the black ink staining the paper without smudges or spots.

"This is all the knowledge I have gleaned over my life that may prove useful in my search for the Wise One," she explained tenderly, then tapped a page, "Can you read this?" she asked Garden.

Garden peered at the words on the page hesitantly, and Vig suspected that he had been overconfident in his reading skills.

"It is Garatin in origin," Lady Serene pointed out, "Do you know what it says?"

"It's... an old riddle," Garden mumbled at last.

Lady Serene nodded in satisfaction, "Yes, I copied this from a scrap found in another book. I believe I know it's meaning but would be honored if you would translate it."

Vig noticed Garden shift uncomfortably.

Lady Serene also seemed to notice, and it occurred to Vig that she was desperate to share her findings with someone who might appreciate them.

"This first word, is I believe, 'Promise'," Lady Serene prompted.

"Promise*s*." Garden corrected.

"Ahh, yes!" Lady Serene seemed genuinely excited to be corrected, "that makes more sense! 'Promises will be broken,'" she read the first line.

"Lies will be... spoken..." Garden tried the next line, "Perhaps, 'lies will be told'."

Lady Serene nodded excitedly, while Vig observed with interest.

"Wisdom will be gained, or curses will be laid," Lady Serene finished.

But Garden shook his head. "This word," he pointed, "It's not 'wisdom,' it's... this tongue doesn't have the right word for it..." he looked away thinking hard. "Dreams, or... wishes would be the closest thing."

Lady Serene blinked in surprise, "*Wishes* will be gained?"

"Wishes will be *made*," Garden corrected again, "And curses will be laid."

Lady Serene bowed her head close to the page to study it again, muttering to herself, "This can't be right!"

Garden shrugged to Vigil, who could not help but chuckle at the woman's outrage.

"The only reason I copied this down is because I thought it spoke of the time of the Wise One- not some nonsense about *wishes*!"

"I must be mistaken," Garden offered anxiously.

Lady Serene straightened and shook her head, "No, I see that you are right. Never the matter! My ignorance has been enlightened." She promptly took out a charcoal stick and forcefully ran a fat black line through the Garatin riddle.

Vigil shook his head with a smile as Garden nervously got up and bowed away, obviously anxious to please. Lady Serene, with tight lips and arched brows, flipped through the pages of her precious book.

Vigil's eyes snagged on the prince again and his smile faded. Theoph had been disturbingly distant since their encounter with the Ancient One, leaving Vigil at a loss. He and Salvage had discussed the encounter in whispered tones every night since, but she was as clueless as he. She had not been given any visions since then, and the whole thing was beginning to feel like it had not happened at all!

"My lady," Vigil spoke suddenly, the words of Voy echoing in his heart, "Does your knowledge extend to curses?"

Lady Serene paused, "I have come across a number of curses in my books and tomes. Why do you ask?"

Vigil wet his lips, "My reasons are... personal, I would know more about the curse of the Heart Stain."

Lady Serene raised her already high brows.

"Have you heard of such a thing?" Vigil prompted.

"I believe I have come across a curse of that name in my studies; I recall it was a particularly hopeless subject. It makes me wonder why you would ask. One does not seek answers to unanswerable questions unless they have need of the answer." She watched him closely.

Vigil refused to comment, meeting her gaze evenly.

At last Lady Serene broke the moment and closed her book, placing it back inside the wooden satchel, "I will think on this and consult what tomes and books I have with me."

Salvage had gone on ahead of the company earlier in the evening, scouting for danger and now stood on a high place with narrowed eyes as she gazed northward.

The path had climbed to the top of the cliff where it skirted the edge of a great forest, to the left was the gorge with the river far below and on the far side of the gorge lay a craggy maze of cliffs and caves. On the right the forest stretched away thick and wild, and above the treeline the slope of a mountain rose, hemming in the valley. Having climbed a rock pinnacle on the gorge edge, Sal had an excellent view of the river gorge as it wound northward up the valley, the path appearing to follow it.

At the far end of the valley stood a mountain, and on its side, catching the sun as it set was an unnatural outcropping that held Sal's gaze. She could not decide if it was just an unusual rock formation or in fact a tower standing watch over the valley. Whatever it was, the path led directly to it and was perhaps a day's walk away. The sunlight continued to fade, reminding Sal that she had better turn back before darkness fell; she and the others were not used to the sun's light failing so early in the evening.

Turning, Sal started back the way she had come when she heard something; was it the whimper of a child? She turned and searched the trees around her, the noise came again. Following the sound deeper into the trees, Sal gripped her spear while her heart beat wildly. The whimper sounded less like a child and more like that of an animal! Cresting an incline, she stopped in her tracks.

Before her, with its hindquarters suspended in the air by a thick rope tied to a tree branch high above, was the largest dog Sal had ever seen. Its legs were slender, ending in large powerful paws, thick, long white fur covered its body. It had a massive, long face, with large blue eyes and pointed ears with tufts of hair making them appear extra tall. It watched her closely.

Sal stepped forward hesitantly. Its lip curled and the dog released a throaty snarl but did not move. Sal took another step, in complete awe. The dog snarled again and tried to leap at her, the movement sent it swinging back and forth, its front paws scrambling frantically for traction while its hindquarters kicked helplessly. At last, exhausted, it came to a stop, its breath coming out in huffs.

Sal had readied her spear in case it got loose and lowered herself to a crouch. "Hello," she breathed, "If I didn't know better, I'd say you were a dog, but since all the dogs on my island could probably fit inside you, I'm going to hope they call you something else."

The dog blinked its great eyes, its eyebrows twitching, resembling a look of fear.

Sal inspected the snare from her safe distance; the dog was not going anywhere in a hurry. "I'd let you loose; but I think you'd eat me," she spoke softly, "I'd put you out of your misery… but then whoever set this trap would know someone was here…" She looked around again, hearing Vig lecture her on making decisions based on cold hard logic- not on whatever her heart felt was right.

"I think I have to leave you," she confessed, feeling not at all right with the idea. The dog blinked again.

Remembering her water skin, Sal looked around for something the dog could drink from, she found a length of curved tree bark nearby. Certain that the dog could not break free, Sal approached slowly. It growled more, and tried struggling, but was clearly exhausted.

When she was still too far to touch it, Sal knelt and poured her water into the bark, then using her spear, she pushed it towards the dog. It snarled more; but did not move. The water seeped through the bark untouched.

Frowning in concentration, Sal cautiously reached out, and poured the last of her water onto the bark, some of it splashing the dog's large nose. At last, its great pink tongue flicked out over its nose, then it sniffed the water with interest. Watching her the whole time, the dog lapped up the water hurriedly.

Backing away, Sal watched the animal with pity. "Don't tell anyone I was here," she said at last, then turned and left, knowing Vig would make fun of her for feeling sorry for a vicious beast.

Dusk had turned into night by the time Salvage returned to the camp, she was met with Verlyance lookouts. Ignoring the smell of dinner Sal stood in the firelight, knowing that Vig would come to her.

"What did you find?" Vig asked, coming out of the darkness.

"Trouble, possibly," Sal informed him in a low tone, they removed themselves from the others so that they could talk without being overheard.

"We're not alone up here, there's people somewhere close by," Sal said as Vig held her gaze, "I found a beast in a snare, an hour ahead of us."

Vig's eyebrows pinched together, "Who would lay traps out here?"

Sal shrugged, "There could be villages in every valley for all we know!"

Vig rubbed his chin as he thought it over, "What kind of beast was it?" he asked absentmindedly.

"Remember the dogs back home?"

He paused and looked at her with a puzzled expression, clearly thinking of the shin high mutts that roamed the island.

"Just think bigger," Sal prompted.

"How big?"

Sal did not answer, he put out his hand at thigh level, she shook her head, he raised his hand hesitantly to waist height.

"You're getting there," Sal encouraged, her smirk widening.

Vig raised his hand to his chest and raised an eyebrow, Sal nodded.

"You can't be serious!"

"Oh I am. Big, white, and very scary."

Vig held her eyes, "Tell me you killed it."

By his tone, Sal knew he had guessed the answer. "I could hardly do that; it would have alerted the snare owner of our presence," she argued, "It was stuck fast, besides, we need hardly be worried about a beast in a snare."

Vig sighed, "Very well. I suppose it's good to know what's out there."

"I also saw what looked like a tower on a mountain ahead of us, the path will take us there tomorrow," Sal added.

"Right, I'll inform the others- you should eat something. Then talk to Theoph, would you? He's starting to scare me."

Vig said it in jest, but Sal knew he was serious. It would be no use though; she had tried talking with the prince; he would not listen to her.

'Your god, your curse.' he had said, and maybe it was true.

Salvage's footfalls echoed out into the darkness, bouncing off the cave walls and back to her ears where her heartbeat added to the din. The wild desperate cry of a child drove her deeper into the darkness, no thought to anything else. Holding her torch ahead of her Sal stopped, her boots scuffing on the uneven floor.

Ahead of her, lying on the ground, wrapped in cloth, was the child, hardly a week old, tiny, helpless, but not alone. The beast from the snare stood over it, hair along its back raised, ears back, head down, teeth bared.

Sal dropped the torch, its firelight casting strange shadows from the floor. Taking a fighting stance, she brought her spear in front of her and locked eyes with the beast, her heart sick with worry for the child. A thick rope was tied about the neck of the beast, restraining it from lunging.

"How do you change the mind of someone who believes a lie?" the beast asked, a snarl rumbling behind its words.

Somehow Sal was not surprised to hear it speak.

"You expose them to the truth!" it barked the last word and the rope snapped. The beast jumped forward, leaping over Sal and her spear. Sal rolled into a crouch, placing herself between the child and the beast. A cloaked figure wielding a red sword had come up behind her in the dark and now battled the beast.

Salvage awoke from her vision to find that it was nearly dawn.

The camp was still asleep, exhausted from mountainous travel, Sal's own body protested as she sat up. Vigil was not beside her, meaning he must have the last watch, and was guarding over the perimeter of their camp. Rubbing the back of her neck, Sal paused and narrowed her eyes; Prince Theophany was also awake and sitting up.

He had lifted his tunic up over his shoulder and was removing his stealthy bandage from his upper arm, revealing his wound from the battle with the pirates. Even in the dusk Sal could see that it had not healed properly.

Sal got up swiftly, alerting Theoph to her presence, he turned away, trying to hide his wound.

"That's infected," Sal said, kneeling at his side, and seizing his arm.

"It's fine!" he hissed, glancing at their sleeping company.

"It's been neglected; more warriors die from untended wounds than in battle," she warned and grabbed her pack, removing a leather pouch she produced a poultice.

"I'm not exactly a normal warrior," Theoph insisted but allowed her to apply the healing poultice like a bandage. "Death is for mortal men," he proclaimed in a low, serious tone.

Sal worked quickly, knowing that she shouldn't question him on the subject, but she couldn't allow his comment to go unchallenged- not after her vision! "Do you believe that?"

Theoph did not answer, and Sal felt his eyes boring into her, at last she raised her eyes to his; she didn't like what she found.

"I am Theophany," his words were heavy with meaning, "The Victorious, proclaimed by Tylus to rise above all others. I am not bound to mortal ways; not wounds, not fear… and not curses."

Sal held his gaze unflinchingly, "You're wrong!" her words louder than intended.

Nearby the youth, Rend, awoke, his arm knocking his bow. It skidded across the rock ledge towards the edge. Like the inexperienced boy that he was, Rend threw himself needlessly after it. His hands grasped it easily, but his momentum sent him hurtling towards the edge.

With calculated movements, Sal reached out and snagged the youths ankle, saving him from the fatal fall.

Theoph hurriedly replaced his tunic. "You need to be more careful," he warned Rend, but his words were for Sal.

Rend backed away from the cliff edge on his hands and knees, then aimed a sheepish grin back at Sal and the prince. "I wouldn't have fallen!" he assured with youthful ignorance.

Sal rose and released a tight exhale, "I have no intention of letting you fall." Her face heating up with unreleased passion, she turned her back and set about packing her bedroll.

Rend watched her with a bewildered expression, while Theoph turned his own back. Around them the camp was awaking.

Soon Vigil came into camp from along the path ahead of them, whistling a tune. He came to Sal's side and started packing up his things, "Well, good news is we weren't eaten by terrifying beasts in the night. Bad news is they will have many more opportunities," he jested, but Sal wasn't in the mood.

"We shouldn't have brought the boy, Rend, with us," she said tightly, feeling her emotions rising.

Vig paused and rolled back on his feet, measuring her for a moment, he glanced at Rend before fixing his narrowed eyes back on her, "He seems to be managing fine."

Sal aggressively tightened the strap around her bed roll, "He'll get himself killed."

Vig placed his hand over hers, "What's wrong?"

She took a moment to steady her breath before meeting his gaze, "The prince has lost his mind."

"You tried to speak with him."

"He blames me for his curse yet in the same breath claims that he is beyond death's grasp." She half turned away and attached her bedroll to her pack.

"He's lost and I don't know how to help him. At Fishers Hamlet, Voy said that I could help him… I hardly see how though," Vig shared soberly.

Sal swallowed hard, "I was given a vision- I think."

"What was revealed to you?"

Sal frowned. "It wasn't all that clear," she resisted the urge to touch her stomach, "But... I was told that to change the mind of someone who believes a lie, you must show them the truth."

"Then, perhaps it's time for *this,*" Vig carefully pulled forth the enchanted mirror shard that Voy had given him.

Sal rolled her lips in, "I'm not sure he's ready to listen."

"I can wait," Vig decided and put the shard away.

An hour after dawn the company started out again on their journey along the cliff ledge. Theophany's group led the way with Sal and Vig, while Lady Serene on her gillup rode in the middle, the slaves leading the gillup with their supplies and Lady Serene's guards took up the rear.

As the sun rose higher, it's light touched the surrounding mountain slopes and peaks, and the roar of the river far below them became more distant as the path climbed to the cliff top and led them into the trees. Here Sal, Vig and the other warriors readied their weapons and searched the woods for any sign of large, hairy beasts. But it was hard to imagine sinister attacks when birds sang in the branches above them and all the while the beauty and majesty of the Honorfell Mountains surrounded them. Salvage's temper and emotions cooled as she walked with Vig, he always had that effect on her, but the prince continued to be solemn and aloof.

"There it is," Sal announced as she and Vig left the treeline behind and the mountain with the strange shape on its side came into view. In the morning sunlight they could clearly see that it was a man-made structure.

Vig tilted his head to the side, "Well whatever it is, we'll come to it today."

"It looks like a temple!" Rend said as he came up behind them.

"Your eyes are probably better than ours," Sal said by way of agreement.

"If it's a temple Lady Serene may want-" Vig never finished what he was saying, for a shout of alarm sounded behind them.

Sal and Vig spun about, weapons at the ready; their company was being attacked by mountain men in heavy fur cloaks. The Verlyance warriors met the ambushers head on, while Lady Serene's men formed a protective circle around her, Garden and the other slaves cowered amongst the gillup a few paces behind. Rend bravely charged ahead with a mighty war cry, swinging his short sword about, and catching a mountain man on the shoulder, the heavy fur he wore protected him like armor.

"There!" Vig called sharply and charged to aid the prince who was being overtaken by four of the mountain men. Sal joined him in the charge, falling upon the attackers swiftly. One fell instantly, pierced by one of Vig's throwing knives, while another took a nasty blow to his chest from Sal's spear, he stumbled back in a retreat. Theoph was tackled by a third, they fell to the ground, struggling for control over a dagger.

A fourth attacker jumped Vig from behind and seized him in a fierce lock, bending his sword arm backwards till the blade fell uselessly. Vig's free arm scrambled to strike his attacker, but he could do nothing.

Sal heard his struggle as she retrieved his throwing knife, spinning about, she saw both the prince and her husband caught in death struggles. Catching Vigil's eye, Sal ran up to the prince and threw the knife at Vigil's shoulder, he caught it with his free hand and in one sweeping motion, brought it down and stabbed his attacker in the thigh.

Sal skidded to a stop and heaved her spear; its shaft left her fingers and moments later it's point drove into the mountain man atop the prince.

Theoph pushed the man off and scrambled to his feet while Vig overcame his attacker and reclaimed his weapons. The three of them stood together and heaved air into their lungs as they surveyed the battle; their men were being overpowered.

"We're outnumbered," Theoph realized.

Sal's breath caught, she locked eyes wildly with Vig, "Do you trust my visions?"

"I trust *you*," Vig responded without hesitation.

That would have to be good enough, "I won't be long!" Sal promised, then ran headlong into the woods. She ducked under branches and leapt over bushes, twice she used her spear to vault over dips in the terrain. At last, she skidded to a stop, mere feet from the front paws and powerful jaws of the snared beast.

It watched her with eyes Sal would have sworn were intelligent. The sound of the battle behind her urged her on. "Will you fight with me?" she breathed, half expecting the beast to speak as it had in her vision.

Theoph ducked and rolled out of the way of a large axe that thudded into the ground beside him. Landing a blow to the axe wielder's arm, Theoph maneuvered himself back to Vigil's side, knowing that his friend's skill in combat would be the only reason he survived.

The mountain men seemed bigger, and thicker than normal men, they had skin like tanned leather, and all wore gruff beards. Their raven hair was long and often braided, while their armor and weapons were made from a dark red metal.

Theoph's company was outnumbered two to one and they were losing warriors every moment the fight went on. Theoph was pulled off his feet and thrown to the ground, air leaving his lungs from the impact. The axe wielding mountain man stood over him, axe raised above his head, and eyes wild. The axe was grabbed from behind by Vigil and the mountain man dove to one side, coming to his feet with a dagger in his hand to meet Vig.

Theoph scrambled to his feet and collected his sword from the dirt, his eyes snagging on the mountain man's other hand; he held a satchel. Theoph's hand flew to his belt, "He has my satchel!" he gasped.

Vig drew his own dagger and locked eyes with the mountain man. Theoph flanked from the other side but realized with fright that his hands were shaking, memories of the battle with the pirates and Courteous's death threatened to overwhelm him.

With a throaty snarl and a white blur, something massive darted past Theoph and collided with the mountain man, he fell to the ground, his weapons useless as a huge beast attacked him.

Sal was suddenly at Theoph's side, her face flushed and eyes wide. Vig joined them and they retreated backward from the beast as the man's screams brought a moment of hesitation to the battle.

"TO ME!" Vigil called, "Protect the prince!" Those who were able came scrambling to surround Theoph.

Lady Serene and her guards broke free, and they swarmed around the Verlyance warriors.

"Onto the gillup!" Lady Serene exclaimed, "We must flee!"

"She's right- we can not stand against them!" Vig said shouldering past his men, "Everyone to the gillup and ride north!"

Sal placed a hand on Theoph's shoulder, "Stay close!"

"The treasures for the Foretold King- he took them!" Theoph pointed to the still form of the mountain man. The beast had abandoned him and was lunging at a group of other mountain men who had rallied together against it.

"Here!" Garden was suddenly beside him, panting, a bloody wound to his temple, he held out the lead to a gillup.

"Get on!" Sal ordered, half lifting Theoph onto the hooved animal, Theoph grasped the horns of the creature as best he could as it bolted through the company and out of the trees along the path. The gillup bounded effortlessly from rock to rock and bounced off tree trunks. Theoph tried desperately to wrap his legs about the creature's belly, feeling his grip on the horns slip. Mercifully the gillup slowed to a stop, allowing the prince to readjust. He glanced back and saw his warriors following, two more riders on gillup bounded up beside him.

"DON'T STOP!" Lady Serene bellowed and spurred her own gillup faster with a kick to its flanks. Theoph caught a glimpse of Vig bursting through the treeline atop a gillup. Theoph kicked his own mount and started bounding along the trail again.

His heartbeat fluttered at the foreign sound of a horn blast- the mountain men calling for reinforcements? It was cut short with the hair-raising snarl of the beast.

Vigil was exhausted; clinging to the top of a gillup as it recklessly bounded along the mountain terrain used every muscle in Vig's taxed body. But its speed meant he could easily outdistance the mountain men. Shortly after breaking free of the battle, Vig was able to direct a few of his warriors to follow the prince and make for the temple on the mountain ahead of them. Then Vig had doubled back to find stragglers. It broke his heart to know that at least two of the Verlyance warriors had been struck down in the ambush; far from the sea. Who would give them death rites?

Instead of his own people, Vig ran into the mountain men, slipping from their grasps, Vig led them away from his retreating company, deliberately slowing down every hundred feet so as to not lose them too quickly. This worked until the mountain men stringed their bows and sent arrows after him. feeling that he had led them far enough away, Vig left them far behind and tried to find his way back to the path.

"Do you know your way around?" Vig muttered to the gillup as they made their way through another wooded slope. The river could no longer be heard and Vig could not find his bearings from the sun's position as the sky was becoming overcast at an alarming rate. "Well, a steady rain will hide our tracks…" he pointed out to himself half heartedly.

"We need to get higher," he decided, and pulled the gillup's horns to the right, directing him up the slope. The beast seemed tireless, but Vig feared its strength would not last long enough. They climbed and zigzagged till they reached a rocky clearing with a view of a valley below them, "Right… that's very helpful…" he mumbled as he searched for familiar landmarks.

His gillup opened its mouth and seemed to respond with a hearty bleat, it echoed down the mountain side for what seemed like hours.

Before it quite faded away it was answered with a howl from the white beast. Vig flinched and the gillup bolted, it was all Vig could do to hang on as they hurtled headlong through the trees and past boulders. A sudden drop off appeared before them, the tops of trees a few feet below. The gillup did not hesitate but threw itself over. Vig lost his grip and found himself falling through the tree branches as they broke beneath him.

The ground met his body with enthusiasm, his lungs giving up their air and his head spinning from the impact. He lay on his front, stunned, gasping to refill his lungs until strength returned to his limbs and he pushed himself up to his knees.

Nearby the gillup gracefully jumped to the ground from a sturdy tree limb, apparently as comfortable in a tree as on a cliff side.

Checking to make sure his weapons had not been lost, Vig took a moment to breathe and rub his sore chest.

A twig snapped in the surrounding woods. Hastily, Vig drew one of his throwing knives and his sword.

The gillup froze, but did not bolt, meaning that it probably wasn't the white beast nearby. Now on his feet, Vig swung his blade in preparation, and made sure the cliff face was to his back.

Garden stumbled into sight, his chest heaving, and blood smeared across his pale forehead from his wound. He flinched and almost ran when he saw Vig.

"GARDEN!" Vig cried in relief, "You got away!" he rushed forward, arms wide, hardly believing the old man's luck, "I thought surely you would perish!"

Garden heaved his chest with effort, "I will not die before I see my homeland again!"

Vig laughed and sheathed his weapons, then he checked Garden's forehead. "A minor wound," he assured him, but Garden did not seem concerned about it in the least. "We must keep moving- that white beast could be close by," Vig warned turning back to the gillup, "I've lost my direction- do you know where we are?"

Garden nodded, "Aye, the temple on the mountain side is that way," he pointed into the woods, "But I have not seen anyone else since we fled."

Vig nodded, "Alright, you ride the gillup, and be swift, it can outrun the mountain men."

Garden halted, his chest still heaving. "I can not leave you," he stated, "I am the servant, you the master."

Vig wet his lips and collected the gillup. "The gillup can't bear us both. You are the old one, and I the young; I can go farther on my feet than you." He glanced the way Garden had pointed, "Now that I know the way, I shall be fine." He locked eyes with the Garatin; the old man set his jaw stubbornly.

"Don't make me force you, old one." Vig said with a grin, "I can hardly leave you here, besides, I can't take much more of this thing," he insisted lightly, taking Garden by his arm, preparing to lift him onto the gillup. "When you find the others, tell them I'm on my way- and tell Sal I'll have a new song for her when I come." Garden resisted slightly, but Vig had little trouble lifting his small frame onto the gillup's back. "Hold on tight- and don't let it jump off any more cliffs!" Vig instructed then slapped the beast's flank, spurring it forward before Garden could protest further.

Vig watched as Garatin disappeared into the woods, then he closed his eyes, forcing his worry for Sal and Theoph from his mind. Then he set out in a jog in the direction Garden had shown, keeping an eye out for mountain men, and other things with larger teeth.

* * * *

"Be sure that you pile the stones high! At the very least my last resting place should be noticeable!" Lady Serene instructed sharply, her hands trembling as she gripped her staff, betraying how shaken she was. Her guards had been a tremendous help in the escape and together with the Verlyance warriors they had found a place to rest among large boulders halfway up the mountain side where the tower sat. The sky had turned very dark, leaving no trace of the evening sun and now a light rain was falling on the unfortunate travellers. The eerie echo of the mountain men's horns could be heard off and on, reminding them that the danger had not passed.

"And what to do with my books!?" Lady Serene bemoaned, she had been planning her burial for a half hour, "To leave them with uncouth peasants would be as much a waste as to have them buried with my body!"

"We're not dead yet," Garden assured humbly. "We have breath left in our lungs." He had ridden up to them out of the wilderness bringing news that Vigil was alive, and on his way. This news had brought the company to their present halt.

Theophany did his best not to listen to Lady Serene's tirade, and instead focused on the landscape behind them, hoping for a glimpse of Vigil.

"Sire, we are at risk here," one of his warriors pointed out in a low tone, exhaustion showing on his features as it was on everyone's. "We should go on and find refuge in the tower. I know you worry for Vigi-"

"I do not worry over the fates," Theoph cut him off sharply, and turned away from the path. "We continue on to the tower," he announced to the company.

Lady Serene was mid sentence and snapped her mouth shut to stare at him, "And what of your companions!?" she questioned pointedly.

"If they are still alive, they will find their own way to the tower," Theoph answered, satisfied with the degree of chill to his voice- it dulled the pain of his worry sick heart.

Lady Serene shook rainwater from her thin hand, "I won't deny the wisdom of your decision, I admit that I am much shaken from the trials of this day and beyond divining wisdom of my own." She signaled to be helped up.

Shaking water from his eyes, Theoph readied himself to mount his gillup, pushing the thought of the stolen jewels from his mind. The rain intensified and they were thoroughly drenched when they came level with the tower. Now they could clearly see that it was indeed a temple; the tower was carved from the mountain rock and rose high and lonely, while a humble structure of stone and wood stood about it. Past low stone walls was a courtyard with flagstones arranged in strange patterns and shapes. Strips of red, blue and yellow cloth were tied to poles, hung on nails and pinned under rocks; they lay limp in the rain.

Taking a breath, Theoph dismounted his gillup while his warriors ventured cautiously into the courtyard.

"Take caution," Lady Serene warned, disdain evident in her tone, "I believe this is spirit ground."

Before Theoph could respond, a door from the temple opened and three figures in brown robes and red beaded headdresses came out into the rain to meet them.

"Who goes?" asked one who held a lantern on the end of a pole.

Theoph was surprised to hear them speak in the common tongue.

"Travellers seeking safety from bandits on the road," one of the warriors answered.

The strangers came closer, shining the lantern light on the faces of the weary travellers, Theoph expected them to show more surprise at such diverse faces, but they showed no reaction. "Come and welcome, we turn away no one, but be warned, you will answer to the spirits for any violence committed here by your hand," the leader of the three bowed slightly.

Lady Serene scoffed, thankfully it was muffled in the rain.

"Your gillup can be fed and watered in yonder door," the leader pointed to the side of the tower where a second structure stood, then he beckoned Theoph and the others to enter the tower.

The interior was not at all what Theoph expected of a temple, instead of stone carvings and tapestries on the walls, there were only functional wood furnishings and a simple lantern hanging overhead on a chain. There were a number of doors that led off the main chamber, all were shut, while an arch led to a flight of stairs that curled upwards, the tower stairs. Three large men wearing strange clothing with skin like the night sky stood on the steps, arms crossed and faces set.

Theoph shook his cloak and allowed his eyes to pass over the men on the stairs- they did not seem to fit with the other residents of the temple. The three temple priests stood and waited for Theoph and his company to take in their surroundings. They looked like the mountain men, and Theoph wondered how safe they would be.

"You are not the only guests of the temple, but your company is welcome to what space you may find here," the temple priests explained. "There are two rooms with beds you are welcome to. The air in one, I'm afraid, is thick with dust from books," he indicated one door.

Lady Serene's eyebrows soared upwards. "Books you say!? Show me," she commanded and was led away with her guards following.

"I am Prince Theophany of Verlyance," Theoph said, his more elaborate title fell flat on his tongue.

"Many come here from afar," the priest assured.

Theoph glanced again at the strangers on the stairs. "I and my companions travel through these mountains northward to reach a land called Garatin. Have you heard of it?" Theoph asked, driving the thought of Vigil and Salvage from his mind.

The priest nodded, "Aye, the road ahead is very long." His words gave Theoph little comfort.

"We were attacked this morning by bandits, some of my warriors are still missing…"

This time the priest bowed his head as if in shame, "The Honorfell Mountain tribes turn to thieving travellers when they are not warring amongst themselves. Have no fear for your safety here though, no tribe would risk the wrath of the spirits by coming here with fresh blood on their hands."

Theoph swallowed hard but the image of Sal's blood was interrupted by the howl of the beast, crying out through the night, carried on the wind.

The priest paled slightly, and went to the door to look out into the rain, "The baine wilk, however, have no fear of the spirits- was it hunting you?"

"A giant white dog? Aye, since this morning."

The priest nodded and shut the door again. "I would offer you the use of the tower to pray, but it is already in use by our other guests," he said, glancing at the men on the stairs.

"Where are they from?" Theoph asked in a low tone, his curiosity getting the better of him.

"The city of Estewryn in the Niben Weald."

Theoph frowned, the names meant nothing to him.

"Rest now," the priest invited, "Those of you who are here, are safe, and you can do nothing for those who are not here."

The wind blew the rain about the mountains and foothills like waves in the sea, and the hours dragged by one breath at a time. Theoph sat, elbows on knees, head bent, in a humble cell like chamber, waiting… The words his father had spoken to him echoed about in his head like the rain in the wind.

'Become a god in their eyes and your namesake will live till the end of time!'

What kind of god allowed his heart to become sick with worry for the fate of warriors meant to give their lives for him? But the idea of Vigil tumbling from a cliff top in the rain, or Salvage tortured by mountain men haunted him. How would he go on without them? Even *if* he still had the treasure for the Foretold King, the whole quest seemed hollow without Sal and Vig. Theoph's throat constricted when he thought of Dynasty standing on the shore of Verlynn Nel, bidding him farewell.

"Grief is madness of the soul, don't you remember?" Vigil spoke from the door.

Theoph jumped to his feet. "I thought you dead!" he exclaimed breathlessly, clasping his friend by both arms.

Vig leaned against the door frame, he was wet to the bone. "Not yet," Vig managed with a slight grin, "I expected to hear Sal weeping from a mile off; where is she?"

Theoph hesitated, "No one has seen her since the ambush."

Vig's tired grin seemed stuck on his lips, at last he turned away, stepping back into the main chamber where his warriors stood about smiling at his return.

Before following him, Theoph realized that tears were shed on his face, he took a moment to erase them.

"The tower- are there windows?" Vig asked, looking past his warriors to one of the priests.

"Aye, they look out on all sides- but you will not see your missing comrade in the dark." they warned.

Vig sighed heavily, "This night has already lasted for an eternity, the dawn can not be far off now." His carefree tone may have tricked the others into believing he hadn't a care, but Theoph could hear the edge in his voice. Vig turned to the stairs only to be met with the three silent strangers. They did not move.

"Their lady is aloft praying," Theoph warned, laying a hand on Vigil's shoulder.

Vig sighed again, "I only want to look out the tower windows, I have no wish to disturb anyone." He addressed the strangers in the common tongue, leaning against another wall.

The biggest of the strangers stepped forward, he had an enormous build, with strong arms and a thick neck supporting a bald head. Unmoving eyes studied them silently.

"Do they speak the common tongue?" Theoph asked, turning back to the priest.

"You would search the landscape for one of your nitora?" The large stranger said in a thick, rich sounding accent.

Vig looked at him with raised eyebrows, "One of my *what*?"

"It means warrior," the priest volunteered.

"Yes…" Vig answered, "They are lost, and possibly being hunted by man and beast. Will you let me pass?"

The stranger looked him up and down. "I will go ahead of you to see that there is no treachery," he conceded.

"I will be going with him," Theoph stated.

The stranger shifted his stance, "Then I will bring another with me."

Theoph felt the tension rising, "Vigil here is exhausted, he could hardly do you or anyone else damage in his state."

"Don't be rude," Vig muttered under his breath.

"So, I will bring with me another warrior," Theoph decided, waving one of the stronger warriors over to him.

The stranger smirked, "Yes, I'm sure he will be of great help." He crossed his large arms, causing his muscles to bulge.

Vig straightened, while Theoph tried to think of how to respond to the veiled threat.

"May I remind you that if there is violence, you will answer to the spirits!" the priest insisted with a high-pitched tone.

"As a show of good faith," the stranger said, as he and his equally large friend removed curved blades from their wide belts and handed them to their third companion.

Vig removed his own throwing knives with impatience, "Right, can we go now?"

Still smirking, the two strangers started up the steps while the third stepped aside to allow Vig and Theoph to pass. Their third warrior followed closely behind them. Vig climbed the stairs with exhausted yet steady determination, there was just enough room for Theoph to climb beside him, ready to support him if need be.

"How many did we lose?" Vig asked after the first dozen steps.

Theoph glanced at the stranger ahead of them, "Three fell in the ambush, Lady Serene lost a slave and a guard somewhere along the way. Several are wounded, but none seriously. With you back, all that's missing is Salvage and… the boy."

Vig hesitated on the steps, "The boy Errand?"

Theoph nodded, and Vig cursed under his breath, "What of the warriors, how are their spirits?"

Theoph glanced backwards and lowered his tone as they continued, "I suspect they are not at peace with leaving the others without giving them a death rite."

Vig nodded but said nothing more. They climbed in silence till they neared the top, then the stranger with the thick neck turned to them, and Theoph noticed Vig's hand hovering over the empty sheath of his throwing knife. It had been lost in the ambush.

"Our mistress is praying and will not be disturbed. Do not speak to her, stay on the far side of the pillars and we will not have to face angry spirits today."

"You're very convincing!" Vig assured him, "I'm sure everyone back home finds you charming."

The stranger smirked again and ascended the last few spiraling steps. There was no door at the top, only a circular room with a domed roof, a single lantern hung from it. Six windows looked out on the mountains and six pillars behind them created an inner circle in the room. In the center of the floor there was a pattern of the moon and sun.

A slight figure with a white shawl over her head, sat in the center of the room, her legs crossed, and her hands resting limply on her knees.

The two large strangers entered to stand on either side of the figure, and the one who had spoken with them knelt to speak to his mistress.

Vig gestured that their warrior wait by the doorway, then he and Theoph entered the room, staying on the far side of the pillars as instructed, they walked along the wall to a window.

"Well now I'm all turned about," Vig muttered in annoyance as he leaned on the windowsill and took a moment to catch his breath, the wind wet his face with rain.

Theoph stood by his side, he could not help but stare at the mysterious mistress of the strangers. She was very slim, and her shawl was pulled so low Theoph could not see her face. But the sight of her hands and forearms gave him pause. While her men were dark like the night sky, her skin was pale like bleached bone!

"Well, they were right; I can hardly see a thing." Vig complained and moved to the next window.

Theoph was slower to follow and kept his eyes on the pale mistress. Her guard bent low to whisper to her, then she turned her head and peeked at Theoph with eyes the color of blood. Theoph flinched in shock.

"It's as I feared," Vig muttered, "Look, those mountain men must have torches- can you see them flickering there? Why do they still search for us?" he turned to Theoph and noticed he was paying no heed to him.

"She's a child!" Theoph breathed in disbelief. And the girl turned back to whisper more to her guard. He looked up at Theoph and Vig, then stood, fixing them with a hard gaze.

Vig tensed.

"My mistress would know who you are," the stranger said.

"This is Theophany the Victorious," Vig offered freely, "Prince of Verlyance. And I am Vigil, the exhausted," his jest fell flat.

"And who are you?" Theoph asked, still shaken by the girl's bone white face and red eyes.

"I speak for my mistress, I am Dire," the stranger said, his deep voice filling the room, obviously displeased to disturb the girl's praying.

Theoph glanced at the girl who had once again bowed her head from sight, "Who is she?"

"Lady Roam of the Niben Weald, daughter of Command, brother of Golden, the king of Estewryn." Dire answered with pride, but his words meant little to Theoph, who was beginning to realize just how little of the world he knew.

'What is wrong with her?' was on the tip of Theoph's tongue, but he stopped himself in time.

Vigil had refocused his attention back out the window, while Lady Roam again whispered with Dire.

"Why would they be so persistent in hunting us?" Vig muttered again as he watched the flickering of torches far below them in the hills.

"The mountain men do not hunt travellers for long," Dire commented, "Unless there are riches to be won."

"They'll be disappointed to find they already got the lot," Theoph spoke bitterly in the Verlyance tongue.

Vig bowed his head as if just remembering what had happened in the ambush to Theoph's satchel. "All is not lost," he tried to comfort.

Theoph scoffed, "Without those jewels, what have we to offer the Foretold King? Nothing. I have failed before even starting." He turned away.

Chapter 7 Dawn and the Dusk

Salvage suppressed a shiver as she crouched among wet boulders, around her the rain came through the tree branches and formed large puddles. The hunting horn of the mountain man sounded again, this time closer.

'Where is that tower?' Sal wondered again, her optimism wilting within her. Rising on fatigued legs, Sal prepared to continue her hopeless climb up the mountain, but the hairs on the back of her neck stood on end, warning her that something was waiting for her around the boulders. Sal adjusted her grip on her spear, directing the tip outward, and crept along, rounding the boulders she had been hiding behind.

Sal froze, her heart hesitating in her chest; the beast faced her in the near dark, its white fur matted down with rain and its teeth bared in a snarl. Under its giant front paw was Rend, trembling in the mud. Sal bent at the knees, spearhead out, eyes locked with the beast; Why hadn't it killed Rend yet!?

The snarl on the beast's snout faded, and it licked its lips, and removed its paw from the youth.

"Don't move, Rend," Sal warned in a low tone.

Rend obeyed, petrified. The beast turned, before disappearing into the trees, it turned and looked back once more, then trotted away.

Sal let her breath go, and went to Rend, her eyes still on the spot the beast had been last. "Get up," she instructed and lent a hand to the youth, "Can you walk?"

"Yes," Rend managed to get out.

Sal cursed herself for arguing that the boy should come with them. He could be safe at home if it weren't for her!

"We need to keep moving. Those mountain men aren't far behind, they'll know we're trying to get to the tower."

"Will we be safe there?" Rend questioned with a trembling voice.

"Of course, we will, just start moving," Sal prompted, hoping her encouragement did not sound as hollow as it felt to her.

They climbed through the trees at a painfully slow pace, never seeing far in any direction in the dark, and Sal's fears of being lost grew. Twice more they heard the horn blast of the mountain men, closer each time. Rend was exhausted and soon fell behind.

"Come on," Sal encouraged as she stood above him on the slope, her chest heaving and water running off her face. 'I'm giving him false hope,' the despairing thought captured her mind like the jaws of a beast. The Ancient One had abandoned her…

"What if we've missed the tower?" Rend questioned, stopping to lean against a tree.

Sal could think of nothing to say and felt her knees giving way beneath her, wanting nothing more than to give up. A menacing growl sounded in the dark. Sal tensed and brought her spear back up, searching and seeing nothing. The growl came again- dangerously close.

"MOVE!" Sal commanded Rend, he scrambled up to her side, eyes wide with fear. Sal pushed him past her and began backing away.

"Why doesn't it just kill us?" Rend breathed, clinging to the small leather flask of salt water about his neck.

"Start running, the tower *must* be close," Sal instructed, knowing that she was only prolonging his death, "GO!"

Rend obeyed, fear giving him new strength, he bolted up the slope and into the shadows. Sal backed away after him, her spear ready to thrust if the beast should lunge at her from its hiding place.

The sound of someone else crashing through the under bush came from Sal's right. She dared to divide her attention and looked; three mountain men barrelled towards her!

She met the first by deflecting his sword with a sweep of her spear, then spun it around and struck him on the head with the back end of the shaft. He stumbled aside and before the second attacker could get close enough to touch her, Sal thrust her spear, stabbing his shoulder, piercing his armor. In the corner of her eye, she saw the first attacker come charging back at her. Pulling her spear out, Sal frantically tried to get its point between her and the first attacker. A split second too slow, Sal ducked under her spear, and the attacker's sword came crashing down onto her spear shaft. The shaft snapped in two.

Drawing her knife Sal was rammed into by the third attacker, they rolled over each other, mud and forest debris clinging to them. Throwing her body weight at the right moment Sal ended up on top and delivered a fatal slash with her knife. Springing to her feet Sal, took a precious moment to orientate herself, seeing that her remaining two attackers were not in range, she turned and charged up the mountain. Ducking and weaving between trees that loomed out of the dark inches from her face, Sal's heart pounded loud enough to drown out the sound of her breath.

Ahead a warm light flickered between the trees, and Sal caught the silhouette of Rend racing towards a low wall beyond the treeline; they had found the tower!

Something heavy hit her legs and Sal's stride was cut short, she fell face first, her hands barely breaking her fall. Rolling over Sal found a strange weapon wrapped about her legs. She scrambled to untangle herself, but the two mountain men were charging at her, weapons ready.

The beast sprung from the shadows and seized the first attacker with its massive jaws, it threw him aside like a doll. Sal, still tangled up, scrambled backwards, eyes wide as the beast attacked the second man, his screams urged her to run.

Kicking madly, Sal untangled herself, without waiting to see the outcome of the fight, she ran towards the tower's safety. Bursting from the treeline, she scrambled up a rocky road, the tower loomed overhead.

Rend called to her from behind a low wall as the rain stung Sal's face. Strangers in robes and headdresses appeared in a doorway. Reaching the wall, Sal vaulted over it, Rend met her with wide eyes.

"Inside!" Sal warned and a snarl from the beast accompanied her words.

"Baine wilk!" one of the strangers cried out in alarm.

Sal and Rend were herded inside without a moment's hesitation. The door was shut fast and bolted behind them.

"Salvage!" someone cried in surprise.

Sal turned and realized that the Verlyance warriors were there. Relief flooded her body, leaving her limbs weak and shaky. "Vigil and the prince!?" she asked, heart still pounding.

"Aloft in the tower."

The answer felt like someone had lifted a great boulder from her shoulders. Sal heaved air in and out of her lungs and crouched down where she was, closing her eyes she whispered a prayer to whatever force had seen to their good fate.

"Well, go and fetch them," Sal ordered casually.

There was a moment of hesitation amongst her warriors, and she realized that there were others among them, large men with very dark skin and strange raiment.

"I think it best that we wait; things are complicated," one of her warriors explained and handed her a water skin.

Sal drank and rose to her feet. "Complicated how?" she asked, moving further into the crowd of her people and away from the strangers.

"Those men say they are from the Niben Weald, they travel with a mistress who was praying in the tower when we arrived," the warrior explained. "They allowed Vig and the prince and one other to ascend with an escort- They won't take kindly to someone else going up."

"Why did they go up?" Sal asked, noticing Rend leaning against a wall breathing heavily.

"To search for you."

Sal smirked at the answer, "Very thoughtful."

"Salvage!" Lady Serene exclaimed from a doorway, despite the late hour, she like everyone else was fully dressed and did not appear to have been resting, "I *am* pleased to see you unscathed."

Sal smiled and bowed her head, "Likewise, my lady."

Behind Serene, Garden poked his head around the door, his arms loaded with old books and tomes, as so often in the presence of women, he looked thoroughly bewildered.

Lady Serene noticed Sal's gaze, "I hope you don't mind; I've made use of Garden's help. They have a marvellous collection of books here!" she sounded truly gleeful.

"As long as you don't bury him in parchment," Sal joked, still breathing heavily. Sal took the next few moments to steady herself and tried to reassure her pounding heart that all was well. Now that all were accounted for, some of the warriors at last relaxed and settled down on the floor to sleep. Sal had lost all concept of time but supposed that the dawn could not be far off; they would not be making much northward progress that day.

The Niben strangers, there were about a dozen of them, settled down to rest as well, leaving a few awake to guard the tower stairs and watch for treachery- as Sal was doing, despite her fatigue. Footsteps from the tower stairs brought wakefulness to the assortment of warriors, and Sal tensed till Vigil appeared, the prince at his side.

Vigil's unguarded face registered shock, surprise and relief before he could mask it all. "Salvage! About time you showed up," he commented lightly. The Verlyance warriors smirked and chuckled, used to their interactions.

"I had to track down a few things," Sal explained, gesturing to Rend's sleeping form, this time Vig only allowed a bit of relief to show.

"Well, you could have sent word that you would be late," Vig suggested, refraining from taking her up in his arms.

Sal smirked, "Sorry my love, I can only do so much. I had mountain men on my heels, and apparently a baine wilk stalking me."

"Your safe return would be welcome even if you had been a week late," Theophany assured, betraying the amount of relief he was feeling.

Sal allowed him the moment without drawing attention to his emotions. "I believe this belongs to you, sire," Sal said quietly and removed a small satchel from her belt.

Theoph accepted it with bewildered eyes and hesitant hands. Opening it, he first gazed at the contents then at her, "How?" he breathed.

Sal shifted, "My presence went unnoticed when you and the others fled on the gillup, and I was able to retrieve your belongings."

Raising her voice, Sal addressed the rest of her company, "I was able to give our fallen warriors proper death rites with the salt water they carried."

There was a noticeable sigh of relief among those gathered; the souls of their fallen comrades had hope of finding their way back to the sea.

Theoph frowned. "But you've forsaken Tylus," he pointed out, his voice only loud enough for her and Vig to hear.

Sal smiled sadly, "They hadn't."

"Come," Vig said, abandoning the subject, "It's time we all rested." He directed Theoph to the only available private room left.

After setting up a shift of guards to stand watch at the prince's door, Sal and Vig settled down in one corner, but neither could sleep and instead they sat, knees touching, and heads bowed as they related to each other what had befallen them since the ambush. As they talked in hushed tones, Vig worked with gentle hands to clean and bandage a cut on Sal's arm. Their sleeping comrades took no notice of them, and despite their close quarters, Sal and Vig conversed as if in total privacy.

"Why didn't the baine wilk kill us?!" Vig pondered as he tied Sal's bandage in a knot.

She shrugged and allowed her arm to rest in his hands.

He searched her face, "In the ambush, you asked if I trusted your visions; did you foresee the beast helping us?"

"In a way, I couldn't be sure though." Sal confessed, thinking of the other elements of her vision.

"If the Ancient One is responsible for your visions," Vig said softly, "Then he is also responsible for bringing you back to me; for that alone he has my loyalty."

The corners of Sal's lips tipped upwards, "*I'm* supposed to be the Believer," she joked, "And you the Seeker."

Vig smirked in return, "I *am* seeking, can I help it if your faith is the only thing that rings true?"

Sal's smile fell slightly, "My faith is lacking; I thought I would die tonight. I thought I had made a mistake… I would have died if it weren't for that beast, the beast from my vision." She swallowed hard, ashamed of her own despair, "I would have died and never have told you…"

Her words dried up in her mouth, but he ran his hand along her arm gently and waited with a patience that said he would accept anything she had to say.

"My visions…" the words slipped from Sal's grasp, and she hesitated, realizing that she had to come out and just say it, "I think I may be with child."

Vigil's eyebrows drew together, after a moment he responded, "I thought that was impossible for us."

He was being kind; it was impossible for *her*. Cursed is what she was, barren.

"I thought it was impossible too," Sal breathed, "But every vision I have had since before even leaving Verlynn Nel, there has been a child crying. Each vision I search for the child but can never reach it. The further north we travel, the closer I get. Whether I am with child now, or will be soon, I am convinced that is the meaning of the visions; I can think of no other explanation."

Vig searched her eyes for a moment before sighing, "Did you keep this from me because you were uncertain, or because you knew I would make you stay behind in Verlynn Nel?"

Sal allowed a mischievous grin to form, "A bit of both."

Vig sighed again and squeezed her arm, "Now I have more things to fear losing."

"When you have something, you fear losing, you know it is worth having." Sal leaned forward and rested her forehead on his. They sat, secure in each other's company.

Theophany's body was stiff, every muscle ached, but hunger drove him to rise and leave his small chamber. It was late morning, nearly midday, yet many of the warriors were still sleeping, stretched out in the entrance chamber. Lady Serene's guards were clustered about her closed door, and the Niben nitora were clustered about a third door.

Several warriors were sitting up eating from wooden bowls and tending wounds from the day before. The guard on Theoph's door followed him as Theoph crossed through an archway that led to a kitchen of sorts. To one side Theoph took note of another door through which he glimpsed the gillup. He supposed it was wise to keep animals inside when there were such things as baine wilk about.

"Hungry?" a temple priest asked cheerfully. He appeared to be younger than the others at first glance, but Theoph had a hard time pinning down the man's age

"Very," Theoph answered. There was no one else in the room, and Theoph wondered where the other inhabitants of the tower were.

The priest prepared two bowls and handed one to Theoph and one to his guard. The bowl held a lumpy brown mixture that was a mystery to Theoph, but he was past caring and began drinking it from the bowl, "What is this place?" he asked after a moment.

The priest paused in his busy work about the kitchen and smiled happily. "It is the Honorfell Temple," he answered brightly.

Theoph smirked, "Why build a temple here? Is there a town or city nearby?"

"The roaming Honorfell tribes are the only people you will find here, aside from travellers such as yourselves."

"Then why build a temple here!?" Theoph questioned again, silently believing it foolish.

"This is spirit ground." The priest pointed out like it was obvious. "This mountain allows the prayers of the faithful to reach whichever god they seek."

"This temple is for *all* gods?" Theoph asked, baffled by the idea.

The priest's smile widened, "Indeed, see the paintings," he pointed to the walls where high up along every wall were fresco paintings of gods that Theoph had never seen before, one even depicted Tylus.

"Because of the spirit ground, anyone can come here and reach their god; few leave unsatisfied," the priest insisted.

Theoph's scepticism halted, "Do you mean that we are closer to the realm of the gods here?"

The priest nodded with a wide smile, "That is why travellers come from all reaches of the map to pray here."

Theoph set aside his bowl, the rest of his breakfast forgotten. He left the kitchen and the priest without explanation. Searching for Vigil, he found his loyal friend asleep in a corner, Salvage's head in the crook of his arm.

"Vigil, awake," Theoph said, aware of the urgency creeping into his voice and the hopeful flutter in his stomach.

Both Vig and Sal woke, they sat up quickly and took in their surroundings like under threat of attack.

"I must go up the tower again," Theoph explained.

Sal lay back down while Vig moaned and rubbed his face. "Very well," he got up with difficulty, "I wasn't doing anything important," he added under his breath. After grabbing his own breakfast, he followed Theoph as he climbed the steps of the tower with an eagerness that he barely understood.

"Do I want to know?" Vig asked as he finished the contents of his bowl and set it aside to collect on the way down.

"I was told that the spirit ground this temple is built on allows men to draw near to the realm of the gods," Theoph half explained.

Vig did not comment.

"Vigil," Theoph said breathlessly, turning to him on the stairs, "don't you see?! My destiny is within reach!"

Vig did not respond in the way Theoph expected. "You'll see." Theoph started climbing again, his old doubts hanging about in the back of his mind, reminding him of all the times before he had tried, and failed to reach Tylus. The haunting image of his rotting form in the mirror of Voy mocked his unsteady confidence.

The warm sunlight filtered through Salvage's closed eyelids and lulled her back to sleep, the absence of Vigil's body next to her created an odd discomfort. Sounds from the warriors about her waking and eating grew ever distant and Sal knew that a vision was upon her.

Her hands were stained, and her heart ached. Sal was in a village, a large village, everything seemed larger than it should be. Far away there was the sound of a river, and nearby, a well with a clay jar sitting beside it.

Sal picked up the jar, intending to fill it with water from the well, but instead of a rope to pull up a bucket, the well was full to the brim with cool fresh water. Anxious to wash her stained hands, Sal dipped the jar into the water, causing some to spill out onto the paving stones. Filling the jar Sal held it up and realized that the vessel was broken; the water gushed out of wide cracks. She tipped the jar to pour onto her hands, but the water was all gone.

The jar slipped from her hands and fell into the well, but it was no longer full of water, instead a gaping hole stared up at her, and the jar fell forever into it. The cry of a child echoed up from the well, sending Sal's heart into a flutter.

"What have you to fear?" a voice spoke behind her.

Turning, Sal found the baine wilk. "I have much to fear," Sal insisted, "I only *have* one life."

"You were in danger but never at risk; I was there!" the baine wilk proclaimed.

The vision faded from Sal's grasp before she was ready to let go, and she returned to the mountain structure with her warriors. More had woken and life was returning to the company. Sal sat up and stretched her sore limbs, she pondered her vision with a frown as she rose and sought out breakfast.

Lady Serene sat against a wall, perched on pillows, she looked haggard and in bad humor. Garden sat at her elbow, looking bewildered as always.

Sal was handed a bowl and she tested the contents with curiosity.

"A fine mess this is," Lady Serene commented indignantly and brushed aside some of her hair.

"It could be worse," Sal commented brightly, "We could be wandering about the mountains lost and half dead right now."

"A lot of good a safe refuge will do us if we can't ever leave it!" Lady Serene's lack of pithy sayings gave an idea as to how stressed she was. "Surely those horrid mountain men have guessed where we fled to; the moment we try to leave this place they'll attack us again!"

Sal refrained from commenting on their precarious situation; although she knew everyone else had come to the same conclusion, it was dangerous to utter such things aloud.

Garden tried to take the opportunity to leave, but Serene stopped him without comment by quickly laying her hand on his arm.

"Where is your husband?" Serene asked suddenly, her attention back on Salvage.

Sal nodded upwards, "The tower, with the prince."

Serene rolled her eyes in disgust, "Ugh! They aren't praying, are they?"

"What better time is there?" Garden asked humbly.

Serene fidgeted uncomfortably, while Sal tried to hide a smile.

"Right you are, I suppose," Serene conceded, "If one believes in such *things*." She glanced at Garden sideways, "Do you?"

Garden worked his mouth for a moment. "A slave hardly has a right to a god," he said at last. "When I was a boy, I…" he frowned and shook his head, dismissing whatever thought he had.

His uncertainty did not go unnoticed by Lady Serene. "And what of you?" Lady Serene's attention was again on Salvage, "I suppose you believe the same as your warriors. A *sea god* and such things." Her disdain was clear.

Aware of how her fellow countrymen would react to her plainly denying their faith, Sal shrugged and hoped it would be enough to satisfy the woman.

Serene eyed her suspiciously, "Even the foolish are wise when they keep their own counsel."

Sal tried not to take offence at the woman's slight and decided that Serene must be feeling better.

"I, however, will be free with my own counsel," Serene declared, "If we do not perish by the hands of mountain savages, then we'll surely starve when the food supply runs out here! And I shall never finish my quest."

Sal sighed inwardly, knowing that her warriors were listening.

"Perish here if you wish, but I will not die before I see my country again," Garden said, unexpectedly confident.

"I suppose we must simply forge northward then," Sal joined in, "The mountain men will have little choice but to let us pass with you leading us."

Garden nodded staunchly, while Serene refused to be cheered.

"You travel north?" a deep voice interrupted.

Sal turned to find that the mysterious Lady Roam had emerged from her room, and Dire had taken up position beside her.

"Aye, that's right," Sal replied. Vig had told her about the strangers, and she was intrigued as ever to see the pale girl. Vig had said she was young, but Sal was still surprised to see that the girl was hardly more than nine! She was wrapped up in white robes, with face bowed as if uninterested in the proceedings, but a flicker from her red eyes told Sal she was paying close attention.

"How far?" Dire asked, and Sal wondered if he was speaking for his mistress or out of personal curiosity.

"We will find our journeys end when we reach the country of Garatin," Sal answered.

Dire bent low and Lady Roam raised a pale hand to cover her mouth as she whispered to him, he nodded and whispered something back before straightening, "It seems we share a destination; I propose that we travel together, our combined numbers will lend further protection from the mountain men."

Sal shifted her feet; she could not deny the logic of his suggestion. Vigil's voice in her ear urged her to be cautious, "Do you travel home to Garatin?"

Dire smirked, "Far from it, we are on a quest."

Sal raised her eyebrows, "A quest? May I inquire the nature of this quest?"

Dire exchanged a look with his mistress, "We seek the reincarnated Prince of the Dawn and Dusk."

"Oh, for the love of all things decent!" Lady Serene burst indignantly. "This is becoming ridiculous!" she muttered.

The old woman's outburst roused a response from Lady Roam, who peeked at her curiously.

"Forgive my travel companion," Sal said, doing her best to hold back a smile, "We are both astonished at the coincidence. For both the Lady Serene and my prince are on separate quests of similar nature to yours!"

"*You* seek the Prince of the Dawn and Dusk?" Dire asked in baffled astonishment.

"If one more person assumes I seek a king, prince or other such finite figure- I'll go *mad*!" Serene muttered with barely held rage. "No! I am *not* seeking this prince of yours; I seek the Wise One. The days of the Wise One are upon us, and I shall see them ere I breathe my last!" she huffed and crossed her arms, looking away as if too infuriated to continue.

Dire looked amused, then aimed a questioning look at Sal.

"Prince Theophany seeks a Foretold King, one of great prestige. It was revealed to us that he has come into power, and none will stand against his might. My prince seeks to make an alliance with him," Sal explained.

Dire again exchanged a look with his mistress, "A strange coincidence indeed. However, unless the man you seek is the reincarnation of a prince that ruled the Niben Weald many centuries ago, who has returned to deal judgement on his enemies; this is just a coincidence."

Sal actually laughed, "A strange twist of fates this is! I can not speak for my Prince, but I will advise him on the wisdom of joining companies as we travel northward."

Dire nodded his head regally.

The sun poured golden light down on the wooded hills and mountains, bribing the landscape into forgetting the storm of the night before. From the tower's window Vigil could see for miles, and he studied the lay of the land, noting the river gorge that they had traveled along and the valley they had fled through during the night. It was hard to tell, but it seemed as though Sentinel's Pass turned and wound round the mountain that their tower refuge rested atop.

Through the north facing window Vig searched for any sign of the continued path, but the hills and trees revealed little. He debated if they should travel back into the valley to pick up on the path where they had left and risk running back into the arms of the mountain men, or if they should instead risk losing their way altogether by striking out north and hoping to find the path beyond the mountain. These thoughts served to distract him for a time, but the matter of the prince could not be held off indefinitely.

Prince Theophany kneeled in the center of the tower the way Lady Roam had in the night. His eyes were closed but his face was far from peaceful as he sought to force his way into the realm of the gods. He kneeled for so long, Vig began to fear that he would sustain damage to his knees, yet still the prince did not move.

Vig watched him with concern, wondering what he could do for his friend. Quietly he withdrew the enchanted mirror shard, and peered at his reflection, wondering not for the first time if they had imagined the prince's deformed shape in the mirror that night.

"You believe I am cursed," Theophany spoke, startling Vig.

Vig met his eyes, and handled the mirror shard deliberately, "The Ancient One seemed to think you were."

"What power has the Ancient One over me? I, the chosen of Tylus."

Vig hesitated, his fingers sliding over the sharp edges of the mirror shard, "Did you… reach the sea god?"

Theoph averted his eyes and breathed deep, "The gates of the immortals remain closed to me- but it will not always be so. I will claim that which is mine."

Vig couldn't keep a disappointed sigh from escaping his lungs, after all this he still clung to hope. "Perhaps you must consider what Voy said."

Theoph's gaze cut through the air to Vig.

"I have never failed to serve you, sire. Voy said that I should seek the truth to help you-"

Theoph stood angrily and started for the stairs.

"Theophany you can not run from this!" Vig went after him, holding out the shard.

Theoph turned sharply and came within inches of the mirror. His eyes widened in a moment of fear, then he forced the fear out. "I am not bound to mortal ways, and I will not bend to the will of the Ancient One- or any other!" he turned once more and started down the stairs.

Vig grit his teeth in anger, regretting his words and wishing he could try again. Putting the mirror shard away, he started after the prince only to find Theoph had paused on the steps.

"I do not blame you, or Salvage for what happened in Fisher's Hamlet." He spoke over his shoulder, "I know both of you are loyal to me, and I… am grateful."

Vig watched Theoph's back as he restarted the descent, astonished at the surprisingly heartfelt words. Perhaps not all was lost.

They descended the rest of the way in stiff silence, each either caught in his thoughts, or running from them. When they reached the bottom, they were met with expectant faces from everyone.

"I have good news if you were feeling lonely or bad news if you were feeling crowded on the road." Salvage greeted them, the turn of her lips betraying her contained humor.

Vig scanned the faces of the others, trying to guess what she was getting at.

"What is it?" Theophany asked.

"We too are bound for the northern lands of Garatin and would travel with you and Lady Serene; if you are not opposed to our company," Dire of the Niben Weald answered.

Vigil raised his eyebrows, "What!?" he exclaimed.

"They are on a quest from the gods," Sal explained, her amusement shining through in her face.

"It's ridiculous I know!" Lady Serene chimed in, "Who would have thought such things were so commonplace?"

"Our combined numbers would be a formidable defence against further attacks," Dire pointed out.

Theophany hesitated, as if wanting to seek Vigil's advice, but he did not. "Very well," he decided, "Shall we discuss plans for leaving our refuge?"

* * * *

"This kingdom of the Niben Weald," Salvage spoke as she and Dire ventured into the forest, weapons ready, "Is it a large one?"

Dire grinned, matching Sal's comfort level for banter while risking danger. "Have you never seen it on a map?"

Sal shook her head slightly, as she scanned the surrounding woods, "Verlyance has no need for maps beyond the sea," she explained.

"Yes," Dire answered her question, "The Niben kingdom is vast; one could travel for a month and still not see it in its entirety. King Golden, Lady Roam's uncle, rules in the city of Estewryn, he currently holds the loyalty of over half of the Weald tribes."

Sal looked him up and down with a frown, "And the other tribes?"

"We have been at war with them for many years," Dire explained as they made their way through the trees.

"Do you seek the Prince of the Dawn and Dusk to fight against these tribes?" Sal questioned, genuinely curious.

Dire cast her a sly look, "The prince does not offer aid of that sort."

Sal stopped to listen to the wood about them; they were nearing the place she had been attacked the night before. "What sort of aid does he offer?

Dire's only answer was a knowing smile; Sal wondered if his secret would prove trouble for her and the others.

"Here we are," Sal said as they came upon a section of the wood where the ground was disturbed and underbrush damaged, "There should be a body here." Sal said, scanning the area.

Dire studied the ground, "Perhaps your attacker was only wounded."

Sal readied her knife in her hand. "I slit his throat," she argued, "They've been here to collect his body."

Dire scanned about them with dark eyes, "Unless they've given up and moved on; they must be camped nearby."

Sal stooped and collected the shattered remains of her spear, testing the tip, she found that the living coral spear head was still securely mounted on the shattered pole. She gripped it like another knife and ventured forward, "Let's find out."

They crept through the trees together, pausing now and again to listen. Sal took note of how Dire appeared to be at home in the wooded surroundings, and she wordlessly allowed him to lead the way, bowing to his superior experience. Despite his impressive size, the man moved confidently and smoothly, his choice of clothing blended easily with the surroundings and Sal imagined that at a distance it worked quite well as camouflage. His weapons consisted of long knives at his belt, a quiver strapped to his hip holding arrows fletched with vibrant green and black striped feathers, and the largest bow Sal had ever seen. All his weapons were crafted from rich black wood that gleamed in the sunlight. He carried his bow with an arrow to the string.

Together they scouted the area for a half hour before finding their quarry; a camp of mountain men swarmed about the woods, out of sight of the tower windows.

Sal and Dire snuck up, and crouched behind tree trunks to watch them, "They appear to be arguing," Salvage observed, although she could not understand their language.

"They must fear the spirit ground of the temple," Dire decided.

"At any rate, their numbers have grown from when they ambushed us," Sal pointed out darkly, "I count over thirty."

"A fair fight with our combined numbers," Dire commented, "It does leave the question; why do they want you so bad? Your prince said that they had already robbed him of what wealth he had."

Sal took her time to answer, "Perhaps they think there is more to have." She decided against sharing that she had in fact saved the riches. "They may even know about your company; it could be they are after *your* wealth," she suggested, watching his reaction closely.

Dire's face was impassive, "It could be."

Sal smirked; they would both keep secrets then.

"Let us retreat now, before we are discovered," Dire suggested.

Sal nodded and they crept backwards noiselessly. Allowing her to take the lead, Dire lagged behind a few paces. There was a shift of shadows by Sal's side and one of her knives was suddenly knocked from her hand by the blade of a hidden mountain man.

Salvage took a step back but was a moment too late. The mountain man seized her, pinning her arms to her sides, and held his blade to her. The mountain man opened his mouth to raise the alarm but was silenced by Dire's arrow. Sal slipped from his grasp and turned on him, knife in hand, but the mountain man fell limp to the forest floor.

"A scout, we must have slipped past him earlier," Dire said as he came forward and retrieved his arrow.

Sal came close to gaping at him, "You saved my life just now; not many have had the chance to do so."

Dire allowed the corner of his mouth to turn upwards, "We should go now. There may be more scouts."

Sal retrieved her fallen knife and the two of them made a hasty retreat, meeting no further resistance. Before returning to the tower, they circled the temple to make sure an attack was not imminent.

The entrance chamber and hallway of the tower temple was crowded with warriors and nobility alike. The afternoon sun had not yet sunk behind the mountains and still lit the proceedings inside the temple.

Theophany stood with arms crossed, every fiber of his being striving to prove himself as the clear leader amongst all gathered; he was having little success. Vigil and Salvage stood on either side of him.

Lady Serene sat in a chair gripping her staff, and casting refined disdain at everyone else. She would not admit so, but she was still badly shaken from the events of the day before. Her guards clustered about her, staying mostly mute through the discussion.

The silent and mysterious Lady Roam sat on another chair, with Dire at her right, speaking for her with confidence. Her warriors, called 'nitora', stood with arms crossed and mistrust in their dark eyes.

The temple priests edged in on the three groups humbly, a contrast of peace and humility amongst the otherwise tense atmosphere.

"How much of this back road is on spirit ground?" Dire asked the temple priests.

"Only a short distance," one of the priests answered, "And it will join up again with Sentinel's Pass, I assure you."

Theoph nodded, considering his options, which were limited, "It seems like a reasonable escape."

"You said that the mountain men know of this road, surely they will expect us to retreat on it," Vig directed his question to the priest.

"Aye, but they will not enter the road on this side of the mountain for fear of angering the spirits," the priest pursed his lips. "They have angered the spirits in the past and paid heavily for it. They will likely try and cut you off on the other side of the mountain, but it would take them a full day and night to circle the mountain to the other side. Something they haven't done… yet."

Theoph nodded, hoping the others viewed him as competent, "Lady Serene, what say you?"

"Me!? Why ask me!?" Serene exclaimed, "I am hardly a battle strategist!"

"You are the wisest amongst us," Theoph pointed out.

She huffed, but seemed placated by his complement, "When a woman only has one option, her wisdom or folly can only be revealed by the outcome."

Dire narrowed his eyes in confusion, and Theoph held back a smirk at the woman's strange answer.

"I agree," Theoph said, drawing attention back to himself, "Taking this spirit road is our only choice without meeting these mountain men head on. If we move swiftly, and not rest through the night, we will rejoin Sentinel's Pass and hopefully elude the mountain men." He looked over his unlikely travel companions, "Shall we venture northward together?"

"To find a great treasure, one must risk much," Lady Serene declared and rose to her feet, but her words gave pause to Theoph; Voy had said something similar.

"Northward and may the Prince of the Dawn and Dusk look upon us with favor," Dire agreed, bringing Theoph back to the present.

"Let us make preparations then," Theoph instructed, still distracted. The three groups split up and the temple was busy with movement. Theoph stood aside and allowed Vig to give his warriors directions.

"Sire," Sal spoke softly at his side, "please, allow me to look at your wound again while we have a chance."

Theoph agreed grudgingly, and the two withdrew to his chamber. Sal closed the door while Theoph removed his tunic and sat. The bandage Sal had applied the day before was soiled and stained. She removed it without comment and began cleaning the wound.

"It looks better," she commented lightly.

Theoph remembered their tense conversation when she had last dressed his wound, "Thanks to you."

She let the complement pass without comment.

"I would be truly lost without you and Vigil," Theoph went on, finding his pride bitter to swallow, "I've been… rash with my words to you of late."

Sal raised a single brow as she worked on his arm, "Sire?"

Theoph sighed; she would not allow him any shortcuts in his apology, "I blamed you for what happened at Fishers Hamlet. I blamed you for the curse. I was wrong to do so."

Sal finished bandaging him before responding, she lowered herself down into a crouch and looked up at him, "I am your loyal servant, sire, and I will do all in my power to help you. My visions-"

Theoph silenced her with a movement, "I will always count you as a friend, but I want nothing to do with your visions, *or* your god."

Sal bowed her head for a moment, then stood, "Very well, but you can not stop me from trying to save you from your own folly."

Theoph flexed his jaw in annoyance; she never did know when to give up!

* * * *

Vigil tilted his head to one side in question as Lady Serene beckoned him into her chamber.

"Oh, don't look at me like that!" Serene scolded once he was inside, she shut the door and sat down on her cot. Her chamber was dusty and smelled of old books. The walls were lined with shelf after shelf of tomes while scrolls were slipped neatly into slots.

"I found what you were after," Serene boasted.

Vig frowned, "What was I after?"

Serene rolled her eyes and heaved a large book onto her lap, "You asked me to look into the matter of curses- the Heart Stain to be exact."

Vig's eyes fell to the book and his heart beat a little faster.

Serene looked extremely pleased with herself. "I knew I had come across the Heart Stain curse before, it was mentioned in a list of forbidden enchantments in the dark arts of ages past. But last night I discovered more." She patted the book on her lap, "I couldn't sleep because- well you know why, and so I began reading the books around me. This one is an account from a priest who lived many years ago, mostly prayers and other such nonsense, but in one part he tells of a traveller who came to this temple hoping to be cured from a curse."

"A Heart Stain?" Vig prompted excitedly.

Serene nodded, looking even more pleased with herself, "Unfortunately the book doesn't describe what the curse looked like."

"No matter, I've seen it," Vig muttered.

Serene paused, looking disturbed, "Not up close I hope."

"Why?" Vig asked, fearing her answer.

"The book says that the traveller died; found him aloft in the tower. Obviously, their prayers weren't answered," she ended with morbid humor.

Vig's mind reeled with the information.

"Quite the coincidence if you ask me," Serene muttered.

"What do you mean?"

Serene tilted her head regally, "The book says that the traveller was praying to the Dawn and Dusk King -or whatever- the same deity that our friends from the Niben Weald worship."

Vig wet his lips, perhaps Dire would know more of the heart stain!

"Now if that's not cause for discomfort, I don't know what is," Serene went on. Vig cast her a confused frown. "The book records that the temple priests welcome all, as is their creed, but the author of this book records that he and his fellow men found extreme discomfort at welcoming a worshiper of the Dawn and Dusk King, stating that they disagree with several of their practices. He refrained from giving specifics. Makes me wonder what practices would make these priests uncomfortable."

Vig's frown deepened; just one more thing to worry about.

Serene looked at him with curiosity, "Well? Does this help you?""

He sighed, "Yes, thank you, I am in your debt." He turned away; how could he help Theoph now?

Chapter 8 Disdain

Dust from the training yard coated Courage's chest and arms, and the air was thick with the musky scent of sweat. The yard was crowded with soldiers who stood shoulder to shoulder, creating open spaces for wrestling matches, while above them leaning on the railing of the gangway from the sleeping quarters, officers watched with interest.

Rage glanced upwards to aim a grin at Captain Farious; surely the man was impressed. Courage's new opponent stepped out from the crowd, and eyed Rage with clear apprehension. Rage chuckled and placed his hands on his hips, "Whenever you're ready."

His opponent flared his nostrils a moment before charging, giving Rage a second of warning to respond, he feigned to the left and stuck his foot out catching the others leg as he rushed past him. Rage delivered a shove to his opponent's shoulder as he stumbled, sending the young man face first into the ground.

"Who's next?" Courage asked arms out and palms up; he had faced eleven of his fellow soldiers now. None had yet to beat him.

The men surrounding him looked to each other and bravely invited others to take on the challenge, but no one did.

"What!? No one?" Rage asked boldly, a comrade tossed him a rag and he wiped off his face. "Very well, I'll accept the title of champion and represent you all in the tournament."

"There's one other soldier who has bested all his opponents," Captain Farious interrupted from his viewing point; he bore a sly smile that made Rage uncertain.

Someone was pushed through the crowd towards Rage, and the soldiers stepped aside for the second champion to approach. Wilderness didn't look the least bit surprised to see who his next opponent would be.

Rage glanced up at Captain Farious, remembering the stiff reprimand he and Wilder had received the week before about brawling in the barracks- now they were invited to fight?

"The winner of this final match will represent my men in the wrestling matches at the tournament. May the best man triumph," Farious instructed.

Rage met Wilder's eyes with heated intensity; he would not allow a hedge-born Garatin to represent him!

Wilder began circling him, nothing on his face betraying emotion, it unnerved Rage; a man wasn't meant to be so calm in a fight- where was his passion!?

Rage casually began circling too. "Did you bribe your other opponents to get this far?" he asked, hoping to rile the Garatin into making a mistake, "I can't imagine you had much to offer them, being a mongrel peasant after all."

Wilder's façade of calm melted in the heat of his anger and the Garatin charged, Rage didn't have time to dodge this time and was nearly knocked off his feet. The two men grappled with each other, each trying to throw the other off balance. But Rage had the advantage of a bulkier build, and his feet remained planted firmly on the ground while Wilder struggled and slipped.

Forcing a bit of distance between them, Rage brought his knee up into Wilder's stomach. Wilder's concentration was broken, and with a roar of effort, Rage knocked Wilder to the side and slammed him into the dirt.

His comrades cheered and rushed towards him, blocking from view whatever expression Wilder's face choked on.

"Courage will represent us in the tournament wrestling matches!" Captain Farious declared, and Rage drank in the sweetness of the Garatin's humiliation.

The celebrations were short lived however as the captain's voice cut in on the excitement of the soldiers, "Enough time wasted for today, prepare for a full barracks inspection at nightfall."

There was a suppressed groan from everyone, but all knew better than to complain. Sweaty and tired as they were, the soldiers set about cleaning and straightening the barracks. Some went to the stables to look after the horses and see that all the tackle was in order, while others went to the armory to clean and inspect the weapons. A full barracks inspection meant that every aspect of the building and grounds would be scrutinized, punishments were common when something was found amiss.

When Courage was done oiling swords and knives, he joined the other men in the sleeping quarters; the last place to prepare for inspection. It was nearly sundown and the men, including Rage, were weary of the day.

One of Rage's friends, Gid, carelessly threw his blanket onto his bunk, "How long will they keep us here training!?" he questioned impatiently, "None of us are novice soldiers- why won't they just deploy us?"

"Maybe Farious really wants his men to do well in the tournament," another soldier suggested as he lounged on his bunk.

"We could prove our mettle by actually serving! Instead Farious keeps us locked away training!" Gid pointed out as he half heartedly straightened out his bunk. "The tournament is still a month away- we should be patrolling the city! Even escorting officials would be better than this!"

"Obviously Captain Farious has something else planned for us," Wilderness broke in on the conversation from his corner bunk, everyone cast him unwelcoming gazes.

"Like what?" someone asked with disdain.

Wilder paused in straightening out his belongings (his bunk and area was always impeccably clean and orderly), "Something other than serving as regular soldiers; he is testing us, weeding out those unfit to his purpose. Why else do you think Entin, and Main were sent away after being summoned to speak with the captain?"

No one answered as unease gripped the room.

"Soldiers don't question orders," Rage said in a warning tone to his comrades.

"*We* haven't been given orders," Wilder dared to continue, "*We* haven't been told anything."

Rage straightened out his shoulders and pointed a disdainful look at Wilder. "Keep a civil tongue before I remove it entirely," he threatened.

Wilder's jaw flexed, but he said nothing more.

'Good' Rage thought, 'the half blood is already learning his place.'

"Captain in the quarters!" a soldier announced sharply as he opened the door and stepped in. Everyone scrambled to stand erect by their bunk as Captain Multifarious limped into the room, he paused to sweep the room with a penetrating gaze and Rage wondered if he had overheard anything.

"What do you want?" Captain Multifarious asked from his desk as he went over paperwork. Mid morning sun rays lit the room and the sounds of the city drifted in through the windows.

Courage stood before his captain confidently, "I'm requesting day leave, captain."

Farious finished folding and sealing a letter before glancing up at him, "What for?"

"My mother has returned from our summer manor and has asked to see me," Rage explained.

Farious filed the sealed letter then leaned back in his chair, "Will this be the first time you've seen your mother since your father died."

Rage was taken aback; did Farious know personal details about all the soldiers? "Yes, captain, I have not seen her in many years."

"Do you have other kin in the city?"

Rage was beginning to think he wouldn't be allowed to leave for the day. "No. Aside from my mother, an uncle in Larsanne is the extent of my living kin."

Farious nodded, seemingly deep in thought. "Well, we must all do what we can to please our mothers; You will return tomorrow morning," he said at last.

Rage saluted, baffled by the strange conversation, "Thank you captain."

"How are the soldiers doing?" Farious asked, halting Rage from leaving.

Rage hesitated to answer, "They are doing well, captain."

"I ask you because I know the men look up to you," Farious explained.

Rage was not sure if he should thank him for the compliment. Farious went back to his papers and Rage moved again to leave.

"Congratulations on winning the wrestling matches," Farious halted him again. "You fight with uncompromising determination, I'm sure you will win honor in the tournament."

"Thank you, captain."

This time Farious waved for him to leave.

Frowning, Rage stepped out and was met by his friend, Gid.

"Were you summoned too?" Gid asked.

Rage frowned, "No, I have day leave."

Gid patted him on the back as he passed him into Farious's office. "Don't get mugged out there," he advised lightly.

Courage tried not to think about what Wilder had said about men being summoned by Farious. 'Don't question orders,' he reminded himself firmly, and put the matter from his mind.

Going to the stables, Rage prepared his horse and set out into the city streets. His family's castle was not that far from the barracks, but he did not want to make his homecoming on foot. He was twelve the last time he had been home, but he remembered it well. It was a great stone castle in the center of the city and was one of the oldest structures in Garason. Its outer walls surrounded by the streets, and its towers looked down, as if with disdain at those passing by. Rage had very few fond memories of the place, and if not for his mother sending for him, he would not choose to spend a moment inside the cold walls of his childhood home. Riding in through the open gate, Rage found that the building itself was smaller than he remembered. Stable workers approached him waiting for orders.

"Send word to the mistress of the castle that her son has come," Rage said grandly and dismounted. One of the workers ran off to deliver the message. Handing the rains of his horse over, Rage took a deep breath before braving the front doors of the castle.

Once inside, it did not take long for the warmth of the morning sun to be sapped from his bones as the oppressive chill of the castle set in. Rage had taken the news of his father's death fairly well at age fourteen, but now, he felt as though his father was still there, as if his cold heart had remained.

"This way, my lord," a page instructed and led Rage into the fire hall; but of course, there was no blazing fire. Rage had always assumed it was his father who preferred the castle to be kept cold, but perhaps it had been his mother all along.

"Where is my son?" a woman in her forties questioned in refined tones, "I sent away a boy, but a man stands before me." Her heavy dress dragged behind her as she approached him. Reaching out she held his chin so as to inspect his face.

"Hello mother," Rage took her hand and kissed it.

She pursed her lips ruefully, "You didn't mention in your letters that you bore your grandfather's face."

Rage smiled grimly; he didn't remember much of his grandfather, only the gifts he had received from him. Rage stepped back to look at his mother better; he had not mentally prepared himself for how much older she would be. "Have you been well?"

"Well enough," she said with a measured sigh, "Now I hear that your betrothed has arrived and was presented to you?"

Rage dipped his head; in her letters, Rage had gotten the feeling that his mother was not one prone to idle chatter. "Indeed, she was, over a week ago."

"And?" she asked sharply, "Is she suitable?"

Rage felt a moment of embarrassment, Lady Loyal was certainly beautiful, "I believe she is."

His mother huffed, "I should hope so, considering the trouble I went through to arrange things." She turned away and Rage accepted a cup of wine from a page. "I will send for her and see the girl myself," his mother announced, she approached a chair but hesitated to sit. She turned away as if too agitated to relax.

Courage considered sitting himself but thought better of it.

"I hear that you are training under Captain Multifarious," his mother began again and fixed him with her sharp gaze, "What are you being trained for?"

"I have not been told," he admitted, feeling foolish.

"Have you been promised a position, or a post somewhere?" she questioned further.

Rage ground his teeth, thinking of Wilder's theory, "Not yet."

His mother huffed in disdain, "Don't they know who you are? Are they aware of your service in the Five Isles?"

"They are, mother. I don't know why a promotion hasn't been mentioned yet." The more he thought of the matter the more it frustrated him.

"Never matter," his mother declared, "I have arranged something else."

Rage frowned at her in question.

She smiled pleased with herself, and sat down at last, "I have been in correspondence with the clerk of Governor Endure, he has promised to speak of you to the governor. A knighthood was hinted at."

Now it was Rage who was too agitated to sit, "Truly!? A knighthood?"

His mother nodded, "It is well deserved, considering your heritage. With a knighthood from the governor, you would be excused from the king's direct service, and could forget about useless training! In time, the governor may entrust you with soldiers of your own, and of course you would be given land…" she trailed off.

Rage was blown away, a knighthood from the governor was about as far as a soldier could go on this side of the Neenor Sea. He would be able to bid farewell to the duties of a common foot soldier!

Setting his drink aside, Rage went to his mother and kneeling before her he kissed her hand again, "You are a marvel!"

His mother smiled primly, "Don't thank me yet, the knighthood was not *promised*- only hinted. The governor's harvest banquet is next week, I've secured us invitations; if you present yourself well and the governor is pleased, there is a *chance* he will knight you."

A wide grin split Rage's face, "This is perfect! However, will I be able to thank you?"

She leaned forward and held his face. "Win the respect of the court," she instructed without hesitation, "Achieve that, and it will be thanks enough for me."

Rage smiled and kissed her hand once more before rising, his head spinning with his suddenly altered future. He had no doubts that he would be knighted- why wouldn't the governor be impressed with him?

"Next I'll see about securing a banquet invitation for your betrothed," his mother added, "that is, after I see her."

Rage hardly heard her; he would be a knight!

Regime huffed in frustration. Without looking she thrust her embroidery at Dream; it was knotted and hopelessly tangled.

Eam took the embroidery, abandoning her own, and did her best to untangle the mess that Lady Regime had made. Loyal sat nearby working on her own handkerchief, she watched discreetly with guarded sympathy.

Regime kept her quarters uncomfortably warm, in Eam's opinion, the heat from the fire added to a stuffiness in the room that made it hard to breathe. Gime held her hand out for her embroidery.

"I have it nearly sorted, my lady," Eam assured meekly, her fingers shook slightly in her haste.

Gime waited a moment longer before snatching back the embroidery. "Give it here! Useless!" she snapped and impatiently worked at the knot. Her patience wore out quickly and she tugged at the knotted thread till it broke.

Anticipating this, Eam held out a new threaded needle.

Gime snatched it from her and stabbed her embroidery without precision, "Just get out!" she muttered at Eam, "I can't stand your company right now!"

Eam hesitated just long enough to exchange a look with Loy, she then hurried from the room, anxious to leave Gime and her biting words behind. The memory of her rod across her back still in the forefront of her mind.

Leaving Regime's private quarters, Eam breathed freely for what seemed like the first time in hours. Gime had become unbearable since the banquet; obviously her first appearance in court had not gone as she expected. Turning a corner, Eam nearly ran into someone.

"Steady there!" the man exclaimed and steadied himself as Eam jumped back. It was Gime's older brother; Tenacious.

Dream's face turned red in embarrassment, "Forgive me, my lord!" she dropped into a curtsy and winced as the movement pulled at the still raw skin on her back.

"It's alright Eam," he assured easily.

Eam straightened, surprised that he knew her name.

"Everyone's in a hurry to escape my sister!" he added ruefully.

Eam bit back a smile when she met his gaze; she had never experienced the young lord's charm for herself and suddenly understood why so many maidens fancied him!

"We must simply survive her as best we can," he winked.

"Of course, my lord," she mumbled and ducked her head, she caught a parting smile on his dark face as he passed by.

Eam decided to tuck the short conversation away in her memory like a glittering pebble in a pocket, 'it won't happen again!' she thought to herself as she made her way through the castle to the kitchens. Once there, she found her mother churning butter with the other kitchen maids.

Navigate was a sturdy woman with worn hands and an even more worn face. She looked up at her daughter with a frown, "What are you doing here?" she questioned.

"Regime dismissed me," Eam admitted and grabbed a broom from nearby and began brushing potato peels into a pile.

The head cook bustled over and dumped an armful of more potatoes in front of a kitchen maid. "You can run an errand for me," she suggested and took the broom from Eam, "I never have enough help about here- I need an order placed at the bakery."

A servant like Eam never had time to just breathe, either she was breaking her back to please Gime, or racing around the castle. Eam did not mind running errands though, it was a welcome relief to Regime's company, especially when it was an errand to the bakery. Making her way through the streets Dream pulled her shawl closer against the stiff breeze, her thoughts on how Loyal was managing without her. Turning a corner, Eam arrived at the bakery and an honest smile touched her face.

A Garatin girl of seven played with a ragdoll on the front steps of the bakery, her blonde hair unruly and her blue eyes unseeing; blind since birth.

"Good morrow Mayhap," Eam greeted.

Mayhap's head tilted upwards and to one side, a wide grin slit across her face revealing that she had lost yet another tooth since last Eam had seen her. "Eam!" she cried out.

Eam mounted the steps and playfully draped her shawl over the girl's head as she walked by. May squealed in protest as Eam entered the busy bakery. Inside, Eam was met with stifling hot air from the ovens, women with sweaty faces, and the throaty cry of a babe. The cry came from a woven basket that was tucked away in a corner. Eam went straight to the basket and eagerly plucked the babe up into her arms, the little boy was only a month old and was still small enough to be carried one handed. Eam cradled him close, smiling into his little red face.

"All Fin does is cry," Mayhap complained of her brother as she came in after Eam, wearing her shawl.

"A bakery is no place for babes, large or small!" one of the workers complained and stuffed a milk-soaked cloth into the baby boy's mouth.

"I'm sorry," the mother of Fin and Mayhap apologised as she came in from a back room, "Thank you Eam!"

"I don't mind Dol!" Eam assured her friend, smiling down at Fin as he sucked away on the cloth.

"You're about the only one," Dol muttered, glancing about them, "I don't think they'll keep me here much longer if he won't stop crying." The Garatin woman was a serf of Brier Ridge, her husband having died in an accident at the mill many months past.

Eam looked up at her friend, "Head cook was just saying how they never have enough help at the castle- I could ask if they'll take you!"

Dol's weary eyes lit up, "Really!?"

Eam nodded eagerly.

"Would we live in the castle!?" Mayhap asked excitedly, always one for listening closely.

"Enough chatter, if you're here to look after the babe- take it elsewhere!" the head baker cut in.

Eam blushed in embarrassment. "Head cook sent me to make some grain orders," she explained, "The master wants another two bushels next week."

The cook huffed angrily, "That'll mean two less bushels gone to his serfs!"

Eam rocked Fin to distract from the cook's anger.

The woman waved both flour white hands in dismissal, "They'll be delivered along with the rest- now back to work!"

Dol shared a last thankful smile with Eam before going back to her station.

Eam snuggled Fin for a few moments more, "Mayhap- grab his basket- you can look after him on the front steps, can't you?"

Mayhap sighed heavily, but felt about till she found the basket, "I don't know how to keep him happy," she complained as she followed Eam back outside.

"But you can keep him out from underfoot," Eam pointed out, then set the basket next to Mayhap and placed Fin inside it.

"Will we live at the castle with you?" Mayhap asked again as she held on to the basket.

Eam took back her shawl and backed away onto the street, "I hope so."

* * * *

Darkness enveloped the city like a soft shawl, fitting into cracks and drawing back from lit flames. The people of Garason including the training soldiers withdrew from the darkness and prepared for sleep, waiting for the sunlight to return.

No torches were lit in the training yard of the barracks, and a shadowed figure moved about the yard like a phantom. At the far end of the yard, three arrows flew towards a slender wooden post that had been stuck upright into the dirt before a leather hide target. The figure did not pause to see if his aim was true, but kept moving, his feet taking care not to disturb the dusty ground.

A noise from above brought the archer to a stand still, smooth action one moment, invisible the next. A page boy exited from the captain's office and ran to the barracks along the open hallway, his boots pounding on the wooden planks. A moment later and the boy appeared again, this time with a soldier in tow, they crossed back to the captain's office in silence.

The archer waited a moment longer before resuming his target practice, estimating that the soldier would spend four minutes and sixteen seconds inside the office before exiting again, and like all the others who had been summoned by the captain, would pack and leave the barracks without explanation.

The archer withdrew another three arrows from his quiver and held them ready, with a flick of his fingers one arrow swung into position on the string and was propelled towards the target, before it even hit, the second arrow was already notched.

When the third arrow found its mark, Wilderness paused to squint at the barely visible target; out of the two dozen arrows he had shot into the darkness, two of them had hit the target, while the rest studded the slender wooden post.

Wilder glanced at the office, seeing that the meeting was still underway, he crossed the yard to collect his arrows. When he was done, the office door opened and the soldier emerged and crossed back to the barracks, his footfalls sounding heavy in the night.

Wilder began to cross the yard, as he went, he notched arrows to his bow and twisted at the waist to fire backwards at the post. Once on the far side of the yard, Wilder took three arrows and performed his quick shooting trick again.

"Hardly a need for archery matches tomorrow," Captain Multifarious's voice sounded from aloft.

Wilder looked up to find the captain leaning on the railing of the gangway, the outline of his body barely visible in the darkness.

"I know already that you're the best archer we have here," Farious spoke with sincerity, "You'll probably win at the tournament too."

Wilder shifted his feet uncomfortably, "I don't have the funds to enter the tournament matches."

Farious straightened from the railing and made his way to the stairs, his walking cane making distinct knocks on the wooden steps. "I'll pay your entrance fees," he said, less like an offer and more like a statement of facts.

Wilder had a hard time reading the older man's face in the darkness, "You will!?"

Farious came to a stop before him, " I want to be represented by the best."

Wilder felt robbed of speech for a moment, he was always expecting some kind of insult at the hands of the Tarvin, instead he only ever received praise! "Thank you, sir."

From above, the barracks door opened and the soldier who had come from Farious's office exited again, this time with his belongings. He descended the steps, glanced briefly at Wilder and the captain, then left.

Wilder watched the captain's face closely.

"Do you know why he's leaving?" Farious asked quietly.

Wilder considered his words for a moment, "I would suspect it's for the same reason all the others left."

Farious smiled and glanced down, "And what do you think that reason is?"

'A clear mind' Wilder reminded himself, realizing that what appeared to be a casual chance encounter might actually be the captain deciding if Wilder would also be packing up that night. "Whatever the reason, it's beyond my station."

Farious looked up at him with a shrewd expression, "I think you'll go far with that attitude, son."

He turned and made his way back to the stairs, "Pack it in," he ordered briskly, "join the others in the barracks, you clearly don't need any more practice!"

Chapter 9 Dishonor

There was something about Lord Eloquence's son, Tenacious, that unsettled Loyal, she had trouble putting her finger on it though. In the end she decided that it was because he represented yet another barrier in preventing her escape, this decision did not ease her discomfort.

The young lord of Brier Ridge escorted Loyal through the castle's main entrance, Dream followed behind, her meek presence easily forgotten, but Loy was ever grateful for her company. A friendly face could make all the difference in Loy's first meeting with her future mother-in-law.

The mother of Courage stood waiting for them, her raven locks concealed in a headdress that had lost favor in Tarva decades ago, but she held herself with undeniable dignity and commanded undivided attention.

"Lady Quell, good fortune to you and your house"' Tenacious greeted and bowed respectfully as Loyal hung back, not daring to lift her eyes.

Lady Quell did not care to answer.

"I am Tenacious," Acious forged ahead with surprising grace, "Son of Lord Eloquence of Brier Ridge, guardian to Lady Loyal, whom I now present to you." He waved backwards to Loy with a charming smile.

Loyal stepped forward and dipped into a low curtsy, her heavy skirts folding about her. Lady Quell extended an impatient hand towards her, "Come here child."

Loy rose and took the woman's hand, it was cold. Gathering her strength, Loy raised her eyes to meet the gaze of her future mother-in-law; the woman was studying her with critical eyes. After a sweeping glance she turned Loy's hand over and peered at her palm. "Very good," she pronounced, "Walk with me." She turned but hesitated, glancing at Acious, "I will speak with Lady Loyal *privately* for a time, I will send for you when I am done."

Acious bowed again, his smile intact.

Glancing over her shoulder, Loyal discreetly beckoned Eam to stay with her.

Lady Quell began walking briskly down a hallway lined with tapestries, leaving little time for Loy to take them in, as they walked, she glimpsed faded portraits of proud Tarvin men and soldiers in glorious battle. Few depicted women.

Lady Quell stopped abruptly before one of the last tapestries, "My husband, may he never be forgotten, was a man of great vision, he saw to it that our daughter married very well, and that our son should receive the best training in the king's army."

Loy met the eyes of the man in the tapestry, he looked as cold as Lady Quell's hand had felt. Her betrothed bore a striking resemblance to his father.

"My husband is dead now, and it has been left to me to see that his vision for our son is carried out." Lady Quell went on and Loy felt her eyes on her. "A great man of Tarva requires a specific breed of wife, one that will carry out her duty without blemish. One that would rather die than see shame and dishonor laid at the feet of her husband."

Loy did her best not to move, even breathing felt like it might be considered a flaw to Lady Quell.

"I was in correspondence with your father for over a year to arrange this union and was assured that you would outshine all others in the courts of Garason." She paused, but Loy remembered her etiquette lessons all too well, and knew that she was not expected to speak unless invited to do so.

Lady Quell inhaled sharply, "I will not allow anything to damage my son's future and will do what I must to ensure his success in the court. Despite the considerable trouble I went through to arrange your presence on these shores, do not assume that you have been welcomed into my home just yet. Before that can happen, I must first decide if you will further the plans for my son or damage them. *Well?* Are you my ally?"

Loy turned her head gracefully and met the woman's intense gaze. "A true lady of Tarva seeks nought but to please her husband," she recited humbly.

Lady Quell narrowed her eyes, "You obviously have been well taught, come into the fire hall, there you can properly recite Benevolent's etiquette book for true ladies of Tarva." Lady Quell turned and continued down the hall.

Loy allowed herself to breathe; the first test had been passed. Eam took the opportunity to slip up to her side and offer a comforting smile.

Together they followed Lady Quell, and as they passed a tapestry with Courage's likeness, Loy glanced over her shoulder to make sure Tenacious had indeed left; now there was only Lady Quell between her and her next escape attempt.

Loyal spent the better part of an hour reciting passages from etiquette books and classic poems to prove her education, twice her memory faltered but she was able to recover gracefully. Had her childhood governess been there, she would have been proud, and no doubt gloated over how all the tedious hours of Loyal's lessons had been justified.

Lady Quell did little to display if she was pleased or not, but since she had not pointed out any faults, Loy guessed that she had met the woman's standards. All the while Eam stood in the shadows, silent and still, yet her mere presence gave Loy strength. Without her, Loy would have been overcome with agony as her chances of escape slipped by with every passing moment.

"Enough of that," Quell declared after Loy finished reciting the sixteen qualities of a true lady. "On to more practical matters- what do you know of running households?" she raised an eyebrow.

Loy hesitated, sensing a trap, "I learned from observing my mother."

Quell's eyebrow appeared caught in an arched position, "Do you think you will manage this household with skill and decisiveness?"

The trap was set, and Loy strayed dangerously close, "I will fulfill whatever role you and your son have for me."

Quell's eyebrow relaxed, "Quite right, *I* shall remain the mistress of this household, and you will not interfere."

Loy lowered her eyes submissively, "Of course, my lady."

"Naturally, some responsibilities will fall on you solely, such as children; strong sons will be expected from this union."

Loy refused to allow a blush to creep onto her face.

"And you will of course make many appearances in court; being a soldier, Courage will oft be absent, and it will fall to you to remind others that he still holds a position in court." Quell looked her up and down, her face turned colder, "Do not misunderstand what is expected of you though, you may gather the impression from me that a woman should seek to arrange and plan her own future and that of others." She let the words drift in the space between them.

Loy's back ached from sitting up so straight, yet she knew that any movement now could land her in the jaws of the ever-present trap.

"That will not be expected of *you,*" Quell said with finality. "You are to be the embodiment of a perfect wife, mother and lady of Tarva."

"I seek nothing else," the lie passed Loy's lips with the ease of a sea sparrow in flight.

Quell allowed silence to settle in the room, "Excellent." She proclaimed brightly, "I believe you will do quite well indeed. I shall be most displeased if any shadow of shame should cross your name before you wed my son." Lady Quell breathed deep and stood, "Of course the wedding will not take place until Courage has obtained a fitting title in the army, which may take a few years. You will be receiving an invitation to Governor Endure's harvest banquet where he may very well knight my son, I expect you to conduct yourself with grace at the banquet."

Quell waved to her own maidservant whose presence had been forgotten along with Eam's, "Send for Lady Loyal's escort." She cast Loy one final appraisal, then glided out of the room.

Loy did not dare move for a long moment, then she turned to make sure that she had indeed been left unattended; now was her chance.

"Well, that trial is over with," Eam said cheerfully as she came to Loy's side.

"Quickly Eam- is anyone coming!?" Loy asked in a rush.

Eam looked stunned for a moment, then went quickly to the chamber entrance, "There is no one."

Loyal leapt up and rushed straight to a small servant's door, knowing the very seconds slipping by were more precious than gold. The door opened and the narrow hallway beyond was empty, "Will this lead outside!?"

Eam was by her side quickly, "It should yes; we are still on ground level too!" She led the way through the door.

Loy felt a pang of guilt that her friend would so willingly and without question help her- *again.*

Eam hesitated a moment before picking a direction, closing the door behind her, Loy followed, her heart pounding wildly; she would never need be in the same room as Lady Quell again!

Eam picked up her skirts, excitement growing on her face, "Here!" she rushed towards another door, creaking it open she peeked out, "No one's there." She slipped through with Loy on her heels; they were in a main hallway, and around a corner the entrance chamber could be glimpsed.

"There'll be a servant exit close by," Eam assured, looking about, "There!" Together they rushed around another corner and ran headlong into Tenacious.

"Lady Loyal!" he exclaimed, stepping back and looking them both over. "Whatever are you doing?" his eyes lingered on Eam.

Nearby was Lady Quell's maidservant, looking very cross. Unlike the last time, neither Loy nor Eam could think of something to say, but by the sly look that quickly crossed Acious's face, he guessed the answer to his question. "Let us be on our way then, shall we?" he suggested.

"Of course." Loy agreed, exchanging a disappointed look with Eam.

Without further discussion, Tenacious escorted Loyal from the castle and with Eam following, they climbed back into their carriage. Loy's heart pounded as though trying to break free, and her disappointment stung bitterly.

Tenacious wore his pleasant smile as they settled in, and the carriage rolled out of the castle's courtyard. Loy did her best to avoid his eye contact, any time their gazes did collide though, Acious betrayed no judgement.

Beside her, Eam fidgeted restlessly, no doubt going mad with the same tension Loy felt. Before long, their carriage was slowed and noise from a raucous crowd captured their attention.

"More rioters," Acious commented as he leaned forward to look through the dusty window, he aimed a smirk at Loyal, "Rebelling against authority, such deviance is shocking- don't you think so my lady?"

Loy held her breath; he was mocking her. Did he know that she was trying to run away? Would he report to his father what he had seen and would Eam be punished!?

Acious settled back into his seat, his smirk intact but he said no more, leaving Loy in agony over his intentions.

Wilderness adjusted his archery armguard, his back to the rest of the sleeping quarters but listening closely to all his comrades said. It was a habit he had picked up over the years, one that had proven useful many times.

"Where is Gid?" Courage asked, Wilder turned his head to one side to see Rage looking about the room with a confused frown. How could a soldier be that unaware of his surroundings!? Two more soldiers, including Gid had been mysteriously dismissed over the past two days, making four in total. All of whom had been friendly with Rage.

"He left yesterday," another fellow soldier answered to which Rage's frown deepened.

"He said he had been re-stationed in the north barracks," someone else volunteered.

Wilder shook his head, annoyed that no one was acknowledging what was so obvious to him! "Gid and the others talked too much," Wilder pointed out with a level of contempt, "clearly that doesn't suit Farious's plans."

Rage did not challenge him outright this time, and the others seemed less doubtful.

"Well," one of Rage's remaining friends spoke out cheerfully, "We know that Farious isn't picky about bloodlines, otherwise we all know who would have been the first to go!" He cast Wilder an impish smile while the others shared in his humor.

Wilder forced himself not to react, and instead wondered just how much of his sordid history the others knew. With no more talk of disappearing comrades, the men began to file out of the barracks, ready to begin the day of archery matches. Wilder waited to be the last one out, aware that Rage took every opportunity to glare at him. His hostility threatened to shift Wilder's confidence over the matches, and he took a moment to re-center himself before following the others outside.

As before, Captain Multifarious and the other officers stood aloft to watch the matches, sometimes pointing out soldiers and talking amongst themselves, whether because they were impressed or otherwise, was kept a frustrating mystery to those below.

Five leather hide targets were set up at one end of the training yard, and the soldiers were grouped to face off against one another. Any who missed the target, or hit outside the second inner ring were disqualified, while the others continued on in the matches. Due to its nature, the archery matches were much less rowdy than the wrestling had been, but there was still plenty of veiled animosity towards Wilder.

Withdrawing inward, Wilder went blind to faces, and only paid attention to the arrows and targets, whispered words and insults fell on deaf ears as he came out of each match the clear winner. His arrows never strayed from the center ring, and his thoughts were equally as focused.

Again, he notched an arrow and drew the string tight, the arrow flew, and it's point hit dead center of the target, leaving his opponents arrow two inches away, but it might as well have been two miles.

"I believe we have a winner." Captain Farious's voice spoke as if from far away, "Wilderness will represent us in the tournament archery matches."

Wilder broke free from his trance and looked about himself; unlike when Rage had won, there was no cheering. The soldiers wandered away, scowling, and muttering to one another. Courage stood nearby, running his thumb over the red fletching of his arrow, and glaring at Wilder with a gaze like fire.

Captain Farious descended the stairs supported by his cane. "I think this will be the last time anyone is surprised by your skill with a bow," he said to Wilder.

Wilder breathed and further shook himself; he couldn't believe the matches were really over! Glancing upwards he realized that the sun was well past high noon. Somehow, he expected his victory to taste sweeter.

Farious stood across from him with narrowed eyes as the yard emptied, "What's your motivation son?"

"I just want to do well sir," Wilder answered and walked to the target.

"No, that's not it."

Wilder collected his arrow and realized that the arrow of his last opponent had fletching of red. Satisfaction flooded over Wilder and a smile stole across his face before he could control it; he had beat Rage without even realizing it!

"You're out to prove something," Farious stated.

Wilder turned to face him, his smile gone, "Who would I be trying to prove it to?"

"Whoever it is, they were a fool for doubting you."

★ ★ ★ ★

"Will the king be there?" Mayhap asked as she lay on the cot, playing with Eam's rock collection. The sun had long left the city in darkness and Eam's feet ached from her long day.

Removing her outer work dress, Eam made a face, "The king of Tarva hasn't even been to Garatin, he certainly won't be at the governor's harvest banquet!"

Mayhap tossed one of the rocks in the air, it bounced when it landed and skidded across the floor, "Oops," the girl grinned cheekily. "I didn't mean *him*! I mean *our* king, the Garatin king."

Eam sighed, when she had arranged for Mayhap and her mother and brother to work and live in the castle, she hadn't anticipated that the seven-year-old would spend most of her time in Eam's own chamber! "The Garatin king hardly counts- besides, the Tarvin king *is* my king."

Mayhap sat up and frowned blankly, "I thought you were Garatin!" she protested.

Eam brushed her copper hair away from her pale face, for once glad that Mayhap was blind; she was about the only person who would believe that Eam was half Tarvin, "I'm only half Garatin- it's the Tarvin half that matters though." She stooped and fetched the rock from the floor.

Mayhap frowned deeply, "How are you *half* Tarvin?"

Eam scooped up her other rocks from the bed and ruffled the girl's hair, "My father was a Tarvin, you goose!"

Mayhap's face brightened, "Is that why you get to go to banquets!?"

Eam grinned at the child's simplified world view and wished that it was so. She wrapped her rock collection in a cloth and stored it under her bed, "That's right, I'm a great Tarvin lady- didn't you know!?" she joked, tickling the girl who squirmed and giggled. "Now off you go, I need my beauty sleep for the banquet tomorrow!"

Mayhap moaned and went limp on her bed, "But Fin keeps crying!"

Eam poked and pushed the girl towards the door, "Well he needs his big sister!"

The girl paused and a great goofy grin split her face, "I think he would be quiet for a great lady like you!"

Eam gasped at the girl's cheekiness, "Oh go on!" she laughed and pushed the girl out.

Alone, Eam lay down with a smile, but it faded with realistic thoughts of the banquet. When the invitation had arrived for Loyal, Regime had flown into a mad rage that she had not also been invited. Eam had felt like a beekeeper around her mistress ever since, knowing that she would be stung but never sure of when or where. Tenacious would be attending as Loyal's escort, a fact that had enraged Regime further.

"There you are, my lady," Tenacious said as he helped Loyal into the carriage.

Loyal thought it might as well have been a prison though. Spending the night at another banquet where she would be shown off like a new tapestry, and all the while be watched by Lady Quell, was enough to make Loy cry. Dream climbed in after her, and Loy caught the warm smile exchanged between her friend and Acious. Loy gripped her hands in her lap, waiting to be alone so that she could speak freely.

"We may have trouble with more rioters, but you'll be quite safe," Acious assured, then shut the carriage door and joined his father in the courtyard.

"I don't think we need to worry about him telling his father anything," Eam shared with confidence. "Even *if* he suspects that you were trying to run away, he's been nothing but kind."

Eam's comforting words had the opposite effect on Loy, "I fear his kindness is meant as bait." Eam was taken aback. It bothered Loy that her friend did not take things as seriously as she ought to; she was so naïve! "Eam, you can't trust men like him! You must be careful; don't fool yourself into thinking he cares about you."

Eam blinked in surprise and hurt registered on her face.

Loy sighed, "I just don't want you to get hurt."

Eam forced a polite smile but said no more.

Silence lapsed between them, and Loy could think of nothing more to say. To distract her from a nagging feeling of guilt, Loy turned her thoughts to her next escape plan. This time, whether she succeeded or failed, Eam would not be put at risk, for she would never know about it.

The carriage arrived at the governor's castle and joined a line of guests arriving, one by one, lords and ladies were escorted inside. Loy's stomach fluttered uneasily as she thought about what awaited her within, and her turn came sooner than she liked.

Tenacious opened the carriage door and held out his hand for Loyal, while his father, Lord Eloquence waited nearby. Loy avoided making eye contact with Acious or Eam and ignored the charming smiles that the young lord offered.

Once inside, Loy was led into the great hall, it was alight with candles and richly decorated with leafy garlands. There were a great many guests, mostly Tarvin but a few Garatin nobility were present as well. At the far end of the hall, greeting his guests, was the governor.

"There he is, anxiously awaiting our arrival" Lord Eloquence spoke loudly, and the hair on the back of Loy's neck stood on end when she heard the reply; it was her betrothed.

"Lord Eloquence, I assure you I had no doubts that you would be here." Courage wore the striking uniform of a soldier, his appearance drew the gaze of many, but Loy lowered her own eyes.

"Ah but you must have been anxious to see your betrothed again," Eloquence insisted with bravado and waved for Loyal to step forward.

Loy noted that Rage seemed uncertain how to respond, as if uncomfortable, at last he bowed to her, "My lady, you are a vision."

Loy curtsied and knew that he was waiting for her to look up at him, but she could not make herself do it, "You are most kind, my lord," she murmured.

"By the Neenor, you've rendered her speechless!" Tenacious joked, it made Loy's face burn with anger, but she held her tongue through their conversation.

Glancing behind her, Loy hoped to find an encouraging smile from Eam, but her friend stood with head down, and Loy felt even worse for the words she had last said to her.

When she returned her attention to the conversation, Loy found that Tenacious and his father had moved on, leaving her in the company of Courage.

"Walk with me?" he invited, the stiffness from his tone was suddenly gone, enticing Loy to meet his gaze at last; what she found was an open earnestness that surprised her. Nodding, Loy hesitantly took his arm and allowed him to slowly lead her away from the main crowd. Eam followed behind, acting as her chaperone. Holding her breath, Loy dared to hope that her betrothed would unwittingly aid her in escaping by leading her away from the crowds.

"You are very quiet," Courage commented as they reached the edge of the room.

Loy directed her gaze out of a nearby window; the sun's dying light cast long shadows on the city. "Words are best reserved for when there is something worth saying," the impetuous comment left her mouth before she could stay it.

Rage drew back slightly.

Covering her mouth, Loy looked at him in horror, "Forgive me my lord! I am not myself."

A short laugh escaped Rage, followed by a boyish smile, "You are not what I expected!"

Loy bowed her head in shame; her mother would have been mortified, "I beg your forgiveness, my lord! You expected a true lady and instead I spoke rudely."

"You are forgiven," he said easily, still amused, "I find your candor refreshing- but I warn you my mother will not share my opinion."

"I assure you, it will not happen again," Loy breathed; the sooner she could escape the better!

"You are unhappy," Rage said with a sudden change in tone.

Loy turned her gaze out the window, unable to deny his words, wishing he would not pay her so close attention.

"What can I do to make you happy?"

Loy risked a glance at him, genuinely surprised to see that he was sincere, she could think of nothing to say.

"Do you ride? I could give you a fine horse," he offered, his posture and tone shifting to a less humble one.

Loy shook her head slightly, unsure how to respond to him.

"Do you enjoy gardens? The garden of Jes`reel, to the east of the city, are renowned across the country for it's, ah…" Rage seemed to run out of words, betraying how nervous he was.

Loy took pity on him. "Do these gardens have flowering trees?" she asked meekly.

He met her gaze hopefully, "Are they your favourite?"

Loy shifted uncomfortably; she hadn't intended to engage him in conversation. "There is a garden in Tarva, it's filled with cherry trees that turn the city pink every spring," her breath caught unexpectedly as a wave of homesickness washed over her. "I would always go there with Thri- with my childhood playmates."

Rage was silent for a moment, "I'm afraid that there won't be any blooms on the trees here until spring, however, when that time does come, I look forward to bringing you there."

Loy swallowed, pushing melancholy memories aside, "There must be more pressing matters that demand your attention than amusing me, my lord."

He straightened his shoulders and looked about the room as though bored, "I assure you none of them are as rewarding as your smile."

The complement caught Loy off guard, and the smile he hoped for graced her lips for a moment before she could banish it.

He held her gaze with intensity for a moment, before looking away again, as though the moment meant nothing. Loy tried to steady herself, mentally guarding against his charm; enjoying the company of her betrothed had been the last thing she had expected that night!

"Come, we must greet my mother," Courage said after a moment. Loy could have sworn he was as pleased with the idea as she was.

Lady Quell tilted her head elegantly towards Loy as they approached her, and she gave her hand to her son to kiss. "Come we mustn't waste time;

there are many that you must greet and present your betrothed to," Quell insisted briskly.

Loy sighed inwardly and wondered if the night would provide her with a chance of escape at all. Courage seemed to take on a much more prideful and guarded air in his mother's presence, giving Loy the chance to reduce her liking of him back to not at all. In the midst of being 'presented' to members of the court, Loy caught an empathetic smile from Eam, giving her hope that her friend had already forgiven her. Loyal's attention was refocused when those around her bowed and curtsied, she quickly followed their lead wondering who could be approaching.

"Courage, our hero of the Five Isles," Governor Endure spoke for everyone nearby to hear. His voice sounded gray and weak.

"A soldier takes pride not in victory, but in honorable service," Rage responded, his tone anything but humble.

Loy noted the intense gaze of Lady Quell, as if by looking hard enough she could bend the outcome of the conversation to suit her.

"Honorable indeed, Captain Multifarious tells me that you have surpassed nearly all his other men in your training." Endure seemed to be sizing him up.

"You are too kind, my lord governor," Rage bowed his head again.

"On the contrary, I will be kinder still," Endure waved for a page boy, "Bring me a sword," he ordered, "I recognize greatness in you Courage, and your efforts shall now be rewarded!"

The page returned and presented the governor with a sword, Loyal had never witnessed a knighting before, and despite herself, watched with interest.

Anticipating what was coming next, Rage enthusiastically pounded his right fist over his heart and kept it there, his face radiating pride.

"Do you, Courage, swear fealty to the king of Tarva, the empire of Tarva and all its people?" Endure asked solemnly and the crowd grew still.

"I swear it," Rage responded passionately.

"Do you swear to uphold the honor of Tarva, to seek glory for its name and serve her till the end of your days?"

"I swear it."

Endure smiled, "Do you swear allegiance to me, Governor Endure, vassal to the king, and to all governors after me?"

"Till the end of my days I will serve no other," Rage swore.

"Then kneel," Endure ordered. Rage did so and Endure took the sword and touched both his shoulders, "I dub thee, Sir Courage, knight of Tarva."

Endure rested the sword tip on Rage's head, and Rage, looking up with the passion of a million fires, raised his bare hand and gripped the blade till his blood trickled down his wrist, "I seal my oath with blood, may Tarva never fall!"

The crowd cheered and Loy's spine tingled as Rage stood and captured her gaze.

* * * *

"I want to congratulate you on your knighthood," Captain Farious said mildly as he limped behind his desk and sat.

Courage nodded, "Thank you captain, I look forward to serving under the governor. Of course, I will compete in the tournament as planned, but I'll be taking my leave of the barracks on the morrow." His pride and excitement leaked through every word.

Farious nodded, a strange twist touched his lips that wasn't quite a smile. "Yes, well," he hesitated causing Rage a moment of doubt, "I understand how you would be eager to take up duties as a knight, and I'll confess your knighthood came as a surprise to me- not that you don't deserve it though." Farious leaned back in his chair and worked his jaw, like chewing his words before speaking again, "But your training here is too important, and you, too valuable to lose now."

Rage frowned, anger and confusion rising in his chest, "Are you suggesting that you will not allow me to take leave of your service!?"

"I am not suggesting it."

Rage sputtered, his face growing red, "This is an outrage! I have been knighted by the governor of Garatin; I am in *his* service now!"

Farious narrowed his eyes, then sat up and plucked a letter from his desk, "Governor Endure agrees that your training is of more import at present. He explains it here."

Rage snatched the letter and read it over, his anger dissipating at the words, and a distinct feeling of betrayal took its place.

"As you can see for yourself," Farious spoke after a moment, still calm, "as a knight you swore to serve the governor, and you will; under my command."

Rage's eyes lingered on the governor's seal, his anger returned, and he lifted his eyes to meet the captains. "Why is my training here so important?" he asked evenly, "You've never told us the purpose of it."

Farious smiled as if amused, "That will be made clear in time. Suffice it to say that the end goal will only be for the best of my men; those who surpass all others in the training and prove that they can follow orders without question." He held Rage's eyes ominously, "Understood?"

Rage ground his teeth forcing his temper under control, "Understood, sir."

* * * *

The smell of fresh bread permeated the servant quarters and the sounds of a bustling kitchen drove everyone to spring into full tilt for the day. The sun was only just rising but Dream and the other servants of Brier Ridge were well into their daily chores.

Mayhap lingered on the outskirts, doing her best to keep out of the way and listening for when her baby brother would wake. Meanwhile Dol, their mother, and Eam prepared the breakfast trays for Ladies Regime and Loyal.

Eam looked up from her work when a page entered the kitchen, he looked about with purpose, the head cook paused and scowled at him.

"I'll have Lady Regimes breakfast ready any moment!" Eam offered, imagining Gime in a furious state.

"Lord Tenacious sent me actually," the page corrected.

Eam paused, for a moment completely baffled, then her heart fluttered when she recalled all the secret smiles Acious had sent her way at the banquet the night before.

"You are Dream, right? He wanted you to have this," the page held out a yellow wild rose, fresh from the garden. He wore a face that said he was unimpressed with the exchange, but Eam did not even notice. She accepted the flower and bit back a giddy smile. The other servants shared disapproving and knowing glances behind Eam's back as she scurried from the kitchen towards her room.

Her mother followed her and shooed Mayhap away, "What is the meaning of this!?" Avi demanded as daughter and mother reached the servants common area.

Eam turned to her mother and shrugged coyly, "I suppose Tenacious fancies me."

Avi looked at her with an expression somewhere between shock and outrage.

"Mother, he's been nothing but kind to me for weeks now!" Eam insisted. "Surely he is free to choose whom he courts," she fingered the flower tenderly, feeling lightheaded and a little foolish.

Avi's face went white, "What!?"

Eam did not notice the extent of her mother's outrage, "It's a bit of a surprise to me too."

Avi's eyes fell to the flower, "Has he touched you!?" she demanded to know, her tone at last capturing Eam's attention.

"No!" she defended, taken aback, "No, he has behaved honourably towards me!" She remembered how his eyes had followed her- why couldn't her mother see? "I know I am much below his station, and it is presumptuous of me to entertain such a thing, but he doesn't care about that! He fancies me very much, I know it; how could I hope for a better match?"

"NO!" Avi cried as if the thought sickened her, "No, you can never be matched with him!" she snatched the flower from her hands and threw it away, "Tell me he has not touched you in any way!" she shook Eam firmly by the shoulders.

Eam's eyes stung with sudden tears "No, I tell you he has done nothing! Why does this upset you!?"

Avi wheeled away, relieved.

The tears were now escaping down Eam's face, "Surely if he loves me-"

"He is your *half brother*!"

Eam reacted like she had been slapped, "What!? No, he… He can't be! You *can't* be his mother!"

"You share a father!" Avi hissed, shame staining her voice.

Eam stepped back.

"Lord Eloquence is your father," her mother stated.

"But..." Eam blinked rapidly.

"No one but Lord Eloquence knows," Avi said in a low tone. "There was never a reason for you to know," she explained, regret and shame lacing her voice, "This secret must never leave this room Eam." She glanced behind them to make sure no one had followed from the kitchen, "Lord Eloquence would not be pleased."

Eam stared dully at her feet.

Avi took her daughter by the shoulders again, "You must not go near Tenacious again; do you understand me?" she shook her slightly till Eam nodded mutely.

"I must speak to Lord Eloquence at once," Avi said to herself, her eyes drifting away. She hurried to collect her shawl, "Stay here, I will have someone else bring the ladies breakfast up."

Eam could not move, as if frozen to the last place where her world made sense.

Before passing by her Avi stopped and looked intently at her, "Swear to me that he did not touch you."

Eam squeezed her eyes shut, the same thought that had made her giddy a few moments before, made her sick now, "I swear it."

* * * *

"I must speak with you alone, my lord," Navigate said tensely as she stood in the lord's study, the sun's first rays lighting the room.

Lord Eloquence seethed in annoyance over the interruption of his morning; he had always found her presence irritating after she told him of her pregnancy. At last, he snapped his fingers to his two advisers whom he had been talking with. The two men eyed Avi as they left the room.

"You too," Eloquence waved impatiently at the page boys waiting nearby. Soon they were alone.

"You must speak with your son, Tenacious," Avi stated.

Eloquence snorted and lounged further into his chair, "Am I to take orders from servants now? Explain yourself, woman."

"Your son has been giving attention to Dream," Avi informed him in clipped tones. "Your daughter," her anger rising when he did not immediately recognize the namesake.

"So?" he asked flippantly and stood to his feet, walking away to a window, then he paused and asked over his shoulder, "What kind of attention?"

Avi felt her face grow hot, "The kind you gave me sixteen years ago."

He spun about to face her, his dark face draining of blood.

"He has not touched her. Yet," Avi assured with a small amount of relief, "You *must* speak to him," she repeated.

Eloquence stood frozen, his face slowly turning red with anger. "PAGE," he snapped suddenly, a page with a nervous expression hurried back into the room.

"Bring Tenacious here at once!" Quence ordered and the boy ran to do his bidding. A tense silence enveloped the room.

"You will not speak a word, woman," he instructed sharply when Avi shifted, "No one is to know of the girl's parentage."

They waited until Tenacious entered the room, looking bewildered.

"Sit," Eloquence ordered between clenched teeth.

Acious watched his father wearily and slowly sat down, obviously trying to guess where the conversation would lead.

"You have been spending time with the maidservant Dream." Eloquence stated instead of asked.

Acious blinked in surprise, evidently, he had expected a different discussion.

"Do you deny it?" Eloquence pressed when his son did not answer, Avi held her breath; the young lord could claim she was lying.

"No, of course I do not deny it," Acious said easily, "Eam is a lov-"

"I will not stand for it!" Eloquence cut him off sharply, much to Avi's relief; she had no desire to hear what Acious thought of his half sister.

"What!?" Acious exclaimed, not angry, merely confused.

This time Eloquence took a moment to answer. "She is below you; that is the end of it. Do you understand?" he asked, suddenly calm.

"Understand!? Only just!" Now Acious was the one upset.

"If I hear even a rumor that your eyes so much as rested on her for a moment; I will have her removed from Brier Ridge!"

Avi could not stop a sharp intake of breath, but neither man took notice of her.

Acious stood, his anger and frustration rising, "Just so this is clear; you have never once cared which maid servant I spent time with in the past, but you will not stand for it if it's Eam? Why!?"

"She is betrothed!" Avi spoke out, the lie leaving her lips before she could think better of it.

Acious looked at her, as if noticing her for the first time, he seemed slightly stunned. Eloquence glared at her silently warning her to choose her words with great care.

"I will not have shame cast on her namesake," Avi said, head held high.

"That is the end of it," Eloquence said crisply, "Get out."

Acious met his father's gaze defiantly for a long moment before stalking from the room, Avi moved to follow him when Eloquence's words stalled her.

"Woman! I want that girl gone from this castle before the new moon."

Avi's heart sank, "She has nowhere to go!"

"You said she was betrothed," Eloquence said coldly, "I suggest you make it so."

Dream heaved up the full water pail, straining at the weight of it, the morning had dragged by, each second was near agony. Memories of the night before mocking her as she worked. She turned and froze; Acious stood in the courtyard entrance.

Eam ducked her head and approached him quickly, anxious to pass by him without interaction.

"I'm sorry about this," he spoke earnestly.

"I can't be seen speaking with you," she whispered harshly.

Acious grabbed her arm, "If I had known, I would have let you be."

Eam's eyes flew to his face in surprise; she did not think Eloquence would tell him the truth!

He took her eye contact as permission to move closer, "I want to wish you happiness in your betrothal."

Eam held her breath, the word 'betrothal' like the toll of a great bell.

Acious stooped slightly and leaned forward to kiss her.

Eam ducked past him wrenching her arm from his grip and hurried away, the contents of her bucket splashing on the paving stones.

★ ★ ★ ★

"Now I must leave before the new moon!" Eam sobbed.

Loyal held her, being silent through the whole story she finally spoke, "Where will you go?" she asked, afraid of losing her only friend and yet feeling guilty that it was her first concern. Strange that the night before she had been prepared to never see Eam again, but now the thought was unbearable.

"I have nowhere to go!" Eam lamented, her eyes red and puffy. "My mother will have to find me a match; but what hope do I have of ever finding happiness!? The only man who ever loved me turned out to be my *half brother*!" she collapsed back onto Loy to cry some more.

Rubbing her back soothingly, Loy held her extra close and bit back a comment that Acious did not 'love' her and would never have married her; men like him were all the same. But the questionable intentions of Tenacious were hardly important now.

"I swear I'll never smile again at a man as long as I live!" Eam muttered.

"You couldn't have known that he was your brother!" Loy insisted, "It is he who was in the wrong! If he had courted you properly then the truth would have been revealed long before now." She refrained from pointing out that Acious would never have been allowed to court a servant.

Eam pulled back and shook her head, her face a mess, "If the gods exist, it is so that they can mock me!" she declared bitterly.

"Hush now!" Loy said, pulling Eam against her again, "I know it feels as though the world has ended or might as well have." The ache of her own heart thickened her words with emotion, "But when we lose the love we wanted, we *must* go on and..." her words fell short as her thoughts turned to who she had left behind in Tarva; not all dreams were meant to be.

Chapter 10 Another

The air was clear and sharp, while the landscape continued to steal one's breath away with its mere scope and stunning beauty. The mountain slopes robed themselves with trees tall and sturdy, while ominous caves watched from their lofty heights. Although the Honorfell Mountains cut into the skyline like jagged teeth, the sky seemed somehow bigger than ever before, the vastness of it all assaulted the senses of the travellers anew every morning as they trekked northward.

Everything about his surroundings begged Theophany to linger, to sit in the stillness and allow the peace of the wilderness to soothe his troubled soul. They had escaped the mountain men when they fled the Honorfell temple six days ago and had seen no sign of danger since. Theoph felt as though he and his companions were the only people alive in the whole world. It seemed strange to him that the larger his world became, the less people he felt lived in it.

Theoph and his diverse company had come into a small valley the night before, and rising the next morning, they felt as though they had found a secret paradise hidden away in the wilderness. The valley was watched over by three large mountains, and a topaz lake shimmered in the center, its water fresh and bracing.

Wearied from their headlong flight from the mountain men, they had all agreed to rest awhile in the valley and had spent the morning recovering their strength. But now as the morning shifted into afternoon, the company began to explore and spread out. From where Theoph sat on a rocky rise, he could see his warriors on the far side of the lake, their voices carried to him on the breeze, while Lady Serene remained settled on the near shore, basking in the sun. Once it became clear that they would be staying for a time, she had her servants set out her things that she might relax in comfort, although some of her possessions had been lost in the ambush, she still had rugs and pillows to recline on as well as her silverware that was now set out like she was hosting a feast. Theoph thought her foolish.

Lady Roam had settled down a distance from Serene, under the shade of a great tree, she sat unnaturally still for a child, all the while her nitora remained at attention around her. Dire had set out to scout ahead on the road and could be seen returning on the far side of the lake. The gillup, who had shown little signs of fatigue, were grazing in the valley behind where Theoph sat.

For a time Theoph watched Salvage and the youth, Rend, spar in a clearing to the left of him, but Theoph's thoughts were far away, or turned deep inside, he could not decide which. Three things lay in his mind, three things that drove him northward. First to rid himself of the heart stain. Second, to please his father. Third to marry Dynasty. Everything else either got him closer to these or hindered him.

Vigil climbed the rocks towards him, his face held in a frown, "Sire." he greeted, and Theoph knew from the way he worked his jaw he had something on his mind but was unsure how to say it.

"What is it?" Theoph asked tersely, the tension between them had only grown since the tower.

"I think it wise not to linger much longer," Vig answered abruptly.

"Do you think the mountain men will find us?"

"It's possible; they knew we traveled Sentinel's Pass, if they are determined they will find us. But more than that, I feel we must press on; we haven't time to waste."

"Do you know something I don't?"

Vig released a frustrated sigh, "Every moment we waste, the Foretold King's power grows, and we risk losing the chance to form an alliance."

Theoph considered his reasoning, he could see the logic, but he was tired, and longed for a rest from their seemingly endless journey. "We'll leave on the morrow." Vig dropped the issue, but Theoph could tell he had not spoken his mind.

★ ★ ★ ★

Rend panted from the exertion of duelling Salvage, "*Am* I improving?" he asked with despair.

Sal stepped away swinging the new spear she had been gifted from the Niben warriors. "Of course you are," she encouraged easily.

"It doesn't feel like it."

Sal laughed and readied herself to face him again, but a sudden outcry from Lady Serene interrupted. Sal whirled to the lake shore where the elder sat; she was clutching her heart.

Sal bolted forwards, running swiftly down the gentle hill to Serene's side, her guards swarmed her, and atop the rocky hill Theophany and Vigil stood in alarm.

"Oh, this is *it* I fear!" Lady Serene moaned dramatically as Sal reached her, "It's no use," she weakly waved her guards away and held her hand out to Sal, "I have little left to me now, let me spend it in peace with my friends."

Sal knelt and took her hand. She expected the woman's skin to be clammy; it wasn't. "We've hardly had time to become friends," Sal argued, feeling the woman's forehead and searching her face, she could detect nothing amiss.

Serene scowled at her, "I offer the sweet gift of my friendship and you scorn it like filth!?"

Sal relaxed; there was not even a shadow of death touching the old one's features, "Rather, our friendship is more like the sprout of new growth-let's not trample it now."

Serene huffed and readjusted to a more comfortable position on her pillows, despite her scorn, Sal suspected she was enjoying the attention she had achieved. Serene glanced to one side and her face relaxed a bit. "Here is a true friend," she swatted Sal away and extended her hand to Garden who had ventured closer in concern.

Taking her hand with his ever-present air of bewilderment, Garden knelt beside Serene, "Are you ill, my lady?"

"Only dying," Serene assured with a heavy sigh, "I felt my heart stall within me just now."

Grinning at the old one's antics, Sal turned to Rend, "Go tell the prince that everything is alright." Rend nodded and turned away, but not before Serene could aim a scowl at Sal for considering the situation as 'alright.'

Serene's guard brought her a drink of water which she sipped primly.

"How do you feel now?" Sal asked, certain now that there was nothing amiss.

"I shall die presently, I have no doubt," Serene replied casually.

"Surely not!" Garden insisted, "You have not found the Wise One yet."

Serene begrudgingly considered this, "Very well, I will stave off death a while longer. A task made easier through your company," she added smiling cheekily at Garden.

Sal turned away to hide her amused smile at the old man's fearful and embarrassed expression. A white flicker of movement drew Sal's eyes to the shaded hillside where Lady Roam had settled. The child was on her feet watching, her veil hiding whatever expression her face betrayed. It was the first time Sal had seen the child act human, but it was short lived; Lady Roam must have noticed Sal watching, for she sat back down quickly.

"What goes here? I saw a disturbance," Dire spoke as he approached, breathless from running around the lake.

"Lady Serene experienced some… discomfort," Sal explained, watching as the old woman conversed with Garden.

"I'm relieved that she has recovered," Dire commented sarcastically.

Sal smirked, allowing her hand to run along the shaft of her new spear as she planted its end in the turf at her feet.

"I spotted a lone rider on the road ahead of us," Dire reported, capturing Sal's attention, "I judge they will reach us within the hour."

"A mountain man?"

Dire shook his head, "I saw the gleam of polished armor, whoever they are I doubt they are of the Honorfell tribes."

"I'll inform Theophany- perhaps it would be best to call our warriors to this side of the lake," Sal mused, frowning at the far end of the valley where the stranger would soon appear.

Dire nodded and left to give orders to his nitora, Sal watched him approach his mistress and noted that Lady Roam drew her white head covering further down her face. Sal narrowed her eyes; despite liking the Niben warrior, after what Vigil had shared with her about how the Honorfell temple priests were reluctant to welcome them, Sal was uneasy about Dire. The more she thought of it, the more she suspected a dark secret surrounding the pale child.

Speaking briefly with Serene's guard about the approaching stranger, Sal turned and climbed up to Vig and Theoph. Rend was still with them, and the three awaited Sal's approach.

"What's happened?" Vig asked, ever since leaving the Honorfell temple, Sal had noticed that Vig seemed on edge. Even though they had been fleeing for their lives, his behaviour was unusual, and Sal had been worried. He had shared with her that Serene had discovered some disturbing history surrounding the Niben, but Sal suspected there was something more that he had not shared. Whatever it was had replaced her husband's humor with an air of urgency that Sal did not understand.

"Dire returned from scouting ahead, he reports that a lone rider approaches from the north," Sal replied. "He said the rider wore polished armor and thinks it unlikely they are one of the mountain men. The rider will reach the valley within the hour."

Theoph nodded to Vig to continue as he saw fit. It was reassuring, if only a little, that the prince still trusted Vig, even if he couldn't speak freely with him. It was like Theoph was holding them both at arms length.

"Fetch the warriors from the far shore," Vig instructed Rend, who nodded and hurried down the rocks. "I advise not inviting interaction, but rather withdrawing from the path of the road. They may pass by without seeking us out."

Sal nodded.

"What is that!?" Theoph interrupted, his gaze fixed upwards towards the mountain tops.

Sal and Vig followed his gaze. "It's just a bird," Vig commented.

"There's two of them," Sal pointed out, an uneasiness settling in her stomach.

The two birds soared far over the valley, merely black specks in the blue sky. They flew about each other, as though dancing, swooping, and diving. Sal judged that whatever they were, they must be quite large to be able to see them from so far away. Then, one folded its wings and dove towards the earth, the second followed closely.

"Those aren't normal birds," Sal declared as the two shapes grew in size, and now it became clear they were aiming for the three figures atop the rocks.

"We should take cover," Vig suggested calmly and began to herd Theoph and Sal down the rocks.

"That's probably a good idea…" Theoph muttered, his eyes widening as the shape of the diving birds became clearer. The distance between them shortened at an alarming rate.

"NOW!" Vigil ordered sharply, shoving Theoph to the edge.

Sal threw her spear to the ground, its living coral point driving deep into the earth, then she grabbed hold of the prince's arm and, aiming for the grassy turf below, leapt off the rocks. Before they reached the ground the first bird swooped over them, gigantic talons sweeping the air inches from the rocks, followed by large feline paws. Great, powerful wings cast a terrible shadow over Vigil as the creature passed over him. He escaped its clutches by rolling to one side and diving off the rocks. He landed moments after Sal and Theoph.

A sharp eagle-like cry split the air in two as the second creature cut short its dive and hovered for a moment above the rocks.

Grasping her spear, Sal held the prince against the rocks as they wildly searched the sky for another attack.

Vig picked himself up from the ground and rushed to their side, Sal noted with a critical eye that he was limping.

Theoph swore in panic, "What is that!?"

"Terrifying," Sal answered, regaining her composure, and analyzing their situation. Unless the creatures landed, it was unlikely they could be attacked from the sky with the rock formation at their backs.

"GET TO THE TREES!" Vig ordered those who were by the lake edge.

Sal watched as Lady Serene's guards surrounded her, despite the woman complaining earlier about her imminent death, she picked up her skirts and ran across the open area towards the cover of the trees, her guards running with her. Garden kept up with them, his old body stumbling now and again. Dire had withdrawn with Lady Roam, further into the treeline, and all his nitora now had arrows on the strings of their bows.

Across the lake, the rest of the Verlyance warriors took cover in a stretch of trees that nearly circled the lake; Sal judged that they would reach them in ten minutes. But it was Rend that concerned her; halfway between the rock formation and the treeline, he had begun running bravely back to his prince, and was crossing open ground!

"NO REND- GO BACK!" Vig warned. Rend stopped up short, his eyes upwards in shock and fear.

Sal followed his gaze; one of the creatures was again swooping downwards, this time towards the youth. Rend steadied himself, then as the creature's talons swept downwards, he dove forward. One of the creature's talons caught on his tunic and the youth was pulled off his feet backwards, he struggled but was clubbed by the back paws of the creature.

Vig bolted from the cover of the rocks, limping, and brandishing his throwing knives. Thrown off course by the youth's struggles, the creature stumbled to the ground as Rend rolled from its clutches.

Vig raised his voice in the battle cry of Verlynn Nel and threw one of his knives. Faster than logical for a creature its size, the winged beast turned, its furry hind quarters skipping out of the way and its wings swinging about like a cape. Vigil's knife slipped uselessly through the creature's tawny wing feathers and struck the ground at its feet. Rend rolled over and crawled backwards as he came face to face with the hooked beak and golden eyes of the creature.

Vig screamed again, distracting the creature for a precious moment. Reaching the youth, Vig pulled him to his feet and slashed at the creature's head with his remaining knife.

The creature reared back on its legs, its large wings stretching out to either side, then pounced down on the two humans.

Sal gasped from where she and the prince watched, her limbs flinching, trembling to charge into the fray herself, but she was held back by her duty to protect her liege lord.

The creature's head snapped back, narrowly avoiding Vigil's blade. He and the boy lay flat on their backs, pinned to the ground by a front foot of the creature, its talons hooked into the earth on either side of them.

The twang of bow strings sounded, and the creature screeched in pain. Two nitora, led by Dire, advanced from the forest where the others had taken shelter, their arrows sinking into the creatures back right hip.

Vigil stabbed the scaled foot of the creature. It screamed again and lifted its leg, releasing Vig and Rend. Vig rolled to his left, and out from under the writhing creature, but Rend rolled right and was seized again by the creature's remaining good foot.

Vig raised himself up on one knee but was thrust back to the ground by a wingbeat. The creature beat its great wings twice more and pushed off the ground with its feline back legs. Rend cried out as he was carried aloft, captured in the cruel talons.

Dire and the nitora released another volley of arrows, but to no avail. The creature climbed in the air, then darted down the slope towards the lake, the cries of Rend growing faint.

Theoph moved to leave the shelter of the rocks, but Sal held him in place with her hand to his chest, "The second creature is still up there!" she warned. But Theoph would not heed her, he pushed past her and raced towards Vigil.

Sal kept pace with the prince, glancing quickly at the sky as they ran; there was no sign of the second creature.

Dire and his warriors stood with Vigil, new arrows ready and eyes to the sky.

"We must take cover," Dire insisted as Theoph and Sal reached them. "We can not help the boy now."

Vigil's eyes were fixed on the retreating creature as it flew over the lake, his chest heaving.

Everyone gasped when the injured creature dropped Rend and the youth plummeted to the water eighty meters below. Rend's body hit the water, while the creature hovered for a moment then dove after him. It plucked the limp body from the water and soared away.

"ABOVE!" Dire called out in warning.

Sal ducked out of reflex and looked up; diving out of the glare of the sun, the second creature came at great speed. "Get down!" Sal warned, pulling the prince to the ground with her as Vig did likewise. But Dire and his warriors remained standing, and steadfastly aimed their arrows at the incoming creature. Their arrows flew then they threw themselves to the ground.

The creature pulled up, and the arrows whizzed past harmlessly. With great wing beats that pinned everyone to the ground, the creature turned and retreated. Everyone followed its trajectory and their eyes widened in realization; it was heading for the grazing gillup!

"We'll be stranded without them!" Theoph exclaimed and rose to his knees.

Dire jumped up. "To me!" he called to his remaining nitora in the trees. Two stayed behind to protect Lady Roam, and the rest charged towards the scattering gillup. Lady Serene directed some of her guards to help, and together with the Niben they raced after the creature.

The Verlyance warriors from across the lake arrived in record time, "Protect the gillup!" Vig ordered, directing them after the others. "Get him to the trees and keep an eye out for more of those creatures!" Vig ordered Sal, she read the shock, sorrow, and rage over Rend's death on his face. He then scooped up his second knife from the ground and ran to join the others in defending their steeds. Sal took Theoph by the arm and ran with him to where Lady Serene and Roam stood under the protection of the trees.

"Quickly! You'll get yourselves killed out in the open like that!" Serene shrieked as Theoph, and Sal gained the tree cover. The old woman gripped her staff like a club while the other fluttered around her heart, her breathing quick and shallow.

"It's all right," Garden tried to comfort, taking her hand.

Serene squeezed his hand in her own and whimpered at the sight of her pillows and silver abandoned on the lake shore. Sal noted that her precious book was looped over her shoulder.

"They'll be carried away too," Theoph fretted, watching as the warriors reached the gillup.

Some of the gillup had scattered throughout the valley, but most had fled into a rocky nook, and were now cornered. Dire led the way towards them, as the creature circled overhead. Sal turned her eyes away and instead searched for the other creature, she glimpsed it disappearing into the foothills of the valley, taking the body of Rend with it. Forcing her sorrow aside, Sal searched the sky for more threats; she could see none.

Satisfied that they were safe for the moment, Sal looked over the group, despite being the quietest, it was Lady Roam who looked the most terrified. Her veil did little to hide how much her little body trembled. Sal fought the instinct to take the girl in her arms; even Dire was not that familiar with the child.

Sal's attention was drawn away into the woods, and her heart hesitated in her chest; the baine wilk sat in the shadows, its large solemn eyes meeting hers. Then it turned its gaze to the far side of the lake and Sal flinched, for a terrible sharp cry ripped through the valley. It was the same scream that the winged creatures made, only louder, and more terrible.

Sal and the others ducked and covered their ears as the scream echoed back across the valley. She searched the sky frantically, imagining the monstrous size a creature must be to make such a sound. But the skies were still empty.

Lady Roam gasped, and Sal followed her gaze to where the warriors defended the gillup. Overhead the creature pulled up from a dive, its head swinging towards where the scream had come from, then it flew in the opposite direction, disappearing into the mountains.

The warriors, fearing the approach of an even larger creature, worked frantically to drive the gillup into the trees, shouting and checking the sky as they ran.

Sal glanced back into the woods, but the baine wilk was gone. "Move along through the trees to meet the others," Sal ordered, "We're safest in large numbers." The group of them began moving through the trees while Sal watched their flank, she was surprised to see a lone rider on the far shore of the lake.

Running through the trees, Sal and the others passed a few gillup, bleating and terrified out of their wits. Soon they met up with the warriors, who were panting and looking just as shaken as the gillup.

"We need to stay together!" Sal advised, the shock of the attack leaving reason in its wake. "Whatever that *thing* is scared of, may be coming for us now!"

"The gillup have scattered," Dire observed, "The creatures have lost their advantage of surprise- perhaps they will not come back."

"Did you hear that thing!?" Serene shrieked, "I doubt it needs surprise to hunt us down!" she was growing hysterical.

"Look there!" one of the Niben pointed, they all looked and saw the stranger galloping on his horse around the lake towards them. Now that they were closer, they could see that it was a man dressed in fine steal armor, wearing a horned helmet and a great broad sword strapped to his back. As he came nearer, they realized that his horse and indeed *he* was much larger in stature than a normal man.

Sal searched the sky again, fearing that the stranger would be attacked at any moment. "What's he doing!?" she breathed.

The rider pulled back on the rains of his steed, and the mighty gray dappled horse threw back its head and tossed its thick mane. The rider raised something to their mouth, then everyone's ears were again assaulted with the terrible scream of the winged creatures.

"You may step into the open again, friends," the stranger spoke in the common tongue with a deep, rich voice. "The griffins will not return, and you will find no enemy here."

Sal exchanged bewildered looks with Vig and Theoph.

"We are strong in numbers should he prove hostile," Dire pointed out, an arrow still on the string of his bow.

Vig nodded. "Spread out your archers to either side, I will advance to speak with him," he instructed Dire. His regular cavalier attitude was missing; Sal knew the loss of Rend would weigh heavily on her husband's heart for many years. As it would on hers.

Returning one of his knives to its sheath and keeping a wary eye on the sky, Vigil emerged from the trees. "I am Vigil, royal warrior of Verlynn Nel," he introduced himself in the common tongue, stopping a few steps beyond the treeline. He trusted that the nitora were alert and in position behind him.

"Hail stranger," the stranger replied in a deep, rumbling voice, "I am Sir Fortress, knight of Stonemark." He removed his helmet, revealing light brown skin, high cheekbones and a mane of curly black hair. "You need not fear the return of the griffins; I have made them think a larger beast has come. They will move on from here." He spoke the common tongue with a thick accent that required Vig to concentrate to understand.

"I and my company are indebted to you then." Vig studied the stranger, wondering if he could be trusted.

Fortress dismounted, and his true size became clear; he was huge! Vig felt like a child facing him, and he took a step backwards.

Fortress scanned the trees with a knowing eye, "Let us be as friends, Vigil of Verlynn Nel, and call your company forward."

Before Vig could respond, Serene could be heard huffing about how she wouldn't be going out in the open again for as long as she lived. But Dire and his nitora came forward, arrows relaxed on the string.

"Our company is a diverse one," Vig explained as surprise crossed Fortress's face at the sight of the Niben. "My lord, the prince of Verlyance has joined with many on the road north."

Fortress raised his eyebrows at the mention of royalty and bowed his head slightly towards the nitora. "Verlyance is unknown to me, but tales of the fierce Niben nitora have reached my ears."

"As have stories of giants living in the mountains," Dire replied.

Fortress flashed a smile, but hesitated when Theophany emerged from the trees, escorted by Salvage. "Royalty of Verlyance, I presume." He bowed elegantly.

Theoph bowed his head in return while Sal grinned. "He is," she said, guessing the stranger mistook her for royalty, "This is Prince Theophany the Victorious. *I* am one of his warriors." She rested the butt of her spear firmly in the ground.

Vig enjoyed another look of surprise on the large knight's face; it seemed he, like Serene, found female warriors quite novel.

"We must gather the gillup," Dire said, turning his attention away from Fortress.

Vig glanced again at the sky, a reflex he doubted would go away quickly, "I suggest gathering them into the trees and breaking camp at first light tomorrow."

"Allow me to assist in collecting your animals," Fortress offered. "As a knight errant, I seek to bring glory to my name and give aid to any who would need it."

Vig frowned; 'knight errant' was not a term he was familiar with, but he supposed having the man help gather the gillup would allow them to keep an eye on him. He nodded his consent, then gave orders to his warriors, soon those who were not guarding their lords and mistresses set out to gather the frightened gillup. Everyone was wary of more griffins and crossed open areas as little as possible as they searched.

Sir Fortress went with the Niben astride his large boned horse, and Vig was satisfied that they would keep an eye on him. Leaving the work to his men, and Sal to stand guard by Theoph's side, Vig left the shelter of the trees and returned to where the griffin had attacked Rend.

Guilt assaulted him as he thought of the youth's eagerness to follow him into anything; he would have to bring the tidings of his death back to Rend's kinsmen in Verlynn Nel. Not only was the boy dead, but his body had been lost and no death rite could be performed.

Vig stood over the torn-up grass where the griffin had dug its claws into the ground, the scene playing out in his head. A bit of leather caught Vigil's eye, he stooped in the grass and found a flask of salt water, the chain it hung from felt heavy to his hands. Vig closed his scarred fingers over the token, feeling it press into his palm; it must have slipped from Rend's neck when he tried to roll away.

The boy had collected the water and worn it across the treacherous miles, trusting it would lead his soul back to the sea if he should die, but even that thin comfort had been taken from him in the end. Vigil could not bring himself to blame Tylus for the boy's fate, it was Vig who had failed him.

* * * *

The sun sank below the mountains, casting the valley into early dusk (something the Verlyance islanders still found strange) and a chill came down the slopes, creating an eerie fog in the dark. Fortress had assured everyone that the fog would ensure that there wouldn't be any more aerial attacks, and Salvage wondered if that applied to the baine wilk; she had seen no more of the furry beast and had chosen not to tell the others she had seen it at all. She had thought the beast from her vision was a guardian sent by the Ancient One, but if that were so, why hadn't Rend been spared? If the Ancient One wanted them on this journey, why weren't they being protected? Sal kept her worrisome thoughts to herself, knowing that Vig had enough to burden his heart without her doubts.

After collecting the gillup and tethering them in the shelter of the woods, the company had settled down amongst the trees and started two large fires, one for the royalty and one for the warriors, partly to thaw the chill of the fog and partly to ward off the shapeless fears that lingered in the dark. The bleating of the gillup filled whatever silence there could be had, and the crackling and spitting fires distracted from the dark unknown.

Salvage, Vigil and Theophany were returning to the fireside after ensuring that all was set for the night when several of the Verlyance warriors who were not on watch approached the prince, their faces cast in dark shadow, but their earnest hearts could not be hidden from Sal's discerning eye.

"What is it?" Vig asked as he and Theoph paused.

The warriors glanced at one another before speaking, "We would ask the prince a favor."

Theoph held himself regally before them, "What favor would you ask?"

They hesitated again, "That you go before Tylus and intercede on Rend's behalf. The sea god will listen to you and lead the boy's soul back to the sea even without a death rite."

Sal's gaze snapped to the prince's face.

Theoph said nothing, his face betraying no emotion.

Sal opened her mouth, mustering the courage to chastise the men for asking such a bold request of their prince, but they continued before she could, "You are Theophany the Victorious. The chosen of Tylus, and Tylus *will* listen to you." Their words were those of faith, but Sal saw doubt in their eyes.

"It is as you say," Theophany spoke, his tone challenging their doubts, "Tylus *will* hear me."

The warriors hesitated a moment then thanked him and returned to their own fireside.

"Theoph…" Sal tried to speak.

The prince raised his hand in dismissal and walked away to join the others.

Sal watched him go, frustrated that she could not do more, and fearing that the loss of the boy would reopen the still sore wounds left from the death of Courteous. Would her prince ever find healing?

Sal turned to find that her husband had turned his back and faced the forest edge, as much as she feared for Theoph, she feared more for how the boy's death would affect her husband. She neared him, sliding her hand up his arm to his shoulder.

"Their devotion deserves more than silence from the gods," he whispered, unshed tears dancing in his eyes. "They place their faith in a broken man who batters himself against the gates of the immortals in vain." He looked at her, righteous anger burning him up. "We both know that Theoph can no more save Rend's soul than he can walk on water- and yet he continues to claim that responsibility!"

Sal captured her husband in an embrace and leaned her forehead against his, "He's not the only one who unfairly bears the weight of another's burden."

Vig forced breath into his lungs, his arms trembling as he held her.

"We must trust that the Ancient One will make him whole, that he is being led to the Foretold King for a *reason* beyond what his father intended. Do not forget what was foretold to us in Fisher's Hamlet; he is the broken vessel, I the believer, who passes on what the visions tell me, and you, the seeker, the one who will keep him steady in his search for the truth."

Vig nodded slowly, gathering himself before speaking again, "The sooner we find the Foretold King, the better off we all will be."

They shared a kiss in the shadows, all their words spent, and their hearts laid bare. At last, they joined Theoph by the fire, placing their grief and emotions behind their warrior's mask.

The three different companies had agreed upon and set up a watch system when they started out on the road together, and now the shapes of the nitora and Verlyance warriors were interspersed on the outskirts of their camp along with Lady Serene's guards. While the newcomer, Sir Fortress, lay casually on his side by the fire, his long limbs taking up a large area, while his neatly piled armor gleamed in the firelight by his side. His magnificent horse, whose namesake was Cavern, was tethered with the gillup. Fortress had bragged that if there was any trouble, Cavern would be the first to sound the alarm.

The others of the company sat around the other three sides of the fire in distinct groupings, all eyeing the newcomer, curious to learn about him and what his true purpose was for wandering the wildlands.

"Of course, there's always a chance the brutes will come back," Fortress was saying as Sal and Vig sat down beside Theoph, "But a griffin's hunting ground is vast, and it's unlikely to see them twice in a row- all's the better for that! This trick doesn't always work!" he laughed holding up the strange whistle hung round his neck that had scared off the griffins. The man had a boisterous personality that dominated the conversation, and Sal could not help smiling as his booming laughter rolled out over the fire.

"Why do you traverse these dangerous lands?" Dire asked. Lady Roam sat beside him, her legs crossed and her veil shielding her expressions.

Fortress grinned, a cunning gleam to his chestnut eyes, "A question I would hear answered by everyone." He glanced at the gathering of faces; Sal wondered if he would believe their strange quest. "As for myself," he continued, "I am a knight, seeking what adventure I may find. As all proper knights are at some point in their life, I am on a quest of great magnitude, however, its progress is tedious, and I will not bore you with it's details."

A snort was heard from Lady Serene; Sal was beginning to understand that the woman looked upon all newcomers with contempt. Garden sat with her in the firelight, trying hard not to look interested in the affairs of his masters.

"Rather," Fortress continued, "A more fireside worthy story is why a company such as yours travels these mountains."

"We are all on our own great quests," Theoph answered. Sal suspected he found the stranger intimidating.

"And who are you all?" Fortress asked. "The prince of Verlyance, and…" he directed the conversation by bypassing Theoph and waiting for Dire to properly introduce himself.

"I am Dire, sworn guard of my mistress, Lady Roam of the Niben Weald, daughter of Command, brother of Golden, the king of Estewryn." Dire puffed out his broad chest, evidently Theoph was not the only one feeling small.

Fortress raised his eyebrows as though impressed and nodded, then he turned his eyes on Serene, "And you, old one? You seem much too frail to traverse these lands."

Serene refrained from reacting strongly to Fortress's rudeness, and instead lifted her head snobbishly, "I am Lady Serene of the eastern courts of Fairthin. As the old writings say, better is she who makes well laid plans to step into her inevitable grave, than he who stumbles unwittingly and needlessly into it!" she widened her eyes at the knight as though she could make her words throttle him by doing so.

Fortress returned her gaze, a grin hovering on his lips for a moment, before throwing his head back and roaring in laughter. Serene huffed and muttered indigently to herself while the others hid their humor in the shadows as best, they could.

"By my battle scars, can this be true!?" Fortress exclaimed, and sat up from his lounge, his excitement drawing curious eyes from all.

"What is it now!?" Serene demanded to know, as if the man was an impertinent child tugging at her skirts for attention.

"My quest that I thought would be my eternal disgrace has suddenly begun in earnest!" Fortress cried out with joy, "I was told by a great seer that I would find my true path to glory when once I stride side by side with a prince from far away, a child of purity and a poet of old!" Fortress clapped his large hands together in glee, "And here you are!"

Dire exchanged astonished looks with his mistress, while Theoph allowed his mouth to hang open. Vigil shook his head in disbelief, but Sal joined the knight in his laughter; The Ancient One had heard her doubts, and here was her answer. This quest *was* guarded over.

"NO!" Serene gasped. "I will not stand for any more foolery! This is beyond ridiculous! A prince on a quest from the gods I expected, but then this one comes along claiming theirs is a quest to find some dead deity- and now *this*!?" she ended in sputtering and huffing.

Fortress calmed his laughter and looked about in curiosity, "What is the nature of your quests?"

Theoph took a deep breath and looked at Sal, as if she knew how to answer better! "I seek the Foretold King; a great leader who's coming was prophesied by the sea god Tylus."

"My mistress has been tasked with finding the reincarnated Prince of the Dawn and Dusk. A great hero of old, who will bring salvation to our people," Dire adding his bit. Sal listened closely, noting the new information he shared, she wondered though if it was the whole truth yet.

Fortress turned his eyes on Serene expectantly, she huffed again, "I may be in the company of those who seek deities and kings," her contempt came close to offending the Niben, "But I seek a far greater being. The Wise One!"

"Who is he?" Fortress asked, Sal suspected that he was enjoying raising the old woman's bristles.

"The Wise One, who has *never* been confirmed to be a *man*, was promised and hinted at in many songs and stories of old. They hold great wisdom, and their coming has been confirmed to me through his presence," Serene flung a finger at Theoph, "It shall be the fulfillment of my every wish to meet them and a great relief thereafter when I die- if only to be rid of the company of so many fools!" Beside her, Garden took her hand and did much to calm her down.

Fortress laughed again, "This is a truly marvelous thing, for I seek someone else still; a great Warlord, the greatest warrior these lands will ever see. He will instill fear in the hearts of the wicked before purging them from this earth in his great conquest of the world. Now that I have found you three, whom the seer foretold to me, I know my Warlord will soon begin his work of freeing the oppressed and vanquishing all who stand in his way. There is nothing I would hold back from my Warlord; if my namesake should be mentioned in only the fewest of tales told of our deeds, I will rest in my tomb in peace!"

His explanation left everyone in silence. Sal saw that little Lady Roam especially seemed shaken by the knight's morbid passion. Garden was another who's face had gone quite pale. Serene broke the spell by muttering to herself.

Theoph shook his head in bafflement, "Well, it seems we were destined, one way or another, to aid each other on our quests." He paused and it seemed to Sal that his thoughts turned inward, "May we all find what we seek."

Songbirds heralded the new bright morning, and the woods were alive with movement as the ever-growing company of travellers packed up camp and prepared to leave the valley. Vigil sensed an unease among his warriors about leaving the lake, feeling that it was a comforting link with home, but also an eagerness to leave before the griffins had a chance to return. Vig yawned as he saddled his gillup, the beasts were still skittish from the attack.

"I don't think our warriors rested much in the night," Salvage commented.

Vig looked up; she stood with her new spear in hand, watching him with a knowing gaze.

"It's natural that they be affected by what happened," Vig pointed out, blocking Rend's final cry from his memory, "It…" he found he could not speak more of it.

Sal bowed her head in understanding and Vig wondered if she had been given any more visions. Dire approached them, interrupting anything more.

"Your new spear is satisfactory?" Dire asked Sal.

She smiled and spun the ebony shaft of her weapon with ease, "Indeed, it is a gracious gift."

Dire nodded, pleased with himself. The nitora carried their mistress on a litter supported by two poles, and Dire had revealed that they carried extra poles with them in case one broke, but they also could be easily fashioned into a weapon. Sal had been able to fasten her spearhead of living coral into the end of the pole and had been pleased at the strength and flexibility of the dark wood.

"I prefer my companions to be well armed," Dire explained, then went on to point out the other qualities of the ebony wood native to the Niben Weald, such as the healing abilities in its sap.

Vig excused himself from the discussion and sought out Theophany, whom he found on the forest edge, looking out over the water.

"We are nearly ready, sire," Vig reported coming to stand by his side.

"How many more will we lose?" Theoph asked softly.

Vig followed his gaze to where some of their warriors were praying on the lake shore. He shifted his feet, searching his heart for something to say, "You blame yourself for the boy's death, as I do. But we must go on. Grief is-"

"Madness of the soul. I remember." Theoph set his jaw, "Grief for Courteous has nearly driven my soul to insanity. Perhaps I am broken…"

Vig caught his breath, but his hopes were soon dashed.

"But if my flesh is broken then I must repair it. If my soul is sick with grief, then I will reject it; grief is for mortal men."

Vig felt sick; what drove a man to speak such things!?

"When we find the Foretold King, he will be able to instruct me, then I will not be turned away from the gates of the immortals." Theoph ended abruptly and turned away.

Vig was left standing alone.

Chapter 11 The Tournament

A tournament was as much a chance for women of the court to be admired for their beauty, as it was a chance for men to win glory in the matches. As such, the maid servants of Brier Ridge worked tirelessly to curl and arrange Loyal's thick, dark hair, adorning her tresses with little white flowers. Loy was used to being fussed over, and sat still through it all, her mind far away.

Loy glanced up as Eam entered her chambers, her friend seldom wore smiles of late, and tears were often present in her eyes. A new moon would pass through the sky that night, barely visible yet its presence meant Eam would be leaving the following day. Eam's mother had arranged for her to work in a manor in the town of Pethen, its distance from Garason guaranteed that Eam would likely never see the inside of its walls again. The matter of her betrothal had yet to be resolved.

"Perhaps these would be fitting to wear," Eam suggested and presented three rings to Loy. They were expensive, and it would be unusual for Loy to wear them all at once. She glanced up at her friend, uncertain.

Eam knelt and slipped them all onto Loy's fingers. "They are beautiful," she commented and glanced at the other maid servants carefully, "Any one of them could buy passage to… anywhere!"

Loy's heart wilted a bit inside her, she waved to the other servants, "Thank you, Eam will finish my hair alone." The women hesitated, then all retreated.

"This tournament always attracts gypsies and the like," Eam spoke earnestly, "some come from coastal cities. I can arrange for you to have a peasant's dress to change into, then you can slip away with those returning to the coast and buy passage on a ship back to Tarva, just like you planned!"

"Eam no, I…" Loy frowned, trying to find the right words.

"If I can accompany you today- I can help you get away!"

"Eam, if Lord Eloquence sees you, he'll send you away at once!" Loy found that point easier to argue.

"Perhaps he won't see me! Perhaps we could escape together, and you can go back home, and I… I'll start over, far away from Lord Eloquence, Tenacious and this horrible city!" Tears were springing to her eyes.

"Eam it won't work," Loy insisted, "We'll be caught *again,* and then you will be punished! I won't risk that!"

"I don't care!"

"*I* care!" Loy pulled her friend up to sit beside her, "You wouldn't be happy if you ran away, you would regret leaving your mother for the rest of your life."

Eam buried her head into Loy's shoulder, her impulsive resolve melting away.

"Look, I have a plan to help you- but you must trust me!" Loy held her, afraid that if her plan failed her friend would do something rash.

Eam pulled away, "What plan?"

Loy closed her eyes. "Just trust me," she implored, "I will speak with Lord Eloquence today, just promise that you won't do anything on your own!"

"My lady?" a maid servant hesitated at the door, and Eam got up, cleaning off her face and pretending all was as it should be.

"Lord Eloquence sends his regrets," the maid said, pretending she hadn't seen anything, "He and Lord Tenacious will be unable to escort you to the tournament. A castle guard will be sent with you and Lord Eloquence will meet you there."

Loy didn't need to look to know that Eam was watching hopefully; now there was no excuse for Eam not to accompany her. Perhaps it was for the best after all, then Loy could keep an eye on her. She turned her head slightly to Eam and nodded.

"A gift has also been sent for you, my lady," the maid went on.

Loy sat up straighter, her curiosity piqued. The maid waved in a page carrying a rolled-up tapestry. "From Sir Courage," the page announced, hanging the tapestry on the wall and allowing it to unroll.

Loy inhaled sharply and stood in wonder; the tapestry depicted the gardens of Tarva in full bloom. Threads of pink, fuchsia and rose seemed to pop right off the wall, and Loy felt as though she was among the cherry trees again. She bit back a smile, remembering her conversation with Rage when he had asked if she enjoyed gardens; apparently, he had been listening closely.

"My kingdom of flowers," Loy breathed and stepped closer, her fingertips brushing the needle work. Closing her eyes Loy imagined she could smell the heady perfume of the trees and feel the heat of the sun on her face. Her beloved home was suddenly within reach.

* * * *

The sun cast a crescent moon shadow onto the tournament grounds of the coliseum, it's great stone walls stretching as high as any castle and the wind whistled through circular windows and archways. Wilderness stood with the other men under Captain Multifarious, dust from the hard-packed coliseum floor stirred under their feet and the din of spectators filled their ears.

Brightly colored awnings had been set up in the first row of benches, they cast shade on the nobility who sat with great excitement for the opening events. While the rest of the benches were occupied with common folk who waved banners and cheered enthusiastically. Wilder found the noise and movement distracting and he worried how well he would be able to focus during the matches. He tried to withdraw into himself as the master of events presented Wilder and his fellow soldiers to the crowds with much pomp and fanfare. At the head of their group Courage stood proudly, raising his hands to the crowd, and bowing when his recent knighthood was mentioned. The crowd cheered and Wilder forced his resentment into a far corner of his consciousness.

"Keep a clear mind," he said to himself, his voice being totally lost in the din. The master of events was long winded, and there did not seem to be much hope of the proceedings ending promptly. Wilder bounced on the balls of his feet and raised his eyes to the crowd, his gaze snagged on a maiden with copper hair, Dream.

Wilder's mouth twitched into a smile. The Garatin maiden sat behind her mistress, her pale face standing out among the Tarvin nobility. She watched the proceedings with little interest, but the thought of her presence made Wilder even more eager to do well; would her disinterest be forgotten if he won a match?

Wilder's attention was refocused when Courage approached the wall beneath where Dream and her mistress were seated. Rage bowed and spoke, then raised a spear and rested its head on the wall. Dream's mistress stood and pierced her handkerchief onto the spearhead, her token for good luck. Wilder then recognized her as the poor bride of Rage, he couldn't tell if the young lady looked any more pleased to be there than when he last saw her. Rage retrieved the token and he bowed, then with a flourish, tucked her handkerchief into his collar.

A few other of Farious's soldiers received tokens from maidens in the crowd, then the master of events sent them off and began announcing the next group of contestants. Wilder risked one last glance at Dream before he passed under a great arch of the coliseum.

"Who represents Captain Multifarious in the matches?" a clerk asked, he was seated behind a table, a feather quill in his hand. His voice and the scuffling of feet echoed in the tunnel, while sunlight lit the far end that led out to the countryside.

Courage stepped up to the table, "I, Sir Courage will represent in the wrestling," The clerk's quill scratched on the paper in response, his head bobbing, "Trin represents in the jousting," Rage pointed out his fellow soldiers as he named off those who had triumphed over the others. Wilder waited in the back, expecting Rage to neglect naming him. Rage paused and checked the clerk's list, much to the man's ire. "I believe that's it…" he glanced up over everyone as if confirming. Wilder clenched his jaw and made a single step forward. Rage grinned, "Of course, we mustn't forget our Garatin comrade!" He tapped the paper, "Wilderness represents in archery; we're all very proud of him." The clerk didn't react but there were some chuckles from the soldiers, and Wilder imagined Rage's teeth breaking against his knuckles.

Rage smiled, like it was a good jest among friends, "Come let us prepare." He led the way out to the countryside, pretending not to feel Wilder's heated gaze.

The tournament would last for two days, a third day would be spent by the nobility feasting and boasting about their men who had won, while the soldiers recovered from their wounds and spent whatever they had gained through side bets. Soldiers and guards from every lord, duke and carl in Garason and the surrounding areas had come to represent their lords. The rolling green hills of Dumah where the coliseum was nestled, had been transformed into a sea of tents. The lush turf of the countryside was torn up by horse hooves, speared with tent pegs and trampled underfoot.

The atmosphere amongst the tents was like static electricity, knights and other high-ranking men stood about boasting to one another while their squires polished and made ready their armor. Areas were already being cleared for the open matches where the men could burn off extra energy, practice and otherwise show off. This was also where the soldiers stood a chance at winning a prize purse through bets. If it wasn't for Farious paying Wilder's entrance fee to the official matches, the open matches would be all he could participate in.

Wilder and his comrades were guided through the maze of tents to theirs by the fluttering standards of Multifarious. Next to their tent was another that bore the bold coat of arms marking it as Courage's private tent.

The men who would not be competing in the official matches dispersed among the camp, while others stayed behind in the tents to prepare. Wilder declined the company of the others and took his bow and arrows outside. He had taken particular care the night before to see that his bow was in good condition, that the string was waxed and that the arrows were not damaged. Now he sat on a bench behind the tent and allowed the process of stringing his bow to focus and drown out his busy surroundings.

"Lady Loyal sent me to speak with Sir Courage."

A woman's voice spoke from the front of the tent. Wilder's concentration evaporated and he sat up straight, straining his ears; was that Dream, or was his runaway heart playing tricks?

"What is it?" Rage's voice came next.

"My lady wishes you well in the tournament, and thanks you for your kind gift," Dream answered. But Wilder now second guessed himself - if it was her, her voice sounded different- flat.

"Well, extend my gratitude to Lady Loyal, I am ever her devoted servant." The false humility in Rage's voice was enough to turn Wilder's stomach!

"She did like the tapestry then?" Rage asked, hoping for more information.

"Yes, my lord." Eam's short reply made Wilder smirk. Silence followed, and Wilder assumed Rage had returned to his tent.

His curiosity getting the better of him, Wilder approached the corner of the tent, hoping to glimpse Eam as she left.

He flinched back, and felt his heartbeat quicken; Eam had been kneeling just around the tent corner. She sprang upwards and gasped in surprise at his sudden appearance, her hand flying to her collarbone, and a small stone fell from her hand and bounced into the grass.

"Forgive me!" Wilder dipped his head, silently cursing himself for being unaware of his surroundings; he should have heard her coming!

"Tis my fault, my lord!" she assured breathlessly, then her eyes widened in recognition; she remembered him.

"I believe you dropped this," he stooped and scooped the stone up.

Eam laughed slightly at herself, a pink flush coloring her face, "I thought it might be a fossil."

Wilder examined the stone, "I believe it is." He glanced at her, "Not a very good one though."

Eam had regained her composure, and the flush began to fade, "I collect stones," her eyes meeting his briefly, "I find them interesting."

Wilder frowned a bit, "Not the sort of thing a lady usually spends her time doing." He held his hand out and dropped the stone into hers.

"It seems I'm not very good at doing the usual thing."

"You serve the maiden from Tarva now?" he asked, finding himself trying to extend their interaction.

"For today," she answered. He could have sworn there was sorrow behind her words.

"I found myself hoping she had successfully run away before now." He hoped the reminder of their first encounter would lighten her heart.

"Neither of us can escape our fate it seems," Eam answered, glancing guiltily behind her, "Good day, my lord." He let her pass without comment.

"Eam! I didn't think you would be here!" a man's voice exclaimed, Wilder turned and saw that a Tarvin nobleman confronted the downcast maiden, "My father won't be pleased to see you, but I am." He glanced about then took her by the arm and pulled her out of the open, "I've been aching to speak with you for days!"

Eam's body tensed, her feet resisting, but was dragged along just the same, she cast a terrified look behind, her pleading eyes finding Wilder.

Wilder felt frozen in place; what could he do against a Tarvin lord!?

"Tenacious no! I mustn't speak with you- I'm expected back in the coliseum!" Eam tried as the man pulled her between two tents.

Wilder took a hesitant step after her, his chest tightening and his hand gripping his bow turned numb.

"No one will miss you," Tenacious assured, "Look, I've thought about us a lot and I don't care if you're betrothed, and I don't care what my father says!"

Wilder acted before he could think it through. He sprinted to where the two were concealed behind the tents, "My lord!" Wilder exclaimed, "Captain Farious has requested your presence at once- he's most impatient today!"

"Who!?" Tenacious questioned, he held Eam by her wrist, in the process of pulling her close. Eam watched Wilder with wide eyes as she tried to pry her hand free.

"Captain Multifarious of the city guard," Wilder explained like it was obvious, "You'll find him that way." Wilder raised his bow and pointed past them with it, the large sweeping motion struck Tenacious's arm and broke his grasp on Eam. She pulled away and slipped past Wilder, running from them both.

Tenacious made a swipe at her but was much too slow, he made a sound of frustration and disgust in his throat.

Wilder blinked bashfully, "I'm sorry Sir Courage."

"Idiot!" Tenacious shoved him out of his way, "I am Lord *Tenacious*- not Courage!" he went to stand in the open and huffed in frustration when he could not spot Dream.

Wilder shrugged helplessly, "My apologies."

Tenacious swore angrily, then stalked away while Wilder held back a smirk, but it disappeared quickly; what if he hadn't been there?

He stepped back into the open himself and looked about for Eam, worried that Tenacious might still find her.

"Is he gone?"

Eam stepped from behind a tent, her face very pale.

"Is he the one who's stolen your smile?" Wilder asked, checking to make sure the fiend had truly gone. The stricken look on her face was answer enough. "I'll escort you back to the coliseum."

She nodded her consent, "I did not think he would be so bold." Her hands trembled.

"Come," he escorted her quickly through the tents, avoiding others and watching for any sign of Tenacious. Eam was silent as they walked, and Wilder found his anger rising; if she had been a lady of the court then Tenacious would have faced a reckoning for his actions. But Wilder knew men such as Tenacious seldom faced even a reprimand for mistreating a serving maid.

They reached the coliseum's walls and Eam hurriedly entered a stone arch into a dark passage. "Thank you," she said, hesitating between the sunlight and shadow, "I know that wasn't without risk to yourself."

Glancing about them, Wilder stepped into the archway with her, the cold air in the stone passage instantly reversed the sun's warming effect on his skin, but his chest burned inside him. All determination to keep a clear mind was long forgotten. "Will you be safe from him?" he asked, bowing his head to see her face in the shadows.

Eam hesitated, "His father forbade him from speaking to me; I'm being sent away tomorrow." Her eyes glittered with unshed tears.

"Sent where?"

"A manor in Pethen. I'll hardly ever see my mother again, and probably be betrothed to someone who will take me further away still. All because I smiled at him." Her voice turned bitter, and her gaze turned downward.

Wilder knew a moment of doubt, "Do you love him?"

Eam smiled bitterly, "I thought I did, but I'm told he's my half brother." She watched him, expecting to see a reaction of repulsion, but he held his thoughts deep inside, "And now that his true nature is revealed, I see that I was fooling myself from the beginning!"

Wilder hesitated, now understanding the lack of sunshine in her eyes. "Can I do anything to help?" he asked, realizing that he would do anything she asked.

"Why should you want to?"

Wilder breathed deep, the answer to her question confronted him with an outrageous suggestion. "Perhaps it is merely chivalry," he suggested aloud to himself, but he didn't believe it, "But I swear if you should ask for my help; you will have it."

A smile tugged at the corner of her lips, "I don't think I deserve your kindness, but thank you." She backed away from him offering the shadow of a smile before turning her back.

Wilder watched her till she was gone from view. "What are you doing Wilderness!?" he asked himself in exasperation, his heart beat wildly and his lungs heaved air in and out like he had been holding his breath. He slammed his fist into his forehead, 'a clear mind isn't distracted by the heart!' he scolded himself. But his focus from earlier was shattered, in its place was worry for a copper haired maiden.

★ ★ ★ ★

"You're a fool if you think he'll ever pay you back!" Courage said to his friend as they passed through the tents towards the coliseum. It was some time past high noon, and Rage had already competed in the wrestling match; it had been grueling to face so many opponents, one after the other, but Rage would not accept defeat even if it was handed to him on a silver platter.

"If he doesn't pay up, I'll warn him that I'm close friends with the tournament wrestling champion of all Garason!" his friend bragged cheekily.

The flattery, although obvious, was appreciated nonetheless and Rage flashed a smile.

"Where are you going?" his friend asked, stopping short as they neared the edge of the tents.

"I want to see the archery matches," Rage turned and walked backwards to answer.

"Why!? There's plenty more betting to be made on the open matches!"

Rage grinned and shrugged, "Place some bets for me." He turned his back and left his friend behind. He would have walked faster, but the punishment of the wrestling matches was rather harsh on his body. Entering through one of the cold tunnels, Rage came to a halt at the far end, and leaning a shoulder against the wall, he settled in to watch the archery match before him.

There were over thirty contenders, but Wilderness was easy to spot, not only for his skin, but he stood apart from the others, unwelcome among their ranks. The master of events was introducing the match.

"I would have thought you'd be celebrating your victory," Captain Farious commented as he limped up the passage.

Rage straightened and brought his fist over his heart in a relaxed salute, his muscles already feeling stiff, "Captain, shouldn't you be in the stands?" his anger over being kept under his command had cooled considerably as preparations for the tournament had begun in earnest. But it still weighed on Rage's mind.

"I want to congratulate the winner as soon as the match is over," Farious said, standing beside Rage and fixing his gaze on Wilder.

Rage relaxed and leaned against the wall again. "There are some excellent archers out there," he commented, recognizing several of Wilder's competitors.

Farious raised a brow, "I'll offer you a bet if you think Wilder won't beat them."

Rage smiled ruefully, swallowing his pride never came easy, "I know better now than to bet against his skill."

"That's wise."

On the coliseum floor, the archery match began, with archers grouping off to begin firing at a series of targets. Rage found his eyes straying from the action to seek out Lady Loyal in the crowd; had she cheered for him earlier?

"Eyes on the target, boy," Farious muttered.

Rage started guiltily before realizing the captain had not meant him, Wilder kept glancing over his shoulder at the crowd. Rage frowned; he did not expect the Garatin to be the type who was distracted by an audience.

The first round eliminated four archers whose arrows had hit the targets inches shy of the inner circle. The targets were moved five paces further for the next round.

"Something's gotten under his skin," Farious decided when Wilder continued to be distracted through the second round. "Do *you* know anything of this?" he accused Rage.

"No sir, I haven't spoken to him," Rage assured, finding himself tensing as Wilder survived the second round without an inch on the target to spare. Seven more men were eliminated, they walked away, some hiding their frustration better than others, while the targets were moved further away still.

Wilder took the chance to pace in a circle, swinging his arms restlessly; what was wrong with him? Rage pushed off the wall, and crossed his arms over his chest, while the frown between his brows furrowed deeper.

Farious took in a sharp inhale as the third match began with a little over half the competitors remaining. Rage tried to relax his body but found he could not.

Wilder's turn came, the distance to the target well within his ability to hit in the center, he drew his bow string back and released.

Farious swore explosively while Rage's jaw went slack in disbelief; Wilder's arrow had hit the outer edge of the target. He was eliminated with two others, not even halfway into the match.

Wilder stood, like a statue, his bow suspended in place as he stared at his arrow, Rage bowed his head, feeling the man's shame and devastation.

Hissing another curse, Farious turned and hurriedly limped away, his cane echoing in the darkness. Rage watched a moment longer as Wilder backed away from the others. What had happened to the man's stone set focus?

When the archery match was over and a winner announced, the master of events brought the day to a close and reminded the crowd there was more to come the following day. The soldiers and guards who had taken part in the matches returned to the tents; a long night of open matches and betting was ahead of them. While the crowd began to disperse, Courage mounted the steps to speak with Lady Loyal, trying his best to put Wilder's failure from his mind.

Lady Loyal had just risen from her seat, and was waiting upon her guardian, Lord Eloquence, to finish speaking with another nobleman. Rage's hand unconsciously lifted to his collar where he had tucked Loyal's handkerchief, he wondered if she had planned to give him the token before or after she had received his tapestry.

"Sir Courage," Lord Eloquence greeted, "You should be proud of your victory today!" he offered his hand, and Rage grasped his forearm in return, but his eyes impatiently slipped past him to Loyal; her gaze flicked away to avoid meeting his.

"I must say I was a bit disappointed about the last event," Lord Eloquence's voice forced Rage to refocus, "I suppose I expected too much of the Garatin- he once saved my daughter's life you know." He sighed and looked out over the coliseum floor, "But you can't fight your own nature."

Rage's impatience to move on from the conversation, was suddenly halted and he knew a moment of defensiveness, "My lord?"

"Oh, I'm sure the Garatin is a good enough soldier, but he can hardly be expected to surpass Tarva's best."

"Suffer me to disagree my lord," Rage felt his red-hot passion rising to the surface, "But the Garatin has exceptional skills! It pains me to admit it, but he outmatched me in qualifying to compete in today's archery match. He may be Garatin, but he *is* a fine soldier." Rage stopped to take a breath and wondered at his own words.

"I meant no slight to yourself, of course!" Eloquence was quick to clarify.

Annoyed with himself Rage waved a hand, "Let the matter rest," he glanced again to Loyal, "Did your house enjoy the games?"

Eloquence took the hint and turned to Loyal, beckoning her forward. "I fear that important matters kept me in the city till after the opening ceremonies, but I have been quite impressed with the matches. What say you, my lady?"

Loyal made a quick curtsy to Rage, and shyly met his gaze, "With so many skilled men competing, it must be very difficult to rise above them all."

Rage took her hand and bowed over it, "The task was made easier with your token."

She smiled ever so slightly and withdrew her hand, her every move seemed crafted with grace.

"There's talk among the noble's of entering our men into a weaponless melee as a final event tomorrow," Eloquence spoke, ignoring the tender exchange between the two, "if so, you will have yet another chance to prove your mettle- although you hardly need to."

The idea distracted Rage for a moment; ending a tournament in a melee did not happen every year, and it was the sort of thing Rage excelled in!

Beyond Loyal, her Garatin maid moved out of the way of some others who were passing, she hung back from her mistress and kept her head bowed, but Lord Eloquence noticed her too.

"What is she still doing here!?" he muttered, "Forgive me Sir Courage, I'm sure you can agree that running a castle comes with many difficulties; I had given orders for that maid servant to be sent away." He cast a disdainful look at the maid, who seemed to shrink inward.

"Send her away?" Loyal asked, her voice suddenly confident and bold, "My Lord Eloquence, I will not hear of it! She has become indispensable to me; I would become overwrought if she were sent away."

Rage watched with fascination; he would never have dreamed that the demure Tarvin lady could speak with such conviction!

Lord Eloquence sputtered, "My lady, these are matters that you can not understand, the decision has been long since made."

"I shall come to grief then!" Loy exclaimed; her beautiful face stricken.

"Surely this matter can be resolved," Rage interceded, "I will not have the lady become distraught."

Loyal's lashes bat quickly, and tears glittered in the corner of her eyes.

"Another maid will of course see to the ladies needs," Eloquence offered weakly.

"I don't believe that will do," Rage said with narrowed eyes

Eloquence breathed a nervous laugh, "Of course, if the maid is that important to my lady, then the maid will be my gift to her."

Loyal dipped her head in agreement.

"The matter is settled then," Rage brought the exchange to a close.

"Indeed," Eloquence said tightly, he nodded to Rage then passed by him, descending the stairs to leave.

Loyal blinked away her tears and followed, pausing briefly by Rage, "Thank you," she breathed.

He bowed his head, "It is the least I am willing to do for your sake."

He caught the beginning of a smile as she turned away, her newly won maid following closely behind. Rage watched them go, noticing how the two women's heads drew near to one another as though whispering. Rage was about to leave when Wilder caught his eye; the Garatin was standing several rows over, half hidden by an awning.

Surely, he did not have any business with nobility! What was he doing there? Rage narrowed his eyes, understanding beginning to dawn when Wilder's eyes followed the Garatin maid's figure.

* * * *

"Eloquence gave his word mother- in front of Sir Courage!" Dream emphasized the important part of her story. "If he doesn't honor his word, Loyal said she would send word to Sir Courage, and he will deal with it."

Navigate heaved a sigh and allowed the braid she had done in her daughter's hair to unfurl. She leaned her head against the back of her daughters, "Will there ever come a time when I'll have no need to worry about you?"

Eam anxiously turned to her as they sat on her bed, "Loyal will never mistreat me; she said she'll keep me with her as long as she lives!" a wave of sorrow tried to drag Eam down, "Out of everything that could have happened, this must be the best."

Avi narrowed her eyes as the cool night breeze blew Eam's shutter open a crack. "I was meant to arrange a marriage for you," she reminded.

Eam plucked at her dress, "I suppose you'll have to put up with me for a while longer."

Her mother squeezed her hand briefly then stood; she had never been one for great displays of affection. "Until Lady Loyal marries, and then you leave with her," she pointed out and closed the shutter.

"Loyal said that won't be for quite some time yet," Eam replied.

"Yippy! Your staying!" their intimate moment was rudely interrupted by Mayhap's excited cry, she pushed Eam's door all the way open, revealing that she had been listening at the threshold. "I don't want you to ever leave!" she insisted then darted away, shouting the news through the servant's quarters till she was hushed by her mother.

"That child is going to get herself into serious trouble!" Avi muttered and crossed towards the door, she looked out, shaking her head, "You won't though." Her voice turned suddenly solemn, "Will you?"

Eam rolled her lips in, thinking of how Tenacious had accosted her that day. How she would avoid ever speaking to him was beyond her.

"Some trouble can't be avoided," Avi muttered, then slipped out with one last half smile.

Eam laid back in her bed, her eyelids heavy after her wild day of events, suddenly Wilderness's voice popped into her mind, the low rumble in his words when he asked if she would be safe sent a shiver down her spine. She covered her face with her hands and whimpered, cursing her untamed emotions; they would be the death of her!

Chapter 12 A Strange Duo

The master of events congratulated the winners of the jousting with great fanfare while the crowd responded with enthusiasm, but the noblemen were oblivious as they raised their goblets and guffawed over private jokes. The second day of the tournament was drawing to a close and an air of festivity had taken over the noblemen as they sat with Governor Endure. The bets on the jousting had been intense and now they boasted the feats of some men and bemoaned the failings of others.

"The soldier in yellow deserves more attention," Governor Endure commented as he lounged, "Perhaps a knighthood- is he one of yours?" he asked, glancing at Captain Multifarious who had been invited to sit with him.

Farious could not help but grin, "Indeed he is, my lord, yet another of the promising young men I've been training."

Endure groaned as he shifted his old bones, "Not unlike young Courage."

"I foresee remarkable things in his future, if only he can learn to follow orders without his pride getting in the way."

Endure nodded and sipped his wine, "I was disappointed with your Garatin soldier's performance yesterday."

"Not more than he was, I assure you."

Endure looked at him with sceptical eyes, "You're not still considering him for our plans, are you?"

Farious set aside his own goblet, realizing how important his next words were, "Indeed I am governor- more than considering it. He is the ideal soldier for what we have in mind."

Endure did not look convinced, "You remember the standard of skill I require for this?"

"Believe me, I have thought on little else since you first came to me with the request. Wilderness has much to learn, but I am confident of his potential. As I told you before, after the tournament I will be making my final decision on which men I will be keeping. Despite his setback yesterday, I know Wilderness will not disappoint in the future."

"You know I trust your judgment and discretion, but I can not afford to make mistakes with the men I use for this…" he fell short of naming his plan, "it would already be a risk to use a Garatin."

"His loyalty belongs to Tarva, this is without doubt, and beyond that I will stake my reputation on his superior skill and potential."

Endure raised his brows at the bold statement.

"In fact, I will choose him above all my men to compete in the melee today!"

Endure smirked, "and what of your other man; you must have a team of two for the melee."

Farious turned his eyes on the coliseum floor, "Sir Courage and Wilderness."

"You are certain? There is no shame in your men losing the melee, as every team but one *will* lose, but you will hear no end of the mockery if you choose the Garatin and your team suffers because of him."

Farious breathed deep, doubt gnawing at his instincts about the two men. "I have confidence not only in Wilderness, but in them both," he declared with a tone of finality.

Endure shrugged and raised his glass. "May your reputation survive this," he toasted.

Wilderness slashed downwards, shoulder to hip with his short sword, his stroke beating the tip of his opponent's blade to the ground. Before the other soldier could move in defense, Wilder stepped in close and grasped his sword arm at the wrist, applying pressure to where the bones met the hand.

His opponent's grip weakened and with a twist of his own blade, Wilder flicked the useless weapon away, disarming his opponent and winning the match.

The onlookers all protested loudly, cursing Wilder's opponent for failing and making them lose their bets- bets Wilder had made with them. Their underestimation of his skills was small comfort in the face of his shame from the archery match. Wilder silently collected his winnings, while the onlookers moved on to the next open match.

"Stop mucking around; you're required in the coliseum," Courage said roughly, shouldering past the spectators, he was dressed in the leather breastplate bearing Farious's emblem, as if prepared to compete in a tournament match. He carried a second breastplate and flung it at Wilder before he could speak.

Wilder caught the armor, searching Rage's face for the signs of a malicious joke; he could find none. "What for?"

Neglecting to answer, Rage turned and went back the way he had come, pushing past those who got in his way. Wilder handed his sword to its proper owner and stored his winnings in a pouch before following Rage. Jogging for a step to catch up, Wilder swung the breastplate on as he reached Rage.

"Farious has named us as his team for the melee," Rage answered, his stride carrying him swiftly through the tents towards the towering coliseum.

Wilder nearly tripped in surprise; why would Farious do that!?

The two of them reached the coliseum in silence and entered a passageway, Wilder recognized it as the one he had spoken to Eam in the day before.

Stopping short, Rage turned to face him standing toe to toe, "This situation is far from ideal, and we'll be lucky to last more than five minutes! But we both know we're the best soldiers that Farious has got!"

Wilder eyed him dubiously and grit his teeth, "Agreed."

"So, before I wade into this, I would prefer to know just how much I can rely on you."

Wilder grimaced at his distaste for the Tarvin, "I bested everyone in our garrison except for you in wrestling."

"You also triumphed over us all in archery and yet you bowed out of the match yesterday like a trembling halfwit! I can only assume something shook your focus- so what was it?" he was becoming red in the face.

"It won't happen today," Wilder swore, pushing his way past, his temper was getting dangerously out of control.

"Fretting over a pretty Garatin maid in the stands?" Rage dared to challenge him further, his voice echoing in the passage, "You didn't strike me as the type."

Wilder turned on him angrily, "Do not speak of her to me!" catching himself, Wilder tried to reign in his emotions. "She suffered mistreatment before the match, and I feared for her safety."

Rage scoffed, "The wench probably deserved it!"

Wilder lost control and pounced on Rage, aiming for his throat.

Rage ducked and swatted him aside, "GOOD! That is the passion that will aid us!" he grinned triumphantly, "Don't let your anger distract you; force it to serve you instead!"

"NO!" Wilder shouted, furious with himself for allowing Rage to rile him. "No," he repeated, regaining a little of his calm. "That is what cost me the archery match! Anger and blind passion are like a blunt sword; a clear mind is the only weapon that can be relied on." He breathed deep through his nose, forcing his passion to dissipate into cold focus.

Rage's gaze was like fire in the shadows, but whatever he might have said was lost.

"Move along men! The melee is to begin soon!" a tournament attendant urged them through the passage and into the light.

A ring had been cleared on the coliseum floor; its boundaries defined by pages holding banners. Teams of contestants stood in the ring, sizing each other up, shaking their hands out and bouncing on the balls of their feet. The tension of the coming match permeated the crowd as they laid hopeful bets on their favorites, while ladies glowed with pride over the men who had accepted their tokens.

Wilder risked a sweeping glance at the crowd but refused to let his eyes rest on the copper-haired maiden; thoughts of her would have to wait.

As they walked to their position, a page handed Wilder and Rage leather straps to wrap their hands with. "Just see that our downfall is not due to your distraction," Rage warned.

"I don't intend to lose at all," Wilder replied, withdrawing to that inner place of himself, where faces faded, and movement became clear and sharp in his eyes; the place where *he* was master.

"Ladies of the court, most fair, lords of the court, most honorable," the voice of the master of events carried forth over the coliseum. "We have been witnessing to great feats of bravery and skill these past two days, but to who among these champions belongs the crown of mastery over all else? How can such a thing be decided? By the edge of one's sword? By the speed of one's mount? By the color of one's banner? I say nay! Only a melee can be the true judge!" The crowd cheered in excitement.

"Before us is the melee ring, the best our fine city has to offer will work in teams to triumph over all others. No weapons may be used but the strength of their arms and the cunning of their hearts! Any who can not rise to fight on will be eliminated- yet fear not, my ladies, for killing will not be tolerated in the melee, and any who wishes may take his leave of the ring without blemish to his honor." His tone suggested otherwise, and the crowd jeered in agreement.

"Only one from a team must survive to claim victory, but more glory to the team who emerges whole, and they shall claim victory together! Let the melee commence!"

There is always a moment of hesitation before a fight when everyone tries to guess what will happen first. Wilder preferred to use this time to read the posture of others, plan his first moves and pick targets.

However, the moment of hesitation before the melee did not have a chance to even begin; Courage charged toward the nearest team, catching them by surprise with a startling roar. Everyone else broke into action and chaos erupted.

Wilder raced after Rage, cursing his namesake. An opponent looked to flank Wilder as he ran; seeing him out of the corner of his eye, Wilder stopped up short, ducked down, stuck his leg out to the side and tripped the soldier as he caught up. Wilder did not stop to engage further.

Rage was on the ground, fighting two men, throwing punches, and kicking up dust, he fought with unbridled ferocity and was completely unaware of another team approaching. Wilder had mere moments to predict who would move first; it was all he needed.

With three quick strides, Wilder used Rage's back to launch himself high into the air and landed squarely on one of the approaching men, driving him into the ground. Wilder pummeled the soldier with strikes from his fists and elbows, then sprang to his feet. He was a second too late and was kicked into the dirt by the remaining teammate.

"Dirty Garatin!" the soldier spat at Wilder and stepped closer, drawing his leg back for another kick. Wilder rolled onto his back, fighting his anger over the slur, and grimaced as the kick slammed into his ribs. Grabbing the foot, Wilder pinned it to his side and rolled, throwing the soldier off balance, his arms flailing in surprise before landing on his back, winded. Wilder was on top of him before he could move, delivering a swift elbow across his jaw and the man went limp.

Wilder caught his breath and checked his surroundings; there were no imminent threats. Rage rose, leaving his two opponents moaning and feebly struggling to rise. Pure astonishment crossed Rage's face as he looked at the two other prone men, and Wilder standing before him.

"Are you done mucking around?" Wilder asked, allowing himself a moment to gloat.

Rage smirked as his chest heaved a few times and he shook out his right arm, he nodded, then started out towards his next victims. Wilder fell into step beside him, like the shadow cast by a feral beast.

Courage threw himself into another fight, again ending up on the ground. Dust clung to his sweaty limbs and his chest heaved from exertion, but he never slowed. Emerging the winner, Rage went straight into exchanging blows with a lone opponent.

Wilder was never far from his side, moving in constant circles around him, slipping in and out of the fights surrounding them. He would deliver jabs and blows to joints, weakening opponents, then move on, leaving the injured men to be finished off by others. In this way he spent as little energy as he could and instead used the others to thin the crowd. Men were limping out of the melee ring constantly, while others were dragged out by attendants, and soon the fighting stalled as only the best remained. Aside from Wilder and Rage, three teams were left standing. They all paused to catch their breath and size each other up. The crowd goaded them on, waving banners and chanting a Tarvin victory song.

"Hang back," Wilder instructed, as the others gravitated towards the center of the melee, their movements calculated and cautious. "Let them eliminate each other, and we will take on the victors." His words glanced off his teammate like arrows off a stone wall.

"Come on then!" Rage challenged boldly and walked forward, placing himself in the center of the remaining teams. Wilder had little choice but to follow; the others exchanged glances, a tedious alliance forming as they closed the circle around Wilder and Rage.

"Let us see who is a *true* dragon of Tarva!" Rage taunted. But the three teams would not be tricked, and they instead tightened the circle, waiting to see who would strike first.

Wilder took in every movement, every hesitation, reading his opponents like a sailor does the sky. Each man still standing was a worthy fighter, and none would be defeated easily. A dagger in Wilder's hand would have assured him a quick victory, but he reminded himself that he would pay ten-fold for any bloodshed. A course of action began to unfurl in his mind's eye, accounting for each action and reaction that may happen.

"Would you let a Garatin claim vic-" Rage's taunt was cut short as one man broke formation and rushed in to engage with him. Rage waited till the last second then twisted to the side, allowing the man to pass with a slap on the back to encourage him on his way. While this happened, the second and third teams advanced on Wilder, all four men exchanging glances with one another, each expecting to come out the winner. As they quickened their steps forward, the opponent that Rage had sidestepped nearly crashed into Wilder. As if his movements were connected to Rage, Wilder seized the man's arm and swung him back in the direction he came, twisting his arm up behind his back until he felt it pop and go limp. With a kick to the soldier's backside, Wilder pushed him into his surprised teammate, causing them both to go down.

Wilder faced the remaining team, ducking and dodging, waiting for an opening. A bloody fist slipped past and made contact with his already bruised ribs, causing him to stumble gasping for breath. Before he could recover, his opponents swiftly moved in to finish him off. Exhaustion tugged at his body like heavy nets, but he made the sharp pain in his ribs refocus his resolve. Wilder made every move count as an attack and unleashed a flurry of blows with blinding speed. His knuckles drove into one man's neck and his elbow cracked the nose of another, ducking and pivoting beyond reach with a deft kick to a knee and a leg sweep, he left both of his opponents staggering, allowing him a moment to breathe.

Wilder's focus was shattered as he was grabbed from behind by the opponent he had earlier knocked down. The two before him were quick to recover and re-engage, each fuming with anger. Wilder's failing strength made his struggles futile, and a barrage of vicious blows was delivered to his face and torso.

Courage roared from behind, catching the two before Wilder off guard and slamming into them like a battering ram, driving them to the ground. Still held firmly from behind, Wilder shook his head to try and clear his dazed vision and with a mighty gathering of strength, he hooked one leg behind his opponent's ankle and threw himself backward. Landing hard in the dirt their heads collided. Wilder was released and he scrambled to his feet a moment before his opponent.

Wilder felt his strength ebbing from him and his vision refused to clear, but he could taste victory as surely as he could the blood in his mouth. He met his opponent head-on and drove a series of quick jabs to his abdomen driving the air from his lungs. The man staggered backward giving Wilder some space.

Nearby, even the strength and endurance of Courage was flagging as he grappled with the other two remaining opponents. Wilder spared him a glance but saw him in double while his heartbeat seemed to echo back and forth between his ears. His moment of hesitation left him wide open for his sole standing attacker to tackle him to the ground. Wilder controlled his fall as best he could and threw his head forward into his opponent's face feeling something crack just before he lost consciousness.

★ ★ ★ ★

Courage rose from his limp and groaning opponents, sweat and blood dripping into his eyes and filling his mouth while adrenaline abandoned him, leaving his injuries to throb. He spat into the settling dust as his vision cleared, bringing the arena back to his awareness. The commotion of the crowd had died down, leaving Rage to hope that the melee was done; but what had come of Wilder?

He stumbled forward, knowing that in a moment if he alone were left standing the victory would be given to him - regardless of how much his teammate had helped get him there. Laying in the dust as though on top of someone else, was one of the incapacitated opponents; a white Garatin hand stuck out from under him.

Rage rushed forward and rolled the man off Wilder; the Garatin's head lolled to one side and his eyelids fluttered as he fought to regain consciousness.

Melee attendants were checking downed combatants verifying that none were left ready to fight. At the sight of Courage left standing, a cheer began to rise from the crowd as they waited for the winner to be announced.

"On your feet Wilder!" Rage urged, pulling him up by his arm. Wilder gasped for air and tried to hold his head up. Supporting him with one arm Rage slapped Wilder's face abruptly, "Shake it off Garatin! We've won!"

Wilder shook his head and stood up straighter, weakly he pushed Rage away and looked about with swelling eyes.

"Sir Courage and Wilderness, the men of Captain Multifarious- are victorious!" the master of events announced with excitement. The crowd answered back with thunderous applause.

Wilder turned his eyes on Rage. For a moment they only faced each other, chests heaving and limbs trembling. Rage had never seen anyone fight like Wilder, as the heat of battle ebbed away, a surprisingly strong swell of respect took its place.

Rage stepped forward as the dust finally settled and offered his forearm to the Garatin. Wilder hesitated a moment, then soberly clasped Rage's arm with his own. Courage flashed a triumphant and bloody smile.

★ ★ ★ ★

Dream felt delicate, like a half dead tree holding onto its last leaves, the gentlest breath of wind might as well be a forceful gale. But she set out in the early hours of the day after the tournament, determined to be strong and not let her emotions flood over. Before setting out to the kitchen, Eam checked in on Mayhap and her baby brother, she found them both sleeping soundly, blissfully untouched by the recent turmoil in Eam's life.

The kitchen was already bustling with activity, water was boiling over coals, and in the oven, bread was rising and filling the air with its wholesome aroma. Eam's mother came in from the chicken coop and began emptying her apron of eggs while Eam set out Loyal's breakfast tray; she found it strange not preparing Regime's meal, but that duty belonged to another now.

"What's this?" the head cook asked.

Eam looked up to see a Garatin stranger standing in the garden doorway, a large sack of flour thrown over his shoulder, and a felt wide brimmed hat casting a shadow on his face.

"Flour from the market, fifteen copper." The man shifted the sack on his shoulder, flour dust drifting off it.

The head cook clucked her tongue in annoyance, "Brier Ridge has its own mill! Get off with you!" she shooed the man away.

The man discreetly scanned the kitchen from under his hat, his eyes hesitating on Eam, "I just thought a bit of extra help might be wanted here, is all." He edged backwards.

Eam opened her mouth in surprise.

"I said be off with you!" the head cook shooed him with both arms.

He ducked his head and turned away, while the rest of the servants continued with their work.

"Enough daydreaming," Navigate scolded her daughter as Eam stared at the now empty door.

"I'll just go fetch a flower for Lady Loyal!" Eam explained hurriedly and scuttled through the kitchen and out the door.

The rising sun had only just begun to cast light throughout the castle grounds, and noise from the street beckoned from around the path corner. Plucking a flower as she went, Eam skipped a step and rounded the corner.

The man with the flower sack walked before her, but upon hearing her footsteps stopped and turned, blue hopeful eyes meeting hers from beneath his hat.

"Wilderness!" Eam exclaimed in astonishment, "What are you doing?!"

He shifted his feet and ducked his head, "I swore that you would have my help if you should ask for it."

Eam stepped closer, "Did you truly come all this way just to offer your help? In a disguise no less!?"

A smile lay half hidden on his face as he peeked up at her, "I heard you had become a maid servant to Lady Loyal. I wanted to be sure that you were safe."

In spite of it all, Eam smiled, "My fate seems to be kind to me once more; I will no longer be sent away. Your offer of help *is* appreciated, all the same."

"My promise remains, if ever you should find yourself in need." He glanced behind her at the castle, and she was reminded of her trouble with Tenacious. But somehow Eam could not make herself fear him, not when Wilder stood before her.

"Now I know I don't deserve your kindness!" she stepped closer still, feeling like her heart was filled with more bird song than the surrounding garden ever could be.

Wilder hesitated awkwardly then held out his gloved hand to give her something, "To add to your collection." He sounded downright breathless.

A green crystal quartz dropped into her hand, Eam inhaled in surprise, but had no time to admire the gift, for Wilder was making a hasty retreat.

"Thank you!" Eam called after him, wishing he would stay longer, she was rewarded with a flash of a shy smile from over his shoulder.

* * * *

"I told you they wouldn't buy flour from a peddler," the old door keeper said cheekily as Wilder approached.

Wilder flipped him the second half of his payment for allowing him to enter the grounds and left without speaking, his stomach felt like it was tied up in knots; why did Dream turn him into a complete fool!? It was worth it though, now he would be able to sleep knowing that Eam was not about to be sent beyond where he might see her again.

Thinking of her surprised smile and the blush rising in her face as they spoke drove him to distraction as he made his way out of the richer district of the city. The streets came to life as he walked, and he stepped to one side to allow a wagon to pass, his body protesting the abuse it had suffered in the melee the day before. Rising early that morning had been a struggle, even so he was one of the first to rise since the others were sleeping off their celebrations from the night before. Captain Farious had given all his men leave to waste the night and following day as they pleased after their admirable performance in the tournament, but Wilder had not been interested in joining the others in the tavern.

Nearing the barracks, Wilder paused when he caught sight of two dirty faced boys poking through a rubbish heap. He watched them for a moment till they noticed and returned his gaze, "Know where you could sell this flour?" Wilder asked.

The boys came closer, curious. "There's a bakery around the corner," the older of the two pointed.

Wilder nodded, "Don't let them swindle you." He shrugged the flour sack off his shoulder, the small amount of effort it took felt like he had instead lifted a wagon above his head. The sack landed with a thud and a cloud of white powder at his feet.

The older boy did not question Wilder's generosity as he came to collect the sack, the younger boy followed him shyly.

With a wince of pain, Wilder removed his hat, and placed it on the younger boys' head; he instantly snatched it off to inspect it with a wide grin. Wilder knew the hat would be better appreciated by the boy than whoever Wilder had stolen it from earlier. The older boy hoisted the sack into his arms, then they both looked up and froze at Wilder's bruised and swollen face.

Wilder could not stop a grin as he removed his gloves, revealing swollen and cut knuckles. "The other guy looks worse," he assured and handed his gloves to them. The exchange stirred old emotions of the soldier, Endor, showing him kindness when he was a mere stableboy, anxious to prove himself. That old soldier would be proud to know how far Wilder had come.

Entering the barracks, Wilder noted that no one seemed to be awake yet. He loathed the idea of spending his morning in his quarters with the other men, but he had nowhere else to go.

"Wilderness, a word," Captain Farious called from above. Wilder mounted the wooden steps as quickly as his limbs would allow.

Farious beckoned him into his office, and Wilder pulled out his coin pouch, eager to repay his entrance fee to the tournament.

Farious eased himself down behind his desk and gave Wilder's coin pouch a clueless look.

"I don't like leaving debts unpaid," Wilder explained, dropping his winnings onto the desk.

Farious raised his brows, "You did well for yourself. But the bets I made on the melee repaid your entrance fee." He flicked his hand for Wilder to take back his money.

Wilder hesitated before doing so, surprised that the captain had bet on him at all.

"You're not permanently injured," Farious inspected him as he lounged back, "Are you?'

Wilder forced his body to straighten, "No sir, I'll be fit to resume training at your order."

Farious worked his jaw and nodded, "Very good, rest today then- and get a poultice for your cuts."

Wilder left the captain's presence and before returning to his sleeping quarters, retrieved a poultice from the kitchen as Farious had advised. The poultice consisted of bitter smelling herbs and a thick green paste, swallowing back his distaste for the smell, Wilder smeared the mixture over his various cuts, then entered the sleeping quarters.

Many of the other men had not risen yet and the room hummed to the rhythm of snoring. Wilder made his way towards his bunk, his thoughts again returning to Eam.

"Where did you go?" Courage asked, his voice a bit groggy sounding, he was stretched out on his bed, and watched Wilder with half closed eyes.

"I had some debts to repay," Wilder answered quietly, wishing Rage would leave him be.

Rage smirked, "The others thought you had been dismissed."

Wilder hesitated and looked back at him.

Rage shifted into a more comfortable position and closed his eyes, "It was a nice thought while it lasted."

Chapter 13 Repayment

"You are all dismissed from my service. See my clerk to receive your transfer papers," Captain Farious stated abruptly as he addressed his men from the top of the gangway stairs. He pounded his fist over his heart once, then turned and limped into his office.

Courage blinked in shock, his lips opening for words that dried up in his mouth. His fellow soldiers stood for a moment, utterly dumbfounded, then began turning to one another, their disgruntled and confused mutterings wafted over Rage like a sour breeze. He turned his head and met the gaze of Wilder who betrayed nothing of his own thoughts.

The soldiers began filing out of the training grounds towards their quarters to pack, along the way they were handed their transfer papers from the clerk. Unable to speak, Rage joined the line next to Wilder.

"The captain has asked to see you both," the clerk informed them abruptly when they reached him.

"What in blazes is happening?" Rage could hold his tongue no longer.

The clerk paid him no mind and Wilder nudged his elbow as he backed away towards the stairs. Rage threw up his hands in frustration.

"Keep a clear mind," Wilder spoke quietly as they climbed the stairs. Three days after the tournament, the two of them still moved stiffly.

Rage muttered under his breath angrily but managed to silence himself as they reached Farious's office.

"Enter," the captain called after their knock. He sat at his desk organizing and scanning a pile of documents.

Rage stood by Wilder's side before the desk, remembering the last time they had stood there.

"I should have liked to continue training you and the others," Farious began, his eyes still on his papers, "but, some lessons are best learned through trial." He looked up and scanned them with critical eyes.

It took all of Rage's will power to remain silent; how did Wilder do it so easily!?

"Garatin rebel's have been causing some amount of trouble in recent days," Farious informed them as he leaned back in his chair. "They have been ransacking farms in the countryside and two days ago attacked the manor of Foxwood; they did so when the majority of the main guard were escorting an official through the city. The rebels could not have known this as the guards of Foxwood were ordered to do so mere hours before. As a result, the manor was completely sacked and stripped of weaponry. The lord of Foxwood is also a captain of the center barracks in the city; I believe there to be a spy among his soldiers who is feeding the rebels information."

Rage resisted glancing at Wilder to see what he thought; it's not as if he would have been able to guess from his stone-like expression anyways.

"I want the spy caught and killed; no matter who he be," Farious took up a letter from his desk and held it out to Rage. "I am sending you to the center barracks to serve under Captain Splendor, these transfer papers say nothing of your mission; beyond these walls this mission does not exist, understood?"

Rage took the letter and glanced at Wilder. As expected, the Garatin betrayed nothing on his face.

Farious also looked at Wilder and seemed to hesitate a moment, "As for you Wilder, your heritage allows you to do what no other Tarvin soldier can do; I want you to infiltrate the rebels. Gain their trust and find the source of their information; it is possible they have spies in more than one barracks in the city. Whoever they be, stableboy or traitor; I want them dead."

Farious allowed silence to stretch out in the office. "You are to carry nothing with you that could link you to the Tarvin army, if discovered, consider it your last act of service to die without revealing your orders. For this mission, you are on your own. Neither of you are to contact me until the job is done, wait two days before coming here to report. Avoid passing information between the two of you as well; I'll be disappointed if either of you should be killed on your first mission."

The captain paused, allowing Rage a moment to understand what was happening.

"Courage," Farious spoke again, "go and report to Captain Splendor, and Wilderness… take to the streets. You are dismissed."

Rage and Wilder saluted stiffly, then exited and made their way to their quarters in silence. The others had already gathered their meager belongings and left, the empty quarters felt barren and haunted. Wilder crossed to the far side of the room to his bunk. Rage watched him separate his personal belongings from his soldier's gear; there was not much for him to take with him.

"Did Farious just make us into assassins?" Rage asked, his voice shattering the silence.

Wilder paused, glanced up for a moment, then nodded mutely.

Rage stood dumbfounded, rooted to the floor.

Wilder seemed unphased as he looked over his gear, then walked away, tucking a single dagger into his belt.

"Is that *all* you're taking with you?" Rage asked.

"I've had it since I was a boy; it's all I'll need," Wilder assured. As he got to the door he paused then turned and looked Rage straight in the eye. It was only a moment, fleeting, yet real nonetheless when a glimmer of mutual respect passed between them. "May you have good fortune… and good hunting," he said quietly, then left, looking for all the world like any other Garatin commoner.

* * * *

Captain Splendor scanned Rage's transfer paper as they stood in the courtyard of the center barracks. Unlike Farious's training barracks, the center barracks was built more like a fortress, and bore the signs of much older architecture. As its name suggested, it was situated in the center of the city and served to lock up many a troublemaker. Stone ramparts enclosed a courtyard and several buildings including a guard house and stable. A mighty portcullis currently stood closed to the busy streets, and a handful of soldiers mulled about the gatekeeper's door.

"Sir Courage, eh?" the captain asked, "The same who competed in the tournament?"

Rage grinned, unable to resist, "That's right."

Captain Splendor nodded and folded the transfer paper, "It's about time I received reinforcements, even if it's only one man," he squinted up at the sun. "We deal with the highest level of crime and violence in the city and yet are given little credit or assistance." He smiled tightly, "I'll be glad of your expertise here. As a knight you may have private quarters…" he gestured to the guard house.

"I prefer to sleep with the rest of the men, captain," Rage interjected, holding his breath; how could he gain information if he were kept from the other soldiers?

Captain Splendor raised a dark brow, "As you wish," he looked him up and down, "You've been serving under Captain Multifarious…"

Rage shifted uncomfortably.

"What did he have you doing?"

"Extra training," Rage managed to say, the words feeling forced and stiff.

Captain Splendor smirked, "Right." He turned to his men about the gatekeeper's door and gave a shrill whistle to gain their attention. "Sir Courage will accompany you on your patrols today," he ordered, gave Rage one last curious glance, then turned away. He must have been near the same age as Farious, but walked like a young man, and Rage assumed he could give any man a fair fight.

Rage turned his eyes on his fellow men; did any of them suspect there was a spy among them?

* * * *

Wilderness rubbed his thumb over his hand as he walked the country road; another splinter had nestled into his skin. His hands were raw and chewed up from handling wood all day on the kiln farms outside the city. He had been working as a day laborer for three days and had yet to find the Garatin rebels. The raids and riots in the city had all but ceased, suggesting the rebels had disbanded, but Wilder believed otherwise. They were a cautious lot and must surely be plotting in the shadows. Wilder had high hopes of finding them that evening.

Stooping his head to enter a low doorway, Wilder looked about the interior of a country alehouse; it was built into the earth like a cellar, stone walls sloped into a curved ceiling where all manner of goods hung to dry out. An open fire pit and a few stray candles cast light on benches and barrels used as tables. Farmers and other day laborers filled the room with chatter and life after the day's work. Every face to be seen was Garatin and Wilder had to remind himself that he looked no different.

He made his way to a group of men he had been working alongside and joined them at their table. They accepted his company easily, and hardly gave him any mind as he listened to their conversation. They were a motley crew of various ages, all of them were lean enough to stand in a field as a scarecrow, and most of them bore the scars of the pox on their faces.

An older man downed his cider and wiped his mouth. "There goes my sweat and toil of the day," he bemoaned, gazing into the bottom of his drink.

"Meanwhile the Tarvin masters eat their fill," another complained.

"Beside fires burning the charcoal we labored over," Wilder took the chance to add.

"Here, here!" The group agreed with little enthusiasm but plenty of venom. One of them squinted at Wilder, "Haven't seen you about before now," he commented, a shadow of mistrust on his face.

"I'm Guild," Wilder offered humbly, learning to go by a different namesake had been tricky, but he did not want to risk someone knowing him from the tournament. "My kin are north of here; I came because I understood a man could be his own master here in the city. I didn't know that was only for Tarvins."

His explanation was met with more grumblings, but no one took the bait, so Wilder kept trying, "Something's *got* to give soon though."

"Change is like a boiling pot," the oldest of them said with a sour expression, "it'll never boil when you're watching." There was another round of muttering agreement.

Wilder found himself disgusted with their lack of initiative, "It never will boil unless you set a fire under it!"

They all paused and regarded him with weary eyes, Wilder swallowed hard and cursed himself for not holding his tongue; Rage's impulsiveness had worn off on him!

As a group, the men put down money for their drinks and got up, casting Wilder vaguely fearful looks before abandoning the alehouse.

Swallowing a sigh, Wilder cursed himself again.

"Guild, was it?" the alehouse keeper asked as he inched closer, looking like a raven after a shiny trinket. "Nary mind them, they grumble lots but are too lily livered to do any good!" He looked Wilder up and down, "You wanna help the 'pot boil'?"

Wilder stiffened eagerly, "Aye!"

"Come back ere tomorrow night after dusk, and then you'll see what's going to set the fire." He winked, then went about his business.

Wilder did as he was told and returned to the alehouse the next day as the evening dusk made way for the night. He was stopped at the door by a twitchy looking farmer, "It's closed for the night." he insisted, glancing up and down the dark country road.

"The alehouse keeper told me to come. I am Guild," Wilder explained.

The farmer cracked a grin, "Guild, eh? I 'erd you were full of fire the other night; that's what we need." He waved Wilder inside.

Wilder scanned the room quickly and came up with a head count of fourteen Garatins- farmers and serfs, there were even a few women among them. Several carried rough hunting knives stuffed into belts and two pitchforks had been left by the door. There was an overall air of anticipation and anxiety; Wilder guessed that this was not the main body of rebels.

Thanks to his pale complexion and vagabond appearance, Wilder went unnoticed, and he found a spot to stand with his back to a wall. An exit plan was always at the forefront of his mind in case he was found out and he mapped out an escape while the room settled and a few more stragglers joined them.

A hush fell on the room as a man mounted a box and addressed the crowd. "My countrymen, hard and honest workers, you have come because you know in your hearts that all is not as it should be. Tarva marches across our lands and burns what will not submit, while our countrymen are content to bow under their sword like sheep to the slaughter!" This man bore the scars of conflict; he was no farmer. "How much longer will you tolerate the desecration of our lands, our homes and our freedom? We have no king who will fight for us, instead we must rise up and drive out the invaders like the vermin they are!"

Wilder noted how the man's words affected the crowd; they were like wilting plants in a downpour.

Surprisingly, the man stepped down and offered his hand to a woman who mounted the box; she was young, hardly a full woman yet. Two long, blonde braids down her back added to her youthful appearance and her blue eyes looked over the crowd with fevered energy. The crowd stirred at the sight of her, a wave of whispers rolled outward among them, and the words 'Rebel Queen' passed Wilder's ears in a hush.

"I am Manifest, the one you have heard rumored of by firesides in the dark of night," she spoke out of the side of an honest grin, like sharing a secret with a dear friend, "Like you, I grew up on the stories and promises that one day we would be free again, that Eloi would remember us and lead us to victory over our foes. My brothers, my sisters, I stand before you and tell you; that time *has* come!"

"There is a song of freedom rising from the tongues of our countrymen in the streets of Garason, it's rolling out towards you, sparking fire in the hearts of every ear that hears it; can *you* hear it!? I know our time has come, the rebirth of our country is in our hands, and yes; there will be blood, there always is during birth. But Tarva has long demanded the blood of our sisters, our fathers… our children. It is time *they* bleed for us! Join me, my countrymen, and become a part of this coming age. We can offer little, aside from your freedom."

The crowd cheered and turned to one another to share excitement and convince the hesitant. Manifest stepped down from her box and began greeting everyone individually.

Wilder took in a sharp breath to recentre himself; for a moment he forgot that he was Tarvin.

Manifest was slowly making her way towards him, she spoke with each person along the way, asking their namesake, and encouraging them to join her. Wilder sensed little resistance from those gathered. He had been wrong; this was not a room of wilted plants, but rather, dry kindling before a flame.

At last Manifest turned to Wilder, her eyes bright and smile inviting, "What is your namesake brother?" she asked, clasping his forearm with her hand.

"Guild, I've just come to the city, had I known of you Manifest, I would have come sooner." He put forth a boyish eagerness and found it easy to feed off her energy.

She smiled widely. "Call me Anifest, I know we will be glad to have you by our side!" she looked him up and down quickly and her smile faded slightly. "New to the city and it seems you have already come to grief. Was it a Tarvin who gave you the black eye?"

Wilder could not stop a grin from sneaking onto his face, "That's right, a gang of soldiers actually."

She shook her head shamefully, "I'll wager the cowards were given no reckoning for their mistreatment of you. It is injustice like this, that we will set right!"

"I look forward to it."

"How did they get in?" Courage asked as he scanned the manor of Foxwood; it was a fortress!

"I heard a sally port was stormed and overwhelmed," one of the three soldiers Rage patrolled with answered. "They ransacked the armory and disappeared, but not before the servants in the courtyard were killed, and good old Captain Splendor fought 'em away from his women folk."

"The captain was at home?!" Rage asked in surprise.

"Aye, he has a nasty gash across his chest to prove it! He ordered most of his manor guard and many from the barracks to escort an Ambassador from Jarg into the city," the soldier spit in contempt as they turned away from Foxwood. "As if the barbarian giant couldn't look after himself just fine- babysitting him cost us Tarvin lives!"

Rage scoffed, "An untrained mob could never pull off that kind of thing, they *must* have had help!"

His comrades stopped short, and turned on him with unfriendly faces, "Are you saying that one of us betrayed our captain and fellow men to the Garatin filth?"

Rage could have bitten off his tongue in frustration, he took a step back and tried to subdue his unfiltered passion. "Far from it, friends, I only wonder how the rebels could be so successful," he tried to sound humble- it was a stretch though.

His fellow soldiers chose not to respond and instead turned away. Rage swallowed hard and grit his teeth for the rest of the patrol, all the while going mostly ignored by the others. Nearly a week into his mission and he still had not gained the trust of his comrades or learned anything that might point to a spy. He hoped that Wilder at least was having better luck.

They completed their patrol and returned to the barracks to sleep, the next morning as Rage crossed the yard on his way for another patrol, Captain Splendor called to him from inside his office. Rage hesitated a moment before stepping into the captain's office; unlike the office of Farious, this was also Splendor's sleeping quarters and as such was cramped with personal items as well as official.

Captain Splendor had not yet donned his officer's armor and his loose tunic allowed for the display of a bandage across his chest; the wound he had received while defending his manor nearly two weeks before.

"I hear there has been some tension between you and my other men," Splendor started without preamble.

Apparently, the captain's men hid nothing from him.

"They took offence at my suggestion that someone privy to their orders had betrayed them in recent events," Rage answered, "It wasn't my intent to rile them, sir."

Splendor eyed him for a moment, then heaved a sigh, "No, of course not. It can't be helped though; a man of your station will have come to the same conclusion as I have. There is a spy in my ranks."

Rage opened his mouth and nearly asked if Farious had confided in him, but he managed to hold his tongue.

"Don't look surprised, it is what you suspected as well." Splendor glanced out his window. "I understand the men don't necessarily like you at the moment, but I could certainly use a spy of my own." He met Rage's gaze, "Keep your ears open, poke about if you can and report to me if you find anything."

Rage shifted to stifle his humor over the irony of the situation, the captain took it for discomfort, "I know it's hardly what you imagined you would be doing as a soldier, but we all must do our part."

"Of course, sir," Rage managed to say with a straight face.

"And don't leave anyone beyond your suspicions, I know it's hard to believe one of our fellow men could be betraying us to the rebels, but a bribe can go a long way to corrode a soldier's loyalty."

* * * *

Wilderness dropped softly from the wall top into the blacksmith courtyard, the nearby forge made the air stifling. It hadn't been easy to slip past the rebel lookouts posted on the street, and he feared he had wasted too much time slipping past them.

Running along the length of the wall he crouched beneath a window that looked into the blacksmith's working area; Anifest and her right-hand man talked with the smithy inside.

"Aye, they will join us," the blacksmith was assuring, casting cautious glances to the open street where there was heavy foot traffic, "I had to swear to them that we wouldn't all die though."

After his first peek to verify his targets were inside, Wilder sank down out of sight and listened intently, he could imagine Anifest flashing her lopsided smile when she replied, "That is all we can ever do, brother. You have done well. Tell them to be ready at noon tomorrow.

"What of weapons?" the blacksmith asked, "how will we defend ourselves?"

"Anifest has seen to everything," the second rebel assured. "There will be swords to spare, and our escape is well planned."

"How!?" the smithy was sounding less confident in their leader's plan. "After we set up the barricades, we'll be as good as trapped inside- if the people don't join-"

"Have faith brother!" Anifest interrupted him. "I do not expect the people to join us- not yet. That will come. Tomorrow is another step towards our freedom, but you must have faith in me! I have been assured we will be able to escape. Eloi will not abandon us."

Wilder narrowed his eyes; who had assured her of an escape? Who was the spy!?

"Remember, all who are with us must be in the courtyard of the Vase tomorrow at noon."

Wilder heard Anifest and the other rebel leaving; what exactly were they planning? Slinking away, Wilder scaled the wall and dropped unnoticed into the street on the other side. Using a passing cart to hide behind he checked to make sure the lookout on the corner hadn't seen him. Now he had to race ahead of Anifest and return to their hideout before she did.

Wilder moved through the streets quickly, using narrow alleys and climbing to the rooftops till he reached the butcher's shop. Above the shop was one of the many hideouts that Anifest used, and where she had left Wilder not long before. Crossing the rooftop of a house beside the butchers, Wilder glimpsed Anifest entering the shop from the front. Wilder made his way to the back corner of the roof and stood opposite the window he had escaped from earlier. Leaping across the gap between roofs, Wilder stood above the window and swung himself down and inside.

The room was as he had left it; empty beds lining the walls with piles of provisions here and there. Outside in the hall he heard Anifest's voice asking another rebel if anything had happened. Wilder stepped to one side and lay down in one of the beds, as if he had been napping. Anifest opened the door, "Still sleeping!?" she asked with a laugh.

Wilder startled and sat up, "How did it go?" he asked eagerly.

Anifest shook her head at his boyish energy; at least he had her fooled, "It went well Guild; we'll have nearly forty of our countrymen to aid us."

"Aid us in what? You haven't actually told me yet," he prompted sheepishly.

"That's because you don't need to know," the other rebel said grudgingly.

Anifest considered Wilder for a moment, "You will find out tomorrow, brother."

★ ★ ★ ★

"What do I do with this!?" Wilderness asked, pretending he did not know how to properly hold the sword he had been given.

"Use it," the rebel said with a level of disgust.

"You know, no one has told me what it is we're doing," Wilder complained as he and the scrapy looking rebel waited in an alley looking out at the Fort's courtyard.

The rebel rolled his eyes in annoyance, "We're not likely to trust new recruits with everything, now are we? Just wait for the signal. Anifest knows what she's doing."

Wilder found no comfort in this. He tested his sword and found that it was a fine blade of Tarvin make, where had they gotten such a thing?

They waited in the alley, watching people on their way to market, the devote coming to the Vase, or Tarvin's coming and going from the many official buildings that faced the impressive marble fort that housed the Garatin artifact of the Vase. Wilder had spotted many of the other rebels hanging about the crowd, waiting.

"There's the signal," his mistrusting comrade whispered and shrank back into the shadows of their alley. "A two-man patrol of soldiers will come around the corner in a moment; kill them quickly."

Wilder bowed his head to take an even breath; he hoped neither of them would be men he knew.

The two soldiers came into view, talking to one another, their guards down. Wilder and his comrade reached out, each grabbing a soldier and pulling him back into the shadows. Wilder found himself hesitating, as if straining to open a bolted door. The soldier struggled against him, and Wilder's hand slipped from his mouth, the soldier inhaled sharply to sound an alarm.

Wilder drew back his sword arm and drove the blade into the soldier's back, slipping under his tough leather breastplate, and upwards through his body. The blade met precious little resistance, and Wilder was left astonished at how easily he had killed the man. He withdrew his blade, adrenaline flooding his limbs, weakening his legs. He allowed the dead soldier to fall to the paving stones and stepped back from the growing pool of blood.

"Kill or be killed," his comrade said with a sniff, the other soldier dead at his feet.

Wilder nodded mutely; would he tell Captain Farious what he had just done? Would Rage understand?

His comrade held his own bloody blade behind his back and stepping out from the alley he raised his free hand. Wilder caught a glimpse of someone else across the courtyard doing the same. Had they also just killed a patrol?

A hay cart rolled into the center of the large courtyard and stopped. Anifest drove it and now stood on the bench and raised a hand to the sky. Her lopsided grin was absent.

'She's a clear target for any archer standing up there like that!' Wilder thought before he could remind himself whose side he was on.

Anifest scanned the area, making sure all her rebels were ready, then dropped her hand and watched her plan unfold. At her silent command, strategically placed carts of barrels, and carriages were rolled across all the street entrances, blocking traffic, then the wheels were hacked off in a frenzy and the carriages and cart beds fell to the streets with alarming booms. To fill in any gaps, fences that had been hidden nearby were carried into place, rebels made quick work of securing them with nails. It seemed Anifest had planned every movement.

A crowd of people, Tarvins and Garatins alike had been trapped in the courtyard, realizing what was happening, some tried to escape before gaps were closed off. Several carriages of Tarvin lords were being defended by their escorts.

"Come on!" Wilder's comrade urged as he and other rebels ran towards Anifest. Their leader kicked the hay from the back of the cart onto the paving stones, revealing a stack of swords. Anifest began handing out the weapons and giving orders, her smile returning.

"Well done!" Anifest beamed as her rebels reached her. "We will have little time before soldiers arrive, and we have much to do! Guild, join the others in subduing those guards! Gather our hostages in the middle of the courtyard, separate the Tarvins from our own countrymen; there is no need for them to suffer more than they have already. Find the richest of the Tarvins, they are our protection should the barricades fall."

Wilder was astounded at how well Anifest had prepared- but what was her goal in all of this? Before following her orders, Wilder noted that she selected a group of her core rebels to lead into one of the Tarvin buildings; it was a ceremonial hall for hosting councils.

Seeing a bow and quiver of arrows in the cart, Wilder left his stained sword in favor of the bow; in the large open area, its range would serve him best. He began thinking of how he could help the Tarvin soldiers get past the barricades when they arrived, but his thoughts came to a sudden halt when ahead of him, some rebels dragged four maidens from one of the captured carriages; two of them were Lady Loyal and Dream.

Wilder turned away before Eam could see him, his heart pounded erratically, and his focus shaken.

A rebel grabbed Loyal and dragged her away from Eam's protective arms, using her as a shield against the frenzied guards of Brier Ridge. Eam reached for her but was held back by Regime who screeched and sobbed in fright. One of the guards charged the rebel holding Loy, a frantic attempt to kill the rebel, but he was blind to Loy standing in the way. Eam screamed.

An arrow thudded into the guard's chest, halting his attack. Eam's eyes searched for the archer and stared agape as Wilderness approached. His kind face bore all the chill of an evening's frost, while tension filled his posture and blood stained his tunic. He was not wearing a soldier's uniform.

He met her gaze and raised a finger to his lips, begging her to say nothing. Eam jerked her head away and stared at the paving stones, beside her Regime clutched at her as she trembled hysterically, despite her handmaiden's best efforts to calm her.

"Anifest said to gather the hostages in the middle of the courtyard, separating the Tarvins and Garatins," Wilder informed, as the rebel's dispatched the other guards quickly.

Eam risked glancing at him; he had joined the rebels!?

"My father is the lord of Brier Ridge and will pay handsomely for my safe release!" Regime exclaimed, holding Eam and her handmaiden in front of her like a shield.

The rebel holding Loyal smirked without humor, "Aye, I'm sure he's dying to have you back, love!" he handled Loy roughly, but she refused to react, keeping her eyes averted. He directed her away towards the center of the courtyard.

"I will not be separated from my mistress!" Eam dared to speak, risking a glance at Wilder as she evaded the grasp of another rebel who was herding the Garatins to one side.

"Very well then," Wilder agreed grudgingly. He deftly took Loy from the other rebel, her eyes widened when she saw his face. Ignoring her, Wilder took hold of Eam with his other hand and began walking them away to where the other Tarvin hostages were being forced to sit on the paving stones.

"Don't say a word," Wilder warned in a whisper, "Keep your heads down; I *will* get you out of this."

A thousand questions spun through Eam's mind, but her tongue felt numb in her mouth, Loy was equally mute. They reached the other hostages and lowered themselves to sit, Wilder released them, but his hand lingered on Eam's arm, she wondered what exactly he was trying to tell her, 'don't be afraid'? Or 'forgive me'?

Regime was also brought over, whimpering and sobbing, she refused to be comforted by her handmaiden. Loy gripped Eam's hand with frightening strength, but her face betrayed little of her emotion.

Wilder was never far, but did not try to speak to them again, his gaze often resting on Eam. Activity among the rebels seemed to come to a stand still as those manning the barricades waited for soldiers to arrive. Eam's eyes were inevitably drawn to the Fort, its marble walls reaching high, and white banners fluttering in the wind as if to proclaim the rebel's victory; were the rebel's trying to reclaim the city for Garatin?

The rebel's guarding the hostages began to take their coin purses and jewels, Loy hastily removed her rings, ready to hand them over. "Don't resist them," she advised, but Regime would not heed her.

Eam watched helplessly as a guard took Regime's rings and necklace, she fought against him, scratching and kicking. Wilder stood at a distance helpless to intervene- or choosing not to. While they were distracted, Eam was wrenched to her feet by a rebel with rotten teeth.

"I have nothing!" Eam assured, eyes wide.

"Shhh!" the man hissed, holding her uncomfortably close, "You're a servant in a Tarvin lords manor- aye?"

Eam tried pulling back from him while nodding her head.

"You have no love for rebels?"

Eam's mouth hung open, "Of course not. You should all be ashamed-"

"Good!" he hissed, "You must see that the Tarvin governor is warned- Anifest plans to ambush and kill him! soon!"

Eam searched his face in shock.

"Just see that he is warned!" The rebel hissed then released Eam with a push. Nearby Regime was thrown to the ground, deprived of her jewels; no one had noticed Eam's interaction with the rebel.

* * * *

"I want four soldiers to guard each barricaded street- don't engage the rebels! They are contained for the moment- keep it that way," Captain Splendor ordered calmly. Courage admired that about him. "Reinforcements from other barracks are on their way, all we have to do now is keep the rebels from moving."

Soldiers rushed off to follow his orders while Rage remained with the main body of soldiers and the captain at the largest barricade. They could not see into the courtyard beyond- but all seemed quiet. Courage itched to get a better view of what was happening; was Wilder with these rebels? Had he found the informant? Or would the rebels succeed in their plot because someone was still aiding them?

"Look alive- they've sent someone to negotiate," Captain Splendor spoke aloud confidently, as an opening in the barricade was made and a lone rebel peeked out with raised hands- seeking a parley.

"Archers, keep him in your sights- but do not fire unless I give the order," Spender directed, then bravely stepped out in full view of any possible hostile archers. He waited for the rebel to leave the safety of the barricade and meet him.

Rage stood with the archers, arrow to a taut string, sword on his hip and eyes trained on the rebel as he approached the captain.

"My men surround your barricades as we speak, and reinforcements are on their way; we will quickly outnumber you," Splendor spoke. "Surrender now while you still have something to gain."

"It is the Tarvin lords who have something to gain," the rebel replied. "We hold captive the young son of Lord Errand and the fair ladies from Falcon's Hall and Brier Ridge."

Rage inhaled sharply, his aim faltering.

"If they are to leave here alive, we will require payment. A king's ransom will do, or whatever the lives of our hostages are found to be worth."

"This is no rebellion," Splendor growled, "It is an assortment of cowards!"

The rebel backed away, "That title belongs to those who will not act." He slipped back into the barricade, the gap closing after him.

Splendor cursed under his breath and turned on his heel, "Raid these streets and collect every trunk and chest you can find," he ordered quietly, "Fill them with rocks and let not the rebels see you- quickly!"

Rage was taken aback, then his anger flooded over him, "Sir, my betrothed lives in Brier Ridge!"

Splendor raised his brows and looked him up and down, "Empty your coffers if you wish; but I do not intend to give the rebels anything, coin *or* victim."

"I will not allow you to risk the life of my betrothed!" Rage challenged, his face going red.

"Courage, I will deliver your lady love to you on my honor; but you *will* follow my orders first." He turned away, leaving Rage feeling powerless; what would he do if Loyal came to harm?!

Splendor quietly addressed his gathered men, "Send for the soldiers around the perimeter; we can not wait for reinforcements. On the pretence of delivering the ransom, we will make a full-frontal attack and storm this barricade, kill the rebels in your path, but find and protect the hostages at all costs." His orders were carried out with haste.

The minutes dragged by like rusty hooks in hard packed soil. Floods of nausea and fear washed over Rage unexpectedly, and memories from the Five Isle uprising haunted his mind; how many would die? His fear ebbed to distant anger against Spender for being so reckless.

The soldiers from the perimeter arrived just as the rock-filled trunks did, and Rage realized that the rebels would be suspicious that they had collected the ransom so quickly- didn't Spender see that too?

Splendor had his men ready to surge around the corner at his word, then brought several men with him to carry the ransom towards the barricade, "Come collect your money- if you're not too ashamed!" Splendor called out.

Rage set aside his bow and silently drew his sword as he and the other men waited, not daring to peek around the corner.

"Step away." The voice of the rebel called out, and Rage tensed.

"You have your ransom- deliver the captives," Splendor pressed.

There was silence, then a horrible moment of hesitation after Splendor called, "Attack!"

Courage remembered pushing past a lone rebel, using the trunks to jump off of and climbing the barricade. He did not remember falling to the other side, nor could he recall what his fellow soldiers did. Instead of a line of rebels meeting them with blades, the courtyard was empty aside from the captives huddling in the center.

Rage hesitated, suspecting an ambush, but the captives were out in the open- the rebels could not sneak up on them. He scanned the windows and rooftops for archers- but there were none.

Throwing further caution to the wind, Rage rushed forward, his eyes locking on the kneeling figure of Loyal. The other soldiers fanned out in the courtyard, searching for the rebels.

The captives rose to their feet and watched with mouths gaping- some pointed frantically to the other end of the courtyard, they spoke in a jumble, their meaning lost.

Loyal and her Garatin maid rose to their feet, clinging to each other, Loyal's eyes widened in surprise and relief when she saw Rage running towards them.

"My lady! Are you harmed!?" Rage asked, reaching them.

Loyal pointed the same as the others had, "The rebel's have fled!"

Rage followed her finger and saw that the barricades had been pushed aside, and left abandoned on the paving stones were swords, daggers, and arrows; the rebels had left behind their weapons.

Splendor sent men after the rebels, but the city streets were crowded, and they found nothing. The only rebel they had was the one who had come to receive the ransom; he was put under guard and interrogated, but he would reveal nothing.

"He'll talk," Splendor assured with quiet certainty when the rebel was loaded into a prison wagon.

It took longer than Rage liked to arrange for a carriage, driver, and escorts to return Loyal back safely to Brier Ridge. Even though the courtyard and the surrounding buildings had been searched thoroughly, Rage feared an ambush and was anxious that Loyal and the others leave as soon as possible. He aided first Lady Regime and her handmaiden into the carriage, both were very shaken, then he offered his hand to Loyal. The emotion on her face was beyond him to interpret, and she climbed into the carriage without comment.

Rage offered his hand to Loyal's handmaiden next- she grasped it urgently, "One of the rebels spoke to me!" she whispered in a rush, "He said that the rebel leader is planning to assassinate the governor!"

"Are you certain?' Rage asked, stepping away from the carriage and leaning closer to her.

"He said they planned to ambush him- *soon*."

"Who was this rebel- was it Wilder?"

Eam blinked and drew back, "No- but he *was* here. Why is he with the rebels?"

Rage looked away, thinking hard. "Say nothing of this to anyone- especially that you saw Wilder," he directed her into the carriage and shut the door.

Watching the carriage rumble away, Rage's thoughts drove a deep frown into his face; did Wilder know of the planned assassination? With the spy still uncaught, the life of the governor was at serious risk. How could they hope to protect him when a large group of rebels easily slipped through their grasp in broad daylight?

The rest of the day passed without interest. The reinforcements arrived and they, along with Splendor's men began to search for the rebels, but it was a hopeless task. Upon inspection of the government buildings, it was discovered that the rebels had made off with a large amount of money, money that was being kept there in secret. Money that was now being spent as bribes to keep the rebels hidden.

Courage very badly wished to speak with Wilder but had little time or energy to consider how he might go about contacting him, or how that would be going against Captain Farious's direct order. Rage was kept busy the entire day, patrolling the city, looking for signs of the rebels, a thankless task. Because vigilance had been increased in an effort to root out the rebels, nearly every soldier available was out, and were kept out all night, patrolling and raiding any likely hideouts. Rage finished his patrol with one other man well past sundown, and the two began to make their weary way back to the barracks on foot.

"Where are you going?" Rage asked as his companion turned down a street away from the barracks.

"I plan to be far too drunk in the morning to follow orders," he said flippantly, "The least I deserve after a day like this one."

He turned his back and walked down the dark street towards a drinking house that the soldiers frequented. Light from the building spilled out onto the street, but all Rage wanted was to sleep soundly, he shrugged and continued to the barracks.

The streets were very empty and had been for hours as the military presence became increasingly oppressive, Rage wondered if the governor would place a permanent curfew over the city similar to what Tarva had. Thinking of the governor made Rage nervous; were the rebels sneaking into his chambers at that moment to slit his throat? He had sent word to Captain Splendor that the Governor was at risk, but of course had heard nothing in return.

Turning the last corner before reaching the barracks, Rage paused and remained in the shadows; Captain Splendor was walking away, his distinctive Tarvin armor absent. He pulled a cloak tightly about himself and walked quickly, keeping to the shadows.

Rage stood frozen in place. A good soldier follows orders and would return to the barracks to sleep off the long day. A good soldier does not question the actions of his superiors. Before the captain was out of sight, Rage started after him, making his footfalls silent and staying well behind. 'Perhaps he is merely returning to his home,' Rage tried to reason, even still he could not make himself turn back.

The captain led him along a convoluted path, through alleys and doubling back on his progress twice, making Rage wonder if he was just aimlessly wandering to clear his mind. Once Rage nearly lost him and only by luck spotted him again.

At last, when they had reached a section of stone houses with flat roofs where many of the city laborers lived, the captain walked down a long narrow street, at the end he entered a house with an enclosed stable attached to it. This was certainly not the manor of Foxwood. He entered the house without knocking, and before closing the door, he scanned the street behind him. Rage pressed himself against a wall, praying for the shadows to hide him.

Waiting a moment after the captain had closed the door, Rage followed, his nerves causing his hands to shake; what would he say if caught? Dashing through the open, Rage reached the door and listened for voices within; there were none, but he heard another door open and close. Caution was for fools.

Rage opened the front door slowly and was met with a short flight of steps up towards the house's inner door, halfway up these steps was another door that led into the adjoining stable. The passageway was unlit, but a flicker of lantern light came from a small window in the stable door. Rage ascended the steps slowly, forcing his breath to still while his limbs tensed for action.

Reaching the stable door, Rage peered through from a corner of the small window, half expecting to be confronted with the captain's disapproving face. The door led out onto wooden steps that went both up into a hay loft, and down to the stable floor, where one stall housed a humble cow. A single lantern hanging from a hook was the only light.

Captain Splendor had just reached the bottom of the steps, from a window in the back of the stable a young Garatin woman dropped to the floor, her long blonde braids swaying with her movement.

"Are you certain this place is safe?" the woman asked, casting a nervous glance at the door- Rage jerked his head back and held his breath.

"Quite certain; although the family who live here are not willing to join in any protests, they support the Rebel Queen gladly," Splendor replied softly. Rage's eyes widened, and he dared look through the window again, in case his ears deceived him.

"Well, thanks to your plan, this rebel queen now has the means to feed an army. Thank you."

Rage's breath quickened instead of calmed.

"I've worked out an escape plan for my prisoner, it will require another riot. I will send a patrol into the market tomorrow morning, have your rebels start a fight and stir up the people in the market. You and your rebels should leave as soon as the people are rioting. After you have had enough time to leave, I will send in my men. When the barracks is empty, my prisoner will find it easy to escape."

Rage's mouth hung agape; how could Splendor betray his own people!?

'I want the spy caught and killed, whomever he may be' Farious's words urged Rage's stunned mind into action, he tried to open the door, his anger rising up inside him, but the door wouldn't budge, it had been bolted on the other side. The window was too small for Rage to reach through, and he silently cursed; he would have to wait. Splendor heard his movement and looked up, a frown on his face.

* * * *

A Tarvin fraternizing with rebels- worse conspiring with them! The truth made Wilder sick.

Wilder knew he was close to discovering the spy, and when Anifest had slipped away in the night, he had followed her without hesitation. Wilder had silently climbed in through a window into the hay loft. Knowing the sound of the hay would give him away, he had lifted himself up into the rafters and watched the proceedings below with seething contempt. First for Anifest, for all her hatred of the Tarvins only to be working with one secretly, and then for the Tarvin himself. He did not know who the Tarvin was but guessed from the conversation that he was a high ranking soldier, this only infuriated Wilder more, but he resisted his anger and focused his mind. He withdrew his dagger, the one he had been given as a boy, it never failed to focus him.

A sound at the stable's inner door interrupted the two conspirators. The Tarvin looked up at the door, but there was nothing to be seen.

Anifest had missed the disturbance and continued, regaining the Tarvin's attention, "And what of our plans for the governor? When will we strike?"

"When the time is right," the Tarvin insisted, still distracted, "We must be patient."

"I'm tired of being patient while my people suffer under that man's tyranny!" Anifest spoke with the impatience of a child, a side of herself that she kept well hidden from the rebels. "Every moment we wait more farmers are cheated out of their land, servants abused by their Tarvin lords, and taxes raised above reason. The blood of the innocent is spilled on every street corner- all while the governor turns his back! I can feel that my rebels are ready- they have never been so willing to follow me. We must act *now* before their passion dries up!"

"Peace," the Tarvin soothed, "Those who truly believe in the cause will stand by you for as long as it takes to win their freedom. As for those who let their anger motivate them- they will always join a rebellion when it starts. Anger and blind passion are fine enough weapons for them, as their leader, you must rise above them. You will do so by keeping a clear mind."

The words hit Wilder like daggers; he nearly lost his balance in the rafters. The world closed in around him, his heartbeat the loudest thing in all existence. His palms went sweaty and the dagger in his grip felt oddly heavy.

Those words.

Those were the words that had sustained him through his life and motivated him to excel beyond the limitations others set upon him. Those were the words a young soldier had spoken to him when he was just a stable boy, dreaming of becoming a soldier. Those were the words of a man he had idolized and credited for inspiring him.

Those were the words of a traitor.

"Keep your mind focused on the end goal, and we'll get there together," the Tarvin spoke on, oblivious to the worlds his words had once created and now destroyed. "Start the riot tomorrow in the market and I will take care of the rest. Go now, and don't be caught."

Anifest hesitated, then did as he bid, climbing through the window she had come in by, and disappearing. Wilder waited not another moment more; dropping from the rafters, he landed in the loft and jumped down to the stable floor.

The Tarvin stepped back, his eyes opening wide in surprise.

Wilder's mind had never been so clear, nor his heart so enraged. He stepped forward, clapping one hand over the traitor's mouth while the other slit his throat in a quick smooth motion. He pushed him away.

The Tarvin fell backwards, his eyes wide in an expression of shock that would haunt Wilder for the rest of his life.

Wilder looked down at the dagger, a sob tore up his throat. In his mind's eye he could see this man as a young soldier standing in a doorway. He could hear this man giving tips on how to hold this same blade. He felt again his boyhood pride well up inside him when this soldier said to him '*well done.*' Wilder fell to his knees unable to take his eyes off the victim of his first assassination.

"Wilderness!" a voice hissed from somewhere impossibly far away. Wilder looked up and saw the face of Courage through the door's little window. The door rattled and strained against the bolt that had been put in place.

Wilder forced his legs to stand, it felt like there was a delay in his movements and he climbed the steps as though in a stupor. He lifted the bolt and Rage swung the door open, his eyes flying to the body in the flickering lantern light.

"That was Captain Splendor; the one Farious assigned me under. I followed him here… but I didn't think," he looked sharply back at Wilder.

Wilder used his sleeve to erase the tears that were suddenly spilling over from his eyes. "I knew him," he managed to whisper.

Rage studied him for a moment, but Wilder hadn't a clue what he was thinking. "We need to get out of here," Rage concluded at last, "You should leave that here," he gestured to Wilder's outer vest tunic.

A wave of unexpected nausea assaulted Wilder when he looked down; the captain's blood had splattered across his chest. His movements were sloppy and slow as he undid the lacings and shrugged off the stained garment.

Meanwhile Rage descended to the stable floor and cautiously approached the body, with his own dagger he checked for breath on the blade. He returned, satisfied the job was done, but Wilder stood fixed in place.

Rage roughly seized his shoulder and jostled him. Wilder met his silent questioning eyes and nodded twice. The two exited the house, checked that the street was abandoned then slipped into the shadows. Wilder followed Rage's lead dumbly, moving out of instinct rather than purpose; after all he had accomplished, a slit throat was far from the repayment he had hoped to give to the man who had started it all.

"Come on, I could use a drink," Rage broke in on his clouded thoughts, and the Garatin found himself standing out front of a soldiers' drinking house. Light spilled onto the paving stones and the hum of voices showed that many had similar thoughts to Rage.

Wilder shook himself enough to realize the unlikeliness that Rage would suggest they share a drink, and even more unlikely that Wilder should accept. But he entered the establishment side by side with the Tarvin and the two found an empty table.

"I met him when I was a boy," Wilder spoke, caring little if Rage listened, "He taught me how to grip a blade. Told me I would be a soldier when no one else believed I could."

"I liked him," Rage shared after a moment, his tone suggesting his own inner struggle, "Thought he was a good man."

"I think he was."

Rage let the comment fade into the hum of voices around them, "We've completed the mission now. The rebel's will be hard pressed to find another informant who can help them as much."

Wilder nodded, thinking of how Anifest would start the riot in the morning; when would she realize that something was amiss?

"If we had missed this meeting, the governor might have come to harm," Rage shared, and Wilder remembered that part of the conversation in the stable.

"Your Garatin maiden with copper hair warned me of the plot earlier today," Rage commented as he hailed the barkeeper.

Wilder perked up, "Eam!? Was she alright?"

Rage nodded, "Aye, my betrothed handled being held captive surprisingly well and insisted she was unharmed. Do I have you to thank for that?"

"I would have seen them to safety, but…"

"You did well. Eam seemed genuinely concerned that you had joined the rebel's though."

Wilder searched his face for any kind of joke, but found none; would he ever get the chance to explain to her?

The barkeeper arrived at their table, a wiry Tarvin man balancing a tray of mugs, "Here now- you Garatin shove off! I don't serve your lot here!" he said sharply at seeing Wilder's pale face.

"He's with me," Rage explained smoothly as he grabbed two mugs from the tray and passed one to Wilder. Wilder met the barkeeper's flabbergasted gaze coldly then turned his eyes away with disinterest.

"You heard him," another patron joined in, he was a soldier, and his comrades rose to join him, all casting hostile gazes at Wilder, "He doesn't belong here!"

The barkeeper backed away and waved for others to join in, there were now a dozen soldiers on their feet, each one glaring at Wilder.

"I will say this once more," Rage said, heat rising slowly in his face, "He is with me. Now leave us in peace." He turned his back and took a long drink from his mug.

"Stand aside, or you'll get the same as him," the first soldier threatened confidently.

Rage exchanged a look with Wilder and sighed, "Very well, I warn you though; we've had a *very* bad day," he stood and charged.

Wilder closed his eyes for a moment, took a mouthful more of his drink, then rose to join Rage.

Chapter 14 Bainemere

"Why would we turn aside now, when I can clearly see that this road takes us directly to a pass through the mountains we need to get through!?" Lady Serene argued in exasperation.

"As I have said," Sir Fortress's voice swallowed up that of the elderly woman's, "I know well these mountains, and can lead us through a pass to the west that lets out at a better point into the lands beyond!"

"And yet there is no road to this 'far superior pass'! What's wrong with the one I can clearly see now!?" Serene countered with gusto.

The voices of the elder and the giant rang out into the mountain air, their tones of frustration and anger cut through the peaceful morning and grated on the nerves of the other travellers. Vigil stood by Theophany's side through it all, doing his best not to escalate the disagreement, nor to let it frustrate him into anger; this task was proving difficult. Theophany, too, was losing his patience.

"An absence of a road to this other pass is concerning, even so, why wait till now to suggest this other route?" Vigil tried wading in.

Fortress heaved his large shoulders in a heavy sigh, "I did not think of this other pass till now, I have never traversed it-"

Lady Serene sputtered in outrage, "So how do you know it's the better pass!?"

"Because I have heard others speak of it!" Fortress boomed out in anger. Serene refused to back down though and faced him boldly. "As for the road that leads to this pass, it joins with the road we now travel, but we can save time by cutting through the forest here!" Fortress pointed with his large hand to the west through the dense wooded mountain side.

Vigil sighed and squinted at the road they traveled; Sentinel's Pass had not led them astray before- why should they abandon it now? Especially since it had become wider and much more road-like!

They had left the valley of the griffins nearly three weeks past and had traveled along the river from one valley into another, while the mountains became smaller around them, giving hope that they were nearing the end at last. Then, Sentinel's Pass left the river side and led them back into the hills. The company had set up camp in the dark the previous night and awoke to find they had an excellent view of the road as it descended the hill they stood on and wound into yet another valley. But beyond this, they could see a clear strip that led through, what Fortress told them, were the last mountains before the northlands.

"Where does this path lead that you are afraid to go?" Dire asked, breaking his silence. His question stalled Fortress completely and gave everyone else a moment of pause as they considered the question.

"I fear nothing," Fortress bragged, but his words lacked weight.

"What information are you withholding from us?" Theoph asked, narrowing his gaze, distrust suddenly leaping into the companions.

"Yes indeed!" Lady Serene joined in, "What is down in that valley that you don't want to tell us about!?"

Fortress threw his hands up with a roar of frustration, then turned his back and stalked away, leaving the others to stare at his retreating back with outrage and confusion.

Vigil turned away and rolled his eyes in exaggerated annoyance.

Lady Roam giggled in response. She sat atop a boulder watching the whole exchange, her nitora standing close by. The girl had raised her veil to see better and quickly pulled it down over her white face, but not before Vig caught the look of honest childish joy on her face. He winked at her, wondering what other micro expressions she hid behind her veil.

Vigil left the squabbling of the others behind and went through their camp; the warriors of the diverse groups had ceased to segregate themselves from each other and spread their sleeping rolls without reservation for who was next to them. The atmosphere that had come about in recent days was one of comfortable companionship, which made the disagreement over roads that much more uncomfortable. Vig stopped now and again to check in on his warriors, no one talked of Rend's death, but Vig knew it still weighed heavily on the hearts of his countrymen.

Salvage had taken the second last watch of the night, and had only recently woken, she sat with her back to Vig. Her long black locks were growing unruly after their travels, reminding Vig how long they had been away from Verlyance.

"Everything alright?" Vig asked, squatting beside her; she was tense, "You had another vision," he guessed.

She nodded and removed her hand from over her mouth. "It was the child again. Screaming in the dark, I could not find them. The child is in danger- *my* child, and I can do nothing."

Vig pulled her close and closed his weary eyes; the dream of raising a child of his own had died long ago. He had not realized how badly Sal still wanted the dream to be real.

"What of our path, your vision didn't happen to say what road we are to take- did it?" he asked when he sensed she was ready to move on.

She shook her head. "More broken vessels, a road in the darkness… and the child," they drew apart.

Vig glanced back at the prince, who was still talking heatedly with Lady Serene and Dire. "Well, I guess it's up to me then." He reached for his lute, "Perhaps, a lighthearted song about a traveller who couldn't decide what road to take?" He started to pluck out a tune.

Sal smirked ruefully, "You'll get yourself into trouble."

"Come hear the tale of old Smithy," Vig started, drawing bemused gazes from the warriors as they leisurely packed up camp. "He was a man that we all ought to…" he paused pretending he was thinking of a word that would rhyme and looked back at Sal.

She pointed at him, "I'm warning you."

"Pity!' Vig turned away cheekily and began to wander through the camp, waiting for death glares from Theoph. "He went away over the hills in search of what? No man could say. But he died an old smithy who all men do pity, he bided his time for far too long deciding on what path he should take!" He ended his song with frenzied strumming, it was accompanied by laughter and half-hearted applause.

There was sudden movement in the treeline around them. Everyone froze, then simultaneously reached for their weapons; but it was far too late. They were surrounded by a band of giants who carried hunting bows and wore horned helmets the same as Fortress.

★ ★ ★ ★

The transformation from boiling mad to scared stiff on Lady Serene's face was one that held Theophany transfixed till it was too late to react. Dire was faster, he and his nitora formed a protective circle around Lady Roam while the girl ducked in a trained response.

Theoph reached for his sword hilt but refrained from drawing it, instead he glared threateningly out at the strangers. Although the giant's held arrows to the string, they did not have them drawn, it emboldened Theoph, in the back of his mind he knew he should be afraid, but he cast the fear out like it did not belong to him. He saw Vigil scan the strangers with critical eyes, his lute relaxed in his hands while the other warriors scrambled to their feet.

One of the giants stepped forward, instead of a bow, a falcon-like creature perched on his arm, its hind quarters were cat-like, reminding the travellers of the much larger creatures of the same kind. The giant spoke, his voice deep and his words foreign.

Theoph glanced at Serene, who was cowering behind him; her hand fluttered over her heart and from the look on her face he guessed she had not a clue what the stranger said.

"They speak the common tongue," Sir Fortress informed, returning from where he had stormed off to. Evidently his presence had been missed by the hunting party.

"And who are they?" the giant with the falcon asked, his accent the same as Fortress.

"We can speak for ourselves, thank you kindly!" Serene interjected, her anger returning. "We are travellers of the highest distinction! The likes of which do not need to answer to you!"

Theoph raised a subtle hand, requesting that she be still, "We travel north and seek passage beyond the mountains."

The giant smiled slightly, humored by Serene's indignation, his eyes wandered over the rest of the company without haste, leaving them all in suspension. "What business do you have in the north with such a... company?" his gaze lingered on the various weapons the warriors held.

Theoph raised his head higher, knowing his warriors watched, "Our business is our own, we have no quarrel with you."

The giant nodded, his Falcon creature moving restlessly, then he spoke to Fortress in their native language.

Fortress stepped closer to Theoph and Serene, "I travel with them as a companion; they have spoken true."

"Welcome then," the giant said cordially, "I am Sagacious of Bainemere. Accept the escort of humble hunters down to the Keep, you'll find rest and fresh provisions there."

The hunters stood their ground, neither raising their bows nor putting their arrows away.

"We do not require an escort," Dire spoke up, his defensive circle remaining in place.

Sagacious smiled, "But you will accept it nonetheless, as honored guests of Bainemere Keep."

Vigil shrugged, intentionally lighthearted, "How could we refuse?" he exchanged a look with his warriors.

Serene stepped out from behind Theoph where she had been hiding, "I have decided we will graciously accept your most kind invitation. You will of course allow us to break camp." This was not a question, but a demand and she did not wait for an answer. Marching past Dire and into the rest of the camp, Serene began ordering things to be packed up.

Theoph joined Fortress as he stalked further into camp. "Any chance we get out of this alive?" Theoph asked under his breath.

Fortress looked out over Theoph's head at the Bainemere hunters who simply stood and watched. "Just don't mention where I hail from," he muttered back, leaving Theoph with a sick feeling in the pit of his stomach.

Theoph moved towards his own people.

"That's the last time I let you sing," Sal muttered as she passed Vig to stand guard by Theoph's side, her eyes tirelessly scanning the hunters.

Despite his relaxed posture, Theoph knew that Vig was being just as cautious. "If you are suggesting that our new friends have been led to us by the sound of my melodious voice, I take offence to the idea that you won't allow me to sing again. How else will we meet new people?"

"Don't share with them where Fortress is from," Theoph passed the warning on, catching the ear of his friends and that of Lady Serene.

The old woman turned a sharp gaze on their large traveling companion, then snorted, "I see no need for there to be violence. Peace is easily negotiated whereas conflict benefits no one."

"Let's hope the people of Bainemere feel the same," Sal muttered.

Camp was packed with hands always within reach of their weapons and eyes ever on the strangers. Lady Serene clutched her precious book to herself and made sure her other riches were kept out of clear sight. Instead of setting up the litter that Lady Roam always rode on, Dire picked her up and she wrapped her arms around his neck, reminding everyone how young she was.

The gillup were gathered in and saddled hesitantly, as everyone wondered if they would be allowed to ride them, or even keep them.

"Your women folk may ride the beasts, but the rest of you will kindly walk," Sagacious instructed, taking a step closer, his men doing the same.

"Oh, how very thoughtful," Serene muttered as she made ready to mount her gillup.

"If given the chance, make a break for it and escape," Theoph whispered to her, glancing at their passive aggressive captors.

"Yes, I would be in a much better position alone in the mountains while my companions are held captive by giants!" she replied without missing a beat. "Allow *me* to handle this, I'm sure I can make them see reason," she held her head high. "Just don't do anything idiotic!" One of her guards then lifted her onto the gillup.

Beside them Sal helped Garden onto another gillup's back.

"Only women may ride," Sagacious reminded, his falcon stretched out its wings and snapped at the air with its curved beak.

"He is old and unsteady on his feet," Sal defended her actions without flinching, Garden moved to dismount, anxious as ever to not cause a scene. Both Sal and Serene reached out and laid a hand on him to keep him in place. "Surely good hosts would allow such a thing," Sal challenged.

Sagacious tilted his large head to one side impressed by her boldness, Vig tensed and drew closer to his wife in response. But the gaze of the giant was now on Garden. "A Garatin," he commented.

Garden licked his lips and nodded nervously.

Sagacious bowed his head. "May Eloi be with you," his smirk widened, "That is what they say in your country, is it not?"

Garden worked his jaw, and his gaze turned to a far away place, as though a forgotten door had been swung open, allowing a fresh breeze to blow in.

"The country of Garatin is near?" Theoph dared ask.

"Aye, beyond the Dinco Mountains," Sagacious pointed to the last mountain range in the north. He then looked over the large company, "We will move out now, keep a steady pace, and try to stay out from under foot." The other giants chuckled and began to move forward, herding the group along the road. "We will reach Bainemere Keep before midday."

"And after that?" Theoph asked boldly.

Serene hissed at him to be silent, and he clamped his mouth shut as they began their way along the road. Some of the giants of Bainemere moved ahead, while the rest drove them forward from behind, arrows relaxed but ever present on their strings.

The road took them along the hilltop for a time, then plunged down into a valley; any view of Bainemere Keep was now hidden.

"I think you should tell me why hailing from Stonemark is an issue," Theoph asked Fortress, taking up stride with the giant. Nearby, Vigil moved closer to hear the giant knight's answer.

The muscles in Fortress's jaw flexed, "The matter is complicated, suffice it to say our chances of leaving Bainemere alive would decrease should that information be shared."

Theoph studied him for a moment trying to see through his words to what he was not saying, "And Bainemere, what should I expect?"

"A formidable keep, one we will not escape from through force. I have heard tell they settle the smallest of disputes through single combat, the losers being driven out into the night to pray mercy from the baine wilk."

Both Theoph and Vigil looked up at him sharply.

"The baine wilk is a mighty wolf of the Honorfell Mountains, with fur the color-"

"We know," Vigil interrupted.

"We have encountered the creature before. Are there many here?" Vig asked.

Fortress looked impressed, "I have lived in the Honorfell all my life and only glimpsed the creature a handful of times."

"Once is enough for me," Theoph muttered, "You said they are partial to single combat? Perhaps that is our answer. Let us be done with this pretence." He half turned to the nearest giant and pulled his sword a few inches from its sheath.

Vigil tensed and blocked him from charging, "Theoph stop; a peaceful outcome may yet be reached! They haven't even taken our weapons- lashing out would make matters much worse!" Vigil nudged Theoph forward, his face one of bewilderment at Theoph's actions.

Theoph consented and released his blade, "I will not allow these giants to make a mockery of us! Are we but vagabonds wandering the wilderness- or lords and champions?"

Fortress shook his head and smiled darkly. "You will be the death of me!" he scanned their captors, "Our fate may yet be decided by glorious single combat. I would relish the opportunity." His eyes gleamed.

"Or both of you could try and relax!" Vig interjected- they had gained the attention of Sal who kept glancing over her shoulder at them.

Theoph sighed tightly but let the conversation lapse into silence as they walked; Vigil and Salvage would be quick to join him when he made his move- he did not need their approval to act.

They walked along the mountain road, pausing now and again, as the giant hunters said, 'to give the legs of the undersized a rest'. During these times Theoph tried to communicate with Dire, but the hunters kept a close eye on the Niben, wary of their fierce reputation.

True to his word, Sagacious led the company around a bend in the road where the trees fell away to reveal a great stone keep carved into the mountain side below them. Thick walls of jagged stone encircled a castle with sturdy square towers and grand arched roofs. Around the right of the keep, the road of Sentinel's Pass appeared to turn and beyond lead to the mountain pass that they had seen earlier. Great crowds of people mulled about the castle grounds, coming, and going along the great drawbridge.

The sight of it gave Theoph pause, and he knew a moment of doubt. How would they escape such a place? Around him the same fear trickled through his warriors, a few glanced at him; he stood up straighter.

"You have come at a special time," Sagacious said as he came to stand behind Theoph, his deep voice making the prince flinch. "It is Wilkton, our festival to appease the spirits of the baine wilk. You will be among many who have come to celebrate."

"We have not come for festivities, but to reach the northlands," Theoph said stiffly.

Sagacious laughed heartily, "The lord of Bainemere will be thrilled to host you."

They left the hillside and soon approached the keep on a wide road. The giant hunters began to call out and greet others on the road, they spoke in their native tongue, but Theoph could easily tell that many asked about the group of strangers. As they approached more and more people, Vigil and Sal had their warriors gather closer to Theoph, Lady Serene's men did the same while Lady Roam continued to cling to the neck of Dire.

"All will turn out right," Sal encouraged brightly, her optimism drawing sceptical glances from many of the warriors.

"Just let me do the talking," Lady Serene reminded from the back of her gillup as they passed over the lowered drawbridge and entered Bainemere Keep. Theoph exchanged a look with Fortress; the knight nodded and adjusted his shoulders, his massive sword shifting across his back.

With trepidation they entered through the massive gates of Bainemere and under a mighty portcullis and found themselves in a large courtyard. Giants of all ages gathered in groups, to watch entertainers and listen to minstrels, there was even dancing around a maypole. Theoph and the others felt like children among them. Even the tallest in their company wasn't at eye level with these mountain dwellers, only Fortress matched their stature.

The walls surrounding the keep joined to a sheer cliff, as though the builders of Bainemere had cut into the mountain side. A set of doors were set into the exposed cliff side at the far end of the courtyard, one was left ajar, and blackness could be seen beyond, like a gaping maw of the mountain. The castle rose ahead of them, with steps leading up to large double doors that stood wide open.

The hunters of Bainemere brought Theoph's company to a halt before the castle steps while the crowds drew away from them and stared in open curiosity. One of the hunters climbed the steps and disappeared inside, leaving the rest to wait. The gillup moved restlessly while Fortress's horse stamped its hooves. Lady Roam squirmed in Dire's arms, her veiled face turning to look at their large surroundings. Theoph rested his hand on his sword hilt, his heartbeat picking up new beats with every second they waited.

A giant emerged from the castle doors, large feathers adorned his tunic on the shoulders, drawing attention to his large stature, his hair was thick and long, while ragged scars marked his face. He bore himself with unmatched authority and descended the steps deliberately slow, his eyes studying Theoph and the others. Fortress turned his face away.

"The lord of Bainemere," Sagacious announced and his smirk returned with an extra spark of humor, "My father."

A mutter rolled through the travellers, but this information changed nothing for Theoph, if anything, it improved things!

Lady Serene raised her head high and made her gillup step forward, "I am Lady Serene of the eastern courts of Fairthin, I and my company are most honored to be welcomed into Bainemere. As the wise say, let us be friends while friendship can yet be had." She dipped her head slightly in respect.

The lord of Bainemere bowed his head in a similar fashion and began to speak to his son.

"Friendship is a bridge burned by those who force others to cross it," Theoph spoke, stepping forward and drawing his sword, on either side of him Vig and Sal were forced to keep in stride with him. Lady Serene twisted around to give him an outraged stare, while Sagacious only tilted his head to one side.

"I am Prince Theophany the Victorious, the prophesied king of Verlynn Nel, and I will *not* be held here against my will!" Theoph cut the air before him with his blade, forcing his warriors to step back.

"Sire no!" Vigil whispered while the hunters of Bainemere shifted and readied their weapons again, this in turn made Serene's guards and the Niben half draw their own weapons- neither side committing to the violent action.

"Release us or face me!" Theoph challenged Sagacious.

"Do as he says," Fortress advised, stepping up to Theoph's side and drawing his massive blade.

Everyone was now drawing weapons and the crowds shrank back, the celebrations ending abruptly.

"Stop this!" Sal hissed in anger.

Fortress laughed boldly, brandishing his blade "Bainemere will rue this day!"

The lord of Bainemere gasped and stepped back, then flung a finger at Fortress accusingly, "It is the oathbreaker of Stonemark!"

Sagacious turned on them suddenly, an ugly snarl on his face while his falcon took to flight, the other hunters reacting in kind.

Fortress laughed all the more. "Come on then! Your names will be added to the list of my fallen foes!" he lunged out, swinging his sword in an arc, forcing the hunters to jump back, and gaining space for him and Theoph to attack.

Sagacious was thrown a sword and shield and chaos broke out among the travellers. Screams split the air of the courtyard, gillup bolted and steel met steel. Orders were shouted and the sound of the portcullis being lowered added to the clamor. Theoph felt as though fire flooded his veins and he was fearless as he met his much larger opponents. He attacked with a ferocity that he had never known before.

"There! Go! Run!" someone ordered- was it Sal? Theoph did not care. He slashed and cut with his sword driving one of the hunters back while Fortress went head-to-head with Sagacious.

In some part of Theoph's consciousness he was aware of his company running across the courtyard towards the cliff face and the door into the mountain, there was also a great amount of screaming and startled gasps from the giants. But Theoph ignored all this and embraced the frenzied rage inside him. The giant before him parried Theoph's blows with his large bow and backed away without even attempting to return the attacks. For the first time in his life Theoph felt like the god his father claimed he was.

"Theoph!" someone hollered- he paid them no mind and charged another giant, this one returned his attacks. Theoph avoided the heavy blows with ease and slashed at the giant's legs. The giant fell and Theoph pounced atop him and drew back his sword. Before he could strike, he was tackled to the ground by a furious Vigil.

Theoph tried to throw his friend off him, but Vig was unmovable, "Theoph stop this!" he shouted, "We need to flee- you idiot!" he drew back his fist and hit Theoph so hard his vision snapped into darkness and the world spun out of control.

Theoph was heaved up off the ground and flung effortlessly over Fortress's shoulder, then was jostled up and down as Fortress and Vigil began running. Theoph's vision cleared enough for him to glimpse the giants draw arrows to their bows, but Sagacious halted his hunters, his face bloody from a wound Fortress must have given him. "The baine wilk has claimed them!" Sagacious exclaimed, a strange expression of fear and respect on his face, "Let the baine wilk have them."

Theoph lost consciousness and the courtyard faded to darkness.

Salvage led the escape across the courtyard, with the portcullis closed their only hope was the door into the mountain. She saw a moment before what made all the giants freeze in awe and fear.

A baine wilk stood in the open doorway of the mountain side, its white fur laying flat across its back and its noble face watching the scene before it with a calmness that drew Sal towards it. It was the creature she had freed from the snare, the same one who had helped them escape, the one from her visions. Reason would argue that this was unlikely, and she was running into the jaws of a wild beast, but she felt it in the marrow of her bones; the baine wilk was leading them to safety once again. The mighty beast backed away into the shadows before anyone of Sal's company could realize what she was leading them to.

Salvage leapt up the short flight of steps that led to the mountain door, and ran into the darkness, the others following without question. The floor of the passage was rough and uneven, while the daylight ended abruptly a few feet from the door, giving way to darkness. The baine wilk was not visible, but Sal could feel its presence, like the gentle touch of something against her foot while swimming in the deep.

The angry whinny of Fortress's horse as he stomped his way into the chamber tore Sal's attention from the shadows and she doubled back to the large door, noting who had made it and who had not. Reaching the door, she made ready to heave it shut as soon as Vig and Fortress crossed the threshold with Theoph's unconscious body.

The giants in the courtyard stood about with weapons and watched, making no move to pursue, or even shoot arrows at them, their lack of action made Sal question her judgement.

"Close it!" Vig ordered as he bounded up the steps after Fortress, the last of their company. Helped by a few others, Sal pulled the door shut, casting them all into darkness.

"Is he wounded!? Sal asked, reaching out and finding Vig, her eyes taking too long to adjust to the meager light penetrating between the doors.

"Put him down," Vig directed Fortress.

Feeling blindly with her hands Sal leaned over the prince, and inspected his body for wounds, finding none she gripped his face and shook him to wake him, her heart beating wildly. "What happened!?"

"I hit him," Vig admitted beside her.

"We're going to die in here!" Serene shrieked suddenly, "Those brutes will be after us in a moment and we'll all die because *he* was too foolish to hold his tongue!"

Sal did not need to see the woman to know she was flinging an accusing finger in the direction she thought Theoph was.

"Be silent for once!" Dire shouted, while others joined in the panic, their disembodied voices bouncing off the walls. Sal did her best to ignore them.

Theoph moaned and stirred, pulling his face from her grasp, she adjusted her grip to his tunic and shook him. "What were you thinking!?" she hissed, her anger coming out in a sudden burst, "You nearly killed us all!"

Theoph struggled to sit up, unable to see if he looked penitent or not infuriated Sal more and she gave him another shake for good measure.

"You hit me!" Theoph moaned in outrage at Vigil, ignoring Sal.

"And I'll do it again if you ever put yourself in danger like that again!" Vig retorted.

Theoph sat up and shoved Sal's hands away. "I was fine!" he insisted, "More than fine; you stole from me a victory that would have been-"

Vig cut him off angrily, "You were reckless and fighting blind- those giants were distracted and soon would have cut you to ribbons! If I hadn't stopped you, our quest would be at its end!"

"I don't need you to protect me Courteous!" Theoph snapped back, the name of their fallen friend sounding much harsher than any curse word.

There was silence and Sal realized everyone else had grown still to listen to the argument. It broke her heart knowing how ungodlike the exchange made Theoph sound in front of his warriors.

"*Vigil*," Theoph corrected himself, still unable to stand.

"What *did* distract the giants?" Dire's voice came out of the darkness.

Sal refrained from saying that they, like her, had seen the baine wilk.

"A better question is what on earth possessed you, Theoph!" Serene picked up her accusations, her tone changing from a shriek to a trembling whisper. "I told you to let me handle it!"

"Not all blame belongs to him," Fortress's deep voice in the dark made everyone jump. "I too am at fault."

"And blame you we *will*!" Serene was picking up steam again, "What did they mean by calling you 'oathbreaker'? Don't you think a feud with these people is something you should have shared!?"

"I can not express my shame over my actions, although I would gladly walk through that door and lay low every last one of them, I am ashamed that my conquest for glory has put you, my friends in harm's way." Fortress sounded suddenly young and vulnerable .

"Harm's way!?" Serene scoffed, "You will have to do better than that! We're going to *die* in a hole in the side of a mountain or be killed by giants at any moment!" her voice echoed into silence, with only the sound of the still panicked breathing of the travellers and the gillups' hooves on the stone floor.

"Why have they not come after us?" Dire asked the obvious.

Before anyone could answer, the startled gasp and cry of Lady Roam made everyone brandish their weapons and turn to see a dull blue glow coming from out of the darkness.

Chapter 15 The Underway

The baine wilk appeared from further into the chamber, its large paws making no sound on the stone floor while its thick fur emitted the eerie blue glow.

"No one move!" Salvage commanded sharply.

Everyone obeyed, their weapons trembling in nervous hands. Leaving Theoph's side, Sal inched her way through the others to face the baine wilk alone. The beast locked eyes with her calmly, then lay down, stretching its front legs out while its tufted ears twitched into a relaxed position.

"What is it doing?" Dire whispered, his voice harsh in the silence.

"Shoot it," Fortress urged.

"No!" Sal snapped looking over her shoulder, the blue light shone on the fearful faces of her company. "It will not harm us; I have seen this in my visions!"

Vig hesitated a moment, then relaxed his sword. "Peace," he whispered to his warriors. They reluctantly lowered their own weapons. "What did you see in the visions?" he asked.

Sal glanced at the prince, her anger still smoldering inside. "The baine wilk will guide us through the darkness," she said confidently- they didn't need to know that she was guessing at what her visions meant.

"*Guide* us?" Lady Serene spoke, her indignation rising again, "Guide us where!? We're in a hole in the mountain side!"

"No," Fortress interjected, "This must be the Underway; a road under the mountain into the north." His voice lacked the excitement Sal expected over realizing such good news.

"What?" Serene barked, "A road under the mountain!? That's ridiculous!"

"How long will it take to reach the other side?" Vig asked, peering into the darkness beyond the baine wilk.

"It takes three days to travel the pass over the mountain, I expect it should take that same amount under it, but it doesn't matter," Fortress explained dismally.

"We can make it; we just refilled our water supply this morning-" Sal insisted but Fortress interrupted.

"It doesn't matter! Bainemere began digging the Underway two years past, last I heard they had yet to complete it."

"Besides, we'll be eaten by that *thing* before long!" Serene insisted, clinging to the horns of her gillup as she eyed the baine wilk. Oddly enough, the gillup were calm and unbothered by the presence of the beast.

"It will not harm us," Sal insisted, feeling surer of her words each time she said them, "Our quest is smiled upon by the gods, and this baine wilk has been sent to guide us."

"The Underway isn't completed yet!" Fortress reminded, his patience wearing thin, "We'll be stranded halfway under the mountain and then what!?"

"If we wait here much longer the giants will lose patience and come after us," Vig pointed out.

"We must go forward; our path is clear to me," Sal tried again, she glanced at the baine wilk; it had laid its head on its paws as though waiting for them to decide.

Fortress threw his hands up in frustration and muttered about how 'there was nowhere to go,' while the warriors began to mutter their misgivings.

"I'm hardly going to follow that thing! How do we know we can trust it!?" Serene complained.

"You can trust *me*," Sal implored.

There was a moment where everyone looked back at Theoph, as though waiting for him to pass judgment; but he refused to even meet their gazes.

"Salvage has never led us astray before," Vig reminded, looking to gain the confidence of their own warriors. "Whenever our path has been uncertain, she has led us in the right direction." They only muttered and shifted uncertainly, unwilling to commit without their prince to lead them.

"We will follow her," the unfamiliar voice of a child declared in a thick accent.

Everyone froze and looked about in the dim blue light for who had spoken; it was Lady Roam!

Dire still carried his mistress on his back, and he twisted his head to look at her directly. She had raised her veil to see in the semi light and bowed her head shyly. Dire spoke to her quickly in their native tongue, to which she mumbled back.

Looking both shaken and bewildered, Dire spoke to his nitora, in answer they assembled in a tight formation behind him. "We will follow your lead," he announced to Sal, with reclaimed dignity.

Sal tried her best to mask her surprise, "Thank you."

Behind Dire, Roam peaked at Sal timidly.

Serene huffed and looked at Garden, who had managed to stay atop his own gillup. "What do you make of this!?" she demanded to know, as if he was an advisor that she always consulted with.

"To stop now would be to never see my country again," Garden said. "I will go on while my feet still can." He looked down at his mount bashfully.

"Very well, I will not depart from the company now," Serene huffed and waved impatiently for her guards to make themselves ready.

When the Niben and those from Fairthin were ready, they paused and waited for the giant of their company to make his decision.

Fortress eyed them in the blue light, his brow furled deeply, "My Warlord awaits me; I will delay him no longer." Still gripping his great sword, he faced the baine wilk wearily.

All that were left were the warriors of Verlyance, and they waited, faithfully, for their prince to make his decision, but Sal saw the uncertainty with which they watched him.

At last, Theoph rose to his feet and bypassed Vigil, "Let us depart then."

The baine wilk went before them, sometimes walking, its large head low to the ground and its powerful shoulder blades rolling up and down on its back, other times trotting, its strides smooth and effortless. At times the beast went too fast, and the company feared they would be lost in the dark without its strange blue glow. This went on for what seemed an eternity, their frayed nerves becoming ever more fragile as they trusted their lives to the beast before them.

Knowing the longer his warriors continued in fear, the worse their situation would become, Vigil deliberately sheathed his sword and shot a comforting smile at those around him. Like a soothing balm on wounds, his actions released some of the tension, and others tentatively put their weapons away. Vig shared a glance with Sal, she smiled; perhaps everything would be alright.

"How does it do that?" Vig asked, breaking the long silence.

Everyone reacted, but it was a long moment before Fortress responded. "It is said the spirit of the moon fell in love with a great huntress called the wilk and one night gave her the gift of moonlight, so that she would never again walk in darkness." Unlike Vig, he had failed to put away his great sword.

Vig made an impressed sound in his throat, it induced a nervous chuckle from a few of the others.

Fortress glanced at him, and a half-hearted grin broke his stern expression, "The 'moonglow' is more common in these parts than you might think."

Unexpectedly the wilk before them stopped to sit and scratch its tufted ear. Everyone halted nervously, waiting for the beasts' next move.

"Common you say?" Vig responded to Fortress, doing his best to sound casual, "You mean there are other glowing creatures around these parts?"

Fortress matched Vig's relaxed demeanor competitively, "No, but the rocks glow." He stopped abruptly to look around them like he had just remembered something.

Vig raised his eyebrows, splitting his attention between the baine wilk and Fortress, "Glowing rocks? You could have fooled me."

Fortress sheathed his great sword and collected something from his horse's saddle bag, then stooped to the ground and picked up a fist sized stone, "I should have thought of this before now," he said rubbing something onto the stone.

Everyone watched as he poured a bit of water over the stone; slowly, a blue glow radiated off the stone, similar to that of the baine wilk. Not enough to see clearly by, but it was better than nothing.

There was a stir of astonishment and curiosity from the travellers.

"As I said, it's quite a common thing in these parts, if I but had more salt we could create enough light to travel comfortably," he glanced up at the momentarily forgotten wilk.

The beast watched them with what seemed like intelligent eyes.

"Salt you say?" Vig asked quietly.

"Aye, salt and water. The effect lasts for a few hours." Fortress held up his glowing rock to inspect the passage. While the Verlyance warriors all looked at each other, sharing the same thought.

Vig met Sal's gaze while Theoph avoided looking at them entirely; they both knew what Vig was thinking. "Light in the darkness, I can't think of a better use," Vig said, lifting two leather flasks from about his neck. One he had collected himself on the shore in Fishers Hamlet, the other, had slipped from Rend's neck before the griffin killed him.

Knowing the eyes of all his warriors were on him, Vig found two more stones at his feet. Hesitating a moment, he poured the contents of the flasks over the stones; they soon glowed.

"Why do you carry salt water!?" Fortress questioned.

Vig sighed, afraid to look up and face the gazes of his people, "It doesn't matter anymore; I am on a new path." He tossed one of the glowing stones to Sal.

Before more could be said, or outrage raised, the baine wilk stood, and continued down the passage. They were all forced to follow.

"What does wilk mean?" a Verlyance warrior asked suddenly, perhaps seeking to ease the discomfort from Vigil's actions.

"'Wolf' is the word for it in the common tongue," Lady Serene answered, she had calmed considerably.

The Verlyance warrior still looked confused.

"I suppose living on an island you wouldn't have wolves," Serene surmised.

"We have dogs," Vig volunteered, hoping his warriors would not now shun him. "They look the same, only smaller, less teeth, more fleas." To his relief, there were some chuckles from his warriors at the poor comparison.

"We have wolves in the Niben," Dire shared, he still carried his mistress on his back. They had been forced to leave Roam's litter behind in Bainemere, along with several of the gillup. Roam had returned to her silent state, but her veil was still pulled back from her face, and she watched the company from over Dire's shoulder, her red eyes flickering to whomever spoke.

Vig grinned when he thought of how she had spoken earlier, he had assumed that she could not speak the common tongue. Now he realized that she had probably been listening in on all their conversations from the very beginning! He caught her eye and winked playfully. The shyest of smiles played on her pale face.

"Is it true that all creatures in the Niben Weald have antlers?" one of Serene's guards asked, glancing at Dire curiously.

Dire grinned, "Of course; we saw off our own so as not to frighten foreigners."

There was a moment of shocked silence as everyone searched the foreheads of the Niben for any traces of antlers.

Catching Roam's eye again Vig raised his eyebrows in a mock astonishment and pointed to his head, making the motion of antlers growing.

Roam giggled and shook her head in answer. Dire noticed and stiffened, in response Roam's smile dropped from her face and she buried her head into Dire's shoulder.

Remembering the secret that his Niben friends were hiding, Vig had an uncomfortable suspicion that he would not like to find out what the secret was.

They walked on in the semi-dark, their foot falls creating echoes while their voices seemed to be swallowed by the shadows. The passage was wide enough for five of the company to traverse side by side, but the walls were jagged and often slick with moisture, so they kept to the center as much as they could. The passage was straight and hardly sloped up or down, giving the illusion that they weren't moving at all, but the entrance chamber had been left far behind, as was the threat of the Bainemere giants coming after them.

Now and again the passage opened up into natural caves where the ceiling above them towered past what their glowing rocks or even the wilk's light could illuminate. Near the entrance there had been bats that flew above their heads when they passed, but soon the only life within the mountain was what the company brought with them.

After what seemed a lifetime, the wilk paused again, its tongue hanging out, and its blue light revealed a widening of the passage, where wheelbarrows, crates, pots and other supplies of a camp were set up. The wilk glanced back at the company casually, then sat.

"What's this?" someone asked, as they all inched towards the camp in the dark, wary of the wilk abandoning its peaceful behaviour.

"A camp for the workers," Fortress guessed as he passed his glowing rock over several large barrels and a water trough.

"Very good then, only the foolish refuse good fortune and opportunity," Lady Serene announced with a familiar tone. She climbed off her gillup stiffly and directed her guards to inspect the camp. "No use walking on in the darkness forever- it must be close to sundown by now," she added in a mutter.

"Looks like there's plenty of food and water to be had," one of the warriors reported upon inspection of the barrels, "And oil lamps!"

The company set about making themselves as comfortable as possible in the abandoned camp. The first thing they did was light the lamps, illuminating their surroundings at last. The gillup were unsaddled and watered in the trough, while Cavern, Fortress's feisty horse, put forward his complaints over their lodging. When the gillup had been seen to, cold rations were shared among the company and a watch was set, both to guard over the company in case they should be attacked by giants looming out of the darkness, but also to keep an eye on the baine wilk.

Sal remained apart from the company, just outside of the lamp light, the wilk's glow lighting her shape as she crouched across from it. She had offered a bit of food and water in a tin bowl to the wilk who had accepted both with unhurried movements.

Vig left her alone for a time but was anxious to see her rest. "Sal," he called softly, coming up behind her. The wilk lifted its head, its ears perking in his direction. Vig froze where he was, nervous of what the beast might do next. After a moment, the wilk lay down its head once more and Sal smoothly rose and backed away to Vig's side.

"Sometimes it looks at me and I could swear that it knows what I'm thinking," she whispered, her eyes still on the beast, "but then…" her voice failed, and she glanced up at Vig. He touched her arm to let her know she wasn't the only one who thought that.

"Do you think the Ancient One sent it to guide us?" Vig asked, part of himself still in shock that he had forsaken Tylus for good.

Sal took a moment to respond, "Either that, or we've all gone mad."

"Come, you should get some rest," he urged, and they backed away from the wilk.

Sal took her rations and went straight to her sleeping roll, without even glancing at Theophany to see if he needed anything. Vig did not blame her, he had no idea what to say to Theoph, or even how to look at him, it was like his friend had been replaced and someone else now wore his face.

Vig leaned against a crate and let his thoughts rest on the prince, who had lay down in a corner away from the others; what was Vig to do with him?

Dire and his nitora were nearby setting up a place for Lady Roam to sleep, as the girl herself stood to one side, her veil still pulled back. She glanced at Vig, her red eyes unsettling in the semi dark.

"So, no antlers?" Vig asked her mischievously, curious to know if she would speak aloud again.

She covered her mouth to hide a giggle, obviously thrilled by his attention; did anyone ever notice her?

Dire looked over sharply, his face void of humor. He quickly stepped to Roam's side, blocking Vig's view, and escorted the girl to where they had set up a little tent for her. Before she slipped inside, Roam gave Vig one last glance, Dire cast him a much colder one.

"Vigil, won't you come join us," Lady Serene called from where she sat with Garden, along with two of the Verlyance warriors.

Vig reluctantly turned away from Dire, deciding that he would sort out the matter later, and sauntered over to the elderly woman. Vig grinned;

through everything they had been through she had still managed to hold on to her embroidered pillows and fancy silverware. Her tent, however, had been carried on one of the gillup left behind in Bainemere.

"You're about the only one not asleep or behaving like an ignoramus!" Lady Serene eyed him keenly as he sat down with them.

One of the Verlyance warriors sat up straighter with a look of mild outrage, "I beg your pardon," she protested good naturedly.

Serene swatted the warrior, "Hush now." She fixed Vig with a stern gaze, "What is wrong with Theophany!? Does he often act like this?" she asked none too quietly.

Vig glanced at his warriors, they bowed their heads, unwilling to meet his gaze. "My lord the prince is under… a great deal of stress," Vig managed to say, but defending his friend's rash actions did not sit well with him.

"We all feel the strain," the warrior who had spoken before lifted her head solemnly and fingered her flask of salt water. "Much has changed for us since we left the shores of Verlynn Nel."

Vig's heart ached for his warriors, they were far from home and confused about their prince's behaviour. Vigil's own actions earlier had done nothing to put them at ease.

"Not all change is bad," the second warrior said suddenly and met Vig's gaze for a moment.

"Humph!" Serene eyed them all with mild scorn, then turned her sharp gaze on Garden. "And what's the matter with you!? You haven't uttered a single word all day!"

Garden opened his mouth, clearly trying to formulate a response, but Serene kept going before he could speak.

"You've been acting like you've seen a nether world spirit ever since that horrible Sagacious barged into our camp this morning! Surely after all we've been through, Bainemere can't have been the most dreadful of them all." She stopped and stared at Garden pointedly.

The old man worked his jaw a few times but could not seem to say anything.

"Was it *this* morning that we met those giants!?" one of the warriors muttered, rubbing his head tiredly.

Vig narrowed his eyes, "Sagacious spoke to you, Garden, didn't he? Greeted you in the traditional Garatin way."

Garden raised his bushy brows and nodded deeply, "Aye, he did."

"I'd wager Sagacious hadn't a clue what he was talking about. Did he say something offensive?" Vig tried prodding the man, wondering what it was that had shaken him.

"He said, 'May Eloi be with you'," Garden offered, his eyes looking watery.

Serene made another sound of dissatisfaction, "Well, how does one actually greet people in Garatin?"

"I… I don't remember. But that name, Eloi…" Garden's gaze drifted like a tuft of hair in the wind.

"Who is Eloi?" Serene asked.

Garden's attention was pulled back, and he frowned in concentration, "The god of my people… I think."

Serene rolled her eyes, as she often did when such topics were brought up, but the old man did not seem to notice.

"It's been so long, but that name… it stirs old memories in this funny head of mine," Garden smiled and fiddled with his dinner bashfully.

"Well," Serene said sharply, "We shall reach your country soon enough I expect." She reached out and awkwardly patted his hand, "Then all sorts of memories may come back to you."

Vig caught a look of sorrow in the old woman's face, she masked it quickly and held her head high. "And then there is Sir Fortress," her sharp gaze was aimed at the Giant now, who had settled down away from them. "Yes, I am referring to you," she made clear when Fortress looked up. "Come here and explain," she ordered, pointing to an empty spot beside her.

Vig did his best to hide his humor over how Serene treated the man like an errant child.

Fortress eyed them coolly. "Explain what?" he asked as he casually chewed his dinner.

"Why did they call you oathbreaker?" Serene asked plainly.

"Because I broke an oath," he replied, without missing a beat.

Serene huffed in response, while Vig could not help but admire the giant for not backing down. But the secret that Fortress was keeping weighed heavily on his mind along with whatever the Niben also hid.

After everyone had slept, and all agreed that it must be morning again, they traveled on after the wilk. The air in the passage became stale and thick with mildew, and fears that Fortress's prediction of the Underway being incomplete became ever stronger. When they reached the next camp after their journey in the dark, they were all weary and anxious over what awaited them.

* * * *

Salvage was running, tripping, falling, and stumbling after the cry of the child. A sea of chest-high grass bowed and swayed to the command of the wind as she raced ever northward; when would it end? Her footsteps faltered and Sal glanced behind her, wondering if there was yet time to turn back. But a great stain spilled out of the sky, pouring over the mountains, and overflowing into the grasslands, it chased after her with a relentless hunger. The silver song of a river filled her ears- or was it the echoing of an underwater lake?

The cry of the child intensified and on the horizon a figure loomed, dressed in rich robes and wielding a sword; he held the child out before him by the heel.

Enraged, Sal charged him, "Don't you dare harm my child!" she screamed, her spear growing heavy in her hands.

"I will tolerate no threat," the figure uttered, then flung the child away. Sal dove after the infant and found herself falling into a giant, dry well.

"Your time is nearly upon you," a voice echoed after her, it was followed by a snarl and shrieking scream.

Salvage jolted awake and was on her feet before her vision had truly faded. The camp was in chaos.

All the oil lamps but one had burned out, and it cast twisted and elongated shadows of the scene before Sal. The gillup were darting away into the darkness while warriors scrambled for weapons. The nitora had fled with Roam, while Lady Serene's guards rallied around her. Vigil climbed atop a barrel while Fortress faced off against the baine wilk.

The glowing blue beast was all fangs, claws and raised hackles. It lunged and snapped, its shape dwarfing all else.

"To me!" Vigil commanded, then flung one of his knives at the wilk, it struck the beast's flank but did not seem to harm it. The wilk lunged at Fortress but was blocked as the giant's horse, Cavern, pounded towards his master and reared up. The wilk sank low to the ground and scooted around the horse. Cavern's eyes rolled back in fear as the wilk snapped at his hind quarters. Losing all restraint, the horse broke away and charged through the camp nearly trampling over the warriors as blood streamed from its hind quarters.

Fortress roared in anger and swung his sword, aiming to cleave the wilk's head clean off, but the beast was too quick. It lunged, easily reaching the giant's shoulders and sunk its teeth into his neck. Thrashing back and forth the wilk tore away Fortress's cloak- the only thing that saved him from instant death. Fortress dropped his sword and grasped the wilk's head, pushing and prying it off him. He lost his balance and fell backwards, the wilk now atop him.

Sal and Vig charged forward together, Sal's spear head aiming for the beast's side. With impossible speed, the wilk twisted, caught her spear shaft in its teeth and flung it to one side, sending Sal with it. She crashed into her own warriors. Vig barreled onwards and collided with the wilk, toppling it off Fortress.

The wilk thrashed and snapped at Vig while trying to get its feet back under itself. Vig rolled away, dislodging his dagger from the beast's flank. He tried to protect his face with his arms and bumped heavily into the crate where the last oil lamp burned. It tipped over, glass broke, oil spilled, and flames burst outwards.

Vig rolled away, his cloak aflame. He panicked for a moment, struggling to shed the garment. At last, he flung it between him and the wilk, who's eyes gleamed just beyond the fire. The blue glow from its fur had vanished, leaving them to guess at its movements.

"GET BACK!" Vig commanded, his feet snagging his other dagger, now stained with the wilks blood.

Sal was by Fortress's side, expecting the worse, but he gasped for breath and stared back at her in amazement. Sal quickly pulled back his cloak, expecting blood to pour from his neck- but he was unscathed!

"Get up!" Vig warned. Sal's heart jolted in fear; the baine wilk had backed into the shadows, its hulking form barely visible as it slowly circled one side of their camp.

"Up- up!" Sal gasped, as she and her warriors pushed and pulled till Fortress climbed to his own feet and hesitantly found his sword, his eyes hazed over in shock.

Everyone was now on the far side of the flames from the wilk, including all the gillup. Sal spared her gaze from the wilk to assure herself that her companions were all safe; Theoph stood among them, his face registering fear.

"What is it doing!?" Vig hissed as they all backed away, "I thought it was helping us!"

"I don't know!" Sal managed, her own questions clouding her mind.

"My things!" Serene shrieked, "Get my packs!" Her guards hesitated a moment before cautiously venturing back into the camp.

"What are you doing!? Stay back!" Fortress hollered, Serene turned on him, her eyes blazing, "I'll not leave my book!"

Her guards snagged her packs, including her precious book, all the while the wilk loomed beyond Vig's burning cloak.

"Those flames won't last forever," Dire pointed out, breathless from the attack, "We need to move!"

Sal realized that they had conveniently fled in the direction they needed to go; had the baine wilk orchestrated that?!

"Then move!" Fortress huffed, his shock fading when he caught sight of his horse, Cavern, prancing nervously in the passage behind them.

As one, they inched backwards from the camp and the only light they had.

A growl sounded close to their right.

Lady Roam screamed and everyone jumped back.

"There's more than one!" someone shouted in terror.

Those furthest along in the passage began running, followed quickly by the rest. Sal, Vig and Fortress remained behind, guarding their retreat.

"Those things will come after us and we'll be trapped," Fortress warned, "Before long we'll reach the dead end!"

"We don't have a choice!" Vig snapped back.

The wilk on their right lunged forward, scattering them.

"Run!" Sal ordered, facing down the creature she thought was her friend. Fortress hesitated a moment but was urged on by another growl in the dark. Vig remained behind. He creeped up behind the wilk, his sword ready while Sal angled her spear to deflect an attack.

"Why are you doing this!?" Sal hissed, half expecting the beast to answer. Instead, the wilk began to circle her. Shifting her feet carefully, Sal circled the other way and was soon by Vigil's side; they now could flee with the others.

Sal glanced about the shadows, where had the other wilk gone? The one they faced lowered itself to the ground, lips still curled back from its teeth.

"What is *it* doing?" Vig breathed in confusion.

"I think it wants us to run," Sal glanced over her shoulder in the direction her companions had fled; how would they find their way in the darkness?

"Alright, start backing up- watch for others," Vig advised. Placing her back against her husband's, they began their slow retreat. The wilk only watched them, a low rumble in its throat urging them to go faster. Soon the dying flames from their camp only backlit the wilk's crouching form.

"I don't know where the others are," Sal breathed- she could hear nothing in the darkness.

"Get ready to run," Vig whispered, "I'd rather break my neck running into a wall than face that thing."

A moment of hesitation, then they both bolted into the darkness, each stride seemed to fall farther than it should, and they fearfully held out their hands, expecting to feel a rock wall. All Sal could hear was Vigil's breath and the pounding of his feet close to her.

"Fortress!?" Vig called out, his voice echoing back to them abruptly.

"WALL!" Sal warned and skidded to a stop, her hands out in front of her. Her spear struck the wall first and slid upwards before her body slammed into jagged stone. She bounced back and stumbled to the ground, her skull contacting cold stone and consciousness failed her.

★ ★ ★ ★

Vigil fell, tumbling through darkness, limbs bruising against stone, hands clawing and slipping. His feet miraculously hit flat ground and he stumbled forward, his chest hitting the ground and his lungs expelling all breath inside. He lay still, forcing his lungs to work again, while accepting that although he could see nothing, his eyes were indeed open.

"Sal?" he managed to gasp. Silence answered him. Moaning in pain, Vig got one of his hands under himself and slowly rose to his knees, "Salvage?" he called louder, while feeling along for his weapons; his sword was nearby while his throwing knives were still in their sheaths. He marveled that he had not been impaled by his own blade when he fell. He decided that he must have fallen into a natural shaft.

"Salvage!" he called again, then listened closely for any response. Had she fallen too? He began to feel about the floor, hoping to find Sal's body yet fearing what shape it would be in. He dearly wished that he still had salt water to make a glowing rock with, but he hadn't a drop left. At last, after crawling about in the dark for what seemed an eternity, Vig was satisfied that Sal had not fallen with him. He chose to believe that she was alright wherever she was.

Banishing his fear, Vig rose to his feet and searched till he found a wall, then began walking. The darkness seemed to press against him, and he imagined shadow hands pulling at his clothes and rummaging through his pockets.

"Or' the waves and or' the brine till my lady I shall find. Her hair like the night and eyes like the stars, into their depths I shall dare, yet beware the secrets they guard." The sound of his own voice comforted him, and he found a bit more courage. "Though the dark vows to thwart I'll prevail in my plot… No, that's no good," he muttered to himself.

"Vigil?" the tiniest voice spoke.

Vig froze, "Hello?" his heart leaping for joy; he was not alone!

A whimper answered.

"Lady Roam!? Is that you?" he called trying to pinpoint where her voice had come from, "Imagine finding a friend here! How pleasant! Keep talking so I can find you, I seemed to have gone blind."

Her whimper answered again- or was it a giggle? It guided him closer along the wall. "Are you still there?" he prompted; he could only imagine how frightened she was. His feet hit something, and Roam squeaked, nearly falling on top of her, Vig tumbled to the ground. No sooner had he landed, than he felt Roam's little hands on his arm. She was whimpering again.

He pulled her close into his arms, "There we are!" she crawled into his lap and clung to him, "We'll be alright now."

Gentle sobs sounded and Vig felt tears soaking into his tunic, "Anyone else here?" he asked, rubbing her back.

"I can't find Dire!" she whimpered, "I'm lost!"

Vig held her even closer; had everyone gotten lost in the dark? "Well, it's alright now, you've found me! Now we can see about finding the others."

Fearful of leaving behind an unconscious friend, Vig convinced Roam to hang onto the back of his tunic while he felt about in the dark on his hands and knees. He found nothing but jagged stone. "Did you fall down a shaft?" he asked.

"No," her little voice reflected how seldom she used it aloud, "There was another baine wilk and we ran… I got lost."

Vig hesitated; now he really hoped they were alone in the dark. "Alright, I'm sure the others are nearby." He rose to his feet and picked up the child, she wrapped her arms around his neck and hung on tight, leaving him a free arm to feel along the wall. "We can't be that far from the end of the Underway." The unspoken fear that they would find a dead end wormed its way between them and Vig wondered if Roam could feel it too.

Vig walked on with a false confidence, each step landed on rougher stone, and the passage sloped downward, Vig became nervous of hitting his head on an ever-lower ceiling. Perhaps he should have tried to go back and crawl up the shaft?

"I promise I'm not skylarking, is that a light?" he asked, uncertain if his eyes were deceiving him.

"What's skylarking?" Roam asked, squirming about in his arms to look ahead of them.

"Never mind- look!" Vig urged; the gloom ahead seemed to be lightening shade by shade.

Vig began to walk faster, his hope rising as the light strengthened. He could now see vague shapes of the passage wall and the ground became more uneven. "Looks like we'll have to climb."

Roam looked up anxiously as they reached a rocky pile; the light was shining behind it!

"That's daylight," Vig decided, his courage now returned in full measure. He felt about on the rocky pile and found a ledge. "We're going to have to climb now."

Roam resisted a moment but allowed him to set her on the ledge, then he climbed up to her, the light was strong enough to see her face; she had lost her veil and her pale face was streaked with dried tears and dirt.

Together they climbed, their hearts racing till at last the passage opened into blessed daylight. They had emerged from a mountainside that looked down a valley with a wide winding river, the land stretching out beyond the river was flat. Below them, an hour walk away was a great castle nestled into the mountains, much like Bainemere.

"We're in the north!" Vig exclaimed and looked down at Roam. She gazed out in wide-eyed wonder, then blinked painfully in the sunlight and stepped into his shadow.

"Come on, let's hope the inhabitants of this castle are more friendly than the last. We'll need help if we're going to find the others," Vig said. But in his mind's eye he envisioned his companions torn to bits by the baine wilk, laying broken at the bottom of a shaft, or lost forever in the dark.

Sal would tell him to have faith.

Something was pulling at her sleeve and hot breath blew across her face as a splitting headache welcomed Salvage back to consciousness. For a moment she did nothing except try to remember where she was, and why she could see nothing. The thing pulled at her harder. In a rush of panic, Sal reached for her spear, her fingertips found it by her side, and she rolled over, bringing the tip around.

A horse snorted angrily, hooves clattering on stone and Sal flinched then breathed in relief; it was not the baine wilk.

"Cavern, I sure hope that's you!" Sal breathed as she picked herself up and felt about to make sure she had not dropped anything. The giant horse stepped towards her and nudged her chest with its lowered head, nearly knocking her off her feet.

"Alright, alright!" Sal rubbed Cavern's neck affectionately. The horse wore its bridle and saddle. This confused Sal, but she brushed the matter aside for more important things. "Vigil?" she called into the darkness. Her echo was the only response.

Cavern nickered gently as if to say he too was missing someone.

Sal stood for a moment, her heart trembling inside her, "What do I do?"

Cavern nudged her again and her hand snagged on a pack secured to his saddle. "Please tell me you have more salt in here!" Sal whispered, her fingers shaking as she opened the pack and rummaged through it. Finding a small leather pouch Sal first poked the contents, then touched her tongue: salt. Soon she had a glowing rock in her hand and the darkness retreated beyond arm's reach, allowing Sal to feel as though she could breathe again.

She set about searching for any sign of Vig, but found none, it was then she noticed the dried blood and wound on Cavern's flank from the wilk. "We'll get that looked after when we find the others," Sal promised, then she set out, fairly certain she was going the right way. There was no need to take hold of Cavern's reins; he followed her happily.

The light from the moonstone was not nearly as bright or as helpful as Sal wanted it to be, even still she noticed that the further they went, the more rugged the passage became. The floor became drastically uneven while the walls looked less like they had been cut and more like the natural walls of a cave. Although the main passage was always obvious because of its width, offshoots into the darkness became regular, after calling and listening into each one, Sal continued on her way, keeping doubt and fear at bay with silent prayers to the Ancient One.

Pausing in despair, Sal noticed Cavern's ears tip forward. Sal waited, straining her ears; there were voices!

"Hello!" she called, starting forward again.

The voices stopped, and Sal turned a corner; a group of her warriors stood in a large cavity where the passage lost its narrow shape completely. With them was Dire and several of his nitora along with what looked like most of the gillup. All of them were lit in the blue moonglow of stones in their hands; her people… they had done the same as Vigil.

Sal allowed herself to laugh as she was surrounded by familiar faces, but her heart fell after processing who was there, "Where's Theophany?"

Her warriors all looked crestfallen, "We hoped he and Vigil were with you."

"Vig was with me, but we got separated." Sal looked about them, hoping her husband and the prince would step out from the shadows at any moment.

"We've also lost Lady Roam," Dire confessed, his face more distraught than anyone else, "One moment she was with us…"

Sal sighed heavily, thinking of the little girl lost in the dark. "We'll find them," she encouraged, hoping her words were believable even if they sounded hollow to her own ears.

"The baine wilk could have killed her," Dire choked on his words.

Sal grasped his arm, "I don't believe the wilk would have done that. I can't explain why it attacked us, but I refuse to believe that it would harm Roam. I have faith that the Ancient One will not abandon us now, and that I will find Theophany. You too must have faith in the Prince of the Dawn and Dusk."

Dire held her gaze sadly, "The Prince of the Dawn and Dusk will not help me; that would require a sacrifice that I am unable to give."

Sal opened her mouth, surprised by his answer. "What kind of sacri-" Her words were cut off when the bright light of a torch lit the chamber. Sal hissed, words not coming fast enough, but there was no need for orders, everyone's weapons were drawn in an instant as they turned to face the unknown torchbearer.

A stranger, a man the size of Fortress, stood at the far end of the passage, his mouth hung wide open. He wore clothes they had not yet seen, and a whip was coiled at his hip. He spoke in a strange language, his tone conveying astonishment and confusion.

"Well met stranger, we are travellers of the Underway," Sal spoke in the common tongue. Stepping forward and lowering her spear, her heart pounding in excitement. "We encountered a baine wilk recently and got separated from our companions in the dark. We would be glad of your assistance to find them."

"What!?" the man exclaimed in the common tongue, "Travellers of the under-what? Travellers from where? Who in blazes *are* you!?"

Sal and the others looked at each other for help but could not think of an answer.

"Is that a *horse*!?" the man shook his head, "How did you lot get in here!?"

Now Sal was just as baffled, "We… traveled from Bainemere through the Underway- are we on the north side of the Honorfell Mountains?"

The man raised his brows and scoffed, "Bainemere!? You're in the Dinco silver mines of Jarg!"

Sal shrugged helplessly, but Dire's face registered shock, "Jarg?" he exclaimed, "We are in the northlands then!?"

Before the stranger could answer, another giant came along in a hurry, "You're not going to belie-" his words stopped short when he spotted Sal and the others, "More!?" he exclaimed.

The two giants exchanged a flurry of astonished words, while Sal and Dire tried to cut in, "You've found our companions!? Where are they?"

At last, the giants looked at them. "Come with us," they directed, clearly uncomfortable and at a complete loss.

Uncertain what they were walking into, both warrior groups fell into lines behind Sal and Dire, without orders they were ready to fight if things soured. Cavern and the gillup followed without trouble, just as anxious as the humans to get out into the fresh air.

Sal and Dire led their warriors as the giants escorted them through more rough-hewn passages, before long they began to pass slaves working with pickaxes and shovels. They were of different races, some were giants, and some, although their faces obscured in the dark, were Garatin. They all stopped in their work and gaped in awe and confusion as Sal and her company passed by. At last Sal allowed herself to relax and appreciate what must be an extremely odd event.

"How could they not know about the Underway when it leads right into their mines?" Sal whispered to Dire as they walked.

He merely shrugged, his face still bearing the signs of anxiety over Lady Roam.

"You listen here! I am a *VERY* wealthy woman in the eastern courts of Fairthin- and if they hear that the people of Jarg have mistreated me or hindered my quest in any way-!"

The familiar flustered and angry voice of Lady Serene acted like a healing poultice on Sal's nerves. She and the others quickened their pace, nearly overtaking their escorts as they turned a corner. There, waiting in a large chamber, were Lady Serene, her guards, Garden, Sir Fortress, the rest of the gillup and the other Niben and Verlyance warriors.

Addressing them was a very frazzled looking giant who looked like he would rather be facing a wilk than the enraged old lady of Fairthin.

But Lady Serene's face lost all its wrath when she saw Sal and the others. "Oh!" she exclaimed and held a hand to her heart, "My dear girl, you are alive! Tis reward enough for this terrible day!" She held out her arms to Salvage.

Sal accepted the embrace. "Theophany and Vigil- they're not here…" she saw, her worry returning. Nearby she saw Dire go through a similar exchange with his nitora.

Fortress likewise embraced Cavern and inspected the horse's wound with concern. Cavern hung his head over his master's shoulder and refused to let him back away.

"There now, all will be set right," Serene encouraged, patting Sal's back, "With a prayer to your god and a few more words from me, I'm sure these men will aid us." She glowered at the nearby giants.

Sal pulled away in surprise, "A prayer…? But you don't believe in such things!"

"Hush now," Serene brushed aside her comment and fixed her eyes on the giants. "Well!?" she demanded, "Send out men to find the rest of my company! There are still two men and a little girl missing- we must find them!"

"My lady, this is a mine," one of the giants addressed her, "We cannot halt work to search for people."

"Then supply us with torches and we will search instead," Dire answered, stepping forward, his tone and posture at their most intimidating, "Or shall it be known that Jarg opposes nitora from the Niben king?"

The giant's swarthy complexion turned sickly, "Of course not!" But he still hesitated.

Serene huffed, "Who's in charge here!? Take me to your master at once- *Then* I'll settle this!"

The giant looked nervously from face to face, "Yes of course, I will escort you personally into Jarg to speak with my master, Lord Bracer."

"And supply us with the means to search for our companions," Dire added, his tone even deeper.

To Sal's astonishment the giant nodded anxiously. It seemed that Fairthin and the Niben Weald were forces to be reckoned with!

Serene huffed and signaled for her guards to ready a gillup for herself and Garden. The Garatin looked even more run down than the rest of them. The fresh air would do him good.

"I will remain here to search," Sal told her.

Serene nodded in understanding, "I'll have more men here to help before long, I assure you."

"I'll send two of my warriors with you to represent us," Dire explained, directing two of his men to join Serene's guards.

"I too will go with you," Fortress said, gathering Cavern's reins in his large hands. He still seemed shaken from his encounter with the wilk.

Serene nodded then hesitated, eyeing him sternly, "You're not an oathbreaker here too, are you?" she whispered.

"I have never been to Jarg or even this side of the mountains." he assured.

Serene narrowed her eyes. "I'll take that as a no," she turned back to Sal, "Very well, I'll send help shortly." She promised once more then she and those going into Jarg departed with the nervous and bewildered giant.

* * * *

Theophany had awoken before Salvage and had overseen his warriors and the others begin to break camp for the next leg of their journey in the dark. No one had approached the baine wilk or otherwise provoked it.

When the beast attacked, Theoph had panicked with the others. He had run with the others. He had stumbled with the others. He had tripped and called for the others to wait. The footsteps and cries of the others had faded, and now he was alone.

Feeling along the cold walls, his hands became numb, while his feet grew sore from stumbling on the uneven rock. He tried calling out in the dark, but it was to no avail; somehow, he had been completely separated from the others.

After a time, running water echoed through the eerie silence and Theoph's heart leapt in hope; if there was an underground river, then he had but to follow it and surely it would lead him out into the open. He stumbled forward, his confidence returning with each step. This mountain would not defeat him, even the darkness could not deny his power.

The wall he followed fell away and Theoph sensed he was in a larger chamber; the water was nearby. Trusting his instincts, Theoph ventured forward in the dark until his boots splashed into water and relief flooded over him. The smell and echoes of the water in the cave reminded him of the pool beneath the temple in Verlynn Nel. Could it be that Tylus had at last reached out and sent the water to guide him?

Theoph knelt and submerged his hand; the water was frigid, and it numbed his hand further. After a moment he figured out which way the current flowed and felt a moment of doubt; did the river flow from the heart of the mountain and lead into the daylight? Or did it come from above ground and pour into the earth?

"Doubt is for mortal men," he said aloud and turned to follow the current.

"Who are you, if *not* mortal?" an unfamiliar voice asked from the darkness.

Theoph flinched and drew his sword, his heart pounded and the skin on the back of his neck tingled. "Who's there!?" he demanded to know, his voice sounding frightened and weak.

"I am a stranger to you. But I know you well."

Theoph turned slowly, his sword before him. "What do you want?" he asked, sensing it would be no use asking for help.

"An answer to my question. Who are you, if *not* mortal?"

Theoph hesitated; he was being toyed with, but they chose the wrong man! "I am Theophany the Victorious, prince of Verlyance, prophesied king of Verlynn Nel. I do not trade words with cowards who won't even show their face!"

His voice echoed into silence.

Fearing a surprise attack, Theoph moved deeper into the river.

"A warrior, a prince, a prophecy fulfilled. These are mere titles. I ask again; who are you?" the rumble of a threat entered the voice.

"I am more than a title; I am destined to surpass mortal bounds and become-"

"A god?" the voice interrupted, "You think yourself above the ways of mortals?"

Theoph pivoted again, trying to pinpoint where the voice came from, "If I am to lead my people, I must become greater than they are."

"A creature of the sea may aspire to grow wings and fly; but such powers are beyond it. How will you achieve such a transcendence?"

Theoph rejected his old doubts, "The Foretold King has done it; he will instruct me."

Laughter rumbled outward, slow, and pointed. A blue glow appeared before Theoph, growing to reveal the baine wilk in all its glory. It stepped closer, huge paws submerging in the river while its large eyes were on level with Theophany's own. "The Foretold King?" the wilk spoke with the voice of a human, while power and intelligence gleamed in its eyes.

Theoph stepped back, eyes wide.

"You know nothing, not even the worth of your own flesh!" the wilk's lip curled in a snarl, then it leapt at Theoph, its front paws colliding with his chest and forcing him backwards. He hit the water and was pushed to the bottom. Theoph gasped for air and water rushed in. The wilk's head came in after him, its wicked teeth sunk into his tunic and shoulder, and threw him aside.

Theoph landed on the river edge, coughing and sputtering. His hand still grasped his sword and he rolled onto his back, struggling to bring the weapon before him. The wilk was upon him in one great bound, its mighty jaws clamping down on his sword. The blade snapped; the tip flying off into the dark while the shattered hilt was ripped from Theoph's hands.

Theoph rolled over and tried to crawl away, the breath of the wilk hot on his neck. He was pinned forcefully in place by the wilk's paw. "Some will not believe till they have seen," the wilk uttered the words spoken to him in Fishers Hamlet, "others will not see, till they believe."

Theoph struggled to break free, but the wilk leaned more weight on his back, he looked around wildly for a weapon. His eyes were drawn to a silver object reflecting blue light, it lay on the stone before him.

How did the mirror shard come to be here!? Vigil had it last…

In the blue light of the wilk, Theoph beheld his own face; torn and grotesque, rotting flesh peeling away from his broken skull. His terror filled eyes staring back at him.

"I see you plainly, Theophany; and you are no immortal." The wilk tore at his back with its claws and Theoph screamed. Teeth sunk into his arm and flung him aside once more. "A broken man is of no use to me."

Chapter 16 Broken

Hopeless. Salvage turned her gaze from the mine entrance, the early morning light on the mountain side was blinding after four days in the dark and she fixed her eyes on the rocky ground instead. Up the mountain path came Vigil, his face marred with weariness and telltale signs of defeat, with him came those who had been searching along the mountainside; Verlyance warriors mostly, with a few of Serene's promised help from Jarg. Sal did not think she had been hopeful that Vig would have found Theophany, but now she felt her heart sink even lower.

Vig stood before her and made a small, helpless gesture with his hands, the words failing to leave his lips.

"We'll find him," Sal found her familiar role of encouragement extremely draining, and she wondered how convincing her words sounded to the others.

Some of their warriors tried to smile their agreement as they passed her to enter the mine, but the giants from Jarg offered no such kindness.

"Come, we both need to rest," Vig insisted, pulling her to her feet.

"We can't leave the others to search-"

"Our warriors have rested through the night, we have not," Vig cut short her objection, "We'll be no use to Theoph dead on our feet." He began to lead her back down the mountain, "And, who knows? By now someone could have found him and Theoph could be impatiently waiting for us in Jarg."

They were beyond earshot of the others now. "You don't believe that," Sal pointed out, using her spear for support as they walked.

Vig was silent for a few slow strides, the surrounding beauty of the landscape lost on him, "No, but I thought you might."

Their progress was slow, both feeling the strain of their journey, and wondering if their quest had come to an abrupt ending. Soon they passed by run down shacks built of scraps, the ground was littered with stray chains: the sleeping quarters for the slaves that worked in the mines.

As they wound round the mountain and grew closer to the valley floor, the giant city of Jarg came into view and Sal beheld its proud structure, built to impress and welcome traders who ventured down the Arrow river in search of the silver for which Jarg was famous. Yet still, gray, and lonely it looked to Sal's eyes, like the mountains had chased and trapped it against the river. Inside the outer walls of Jarg was a thriving town, growing rich from silver, while richer still the silver barons became. The upper crust of Jarg society lived in the castle itself and ran the town and castle much like a business, for there was no king or even lord of Jarg, only the silver barons. It was one of these men who owned the mine that Sal and the others had found themselves in, and who now acted as their host.

Sal and Vig entered the city through a giant-sized open gate and were greeted with a giant-sized steward who welcomed them on behalf of his master, their host, Baron Bracer. "Friends of the Niben are friends of Jarg," he assured them when they first met. He spoke the common tongue with ease and led them through the town. Sal felt incredibly small in this city built by giants, but unlike Bainemere, there were normal sized homes alongside the giant ones. As they went, Sal half heartedly saw travellers of many different races, though none were from Verlyance.

"I had no idea the Niben were so well respected," Sal commented in their native tongue.

"I understand they're loyal customers," Vig explained, "It's a good thing we fell in with them."

Reaching the castle, they were shown inside to their quarters, Baron Bracer had accommodated them and the others with comfortable, non-giant-sized rooms that all joined in one hallway, meaning that they could easily reach one another. Despite the obviously rich furnishings -most things were either dipped in silver, or even made entirely from silver- Salvage found the castle lack-luster and cold in comparison with the living coral that Verlynn Nel was crafted from. On top of her exhaustion and despair, she felt homesick.

"Have you found him!?" Lady Serene demanded, a note of strain in her otherwise composed voice. The elderly woman must have been waiting for their return, for she appeared from one doorway as Sal and Vig drew near to their own rooms.

Sal shook her head, unable to offer more.

Serene wrung her bony hands in response, "Dreadful!" she muttered.

"Where is Garden?" Sal heard Vig ask as she opened the door to their rooms.

"Sleeping- the poor thing is bone weary," Serene answered. "I told him he'd have more energy if he'd only eat a decent amount-" the woman's voice faded into indistinct murmurs as Sal left the hall. Vig was close behind.

The two of them removed their travel-stained clothes and lay down, feeling as though their feet could not last another moment. They were asleep in mere minutes, but they found little rest.

* * * *

Vigil woke sluggishly. The late afternoon sun on his face and the soft bed under him stole his desire to rise. Even after sleeping the entire first half of the day, Vig still felt exhaustion pulling at his body. He was more tired than he had thought!

Salvage had already woken and now stood on their balcony that looked out over the city; she had not bathed yet and her locks of hair were quite messy. What looked like a tray of roasted meat and giant berries waited nearby, offering a convincing reason to rise. Vig breathed deep and pushed his weariness to the back of his mind.

Forcing himself up, Vig bypassed the meal and went to Sal's side. The balcony afforded him a view of the city streets below and the river harbor where flat bottom boats of all sizes were moored to long wooden docks.

Vig placed a gentle hand on Sal's back- she flinched like a bow string being released, her wild eyes locked with his, "The well!"

"What?"

Sal backed away from him, her face elated and distraught all at once, "the well is on the mountain side- and it's dry!" she began pulling on her clothes muttering breathlessly to herself.

"Sal wait," Vig tried to still her, "you had a vision? What did you see?"

Sal grasped her spear, "Yes; the well- Theoph will be there!" she hurried out into the hall.

Stunned for a moment, Vig hastily pulled on his own clothes and strapped his knives on, excitement flooding over him, he grabbed a mouthful of the roasted meat as he dashed after his wife.

"Quickly Vigil!" Sal urged impatiently at the far end of the hall.

Lady Serene ascended the steps in front of her, guards in tow, "What is it- what's happening!?" Beside her Garden watched with watery eyes.

Sal neglected to answer and rushed past.

"She knows where Theophany is!" Vig explained on his way past them.

Serene sputtered in surprise, "Steward- go with them! Quickly!" she ordered. Vig saw the steward from earlier jump up from a corner and thump after him, a bewildered look on his face.

Salvage did not slow her pace, but charged through the castle, remembering the way on her own, flying past serving girls and ducking under the arms of surprised giants. Vig shouted apologies as he hurried along in her wake.

They burst from the castle and bounded down the front steps. Coming towards them was Fortress, his tired face having little time to register what he thought of their strange race. "We haven't found him yet," he admitted, but Sal shot past him.

"Come! She knows where Theoph is!" Vig called as he and the steward rushed after Sal.

Fortress hesitated, then started after them, his long strides bringing him to Vig's side quickly, "How!?"

"She had a vision."

Fortress threw his head back and laughed triumphantly, "BY MY BATTLE SCARS!" His booming voice drew the attention of towns folk as the trail of people raced towards the mountain gate. Once there Sal slowed to a stop, glancing this way and that, still muttering to herself.

"A well!?" she exclaimed when the steward arrived with Vig and Fortress, "A well in the mountains- where?"

The steward glanced at Fortress and Vig, uncertain, "There is one up on the north glade," he pointed, "we may reach it by nightfall."

"No- closer. Is there a well *closer*?" She was growing frantic.

"Up old miners' road, three miles from here- but it's been dry for years."

Sal's face lit up, "Show me!" and off they went again.

Vigil's heart pounded with excitement and hope, while adrenaline pushed him and the others to cover the three miles in fifty minutes. The path led them into a rocky ravine bare of foliage, at the far end were the crumbling stone walls of the promised well.

Breathless Vig slowed to a stop and scanned the surrounding area, searching the craggy hillsides for a body, or perhaps the opening to a cave. "Search that ridge," he instructed Fortress, "I'll go to far end of-"

"Here!" Sal called sharply, she had gone ahead to the well and was looking into it.

Vig and Fortress rushed to her side, uncertain what they would find. The well would have been deep enough for Fortress to fully submerge in if there had been any water. Although the afternoon sun did not reach the bottom, the shape of a body lay in the gloom: Theophany.

The prince was face down, limbs sprawled and motionless. Sal called to him, her voice ricocheting to the bottom, one of Theoph's legs shifted in response.

Vig leapt up onto the well, "Lower me down," he instructed Fortress and clasped hands with him.

"I have a rope," the giant offered.

"Use it to pull us up," anxious to reach the prince's side, Vig lowered himself down, hanging onto Fortress's large hand and bracing himself against the wall, until the giant could reach no further. Vig held on for a moment, allowing his eyes to adjust, then dropped the last four feet. He stumbled, catching himself with both hands. The ground was wet and muddy; a trickle of water appeared from a dark tunnel and disappeared into an even darker one.

Vig knelt by Theophany's side; his back and shoulder were badly mauled leaving his tunic torn and bloody. He rolled him over, "Theoph!"

Theophany blinked groggily, his face was dirty, scraped and battered, "Vig…?" he moaned, giving Vig hope that a death rite was not necessary just yet.

Fortress's rope uncoiled above them, and one end landed nearby. Sal called down demanding to know what condition the prince was in.

"He's awake," Vig answered while lifting the prince into a sitting position; there appeared to be strange flecks of colored lights laying about in the water. Scooping one up Vig realized that they were in fact the jewels of Verlynn Nel! Vig collected them hastily, knowing their worth and what it would mean to lose even one.

Theoph's head bobbed forward, and he tried to rouse himself. "What happened?" Vig asked.

Theoph could only respond with another groan and a bewildered gaze. As soon as he thought the prince could handle it, Vig fashioned a loop into the rope that then pulled tight around Theoph's chest. In doing so Vig could see the extent of the prince's wounds; it was not the work of a blade or any other human weapon.

Vig watched from below as Fortress hauled the prince up, only when once he was safely on the surface did Vig turn his attention to his surroundings again; Theophany's sheathed sword lay nearby. Collecting it from the mud, Vig realized with a quickening of his heart that there were huge paw prints circling where the prince had lay and drag marks from the dark tunnel where the paw prints led back to.

The rope could not return fast enough for Vigil's comfort as he fearfully watched the darkness. Topside, Sal was checking Theoph over as he sat against the well; he looked much worse in the daylight.

"Go back to Jarg, bring more help and a wagon," Fortress ordered the steward.

"No!" Vig interceded, ripping his attention away from his prince for a moment.

"It would look like a death rite," Sal muttered as she helped Theophany to sip some water and dabbed away at the cuts on his face. Fortress stared back at them in confusion.

"You two go back into Jarg, announce that Theophany the Victorious has been found alive and in good health. Call off the search," Vig instructed, stone faced.

Fortress scoffed, "Alive just barely! He needs a healer-"

"Just do it, Fortress!" Vig snapped, then turned back to Theoph. "The warriors mustn't see you like this," he whispered to Theoph.

"They won't, I'll walk," Theoph managed to say.

"You'll have to."

* * * *

Strings and wind instruments were not common in the court of Jarg, rather the primal beat of drums set a festive and fevered mood in the banquet hall.

Vigil stood on the hall edge, reluctant to join his company at the feasting tables, watching instead from the side like an uninvited guest to the banquet thrown in honor of his own prince. The silver barons sat about a head table, their deep and boisterous voices drowning out all others at times, while their musky smelling mountain ale flowed into monstrous drinking horns.

Accommodated with a long table of 'normal size,' the company from over the mountains sat together looking and feeling small in comparison to the rest of the feasters from whom they sat apart.

Fortress sat at one end of the table, closest to the giants, he joked, laughed, and drank with vigor, his encounter with the baine wilk seemingly forgotten. The Niben were next along the table, the nitora sitting and standing about Lady Roam to create a buffer between her and any drunkard who might wander too close. The girl sat quiet and still as ever, her white veil hiding what she thought of the proceedings, while Dire sat next to her glowering at any rude enough to stare.

Lady Serene was next, she cast lofty and disdainful eyes at everyone aside from Garden, who sat with her. The old man looked vastly uncomfortable, and refrained from touching any food, perhaps only suffering the experience to please Serene.

Then lastly, sitting about the empty chair of honor, were the warriors of Verlyance, they above everyone looked least festive, despite their prince being the reason for the feast. Vig pitied them, they, like everyone else, had been told that Theoph was safe and well, and even though they did not believe this was entirely true, they refused to admit otherwise, even to one another. Vig thought of the salt water that some of his warriors had given up to create light in the caves; had they given up on Tylus too?

Vigil ventured forward, hoping to avoid attention and snag a tray of food to bring back to share with Salvage, who was even now tending to Theoph. Choosing to not make himself known to his company, Vig slipped up to the tables and spotted a likely tray between two banqueters, but his stealth was for not.

"Vigil of Verlyance- where is our guest of honor!?" their host, Baron Bracer hollered from the head table as he stood to his feet- none too steadily. His question was followed with ruckus laughter and hands pounding tables in agreement.

"Come, come-" Bracer went on, "It is not every day we are host to a prince!"

Vig moved closer to his friends, a subconscious response, "My lord, Prince Theophany sends his deepest regrets through me that he can not be here, for our long journeys and trails have wearied him greatly, and he is finding much rest in this, your hospitable castle of Jarg. Truly, tales of Jarg will reach Verlyance on the lips of my warriors!" much to his relief, Vig's countrymen backed up his statement with raised drinking horns and a cheer.

Vig moved to the edge of his warriors close to Lady Serene, in the hopes she or one of the others would take up the conversation and remove any further scrutiny from Theoph.

Instead, Serene cast him a dubious glance, "Weary is one word for it," she muttered.

Theophany had suffered greatly, but his resolve remained, and he walked into Jarg earlier that day, supported only by Sal's spear. It was not surprising to Vig that this façade had failed to fool onlookers. Yet still, Vig was compelled to defend the prince's reputation. "Theophany the Victorious is not bound to mortal ways-" he began to reply in a lowered tone.

"Then why would he be weary at all?" Serene challenged.

Vig was saved from answering when Baron Brace spoke out again.

"Very well, but if we are to suffer the absence of our guest of honor, then may we not learn at last what strange purpose brings you here to Jarg? and! How you were found in the deepest of my silver mines, unaware that you had crossed the mountains at all!" there was more laughter, allowing Vig a chance to formulate an answer.

But there was no need. Fortress released a mighty belch as he stood to his feet, swaying slightly. "A worthy query, my most gracious host, never fear-" he hiccupped, "For there is a worthy answer!" he turned and waved a hand at Vig and his warriors, a wide grin on his less than sober face. "Prince Theophany of Verlyance in the south seas, set out some weeks past, with his warriors mighty, and Salvage fair." Here he winked cheekily at Vig. "They set out in search of the great Foretold King, who's coming was… foretold to them by their sea god."

Vig could not hold back a rueful grin at the giants bumbling efforts to explain their quest, but to his credit, the audience was near entranced.

"Our friends from the Niben joined our company, however, to seek the mysterious Prince of the Dawn and Dusk of legend." He deepened his voice for dramatic effect, gaining a glare from Dire. Vig however, noticed that Lady Roam's head tilted slightly, betraying her close attention.

Fortress went on with another hiccup. "And you have no doubt noticed our aged one!" he flung a hand at Serene, nearly taking out someone behind him. Serene huffed ragefully. "She has sought her whole life, the one known as the Wise One." He paused to down another mouthful from his horn, wiping his mouth and beard before continuing. "Whereas I am on a noble quest to find someone else still, the greatest Warlord in all the lands! I will serve him with my sword and the world will know our namesakes!" he ended by thrusting his horn upwards, this was met with cheering.

As Fortress had spoken, Vig had the vague hope that someone in the hall would jump up and claim to be or know of the Foretold King- even the slave of the Prince of the Dawn and Dusk would raise Vig's spirits at this point! But of course, no one responded to Fortress's speech except to cheer and toast. 'Not till Garatin,' Vig reminded himself with an inward sigh.

Lord Bracer took a long draft of his horn before speaking again, "It would seem to me great sport, if you should find all these titles belong to only one man!"

Fortress along with many others in the hall burst into a round of laughter. "Well said!" Fortress praised and laughed again.

Lady Serene and Dire however, bristled and scoffed at the notion, but Vig did not wish to hear what response they might make. Taking his tray of food, Vig escaped from the hall. As he did, Fortress began to tell of their journeys with more hiccupping, but his voice and the commotion of the hall faded into muted echoes as Vig returned to Theoph's quarters.

He found his wife much as he had left her, slouched in a fur lined chair. Beyond her, through an arch, shrouded in shadows, the prince lay on a bed, his still form looking insignificant.

Sal smirked half heartedly when Vig set the tray before her, "You didn't have to bring the whole thing."

"It won't be missed," Vig assured as he looked past her to Theoph.

Sal frowned, wordlessly agreeing with Vig's unspoken thoughts. Turning his back to Theoph and lowering his voice even more, Vig removed the prince's sword that he had been wearing at his side. "I found this with him in the well." He unsheathed it and saw the same startled expression of alarm on Sal's face that he had felt when discovering that the blade was broken.

He returned the blade to its sheath, "There were wilk prints all around him."

Sal looked pained, "He would tell me nothing."

"Not even to explain why those were scattered about in the mud?" Vig gestured to the pouch of jewels that Sal had been keeping an eye on; they had inspected them carefully and mercifully, found none to be missing.

Sal was quiet, her emotions running wild on her dark face, "Something happened to him in the dark, whatever it was… it broke him."

Silence stretched between them, sodden with unspoken pain and concern.

"I will speak to him," Vig said at last and ventured forward.

Theophany lay propped up, awake. His arms rested at his sides on top of furs laid over him, the bandages that Sal had applied to his arm and hand seemed more painful than his wounds. His face was scrapped, bruised and expressionless as he gazed without focus.

Vig set the sword beside Theoph and expected some kind of response- he received none. "What happened, Theoph?" he asked when he could wait no longer.

Theoph was still for so long, Vig wondered if he needed to speak louder, then a single tear slipped quickly from the prince's eye and darted down his despondent face. It shocked Vig so much he felt the urge to flee.

"I am a lie," Theoph uttered softly, and his eyes turned slowly to meet Vig; it made him uncomfortable. "Courteous didn't hesitate," Theoph went on, "You weren't by his side when the sea pirates attacked- I was. He didn't hesitate, or spare thought for his own safety. He met them head on."

Taking a deep breath, the memories of the sea battle playing out fresh in his head, Vig scraped together a few words. "Courteous was a good warrior… and friend. I know if given the chance he would not regret what he did, because it saved your life."

"I hesitated," Theoph went on as if Vig hadn't spoken at all. "I saw the pirates before Courteous did and I didn't act, not even to warn him. I hesitated because I was afraid… I've been afraid of death ever since the sea stars washed up on shore proclaiming my destiny. I wasn't afraid before then." He turned his eyes away. "Strange that a man should only fear death when once he learns he is meant to be immortal. On that day, the sea priests proclaimed that I would never again know pain, or even bleed…" he took a deep breath, shifting his bandaged arms.

"You warned me what grief does to the soul- and well I know it." His gaze turned suddenly sharp and his tone bitter, "I have known grief, fear and doubt. All these and more that I know I should not, because of who I am. Unbind myself from my humanity- that's what my father bid me to do when he saw my weakness. Strive though I have, I can not do it: I am chained to my grief… my fear. My mortality! I am… a lie."

Vig wet his lips, ransacking his mind for something to say. "We've… we have only to find the Foretold King, he will be able to help."

"I'm sorry Vigil, you above all else have always believed the prophecy about me. But Tylus was wrong; I am just a man and will never be anything more." Theoph dared Vig to challenge the statement with his eyes, but Vig could find nothing worth saying. "I spoke with the Ancient One," Theoph's tone changed.

Vig felt his heart hesitate a beat.

"Through the wilk," Theoph went on, "Or perhaps the Ancient One is the baine wilk; what would I know of the immortals? It challenged my claim to immortality, then stripped the lie from me like the flesh on my back. I am, and only ever was, broken. And all those who ever put their faith in this husk of a man are lost!" Tears brimmed in his eyes, while his voice shook with rage and bitterness- impelling Vig to say something, anything.

"No, we are not lost! *I* am not lost. Whatever you are, broken man, or immortal yet to come into his power; you spoke face to face with a god! All my life I have dreamed of such a thing. I have descended the steps of the temple pool in Verlynn Nel more times than I can count. I have kneeled in over my head in the surf till I have nearly drowned. I have begged any god, friend or foe to hear me and grant Salvage to be with a child- but all I have ever received is silence." Vig caught his breath, shocked at his own honesty, aware that Sal could hear every word. "And now you, unwittingly, have come face to face with a god who not only hears you, but has spoken clearly."

"The wilk spoke very clearly, Vig. I am cursed: I can no more fulfil my destiny than I can redeem my own flesh!" With shaking hands, Theoph tore at the bandage on his arm, laying bare his fresh wound, it was black with rot and stunk of death.

Air hissed past Vig's teeth as he inhaled sharply at the grotesque sight.

"That wasn't there before!" Sal exclaimed, rushing forward from where she had been listening in the archway. She tried to inspect Theoph's arm, but he pulled away.

"Leave me." he ordered. They hesitated. "*Leave* me!"

Vig grabbed Sal's arm, she resisted for a moment, but retreated with him back through the arch.

"What can we do?" she whispered.

"Nothing. Wait, maybe. He must find his own way now."

"The warriors *can't* see him like this- they'll lose faith. They could abandon him!" Sal was working herself into a panic.

"They won't forsake him. They are afraid and confused, but I don't believe they'll give up on him."

"That wasn't natural Vig," she breathed, glancing back to the prince "It's the curse! What if we're too late!?"

He pulled her close and held her firmly in his arms, feeling his own fear rising.

★ ★ ★ ★

Salvage felt like a raw wound left open to a blistering sun, the mere presence of a fly buzzing about would be enough to send her over the edge of an emotional abyss. The noise and bustle of Jarg's river harbor did little in the way of soothing her nerves, and her jaw grew sore from clenching.

It seemed that when they were ready to continue on their journey, they would need to travel down the Arrow river into the flat lands of the north. The boats they would travel on were strange to sea dwellers for they were flat bottomed, had no sails or rudder and relied on long poles to propel them through the swampy sections of the river. Once they reached the plains, they would head due north and reach the Dinco River West marking the borders of Garatin. It would take five, maybe six weeks.

Sal was anxious to be underway again, as she knew many of the others were too. The warriors of Verlyance had rejoiced to be near water again and were eager to sail- if only on a river. Content that early preparations for their departure were indeed underway, Sal left the harbor and exited the city walls. Making her way to the sloping fields where they had been keeping the gillup, she relaxed slightly as the beauty and peace of the country and mountain landscape surrounded her. But this was promptly undone when she reached the fields.

Two men were engaged in a tussle, one was of Serene's guards, while the other was one of her own warriors. Their faces were marred with anger while their blows were meant to do damage.

Spear in hand, Salvage stomped up to them, "Enough!" she demanded. Prying them apart she stepped between them.

Her warrior backed away, breathing heavy and upon recognizing her, he grew shame faced, "I'm sorry Salvage. I bring shame to Verlyance."

She frowned first at him, then at Serene's guard, "Have you nothing better to do than fight amongst yourselves?"

Her warrior bristled defensively, "He spoke ill of Prince Theophany!"

Sal paused and slowly turned her gaze on the accused, inching closer to that emotional abyss.

"I spoke no falsehood," the man defended himself heatedly, "Your prince is a weak fool who pretends to be a god but bleeds like the rest of us- and you're all blind to ignore it!"

Before his final word left his mouth, Sal's spear swung up, the shaft cracking across the man's nose. Blood spurted out in an arch as he fell backwards.

Garden admitted Sal into Lady Serene's chambers, Sal would always find his pale, nearly translucent skin, to be unnerving. It seemed that the bashful old man had been thoroughly claimed by Lady Serene as her personal servant, this further irked Sal.

"She will see you shortly," Garden waved awkwardly for Sal to sit. The chairs in the room had been removed and replaced with pillows instead. Sal declined, her jaw beginning to ache again.

"Salvage, my dear, how kind of you to visit!" Lady Serene glided into the room and placed aside a book she had been reading, "The company of friends is the one comfort at the end of one's life- and mine draws ever closer." She sighed tragically and sank down to sit on the pillows. She gestured for Sal to join her. Sal remained standing.

"My lady, one of your guards may report a broken nose," Sal said without preamble.

Serene's eyebrows rose, "Why might that be?"

"Because I broke it."

"I see," was all Serene said. "In the future, see to it that your men give Prince Theophany the respect he is due."

Serene scoffed, her lofty expression turning to scorn, "Oh is *that* what this is about?"

Sal bristled.

"I will never be able to reconcile why a bright woman like yourself, persists in maintaining the belief that Theophany is some kind of emissary from the gods, sent to enlighten the rest of us! I would say it was pure ignorance on your part, but I know you are far too smart to believe he is somehow immortal; therefore, I must conclude you are simply foolhardy! Now, cannot we talk woman to woman, and leave behind these primitive notions of gods and who knows what else- really you are as bad as the Niben with their Dawn and Dusk Prince!"

Sal's nostrils flared and a fire fought to break through her, "You speak boldly for one who seeks a myth spoken of only in fables for children!"

Serene shot upwards, "How dare you!? Garden, see this woman out!"

There was a pause that pulled them both from their rage when Garden did not respond. The old man had sat down and fallen asleep!

"GARDEN!" Serene called and clapped twice. The old man jerked awake and blinked owlishly at the two irate women. "See her out!" Serene repeated then stormed away.

Garden shuffled forward at a loss, Sal did not wait for him, but instead led the way out into the hall.

"She is an insufferable and self-righteous eel!" exploded from Sal's lips and she immediately felt bad for it when Garden flinched.

"She is… upset over what Baron Bracers said"' he tried to soothe.

Sal glared at him in disbelief and a growing respect; even when he must have slept through the exchange and did not know what had been said, he was still willing to act as peacemaker for Serene! Sal grit her teeth. "What did he say?" she asked at last.

"That we all seek different names and may find that they all belong to one man."

Sal mulled this over for a moment; it was not the first time she had considered this possibility. "What do you think?"

Garden was quiet for a moment, his mouth working without words. "When I was a boy, I was told of one who would come to free my people from the Tarvins, invaders from over the sea. This hero… would become a great king and would be wise beyond all measure. He would be a mighty warrior who knew the meaning of sacrifice." His words were soft, and his gaze grew distant.

Pulled in by the tenderness of his recollection, Sal felt her anger dissipating. "What did they call him?"

Garden shook himself slightly, "If you had asked a week ago, I could not have answered… but that giant in Bainemere spoke a name that seems to fit; Eloi." He worked his jaw for a moment and his watery eyes met hers.

The moment was cut short when the door to Theophany's chamber opened; the prince stood with straight back and head held high. His cursed wounds were hidden under his regal clothing while the bandages on his hands were concealed by gloves. Behind Theoph, trying his best not to look bewildered, was Vigil.

"Salvage, I was about to send for you." Theoph said briskly, no trace of his earlier despair and bitterness to be found. "I understand we'll be traveling down the river- I will inspect the boats we are to take. Is the river fresh or salt? I also want a report on the state of the warriors; I suspect they will be growing restless. I share the feeling." He passed by without pausing and she fell into step behind him with Vigil. Their silent exchange spoke volumes.

The rest of that day and the days to follow, rumors in Jarg abounded about the foreign prince who had been lost, then found, dying one day, and brimming with life the next. 'Perhaps he *is* immortal,' the gossipers said to each other, but these rumors fell flat on Sal's ears; she knew the truth.

Theophany acted as though a different man, or the same, running desperately from himself. He went about Jarg, giving orders, overseeing preparations and generally defying expectations. Serene's men said nothing more against him, and the woman herself kept her council, although she treated all those from Verlyance with chilling indifference, especially Sal. The others in the company also treated Theoph differently, whether from greater respect, fear, or veiled mistrust, they held him at a distance. Theoph did not seem to notice, in fact he appeared to welcome this separation. It was the Verlyance warrior's response that was heartbreaking though, they held their heads high, and never once let on that they knew their prince was pretending. Neither Sal or Vig even tried to talk to Theoph about the curse, or what he had said, the only thing they could do was find the Foretold King as quickly as possible and hope he could make the prince right again.

As a kindness towards the Niben, Baron Bracer provided the company with all they needed for the next stage in their journey with the warning that past the Dinco Mountains (as the Honorfells were called in the northlands,) the common tongue was not spoken, and they would most certainly need to rely on interpreters.

At last, on the eve of their departure, the flat bottom rafts were laden with their supplies, and the gillup were prepared nearby. There was some concern over how well the mountain animals would do in the milder climate of the north, but the company was loath to part with them since they could not imagine returning through the mountains on foot.

Feeling like a bow string pulled taut, Salvage dreamt that night and received her last vision.

It was night and a sky of stars lit a great sea of tall, swaying grass that stretched out to all four horizons. Sal walked northward, alone, till she reached the crest of a small hill, sitting there, with its back to her, was the baine wilk. Without fear, Sal approached and sat next to the huge beast. Together they looked out over a country that was strange to her. A wide river wound its way like a silver ribbon from east to west and beyond it was a great city, glowing in the night.

Glancing up at the massive wilk, Sal realized that there was blood on its muzzle, the prince's blood.

"Why did you do it?" Sal broke the silence.

The wilk was silent for so long Sal believed she would never receive an answer.

"Why did you break the guard's nose?" the wilk countered calmly.

"Because it needed to be done."

This time the wilk only blinked once and continued its watch over the city. "This is the last time you will see me before finding the Foretold King."

Sal's heart quickened at the certainty it spoke with, "Why?"

Again, her only answer was a slow blink.

Sal turned her eyes back on the city; it glowed with the light of a thousand fires and held a hopeful promise. Then, starting faint and growing stronger was the cry of the child. Sal tensed and the wilk's tufted ears twitched forward. It was no longer a single cry, but many -a hundred, a thousand- too many for one heart to bear.

Before her eyes, a black stain leaked from the city walls, with each mile it grew, less cries could be heard and the stars above them began to fall in a shower of silver. At last, the stain covered the whole land and only one, pitiful cry remained.

"A warrior," the wilk spoke suddenly, "Will come to you in your hour of need. Death stalks his steps, but I have claimed him." The wilk stood then, its eyes holding deep sorrow as it turned eastward.

"Wait please!" Sal jumped up and ran in front of it. She found that the wilk was so large it had to bow its head to see into her eyes. And it did.

"The child," Sal pleaded, the single cry in the night breaking over her mortal heart like waves in a storm, "Is it *my* child?"

Whatever was said, from wilk to woman, was not to be shared with any other ear. Before Sal awoke, her forehead was wetted with a lick from the baine wilk.

Chapter 17 The Mission

Courage slapped his leather gloves into his palm impatiently and again scanned the street outside the courtyard of Brier Ridge, where was Wilder?

The horses of the carriage that Lady Loyal and her maid would take shifted, causing the carriage to roll forward a bit. Rage's own horse tossed his head as they waited in the late afternoon sunshine. At least, the sun *would* be shining if there were not so many clouds. Rage glared upwards; he would have liked a brighter day to bid Loyal farewell.

The doors of Brier Ridge opened and Lady Loyal emerged, looking ever elegant and graceful, truly she was the envy of many men. Nothing of the trauma she had endured in the rebel barricade could be detected on her gentle features. Escorting her was a man Rage did not know, and neither did he care, for behind them was the maid servant Dream. All was set then. But where was Wilder?

"May I present, Lady Loyal," the escort said once they were near enough- he was probably a knight of Brier Ridge, it did not matter. Rage bent over Loyal's offered hand then stepped aside to help her into the carriage. Eam followed.

In the back of his mind Rage knew he was distracted and behaving abruptly, he should have said something to Loy, but he excused his own behaviour quickly. He would make it up to her later.

Rage and the escort mounted their horses and soon led the carriage out into the busy street; the whole city was cluttered with people. A Garatin festival was approaching and people from all over had traveled to the city to celebrate properly. Inns were filled, taverns were packed every night and markets were quickly emptied of food. The influx of people meant more riots were bound to follow. It had been four and a half weeks since Rage's last assignment serving under the now dead Captain Splendor, and he wondered what his next assignment would entail.

Once on the move, Rage lifted himself from the saddle and searched the crowded street for any sign of Wilder.

"What is it, my lord?" Loyal's escort asked.

Rage shook his head in dismissal, "Nothing." All the trouble Rage went through to arrange this meeting- on Wilder's head be it if he missed his opportunity!

They made slow progress but once they exited the east city gate, they were able to travel at a reasonable pace towards the gardens of Jes'reel. The sun remained veiled behind clouds, but the air was warm enough to be pleasant and the gardens were coming into their full spring bloom.

The carriage rumbled to a stop where the road curved into the garden, nearby was a popular path where a little stone pavilion could be easily reached. Rage knew the place well, having often visited with his nurse when he was a child. Pink daisies grew in overgrown brambles surrounding the pavilion, providing privacy while the little star-like flowers of Garatin carpeted the ground.

Rage looked one last time for any sign of Wilder, then dismounted and helped Loyal from the carriage, her dark eyes took in the garden while her reserved face lit up; she was stunning.

"I believe I once promised you a tour of the gardens," Rage said, forcing himself to forget Wilder.

"I believe you did, yes." She watched him carefully and he could only guess at her thoughts.

"I ah… realize our last meeting was under less pleasant circumstances."

"I was taken hostage by rebels, my lord. Pleasant is not a word I associate with the experience."

Behind her, Eam stood silent, and head bowed- surely, she had questions about Wilder's involvement. Too bad the scoundrel had not come!

"I will forever extend my deepest apology for what befell you, my lady, and it would still not be enough to convey how I feel. I feared you would come to harm that day." Rage hoped he did not sound like a soldier giving a report.

Loyal averted her eyes, "It was not due to you that my carriage ran afoul of the rebels." She offered him the kindest smile he could have hoped for, "Honestly, I have feared to venture into the city since then. I only agreed to accompany you today because your request sounded so… urgent. I didn't expect you to take me here."

Somehow this soft-spoken maiden had the power to make him feel foolish and crass! Rage cleared his throat, "I confess there are two matters I wished to discuss with you, my lady. I remembered my promise to take you here and thought it most convenient to, ah, well, to come…" he found himself running out of words- what was wrong with him!?

Loyal smiled, "I would be grateful for a tour, my lord," she offered her hand. Rage took it gratefully and they started down the garden path. Loyal's escort followed a dozen steps behind while Eam strayed even further, for this Rage was grateful; he did not need a witness for his feeble attempts at sounding charming.

"These gardens," Rage restarted their conversation with hope things would go more smoothly, "were first planted many years ago and belonged to a keep that has since sunken into the earth."

Loy raised her brows slightly and nodded.

"The history of the keep is fascinating, as well as how it fell into ruin. It belonged to a king many ages past whose lands stretched further than the current borders of Garatin do. He had many sons of whom he entrusted his land to, but they fell into quarrels and warfare broke out. Before he died, the king made a decree that the gardens of his keep should be cared for and maintained so long as there was unrest in his lands."

Loy listened without any sign of interrupting or commenting.

"Generations passed and the keep fell into ruin, but the gardens have always been looked after, as you can see. It goes on further up the hill and is visible to the manors and castles in the city." Rage glanced nervously at the lady by his side and realized with a jolt that he was speaking nonsense.

"My lady, I realise you must have questions about what you observed during the rebel barricade." He interrupted himself and halted on the path.

She said nothing. It perplexed him.

"My presence there must have come as a shock, understand that I was temporarily serving under Captain Splendor of the center barracks, otherwise I would not have been there at all."

Still, she said nothing.

"Then there is the presence of a fellow soldier among the rebels. It must have been disturbing to encounter Wil-"

She inhaled sharply, "My lord, if ever there should come a time when I need know of the work you do in service to Tarva, I am sure you will tell me. Otherwise, I am content in knowing that whatever issues you face, you will overcome them. I have no desire to gossip in court about you; it is surely not my place to know such things or share them."

Rage glanced down at his feet and smiled, "Well said, my lady."

She smiled graciously, "Will you tell me more of the garden?"

Relief flooded over Rage, followed by a sense of ease; she was, without doubt, a true lady of Tarva.

After walking along a path that took them through leafy arches and past stone sculptures, they looped back to the pavilion Rage had envisioned saying his farewell in. But now that the time had come, he was reluctant to utter the words.

"My lady, there is the other matter that I must speak of to you," he forced himself to say as they stopped in the pavilion. He dropped her hand and met her eyes. "I have been assigned a mission in the Cokhawk forest; I will be leaving tomorrow morning."

Surprise registered on her face.

"I was made aware of this mission only this morning, otherwise I would have informed you sooner."

"The Cokhawk," she tried the name, and Rage was reminded that she was still new to the country. "The forest on the west border of Garatin?"

"Yes. I am unsure of the duration of this mission and could be gone for quite some time. My mother of course will remain here in the city to provide you with companionship." He watched her closely, wondering what she had heard of the wild and rebellious forest region.

"It will grieve me to be parted from you my lord, all the more since I can not know the day you will return." Would she really miss him?

"I will… write to you, if that would please you," he offered awkwardly; penning love letters was not something he was proficient in! But her gentle smile was enough for him to commit.

"It would please me, and comfort me to know when I receive your letter that no harm has befallen you."

Then she did know. Rage had not been afraid when he received his mission to enter the turbulent situation forming on the borders of the unconquered Cokhawk, but the idea that Loy would worry for him did give him pause.

"Then I shall write to you daily," he promised and was surprised to find that he meant it. He bowed over her hand and kissed it.

★ ★ ★ ★

Wilderness brushed the large amount of dust from his shoulders that had accumulated due to his precarious position during the carriage ride. Rolling under the carriage and clinging to its underside was a good trick though, one that he would be using again. Rage may pester him that going to such extremes was unnecessary, but if Wilder were to maintain his common laborer appearance among others- then he must never be seen escorting nobility!

The coach and footmen had their backs turned, allowing Wilder to slip past them into the gardens, the top of Rage's head could still be seen as he walked slowly along a different path, Lady Loyal by his side. Making sure he would not be seen, Wilder stepped over flower beds and cut across to a path that ran parallel to the one Rage had taken, a flowering hedge separated the two paths. Wilder stood still and watched through gaps in the foliage as Rage and Lady Loyal passed by; Rage was talking about the history of the garden like a complete fool! The escort from Brier Ridge followed at a respectful distance, then lingering even further behind, came Dream.

His heart suddenly beat quicker, and Wilder found it harder to remain calm than when infiltrating the rebels! He followed Eam, hidden by the hedge, making sure his feet made no sound, and looked for an opportunity to reveal his presence to her without alerting the others.

Ahead a gap appeared in the hedge where damage done many years ago had halted further growth; it would be enough to step through. Reaching the gap before the escort from Brier Ridge, Wilder waited silently and noted a large flower blooming in the gap.

He waited till Eam approached, then reached out, intending to be seen, and plucked the flower. Eam peered curiously through the gap as she passed by, then her steps faltered while her mouth opened in surprise.

Wilder bowed his head, embarrassed, and fiddled with the flower, "Good morrow, my lady."

She breathed an astonished laugh, then cast her eyes fearfully after the escort. "And what are you today? Soldier, miller, or rebel?" she asked boldly, taking a cautious step back.

He was dressed as any common laborer, as he had to be, but he wished he could have donned a soldier's uniform to set her mind at ease, "Whatever my guise, I have only ever intended to be your friend."

"You were among the rebels who held my mistress and I captive," she countered.

"Allow me to explain, please," he held his breath for her response.

She glanced again at the retreating escort, then a daring expression came over her and she stepped forward, "I don't know what to make of you, but you have saved my life more than once, for that reason I will listen." She held out her hand to be helped through the gap.

Wilder smiled in relief and helped her join him. "I am a soldier, and have served alongside Sir Courage, you are not mistaken in this. I am and will *forever* be loyal to Tarva."

Her face changed with realization. "You were spying on the rebels!" she exclaimed too loudly.

He flinched and held up a hasty finger to warn her while glancing about to make sure they were alone. She clapped a hand over her mouth, her eyes wide.

"I do many things in service to Tarva- none of them are for the ears of others!" He found that he had grabbed one of her hands and was holding it tight.

Her face changed under her hand, and he realized she was holding back a giggle, he had to smile too. "How long were you with them?" she breathed, excitement and wonder lighting her face, "Are you *still* with them!?"

He breathed a laugh at her innocent curiosity, knowing full well he could lose his head for telling her anything. "I can not tell you more- you might come to harm because of it."

He watched her, clearly thinking back to the day of the barricade- the day he had killed Splendor… would she accept that part of him?

"One of the rebels warned me the governor's life was in danger," she recalled, searching his face.

He nodded, "The governor is safe now. You had a hand in saving his life."

Her eyes faltered for a moment. "You told us that you would get us out safely," she watched him, her curiosity growing again, "Were you meant to sabotage the barricade?"

"Believe me, the less you know the better!"

She looked at him as if seeing him for the first time, a smile playing at the corners of her mouth.

"I couldn't let you believe that I was a traitor though- please believe it was near torture that day; if it would have made a difference, I would have fought every last rebel to see you to safety!"

"Just me?" she was being playful now!

He held her gaze, willing his feelings to be understood, yet fearing they would be.

She blushed and pulled her hand away, "What about the time you disguised yourself as a miller and came to the kitchen of Brier Ridge?"

He felt his own face growing flushed, "I'll confess, that was not in service to Tarva. Merely to you. I feared that you were in danger from… the young lord of Brier Ridge." The memory of the man made his anger flare for a moment, "I still worry in fact."

"You needn't," she assured, the playfulness suddenly absent. "Lord Eloquence has sent his son away, he does not want Lady Loyal bringing the wrath of Sir Courage upon him," she said carefully.

Wilder allowed a sigh of relief; many a time he had worried over the matter. "I will rest easier knowing you are far from his touch."

Eam nodded, then dismissed the unpleasant topic and returned to her playful demeanor. Rolling her lips in and holding her hands behind her back, she slowly circled him, "Your explanation of your actions is convincing, but it leaves one matter that I am unsure of."

"What is that?" he expected more banter.

"Why should you be so loyal to Tarva?" she asked pointedly, "What have they done to deserve you." Bitterness played behind her eyes. It took Wilder by surprise.

He bowed his head, "It is I who have never felt deserving. You hinted once that your father is lord of Brier Ridge."

Sunshine fell from her face and a shroud of shame replaced it.

"I know well the pain that comes with such a thing." He could not keep his emotions from thickening his voice. It seemed he would never have a clear mind when in Eam's presence! "My father is Lord Avail." He saw the recognition down on her face; Avail came from an old line of lords and was well respected in the court. "He did not marry my Garatin mother, and she died when I was young. I was raised with my half brothers as their playmate." He paused, the memories of the bruises and cuts he received after 'playing' with his half brothers made him wince. "But when we approached manhood, our father denied me his name and cast me from his house."

She watched him with unblinking eyes.

Wilder cleared his throat and managed to meet her gaze, "All I have ever wanted is to prove I am worthy of his namesake, to prove I am a worthy son of Tarva. I may have been denied by Tarva, but I can not deny it in return."

"I was right," she said softly, "they don't deserve you."

Wilder blinked in surprise.

The sound of Courage's voice drew near once more- still talking of the Garden. Eam shook herself and started back to the main path.

"May I come see you again?" Wilder asked in a rush, his heart pounding wildly.

She paused, her gaze downward, "Who will you come as?"

"Myself."

She smiled, "I look forward to it." She understood him, he could tell. No one else ever had, and for that reason, he understood her.

The carriage slowed as it entered the city and the crowds overwhelmed it, Wilder knew that Rage would be parting ways with the carriage soon. His arms began to tremble from holding himself above the road. When he felt the crowds would be sufficient to blend into, Wilder released his hold on the undercarriage and dropped to the cobbled road. He lay still as the carriage rolled over him, then sprang to his feet.

Courage sat atop his horse, hanging back to take a different road. Wilder brushed his shoulders off and approached him, trying his best not to look too smug.

Rage stared for a moment, then laughed heartily.

Bashfully, Wilder took Rage's horse leads as if he was a stableboy leading his master through the streets. "I told you I'd be around."

Rage shook his head, still laughing. "So, you did, you knave!" for a moment the two men allowed the silence to grow comfortable.

Did Splendor's betrayal still bother Rage?

"Well, lead on, my horse needs to be watered," Rage declared airily.

As humbly as he could, Wilder began to lead Rage's horse through the streets towards a nearby inn he knew of that was common for travellers to stay at, so although it would be busy, it was unlikely someone would find the two conversing to be suspicious.

"You spoke to the copper haired maid then?" Rage asked lazily.

It irked Wilder to hear the Tarvin refer to her in such a way- perhaps Rage was aware of it. "Indeed. I'm indebted to you for arranging the meeting."

Rage snorted, "I assumed you would make your presence known- were you there the whole time?"

Wilder allowed himself to smile, pleased that he had been able to fool Rage. "I'll leave it to your imagination."

Rage snorted again.

Soon they approached the inn, the courtyard was cluttered with wagons and carts, the establishment obviously filled, but the water trough kept near the street was full.

Rage tossed a coin to a stable hand and Wilder allowed the horse to drink.

"You know I'll be leaving tomorrow," Rage said as he dismounted and made a show of checking his horse over. To onlookers it would seem the two were only talking about his horse's health.

Wilder nodded, "I suspected as much; where?"

"Cokhawk."

They were quiet.

"Has Multifarious given you another mission yet?" Rage asked, his tone carefully low.

"No, just regular reports on the rebel's movements. They have disbanded mostly, Anifest was badly shaken when… when she lost her informant. But with all the country folk in the city for the festival, I expect her to begin something again."

Rage sighed, dismissing the topic, "Well, I trust you'll keep the city in one piece for when I return."

"If I'm here at all."

Rage gave him a funny look, "What's this? Not afraid the rebels will find you out, are you!?"

Wilder smiled half heartedly and shook his head, he supposed Rage would not understand the unrest stirring in his own heart.

"What other reason could you have for leaving Garason? It's not like Farious will send you elsewhere."

"*I* may decide I've had enough of this tired old city and leave!" Wilder dared to speak the sudden impulse.

Rage was stunned for a moment, then laughed, "Not likely! This city is in your blood- you'll never leave it!" he clapped a hand on Wilder's shoulder.

Wilder smiled, he did his best, anyway. Rage sensed his lack of enthusiasm and cleared his throat, "I should be off, stop mucking around and make a name for yourself while I'm away- will you?"

Wilder grinned, "With you out of my way, it'll be easy."

Rage climbed back into his saddle and looked down at Wilder like an arrogant Tarvin considering how much to pay for the peasant's trouble, "Don't get used to it, when I'm back you'll have to put up with being the second best again." He flipped him a coin then backed his horse away.

Wilder caught the coin single handed and watched with a half-hearted grin as the Tarvin rode away; who would have thought the city would feel colder without him?

The gray clouds overhead grew darker, and rain flew with the wind.

* * * *

The storm broke overnight, rolling thunder and sheets of rain assaulted the city of Garason, but it was not enough to dampen the riots that came in the morning. Angry shouts and crowds of Garatin rioters spilled from the center of the city while Tarvin soldiers did their best to keep them contained. Damage was done to taverns and carriages passing through, the rioters did not care if they belonged to Tarvins or not. Many of the nobility made plans to leave the city and escape the unrest, while others were trapped. Even in the streets surrounding Brier Ridge the occasional groups of young men would pass through, shouting for justice and looking for trouble, all the while the uproar from the center of the city could be heard between the rolls of thunder.

"When will we go to market?" Mayhap asked and jumped in fright when a crack of thunder closely followed a lightning strike on the south end of the city. The simple furnishings of the gatehouse rattled in response and Dream squeezed the girl closer to her side.

"I don't think we'll get the chance today," Eam explained as another group of wet and muddy young men passed by; they carried makeshift clubs.

"No one ought to be going out today- not while this is happening," the gatekeeper said sourly, as he stood watching the street from a window.

"Because of the storm?" Mayhap asked.

Eam reminded herself that the girl could not see the angry faces and bloody weapons of the rioters outside. "And the riots; we'll just have to wait."

"Why are they angry?" Mayhap asked, growing impatient.

Eam glanced at the gatekeeper, "Maybe the festival."

The gatekeeper scowled, "I hear the rebel leader was killed in the night; her head left in the street to be seen by everyone. So much for their rebel queen."

Eam gasped and looked down at Mayhap, the girl had a horrified and disgusted expression.

"The rebels will find someone else to lead 'em soon enough," the old Tarvin gatekeeper muttered as he shut and bolted the window. "You two better go back now while the rains not so bad."

Her mind reeling, Eam took Mayhap by the hand and led her outside, the girl was silent as they ran along the path back to the kitchen door. Suddenly the rain increased, soaking their clothes and hair. Mayhap squeaked and pulled on Eam's hand to go faster; the kitchen door was just ahead of them.

Sheltered from the wind now by the walls of Brier Ridge, Eam glanced up and stopped, her feet planting themselves in a puddle. Mayhap lurched to a stop, held back by their clasped hands, "Come on!" she urged; she could not see what Eam saw.

The kitchen door stood out slightly from the walls, allowing a person to stand under an arched roof just beyond the door. The wall around the door was overtaken with ivy, the leafy vines creating a curtain above the arched stonework of the door.

Parting the ivy slightly, holding a casual finger to his lips, was Wilderness. After meeting her gaze, he slipped back behind the ivy, completely hidden.

"Come on!" Mayhap pulled at her arm.

Eam made herself approach the door, all the while gazing upwards, "You go on and dry yourself by the fire," Eam instructed opening the door and nudging the girl inside. Eam stepped back to inspect the door arch, she discovered the ivy hid a nook above the door.

Wilder gazed down at her, a crooked smile slipping across his face, "You said I could come see you."

"I didn't think you would come a day later!" she smiled broadly, her heart suddenly soaring inside while her mind raced ahead to wonder what would come of this. "How did you know of this?" she questioned, inspecting his hiding place further.

"A soldier must know many things about his environment" he repeated what he had once said to her- it seemed like ages ago! He offered her his hand to pull her up.

Without hesitation this time, Eam took his hand and with his strength to aid her, she scrambled up to sit beside him. It was a tight fit, and to keep from slipping off either side of the arch, they had to sit close to each other.

"You do understand why I must be so secretive- I can't just come to the door," he spoke in soft tones so as not to be overheard.

"Of course, I imagine you would fall into trouble if one of the rebels saw you here." She searched his face in the greenish light that was filtered through the vines and found that there was a sorrow and weariness to be found there. "I heard what happened to the rebel leader…"

He bowed his head, his jaw becoming tight, "Anifest would have led the country into further bloodshed if left unchecked."

"She… she was assassinated?" Eam murmured, wondering how they could be talking of such things.

A muscle in his face twitched and he met her gaze hastily, earnestly, guiltily. A chill ran up Eam's spine; who was this man?

"I do many things in service to Tarva, I thought it was for the sake of loyalty, for peace. I'm afraid of the price I must pay though." Fear, anguish, shame, it was all present on his face.

Eam realized that he had come to her for help, comfort, reassurance. Her heart thudded out of control, "You did it?"

His face broke and tears spilled from his eyes, "I'm afraid of who I am Eam."

"You needn't be," she whispered, laying her hand on his. Though she was terrified, her heart told her she knew the truth. "You have saved my life more than once and have done the same for others many times- I have no doubt! I may not know of your other deeds, but I know what you have done for me. Whoever else you may be, you are a good man! And I'll live with the consequences if I'm wrong."

They searched one another's face, no pretences, no secrets between them. He pulled her into a breathless embrace, his tears falling on her skin as he buried his face into her shoulder. Doubts clamored at her faith in him, but Eam shut her eyes and clung to him in return.

"I don't deserve you!" he managed to say after a moment and pulled away.

"I told you, it is Tarva that does not deserve you. It is this cursed city that will beat us both into the dust before it is satisfied! If I only had the chance, I would leave… All the things that would be different if only…"

"Where would you go? Pethen? Finsin?"

"Oh no, I would go much further, I would go where… where I could run for miles and never see the flag of Garatin or Tarva! Where I would not have to worry about pleasing one person or another. Where I could breathe freely and know I was safe." She closed her eyes, the longing welling up inside her, "Wherever that place is, that's where I'll go."

"That sounds like something worth chasing."

Eam rolled her lips in, her tears spent for the moment. "Would you chase it with me?" she asked, trying to sound lighthearted, but she knew that her heart was laid completely bare before this man. Whoever he was.

The air grew thin, and all need for breathing seemed to have been forgotten. "For as far as our feet may take us," he whispered and hesitantly bowed his head over hers. She met his kiss ardently. The world beyond their embrace, forgotten.

* * * *

Captain Multifarious had never been accused of being a coward, he had been called other, equally unsavoury things, but never a coward. He had served in the Tarvin army since the age of thirteen, patrolled the northern borders for five years, trained men in Larsanne, Nirin and Garason. Fought roving bandits in the north, pirates on the sea and giants in the south. Never once questioning his orders, never once compromising his loyalty to Tarva. Never once acting the part of a coward.

He stood in his barracks office, feet wide apart, facing the window as the steady, now straight falling rain, drenched the street beyond. Dusk would come early that evening, it was fitting. Darkness, for dark deeds.

The riots continued, and would continue through the night, men that he had trained through the years would be among the casualties in the morning. Farious had warned the governor.

They will not be frightened by this, he had said, *it will enrage them.*

But the governor's mind was made up; one last message from the Rebel Queen to her followers. And now the city was outraged, and there was no question as to who was responsible, they knew Tarva had silenced their queen, left her head in the street. There was enough outrage to restart the war.

Maybe that's what the governor had wanted all along. Maybe that's why Farious had received his next order. Farious turned away from the window, a muttered curse on his lips; it seemed he was the only one who wanted peace!

"You sent for me," a quiet voice said from the window.

Farious turned calmly, despite everything, a smile tugged at the corner of his lips, "There is yet need of you."

Wilderness carried a rag he had snagged from someone's window and now lay it down on the floor to soak up the rain dripping from his vagabond clothes. He stepped to one side of the window, in the darkest part of the room where he would be able to duck behind the suit of armor should someone open the office door. No one would though.

"A company of foreign dignitaries and royalty have arrived in the city from the south." Farious could not waste time, "The governor fears these foreigners will stoke rebellion in the people."

Wilder's expression was hidden to him, "Why? What do they want?"

"They came looking for a king newly come into power." The weight of his words dampened the already oppressive atmosphere. "The governor has bid them stay in the city while 'he makes inquiries,' but they have declined and returned to their camp outside the city to the north."

Earlier that afternoon, messengers on horseback running wild had been sent between the Governor's castle and every Garatin lord. A single question demanding an answer; is there a usurper among you?

With Anifest dead, it was anyone's guess as to who would lead the rebels next, if any of them were to rise up and be proclaimed ruler, it would have been her. The uncertainty surrounding the issue made it difficult to make decisions, even still, Farious could not help but feel that the governor had made a mistake. He was glad Rage at least had been able to leave the city.

"You know how volatile the city- the country is at present. If even a drunkard stood up and proclaimed himself king; the people would follow him. Now with foreigners from the far south seeking a new king foretold to them by their gods… these are dark times Wilder."

"What would you have me do?" the man in the shadows asked.

"Find the camp of these foreigners, watch them, infiltrate them if possible. If they contact anyone claiming to be a king, kill him. Quickly, before he can amass a following." Farious caught up his cane from his desk and inspected it, the bitterness of his next words causing him to swallow hard, "It's unlikely this will happen though... are you familiar with the Eloi-man prophecy?"

Farious knew that Wilder did not consider himself to be Garatin, and he wondered how much of the culture he had refused to learn or even take interest in. In the shadow a single nod of Wilder's head was the only answer he received.

Farious wet his lips; further explanation was not needed then. "Your main mission is to watch the foreigners until they have left these lands, and deal with any 'king' they may find. However, if the opportunity presents itself..." Farious drew a deep breath and straightened his shoulders; a soldier follows orders. Wilder, more than anyone knew that; *he* had already killed for Tarva that day. "You are to join the soldiers and private guards of Garason in the cleansing order; kill any Garatin male child, of common blood, under the age of two."

Wilder did not react. Rain beat upon the outside walls and soaked the area before the window.

"This order is to be carried out tonight between sundown and sunrise. Don't be seen; I prefer you to be untainted by this." Farious halted, realizing how hypocritical his words were. "Your priority tonight and the days to follow are to watch these foreigners until they leave, I don't expect you'll have the chance to carry out the second mission."

Farious found he could no longer look at Wilder, he lowered his eyes and swung his cane like a pendulum; the governor would regret this. They all would. "That's all."

Wilder took his time returning to the window.

"I would... keep clear of the city, for a time," Farious advised softly, "I don't imagine it will be a safe place for young men known in the rebel community."

Wilder hesitated, his back to him, and Farious wondered if he would refuse orders. Then Wilder slipped into the night.

Farious breathed deep; Wilder was a good soldier. He did not question orders. No one had ever called Farious a coward, but for the first time in his life, he wished he *were* coward enough to hide from the morning that would follow the genocide.

★ ★ ★ ★

Dream lay awake in her bed, the storm kept the rest of the servants awake, while the memory of Wilder's kiss kept Eam awake. Who was this man she had given her heart to?

She rolled the stone he had once given her over and over in her hands, its edges, rough and smooth, now familiar to her. What would her mother say when she found out about her lover? Even the unpleasant reminder of the last time her mother had reacted to a lover was not enough to dampen Eam's light heart.

A sharp crack of thunder, reverberated through the walls, rattling the simple furnishings of the servant quarters. In a nearby room, Mayhap's little brother, Fin, began to cry. Eam waited to hear his mother comfort him, or for Mayhap to hush him in annoyance.

A startled scream of a woman split the night, followed by…

Eam sat bolt upright, eyes wide, straining through the darkness. Heart thudding rapidly. Ears picking up every last, hideous sound. Paralyzed, Eam had no choice but to listen as more screams erupted, then were silenced. Fin cried no more.

Mayhap's terrified shrieking started next. Eam rose, the stone fumbling from her hand, her movements clumsy and painfully slow. Reaching her door, her hand shook and felt numb, but she pulled the door open just the same.

"Leave her!" Eam's mother demanded, panic and shock lacing her words, while Mayhap still screamed.

A group of Brier Ridges guards stood about, one lantern among them, and swords grasped in each hand. Faceless they appeared to Eam, washed out by the sea of blood spilling from the room Mayhap shared with her mother and brother.

Eam's mother was cornered in the hall, wrapping her arms about Mayhap, who's sightless face was twisted in horror. The guards were in a state of confusion, their swords stained, and their hands grasping for Mayhap and the woman who held her.

A clumsy sword, a man in shock, or an evil plot.

Whatever the reason, Mayhap was stabbed. Her little body swallowing the blade stained with her own mother's blood. The sword passed through with little resistance, and pierced Eam's mother where she stood, pinning them both to the wall.

Eam watched, rooted, trapped, entranced. Every moment lasted an eternity. Every moment tore down a brick in the wall of her mind, exposing her to the dark.

Chapter 18 Foretold

"Where is he?" Vigil asked.

"In there! Oh, do something!" Lady Serene fussed, her hands fluttering from her staff to her heart.

Vig ducked into the tent that Jarg had so graciously given to them, among other comforts that had made their four-week crossing of the plains much easier. Inside the tent, the late morning sun filtered through the orange fabric, creating a warm and cozy atmosphere. Serene's belongings were artfully arranged inside, including her bed roll, crowded with pillows, and next to her bed, was Garden's.

The old, pale man lay under a blanket, his body looking insignificant while his face was sunken, and eyes closed.

Vig hesitated a moment, the words of a death rite springing to his mind. He kneeled beside the old man and found that Garden was still breathing, but it was shallow and weak.

"Garden?" Vig said softly, laying his scarred, warrior's hand on the old man's bony shoulder.

Garden's breath quickened and his watery eyes opened, vague confusion crossed his face until his eyes came to rest on Vig.

"You're sleeping late these days," Vig commented lightly, watching Garden with an eagle eye.

"Just tired, did too much yesterday. I'll be alright…" his frail body tensed as he tried to sit up.

Vig hastened to help, "You gave Serene a fright just now, she thought you had died in your sleep."

Garden sighed, an indulgent smile playing on his face, "That woman…" he muttered.

Vig grinned in return, fully understanding, "It's about time you beheld your homeland in the daylight, wouldn't you say?"

Garden's eyes instantly misted, as if just remembering that they had crossed the Dinco river in the night and were now in the land of his birth. He tried to rise, his limbs shaking terribly and his strength insufficient for the task.

Vig tried to help him for a moment, feeling like a metal worker's tongs trying to pluck a flower, then at last, sensing that Garden was growing frustrated at his lack of progress, and anxious to be outside, Vig picked him up. He carried him through the tent like a child and stooping through the doorway stepped out into the sunlight.

Garden released a gentle, almost pain ridden sigh as his eyes swept over the land before them. The land of Garatin was a fair country of rolling hills blanketed in heather and pocked with groves of broad-leafed trees. It was a country for farmers and herdsmen, where deer, field mice and rabbits abounded in great numbers. The sun shone merrily down on the landscape, and due to the hill, they had camped on, they beheld in the north a great city, rooted in the hills.

To their right, the small village of Marsuthe, haphazardly arranged, sat by the shore of the wide Dinco river. Thanks to the map that had also been gifted to them in Jarg, Vig knew that they were situated along the middle of Garatin's south border.

"Garason," Garden whispered, his eyes fixed on the distant city.

"We should reach it tonight."

"Garden!" Serene exclaimed as she approached them, "Tell me you are all right!"

Garden nodded as best he could, and feeling that he was now up to it, Vig set him on his feet. "I am only tired; I will be fine on the morrow. And how could I not!" a jubilant smile spread across his face as his watery eyes let spill some tears, "I am home!"

Serene smiled with him, but her worries were still present. "Indeed, we are friend- and well on our way to finding the Wise One." She cast Vig an indulgent look, "Or whomever." She led Garden away to where she would oversee him eating his breakfast.

Vig watched them totter away, his own heart heavy with worry.

"Do you realize where Salvage is?" Fortress asked, a humoured expression on his large face as he lumbered over.

Vig frowned, trying to guess at what joke the giant was playing at. "Do I want to know?"

A woman's painful moan came from the far side of their camp, followed by soothing words that sounded suspiciously like Sal.

Fortress raised his eyebrows and tipped his head in the direction of the disturbance, "See for yourself, it's not for the faint of heart though."

With trepidation Vig ventured across the camp, hesitating outside Theophany's tent, then pressing onward. Leaning on Sal's spear was a young woman with the fair skin of a Garatin. She wore the simple, stained clothes of a commoner and her face was marred in pain. She breathed through tight lips and released a gasp. A man by her side, Garatin as well, supported her with both hands, his face twisted in concern.

Bent over, Salvage probed the swollen round belly of the Garatin woman, "The baby is in the right place," she proclaimed, "If you could understand the common tongue, you would know that's good news." She smiled warmly at the couple.

Vigil shook his head in disbelief at his wife; didn't they have enough to worry about?

"Stay with us for a time." Sal insisted, trying to make herself understood, "Rest." Sal backed away, nodding for the couple to stay put; Vig doubted the woman would be able to move much in any case.

Sal turned to Vig, "Where's Garden? I need a translator!"

"Sal, what are you doing?"

Sal huffed, "Helping this poor woman! They were trying to pass by when I heard her in agony."

"What do you know of childbirth?" Vig asked, sensing his wife had already won whatever kind of disagreement this was.

"I know enough to see that she'll give birth soon! Now get Garden! See who among our warriors has experience in this."

"Garden isn't doing well," Vig halted her enthusiasm.

"Is he…"

"He's alright for now- Serene thought he had died in his sleep though."

"I knew he was getting worse," Sal muttered.

Vig lay a hand on her shoulder, "Let them take care of themselves, Garden may have need of your healing abilities before long."

She shrugged off his hand and started into the camp. "I have to help them Vig; what other chance will I have to experience childbirth?" she asked flippantly and turned her back.

Glancing at the couple, Vig threw his hands up in frustration; how was he supposed to respond to that!? He went after his wife in exasperation.

Garden did act as translator, explaining to the couple that Sal and one of the Verlyance warriors would examine the woman. Garden grew embarrassed when he realized what kind of 'examination' they meant. The couple seemed hesitant to accept the offer, no doubt fearful of the dark-skinned strangers, but in the end, the woman went with Sal and her warrior into a tent.

Vig stood nearby, shaking his head and muttering to himself when Theoph emerged from his tent for the first time that morning. He wore gloves and a cloak that he kept close to himself, the warriors were told it was because he had difficulty adjusting to the cooler climate. Vig doubted they believed it.

The cloak was to conceal the growing heart stain that plagued the prince's skin. The very thought of it sickened Vig. Theoph had taken to carrying pouches of sweet-smelling flowers to mask the stench of rot that hung about him.

"What is going on?" Theoph asked in a subdued manner, he had hardly spoken since leaving Jarg, consumed as he was.

"Sal can't say 'no,' that's all," Vig answered, unable to look at the prince for long; their interactions had been curt and tense, "A woman on the road was heavy with child. Sal is tending to her now."

Theoph frowned, "Well, we can't stay long. We need to break camp and reach the city as soon as possible."

Vig bowed his head, "Of course, I'll have our warriors begin packing at once."

Camp was broken quickly; thanks to the practice they had accumulated during the past several weeks. Everyone was anxious to reach the city, anticipation permeated every movement, every breath like a thick fog over a restless sea.

Even as Sal exited the tent with her warrior, the pregnant woman and Garden, (who had been called in after the examination) Vig was helping to take the tent down. "We need to get on the move," Vig urged Sal.

"They're coming with us," Sal informed.

Vig sighed, "Don't we have enough to concern ourselves with?"

Sal was immediately defensive, "Mid and Fav are on their way to Garason, why wouldn't we allow them to travel with us? And Mid will give birth any day- they are far from home- she'll need help!"

Vig surveyed the couple; they seemed harmless and… simple minded. Not concerned with a great burden of fulfilling prophecies. "Just don't forget why we're here," Vig gave in, "by tomorrow we could be in the presence of the Foretold King. Theoph will need us."

Sal nodded soberly.

Lady Serene approached, head held high, worry-lines still deep in her face over Garden. "Who are they!?" she asked, eyeing the Garatin couple disdainfully.

"Just travellers on their way to the city," Vig responded as he helped collapse the tent.

"They're coming with us on the road," Sal explained coldly.

Serene sniffed indifferently and avoided acknowledging Sal.

Vig hesitated in his work, watching the two women nervously, their interactions had been short and brittle ever since Jarg.

Sal and Serene stood about for a moment, avoiding each other's gaze, then both turned and walked in opposite directions.

Vigil shook his head and went back to work.

They made good time that day, even the gillup and Fortress's horse seemed to sense their quest was nearly complete. As the road dipped and weaved through the hills, the city of Garason disappeared and reappeared along the horizon, tantalizingly far until they crested one last hill and found it suddenly close.

Whoever they were to find in the city, be it prince, king, warrior, or aged sage, they would soon come upon them. The road from Marsuthe was well traveled and busy with foot traffic. It seemed a large number of the pale skinned Garatins were on their way to the city, it was learned from Mid and

Fav, the pregnant couple, that it was the time of a festival and country folk for miles were coming into the city.

Garden, having his first chance since he was a boy to converse in his native language, found it difficult and often stumbled on the words; Mid and Fav were patient with him though. This was not the only thing of concern around the old Garatin, he did not regain his energy that day, and rode on a gillup the entire way. A gillup had also been made free for Mid to ride, Sal had insisted, otherwise the couple would have been left far behind.

The diverse company, with their strange mountain beasts, giant on a giant horse, Niben bearing on their shoulders a pale child on a litter- drew many curious onlookers. Many of the other travellers stood to one side to allow them to pass, while others stared with open mouths.

The day, although having started bright and cheery, turned overcast, with great storm clouds building to the west. So that when dusk found them, they set up camp expecting rain in the night. The city of Garason was merely an hour away, but the company decided it best to camp on the road and approach the city in daylight. The city itself was larger than any had expected, its massive walls encompassing castles and palaces beyond count; the foreigners could only guess how many lived in the impressive city.

"We'll have to send someone in to locate whoever is in charge," Lady Serene said as they made plans for the morning. "It won't do to just wander about the streets!"

"Agreed, the less time we spend in the streets the better," Dire added, "I expect it to be quite crowded." Beside him Lady Roam was completely still, her feelings on their journey's end, was a mystery.

"Who will speak for us I wonder," Fortress asked with a smirk, "better yet, for whom will they say we seek?"

Serene huffed, "We will just have to explain who we're all seeking- and then we'll see who we find!" she smiled primly to herself, "I, as the most learned among us will speak on behalf of us all."

Fortress rolled his eyes, "Yes, then you can ask after the Wise One first."

"Oh, the order I ask in doesn't matter!"

"I will speak for us," Theoph interrupted from where he stood, apart from the others. "I have come the furthest, if not for my quest, the rest of you might not be here."

Everyone took offence to this, but Theoph waited for them to quiet again. "It was my presence that gave Lady Serene the direction she was to travel in. If not for our company, Lady Roam and the Niben could have been overtaken by the mountain men. Without us, the prophecy from the seer told to Fortress would have been incomplete."

They tried to argue further but could not.

"I will speak for us," Theoph repeated.

That had been the end of the discussion, no one raised the issue that their interpreter was practically dead on his feet. Vig and Serene held onto the hope that Garden would be recovered in the morning.

Allowing the others to leave one by one, Vigil stood until he was alone, around him the camp was set up while above the stars were completely obscured by the storm clouds. Where was Sal? Vig looked about, realizing he had not seen his wife since the tents had begun to be set up. He could not see her at all. Walking about the camp, he followed the sound of a pregnant woman in distress. He found the Garatin man, Fav, sitting outside the small tent that Sal and Vig had slept in. Fav fidgeted nervously, plucking at the threads on his sleeves and hardly noticing Vig's approach.

Vig placed his hands on his hips; Sal could be heard inside with her warrior, speaking encouragement and instructions.

"Salvage," Vig called, shaking his head at the woman he called wife.

After a moment Sal poked her head out, "Be quick, the baby is coming."

"I can hear that. I can also see that it'll be born in *our* tent."

"I knew you would understand," She smiled cheekily and ducked back into the tent.

Still shaking his head, Vig checked in on Garden, already asleep in Serene's tent; the old man did not look well. Vig left the tent with a deep frown, knowing that Serene would be up all night to make sure the old man kept breathing.

One fire had been started in the camp, and sitting before it, one guard at her side, was Lady Roam. Small and lonely she looked, her veil shielding her face.

Vig saw that Dire and his nitora were having trouble with Roam's tent and were distracted. Nodding to the single guard by the fire, Vig sat down beside Roam, leaving ample space, lest he be reprimanded for being too close.

"This time tomorrow we'll be feasting and celebrating!" he announced to the child; she did not respond.

"I wonder what kind of food they have here?" he went on, hoping to get a giggle from the shy child, "Fish, I hope! I haven't had a good eel in ages!"

He peeked at her, surprised his comment hadn't gotten a reaction; her shoulders trembled, and a suspicious sniffle came from behind her veil.

"Lady Roam, are you alright?"

The sniffling increased and she rocked forward a bit.

Vig moved to hold her, the way he had when he found her in the caves, but he stopped himself, glancing at her guard, he was one of the younger ones. Maybe he could be fooled.

"Lady Roam would like a drink." Vig informed him casually. The guard hesitated. "Well, it's not my job to serve your mistress!" Vig shrugged and turned back to the fire.

The guard hesitated a moment more, then surprisingly, Roam turned and stared at him silently. The guard bowed quickly, then hurried off; they would not have much time.

"What is it, little one?" Vig asked, moving closer to her.

Roam pushed her veil back, revealing her unearthly pale face streaked with tears.

"You can tell me!" Vig encouraged gently.

"I'm scared!" she whispered.

"Of what?"

The Prince of the Dawn and-"

"Lady Roam!" Dire's voice cut in like a crack of lightning. Roam flinched and pulled her veil down swiftly, while Dire cast Vig an unspoken warning.

"Your tent is ready, my lady; you must be well rested for the morrow." Dire picked her up effortlessly and carried her away.

Vig stood to his feet, a protest not leaving his lips. He knew that he should walk away; but he could not. Not again. He waited till Dire emerged from Roam's tent and made sure his nitora surrounded it. Then Dire turned his dark gaze on Vig.

Vig made himself face the large Niben without flinching.

"For the last time, Vigil, I will ask you to not speak directly to-"

"What happens to her when you find the Prince of the Dawn and Dusk?" Vig interrupted.

Dire, ever composed, tilted his head back and took a moment to respond, "The Niben will have peace after a thousand years of war."

"No, that's an outcome." Vig felt his anger rising to a place where he could not keep it in check, "What will Roam have to do to achieve it?"

"She is a gift of perfect purity-"

"What does that mean!?" Vig cut in again, his raised voice gathering observers.

Dire breathed deep, obviously struggling to remain calm.

Vig waited a moment for a response, but received none, "Will she be his bride, his slave- what?"

Dire looked outraged at the question, "No! she is to be his-"

"His what!?" Vig's anger had reached *that* place now.

"His sacrifice!" Dire retorted angrily, louder than probably intended, for he shifted uncomfortably and looked about them while Vig stared at him in shock and disgust.

"Many years ago," Dire spoke quietly again, quickly, anxious to be over, "the tribe of the Niben divided, splintered into the tribes that are known today. They made war against each other, each tribe leader seeking to rule the others, none of them could, until one rose up. He conquered the tribes, cutting them low till all bowed under his banner; he was named the first high king of the Niben. He demanded a peace price from each tribe, a blood sacrifice for their previous opposition. A gift of purity. There was peace in the land for many long years, then the tribes revolted, overthrew him and divided once more." He paused, "Such is the legend of the Prince of the Dawn and Dusk."

Vig searched his face, every fiber of himself revolting at the implications of the story, "You believe he has returned."

"Reincarnated- yes. Thrown from his own kingdom by the fates and come to demand the peace price once more. When my mistress was born with skin like the moon, her uncle the king knew that she would be the perfect gift; one that will buy peace for the whole Weald and unite the tribes again."

Vig was speechless- appalled! "She'll be killed!?"

Dire breathed slowly through his teeth, "For peace; it is the reason she was born."

"You would hand that child over to a stranger to- *to kill*!?"

Dire's face changed, and he stepped back, "Do not meddle in the affairs of the Niben, friend."

Vig held his gaze. Then Dire turned and stalked into the night, seemingly undisturbed by all he had said.

* * * *

Vigil did not sleep that night, laying on the ground in the open with his warriors, his agonized thoughts on the Niben and his heart breaking for the pale child. Through the long hours of the night, he listened to the labor cries of Mid as she bore a child into the world.

The storm broke in the night, with rolling thunder, and bright flashes of lightning. Vig and all the others who slept under the sky were quickly beckoned into Lady Serene's tent when the rain began, while the Niben huddled into the entrance of Roam's tent.

Serene went back to sleep soon enough, apparently unconcerned about the host of half drenched warriors huddled into her tent. She hadn't even raised the question why Theoph hadn't invited his own warriors into his tent. Vig of course knew the reason and dreaded the idea of being cooped up in a tent all night with the smell of the prince's rotting flesh. For a time Vig sat awake with his warriors, whispering about the storm, soon most lay down and fell back to sleep.

Garden however stayed awake, and Vig watched what must be a multitude of memories and thoughts running across the old man's face. At some point after midnight, the storm calmed enough for the cry of a newborn child to reach the ears of those still wakeful.

Garden stirred and looked up at Vig. "I wonder what it is," he murmured, a wistful expression crossing his wrinkled face.

Vig smirked humorlessly, "Whatever it is, if that couple isn't careful, Sal will kidnap the little thing and keep it as her own."

Garden nodded, taking the comment deathly serious, which probably was not a bad idea.

★ ★ ★ ★

Salvage did not sleep; she was not tired. The only thing that mattered at all, was the child in her arms. Mid and Fav were fast asleep, exhausted after the labor, the Verlyance warrior who had helped, had also laid down, but not Sal.

It was a boy, he was so small, so perfect. Sal found herself fawning over every little thing about him, from his long eyelashes to his little fingernails. Only a mere four hours old and already he seemed impossibly strong as he slept while it continued raining beyond the tent. Puddles had long since formed and water dripped from the saturated tent fabric. The sun had risen, hidden as it was behind the storm, there was little light to be had, but the camp was waking, their spirits unshaken by the night in the face of the day's promise, an end to their long search.

Sal could not make herself spare thought for the Foretold King, or even the Ancient One; this child, asleep in her arms, was all that mattered. Could this be where Sal was led to all this time?

Mid awoke, and started in a panic, then she saw Salvage. There was a moment where both women looked upon each other- a moment of uncertainty. Then Sal surrendered the boy to his mother, her arms feeling instantly cold and empty. Tears, unbidden, sprung into her eyes, she did not turn away though.

Nearby, Fav stirred and woke to his wife cradling their son, he glanced at Sal, uncertainty, and fear in his eyes. Sal realized how she must look to them, and with difficulty backed away, wishing she could tell them just what it meant to her to help bring their child into the world. How much it meant to hold him.

"Salvage?" Vigil called from outside, Sal tore her eyes from the child and drew back the tent door to meet her husband, water dripping from his hair and nose as the rain soaked him.

Sal beamed at him, "It's a boy."

Vig glanced past her, "Very good. Fortress has gone into the city; he will be back when he knows where we are to go. Garden would have gone with him but…"

Sal felt her stomach do a flip as her thoughts turned to the fragile man.

"He's still not himself, and very tired. We thought it best not to tax him more than necessary. He ah…" Again, Vig glanced at the couple and their new child, "I think he wants to see the baby."

"Bring him- it'll do him good to see the little one; he's so perfect Vig!"

Vig smirked and shook his head, "Alright, I'll see if Garden can get this far."

Sal waited by the tent door, holding it open. It took longer than she expected, but eventually Vig returned, and by his side, wearing her cloak up over her head, was Lady Serene. Carried in Vigil's arms was Garden. Sal had to hide her feelings of dismay at the old man's fragile and lifeless appearance.

"I understand there is a baby to see," Serene announced, shaking the rain from her cloak. She avoided looking at Sal, but she froze when her eyes stumbled on the family of three huddled together. "Goodness…" she whispered.

Garden worked his jaw then spoke his native language to the couple, they exchanged a few words and smiled politely at the group of strangers.

"They have said it is alright," Garden said weakly. Vig walked forward and placed him next to the couple. Sal watched her husband's face closely to see what he thought of the child, knowing now how much he also longed for one of his own.

Serene ventured forward. "Why is it so small?" she questioned, frowning at the baby.

"I think they all come that way," Vig answered, sharing a look with Sal.

Serene sank down next to Garden, her eyes never leaving the baby, "But… surely he is *too* small! They can't all look like that!"

No one paid her any mind for Garden was crying, great tears slipping down his wrinkled face as he stared at the child. Mid asked him a question, then carefully handed her son into his arms.

Vig stood and backed away to stand by Sal, she had a feeling he was just as moved by the sight of Garden cradling the newborn as she was.

Garden sniffled, "Now my life is complete," he announced happily.

"Is that all it took!?" Serene laughed.

Sal laughed too, but it was not without sorrow, for she could tell; Garden would not live much longer. He seemed to diminish before her very eyes.

The six of them stayed in the tent, taking turns holding the boy, commenting on how precious he was and laughing when Serene tried to hold him. She clearly had never held a baby before and had not a clue how to. The baby started crying and Serene panicked, handing him off to his mother, complaining that she was a wisdom seeker, not a nursemaid.

When the morning was half done, a horse galloped up to the camp, its hoof beats so thunderous it could only be Cavern and Fortress returning. Vig and Sal left the tent, not without difficulty, to be greeted with Fortress's perplexed face.

"What is it?" Vig asked.

"Gather the others, there are things we must discuss." Was Fortress's only answer as he dismounted.

Soon they were all gathered in the Niben's tent, anxious to hear what Fortress had discovered.

"I know where to find the king of Garatin," he announced, "however, he does not go by any of the names we seek. Or so the soldiers in the street insisted."

"Very well," Theoph spoke, his voice subdued and barely audible in the constant rainfall, "we shall have to make our inquiries straight to this king." He held his cloak close about himself and no one stood near him.

"I understand he is visiting the city in the castle of the governor," Fortress explained. "I had one of the soldiers inform this governor that we will be coming into the city soon. They…" he hesitated.

"What is it?" Dire asked.

"The city is rioting."

Everyone paused, then a string of questions followed.

"I could not learn much from the soldiers, their understanding of the common tongue was limited. However, I could see for myself the city is a turbulent place to be at present. We must be on guard."

No one was happy with his explanation, but there was nothing more to be done.

Vig and Dire began giving orders to their warriors, a small group would remain behind in the camp while the rest would venture into the city and find whatever awaited them.

It was in this excitement that Sal realized Serene had not come, instead one of her guards had listened to Fortress's tidings.

"COME QUICK!" Lady Serene's shrill voice broke in on the proceedings.

Sal was first out into the rain, Vig and Serene's own guard close on her heels. Into Sal's tent they burst; Mid and Fav were as they had left them, cradling their son. While Serene was bent over Garden, her hands fluttered over him uselessly.

Sal and Vig went forward while the others lingered in the doorway, Serene whimpered up at Sal and Vig uselessly.

They knelt by the old man to listen to his laboured breath; he watched them with sad eyes. "I have come into the land of my birth," he whispered, "I am complete."

Serene took up one of his hands. "Nonsense! You said you would come see my home in Eastern Fairthin!" she was tearing up and unable to speak clearly, "You haven't even been into the city yet!"

Garden closed his eyes and sighed, "Yes… I would like to see Garason before… to see the Fort," he looked pleadingly at Vig.

"What is the Fort?" Vig asked gently.

"The temple of my people," Garden said, with a self pleased tone, "I remembered it when Mid said they have to take their son to the Fort to be dedicated. I remember going there as a boy; I should like to see it once more."

Vig hesitated, no doubt thinking of their mission that day and the riots Fortress spoke of.

"And so, you shall!" Sal interceded, "We'll take you into the city, we'll find you a healer and get you back on your feet to see this temple!" she spoke optimistically but saw how Vig didn't believe a word of it.

"Sal, we must go and meet with the king and governor," Vig reminded quietly.

Sal hesitated, her duty to Theoph and completing their quest fighting to sway what her heart had already decided. "You and the others will be sufficient to guard the prince, I will take Garden myself and meet you all back here."

"What of the riots- Fortress said it's not safe," Vig pressed.

Sal gave him a withering look, "We'll be fine, and you can tell us both what you discover from the king and governor when you return."

"You'll have to tell me as well," Lady Serene announced, tilting her head high and sniffling away her tears. "I shall go with Salvage," she managed a side glance at Sal.

Sal bowed her head, the hurtful words exchanged between herself and the old woman in Jarg resurfaced in her memory, with effort she pushed them aside. "But you must ask after the Wise One!" she reminded.

"Remaining by the side of a friend when they are in distress, is surely wisdom itself. I will not be parted from Garden now." She gave the old man's hand a squeeze. Her guard stepped forward, mouth open, she stopped him before he could speak. "You will act as my emissary, see that these fools don't muck everything up again!"

No one tried to dissuade the woman further.

Vig bowed his head, "Garden I promised you I would carry you into your homeland if need be."

"And you did," Garden insisted with a weak smile, "You did."

"I would carry you to the steps of the temple…" Vig was obviously torn between his duties, he locked eyes with Sal, "I can not leave the prince or..."

Sal lay a hand on his shoulder, "I will look after him, and bring him back here stronger!" she smiled warmly.

Grand castles to divert from the squalor of the poor. Proud armor to cover the scars of battle. Majestic tapestries to distract from the sordid histories they told. Clean bandages to conceal the rotting flesh beneath. Was there nothing of true beauty left in the world?

Theophany walked tall and stoically at the head of their company as they were ushered into the great hall of the governor's castle. He clung to his cloak, knowing it did nothing to hide the stench of his rotting flesh, all he could do was pretend nothing was amiss; soon all would be put right. By his side, ever steadfast, was Vigil, his eyes ever scanning and assessing their surroundings. Lady Roam, veiled and silent, sat upon a litter born on the shoulders of the impassive nitora, while Dire led them, his face cast in stone to hide a sorrowful secret of his own. Lady Serene's chosen guard stood among them to represent her; his men fearful for the safety of their mistress amongst the riots. Sir Fortress alone exhibited excitement and triumph, his stride confident while his sword hung on his back, ready to be pledged in service to his Warlord.

The company had been met with soldiers of dark skin and escorted through the riots to the castle of Governor Endure. All about them crowds of Garatin's jostled and shouted, riled into anger by matters that did not concern Theoph; all that mattered was reaching the Foretold King.

He would know how to help Theoph pass through the gates of the immortals. He would be able to heal his cursed heart stain. He would make Theoph whole again.

Awaiting them in the great hall, was an old man with droopy eyes and a solemn face, with him was another man, late in life, yet not so old as the other. Only the second man was pale of skin like Garden while the other was darker like the soldiers who had escorted the company. Both men were dressed richly, but neither of them wore a crown, and Theoph realized he hadn't a clue who would be the more important, governor or king?

"Welcome to the courts of Garason, and my home." The older of the two men spoke loud and clear, surprisingly he spoke in the common tongue, and did so with little difficulty, "I am the Tarvin governor in Garason; Endure. Pray tell, to whom I have welcomed?"

His manner of speech was a little confusing, but Vig guessed it was time to introduce Theoph and the company. "Well met, my lord governor, we are honored to be welcomed here. I am Vigil, warrior of Verlyance in the far south sea beyond the Honorfell Mountains, and this is, my lord Theophany the Victorious, prince of Verlynn Nel, prophesied future king, and honored champion of the Verlyance Isles." While Vigil spoke, Theoph saw that both the governor and the younger man took in a sharp breath at mention of his Namesake, but neither moved to speak.

Theoph stepped forward, and nodded his head in the subtlest of bows, "I and my esteemed companions have come far to stand before you, lord governor." He turned to Dire.

Dire stepped forward, made a ceremonial gesture with his hand that Theoph had never seen him do and spoke, "I am Dire and will speak for my mistress. Before you, is Lady Roam of the Niben Weald, daughter of Command, brother of Golden, the king of Estewryn." The governor nodded, and Dire stepped back.

Fortress had no need to move, to draw attention to himself, his deep voice resonated easily in the hall, "And I am Sir Fortress of Stonemark in the Honorfell Mountains."

Next to speak was Lady Serene's guard, who first bowed very low, "My mistress, Lady Serene of the eastern courts of Fairthin has also come but remained in our camp; I am here in her stead."

The governor's eyebrows had risen quite high and when it was clear everyone had spoken, he turned slightly to exchange a look with the younger man, who had yet to be introduced. Theoph noticed though that a servant stood by the man's elbow, constantly whispering, a translator.

"I am all the more honored to be a host now, that I know who my guests are," the governor said. "However, I fear I know not *why* you have come across the mountains to speak with me."

"We each of us set out from our lands on a quest to find someone; our quest has led us here, to Garason, where we believe to find him who we have sought," Theoph explained, glancing at the younger man; perhaps he was the Foretold King! "I seek the Foretold King." The title drifted in the air for a moment then gave way to silence.

"Lady Serene has come in search of one known only as the Wise One," Theoph paused hoping for any kind of reaction, he received none. "My friends from the Niben seek the Prince of the Dawn and Dusk-"

"And I, a great Warlord," Fortress spoke for himself, disregarding the agreement they had made that Theoph would speak for everyone, "I was told by a Seer that I would find him when I joined with these other questers." He gestured to the company.

The governor took a deep breath, "I fear none of those names are known to me..." he glanced again at the unnamed man, "Perhaps I could help if I knew more."

Everyone tried to speak at once, then stopped abruptly, and looked at one another bashfully. Each one of them was growing sick with anticipation.

"Forgive us, lord governor," Vigil spoke, "All of us are anxious to find whom we seek." He looked first to Theoph, then to Lady Serene's guard to speak.

"The Wise One was written of in ages past, my mistress discovered a prophecy revealing that the days of the Wise One have come. Little is known of this person, but whomever they be, they will be known for their vast wisdom in all matters, revered by all."

The governor pursed his lips and glanced again at the unnamed man; Theoph was growing very curious!

"The Prince of the Dawn and Dusk is the reincarnated prince of the Niben Weald; a great hero of old, who will bring salvation to our people." Dire added his part, the excitement and anticipation growing thin as doubt and disappointment took its place.

There was silence as the governor stood before them, refusing to comment, but his thoughts were obvious; he had heard of no such people.

"The man I seek," Theoph spoke, knowing in his heart it was in vain, "Will be a great king, newly come into power. His dominion will reach all the lands and his deeds of valor and glory will be uncountable. No one will be able to stand against him."

Fear flitted across the governor's face so quickly Theoph almost missed it, but there was no mistaking the anger that came next as the man turned again to his unnamed companion. When he turned back to Theoph, the anger was gone, "I am grieved to say there has been no word of any such figure in these lands, my lords."

Theoph nodded, his disappointment already well settled in his heart; it was a fool's quest after all.

"We must do all we can though, to aid you, our guests!" Governor Endure said, suddenly motivated. "I will send messengers to the far reaches of Garatin on your behalf; they will seek the Wise One, The Prince of the Dawn and Dusk, a great Warlord, and… the Foretold King. Rest knowing if any of them are within Garatin, we will find out! While we wait, I invite you to stay here as my guests." He bowed respectfully.

Theoph bowed his head in return and turned to his friends; would they feel the same as him? Fortress's face had lost all its excitement and was studying the governor shrewdly, while Dire frowned deeply.

"I think it unwise, my lord," Vigil whispered and Theoph nodded.

"We would be safer on our own," Dire added.

Fortress flexed his jaw, "Agreed. He will know where to find us if matters change."

Theoph turned back to the governor who waited expectantly, "Your offer is most kind, but our company is large, and we have grown quite comfortable in our camp. With your leave, lord governor, we will continue to camp on the edge of the city."

Governor Endure looked a bit surprised, but after a moment, nodded, "As you wish. Will you accept my soldiers to protect you from bandits and rioters on the road?"

Theoph had flashbacks to Bainemere and chose his words carefully, "Our warriors will be sufficient. Thank you, for your service, we will await the return of your messengers."

The company all bowed as much as they wished, then turned and left the great hall. No one spoke. There was nothing to say.

Theoph avoided Vigil's gaze, the last thing he needed now was sympathy! He knew somewhere in a distant part of his heart that he should try and offer some kind of comfort to the others, but he didn't care enough to even try. They had not lost as much as he had.

"Theoph," Vig tried stalling him softly, Theoph ignored him. Vig placed a hand on his arm, "Theoph."

Theophany stopped and turned on his friend, the others moving pass. "There is nothing to say Vigil!" he snapped in their native language.

Vig did not back away, he opened his mouth but never spoke.

"My lords?" a servant spoke to them in the common tongue from a side hallway.

They both looked, irritated to be interrupted.

"My master, the king of Garatin, would speak privately with Prince Theophany," the man said, keeping his voice in a low, secretive tone.

Theoph glanced at the others as they continued along their way, oblivious. He looked briefly at Vig; he would be ready if treachery occurred. "Very well."

The servant led them down the hall and up a small flight of steps into a chamber littered with instruments, the minstrel's gallery. At one end of the room, curtains covered an opening that allowed music to flow down into the great hall.

Waiting for them was the unnamed man who had received them with the governor. "My lord, King Radiance of Garatin," the servant introduced softly, then went to stand by the king's side.

Theoph exchanged a look with Vig; why hadn't the king been introduced by the Governor!? They both bowed, lower than they had to, toward Endure, this was a king after all.

The king spoke and his servant repeated it in the common tongue. "My lord the king understands that you must have questions, but he warns you to speak softly; there are unfriendly ears everywhere."

Theoph stepped closer, his heart beginning to pound once more; perhaps all was not lost. "Why do you wish to speak with me, my Lord king? What more is there to say."

"Much," thc king said through his scrvant, "I can not speak freely before the Governor. You may have guessed that my country is not what it should be."

"Do you know where to find the Foretold King!?" Theoph asked, stepping forward.

King Radiance lifted his hands palms out, "The matter is much more complicated. The Governor spoke truthfully that there is no such knowledge of the people you seek, but that is where his words strayed from truth. He would rather bury this king under a mountain of secrets than see him ascend to power, or else kill him."

"I do not understand, you speak as if the governor has more power than you."

The king sighed, his discomfort obvious, "Indeed, he does. Word of Tarva's conquest has not reached beyond the Dinco Mountains. I am not surprised, the Tarvin army has always been defeated by mountain ranges."

"Tarva?" Theoph looked to Vig for help, but he was impassive and silent.

"Yes, from over the Neenor sea, they have my country under their boot, my people at their mercy. I, the king of Garatin, have not been allowed to rule in this, the capital, instead I've been banished to the north. My son, Prince Ordained, I fear will never rule in freedom as he should, instead he will be forced to humble himself before the Tarvins and cower before them, even as I am made to do! I can do little for my people, stripped of power as I am, but the words spoken of whom you and your companions seek, are remarkably similar to a prophecy we have here in Garason. I believe *he* is here."

"Who!?" Theoph's heart was thudding fast, "The Foretold King, the Wise One-"

"You will understand better when you hear the prophecy of my people. Long ago it was promised that one would come, sent by our god to free us of our oppressors; the Eloi-man, the warrior returned, the wise king of old, commander of the rising and setting sun, come to reclaim his people and avenge them." The words spoken first from the king in a strange tongue, then repeated by the servant for Theoph to hear, worked like rain that even now fell beyond the castle, running off oiled cloaks, soaking into tunics, dripping from hair and forming puddles. Threatening a flood.

"Can it be?" Theoph breathed in his own tongue, after all this time… could they have really been searching for the same man?!

"I knew the moment your namesake was spoken," the king and his servant continued, "That this prophecy must be coming to pass."

"*My* namesake?" Theoph frowned.

Here the servant looked between his master and Theoph then spoke on his own, "There is no direct translation from the common tongue to ours. The best way to say your namesake is *God Bridge*."

The air was knocked out of Theoph, he had never considered the meaning of his namesake in such a way.

The king spoke again, "So you see, your very coming confirms that our Garatin prophecy is coming to pass; the greatness of the Eloi-man has drawn strangers to our land, even though they knew not his name," the king smiled and Theoph half laughed, his mind reeling.

"That is why Governor Endure will not allow this man to rise into power. I can not free my people, but the Eloi-man, or, as you know him, the Foretold King, can. Our Prophecy predicts he will rule in this city- you were right to look for him here. You must find him before the Tarvins do!"

Theoph nodded, it was all he could do.

"When you do- send word to me," the king invited with a gleam in his eye, "So that I too, can pledge my sword."

"I will," Theoph bowed his head in respect.

"Now go, before Endure finds us!"

* * * *

"There you are!" Fortress's voice boomed across the entrance hall of the governor's castle as Vigil and Theophany joined them. "I was about to come after you." There was no jest in his voice.

"All is not lost friends," Theoph responded with more energy and life than Vig had heard in a long time; it troubled him. "I will tell you in the safety of our camp though." He pushed past the doors and strutted out into the rain, forcing the others to bridle their curiosity and follow.

Vigil wished very badly to speak to Theoph but had little chance to. The prince wasted no time in leading the company from the courtyard, some mounted on gillup while the Niben kept pace on foot, Lady Roam being shielded from the rain by a large cloak that covered her almost like a tent.

In the midst of sorting through all that had happened in the last ten minutes, Vigil felt an immense wave of relief wash over him concerning Lady Roam; surely the Ancient One would not direct them to find a man who would accept the blood sacrifice of a child!

The streets surrounding the governor's castle were cordoned off from rioters but once passing through to the streets beyond, the travellers were pressed on every side. It seemed the entire city was in the streets, shouting, pushing and brandishing crude weapons. The Verlyance and Niben warriors created a barrier around Theoph and Lady Roam, using their spear shafts and longbows to push room for the company to pass through. Fortress on Cavern did a great deal to clear a path; no one wanted to stand in the way of either of the giant or his horse. Serene's guards took up an inner defence, dealing with any who got past the others. Vigil could not have talked to Theoph even if he wasn't busy fending off angry Garatins, the noise alone made conversation impossible.

The company had no way of asking what the riots were about, if they had, they would have learned it was over the murder of Anifest. That same morning, sheltered from the rain behind a curtain of vines, a copper haired maiden was meeting with the man who had killed the rebel queen.

It was well into the late afternoon when at last they reached the edge of the city where the riots ceased. So glad to be out from the jostling and shouting, the group didn't stop but pressed on till they exited the city gate and found themselves on the road back to their camp. Here it was realized that two of Vigil's warriors had received minor wounds from the crowds while one of the Niben had tripped at one point and been trampled underfoot; although winded, they were able to continue on.

Theoph did not give anyone a chance to ask him what he had discovered, but instead made his gillup trot, forcing the others to follow suit until they came within sight of their camp, half sheltered from the rain under the boughs of a large tree.

"Enough Lord Theophany!" Fortress demanded as Cavern pranced over the roots of the tree, the others not far behind, "Keep us waiting no longer; if you have good news, tell it now!"

Theoph reined in his gillup and turned to the others, face flushed and smile wide. Vigil watched him speak, his heart falling within him.

"Our quest is not in vain, friends!" Theoph encouraged, "The second man who met with us but did not speak was the king of Garatin; King Radiance. Not the man any of us seek, but he *has* pledged to aid us!"

Fortress frowned, rainwater running down his dark beard, while Dire watched the prince closely, "How do you know this?"

"It was he who detained me in the governor's castle," Theoph explained. "Told me everything; we have found ourselves in the center of a storm in this country. The Garatin people are oppressed and forced under the rule of Tarva, another land to the west. They are awaiting the coming of a prophesied king to free them."

"Why is this good news?" Dire asked.

Theoph's eyes brightened, "Their prophecy describes their deliverer as the *'Eloi-man, the warrior returned, the wise king of old, commander of the rising and setting sun, come to reclaim his people and avenge them'.*"

The others were just as stunned as Theoph had been.

"Theoph," Vigil said quietly, hoping to intercede before anything else could be said. No one paused to hear him.

"That can't be," Fortress uttered darkly.

Dire exchanged bewildered looks with his warriors, but it was Lady Roam who spoke, once more breaking her silence, "The Prince of the Dawn and Dusk… is a king of Garatin?"

Dire's head snapped towards her, sitting atop her litter, she had pushed her veil back, revealing her pale face struggling to understand.

"Yes!" Theoph exclaimed, "But more than this, Dire- Fortress, don't you understand!? We have all come seeking the *same* man- his coming scattered across the lands, buried in our cultures and whispered to our gods for the purpose of drawing us to him!"

"Theophany," Vigil tried again. Around them, the Verlyance warriors, nitora and Serene's guards listened in astonishment, wonder and confusion.

Theoph dismounted, and stepped towards the others, his face animated with passion, "We have not failed, instead we have found something greater still! All we hoped for has come together in *one man*!"

"Where is he?" Serene's head guard asked, scepticism fading from his face the longer Theoph spoke.

"King Radiance said that the prophecy's all say he will come to Garason; we have only to find him."

"Theophany, wait," urgency grew in Vigil's voice, but the prince would not listen.

"Surely, we will find him among the rioters, biding his time, forming an army before striking back against their oppressors. The Garatin king warned me though that the governor will not allow a new king to rise up- so we must be swift in finding him!"

"Theophany!" Vigil shouted, at last gaining the attention of everyone, "This is not right."

The rain falling on their tents nearby filled the following silence.

"Neither the governor nor King Radiance can be trusted; one strives to maintain power over a rebellious people, while the other is fighting to gain power." Vig regretted that he could not have first spoken to Theoph; it was not good for his warriors to see him contradict the prince.

Theoph blinked as though stunned for a moment. "That is why King Radiance wishes us to find the Foretold King, so that he might help free their people."

Vig huffed, glancing at the others. "Why would he welcome another contender for power? Even if he spoke truthfully to us, that he has been stripped of his power, he also claimed that he has been allowed to rule in the north. If a rebellion broke in the country, no matter the outcome, King Radiance would lose his power. He *will not* allow another king to rise."

No one spoke.

"Trust me, Theophany," Vig implored, "You were once warned to heed my words; we would be better to wander in a desert the rest of our lives than ever set eyes on King Radiance or the governor again."

Theoph struggled inwardly, Vig could see it play out on his face.

Fortress broke the silence by dismounting and striding through the company towards the tents, leaving the reins of Cavern dangling. No one else dared move.

"I must find the Foretold King"' Theoph whispered in their native tongue, "I do not have more time."

Vigil took a steadying breath, "Seek with a heart that is true and eyes that are open, trust the words of the seeker and heed those of the believer… and I believe we will yet find what we set out for."

Theoph returned his gaze for what seemed an eternity. "Very well," he said, then spoke to the others in the common tongue, "Vigil is right, the governor and king can not be trusted."

"Then what do we do now?" Dire demanded.

"We wait for Sal to return with Garden. With his help we can find out the truth about the prophecy Radiance spoke of, only then will we know how to act." Vigil spoke for Theoph, whose hopes had been so cruelly risen like a sea bird on a great headwind, only to be dropped into the waves below.

Fortress returned, pack in hand and face dark. Vigil hesitated to speak to the giant, apprehensive over what the man would say. It was Dire who spoke.

"What are you doing?" the Niben asked, as Fortress loaded Cavern with his pack.

Fortress sighed heavily, then turned to them. "Our path's part here. The Warlord I seek must be elsewhere, for I do not believe he would cower in a crowd waiting for the stars to align." Anger and frustration lined each word, and his gaze did not linger on anyone. "I will journey with you no longer; farewell." He swung up onto Cavern and turned his steed out into the rain.

Vig exchanged bewildered expressions with the others, then started after the giant. "Fortress- wait!" he called, stepping out from under the tree's shelter.

Fortress reigned in Cavern, hesitated a moment, and half turned to Vig.

"You can not give up so easily- the one we seek may yet be here!" Vig blinked water out of his eyes.

Fortress bared his teeth in discomfort, "My friend, I wish that our paths will cross again for I see in you a true brother; but I can not believe the Warlord I seek is also a reincarnated prince from ages past, much less a *poet* in an ivory tower." He cut off his contemptuous words to regather himself, "I hope you find what you are looking for."

Vigil bit back what he longed to say; no words could now change the giant's decision, "May you also find that which you seek, friend."

Fortress bowed his head for a moment, then lifted the griffin whistle from his neck and held it out by its cord, "You may have need of this when you return home through the Honorfell."

Vig took the gift humbly, knowing he would miss the man's rambunctious company. With one more nod, Fortress turned Cavern away and trotted towards the road.

"You there!" he called to a Garatin vagabond stumbling through the mud, "I am a stranger to these lands, is there another city in this country, one where I might find a great warrior?"

The man on the road looked bewildered for a moment then pointed west. "A coastal city on the mouth of the Arrow Sea; Larsanne. Many days ride," he managed to say, his skill in the common tongue limited.

Fortress nodded, and pointed Cavern's head due west, and without looking back, rode off into the gray landscape as evening came upon them.

Vig watched him for a moment, then turned to find the others had left the tree and were now going into their camp. Vig hoped dearly that Sal would return very soon with Garden.

Following the others, Vig did not care how wet and cold he was becoming; little mattered now. What would become of the prince if they could not find the Foretold King in time?

Lightning lit up the sky, drawing Vigil's attention in the direction of the road, he paused; the vagabond who had given Fortress directions was coming towards him. He was a younger man than at first was perceived, dressed in threadbare clothes soaked through to his bones.

"Shelter?" he asked in the common tongue, his eyes darting to the tents.

Vigil looked him up and down; he seemed harmless. He nodded and gestured for the man to follow him into camp.

The man pointed to himself. "Guild," he said.

Chapter 19 Foreknown

While Theophany and the others were being escorted into the governor's castle, Salvage and Serene's guards were fighting their way through the riled crowds. Serene herself rode a gillup and her eyes were ever on Garden who rode beside her, being gently held in place by one of her guards. The old man seemed to fade as the day wore on, each obstacle wearing away at the strength that held him upright. Always by their side was the young Garatin couple, Mid and Fav clutching their newborn son close, as bewildered and overwhelmed by the angry mobs and pockets of rioters as Sal was. Evidently the couple were serfs from farmlands in the north and were unaccustomed to the city. It was with their help, through Garden translating, that the group of them found their way around the streets.

Although the fort was their ultimate destination, they spent the better part of the afternoon searching for a healer to see Garden. After being jostled and bruised in the main streets, they entered a poorer district of the city, where the riots grew distant. Here the grand castles were absent, in their place flat roofed houses were packed side by side, crooked and leaning over the streets till sometimes it felt as though they were passing through tunnels. The streets were practically abandoned, and the group had little trouble finding the shop of a healer over top that of a butcher. A rickety stair led up to the second story where the healer's door could be reached.

"A Garatin leech," Garden said, repeating what Fav read from a sign hanging over the street.

Sal shook water from her face, "A what!?"

"A healer," Garden amended, glancing upwards at the shop.

Sal looked about the abandoned street, "Right, stay here a moment, I'll go up." She mounted the stairs two at a time and pounded on the shop door. No one answered.

"Well!?" Serene called impatiently from below.

Sal wiped rain away from a window and peered in; it was unlit inside, and just as lifeless as the street. She knocked on the glass and was about to turn away when she glimpsed movement; an old Garatin woman had come from a back room, but upon seeing Sal's dark face looming in the window, had frozen in the shadows.

Sal banged on the door, trying to see better, she smiled, hoping it looked friendly.

Hesitantly the woman ventured forward, she called through the closed door, her tone unwelcoming. Sal tried replying but found Fav by her side suddenly. He spoke to the woman, and they exchanged a few words before she opened the door. She stared openly at Sal, spoke more with Fav, then leaned over the railing to look at Garden.

"Ahh!" she scoffed, flapped her hands in dismissal and hurried back inside, shutting her door firmly. Sal looked helplessly at Fav, he shrugged apologetically.

Sal turned back to the door, about to pound it in.

"It's alright," Garden's feeble voice called, "We'll go elsewhere."

"Why won't she help!?" Sal demanded as she and Fav descended the stairs.

Garden shrugged evasively.

Serene huffed indignantly, "We'll go elsewhere indeed! We'll go to a better part of the city- to someone who won't turn up their nose! Ask where to find an expensive healer!" she insisted, adjusting her cloak.

Garden hesitated.

"I will gladly pay whatever the cost!" Serene insisted, "Just ask them!"

A few more words were exchanged, and soon the group moved on. Serene muttering the whole time about what kind of worthless healer that woman must have been to turn away a customer. Sal knew better though; the healer had taken one look at Garden and known she could not help. Even now, the old man seemed to have diminished greatly after even such a small exchange. They were running out of time.

Slowly, through the busy streets, they made their way toward the center of the city, and towards the fort. The rain increased and the crowds thinned out enough for them to move quicker till Fav stopped and pointed towards another shop, this one had a large painted sign and a dragon symbol on the door; it looked quite different from the last healer.

This time Sal did not hesitate, spear in hand she pounded on the door then threw her shoulder into it. The bolt on the other side gave way on her second try. Serene gasped and muttered her disapproval, but Sal paid no heed as she entered the shop; Garden needed help.

"Healer!?" she called, uncaring that they would not be able to understand her. There was no one about, but a stairway in the back looked promising. Sal took two steps forward.

"Salvage! Oh Garden, no, no," Serene called urgently from outside.

Sal fled the shop to find that Garden had slumped forward, while Serene had slipped from her gillup and was holding his hand, tears springing to her eyes. Garden's breathing was shallow and weak but with the guard's help who sat behind him, he managed to straighten slightly and shake his head to Sal, "It's alright... it's alright."

Sal's heart sank, then a final surge of determination drove her forward, "You're not leaving us yet, old one; I promised you would see the temple of your people." She handed her spear to one of the guards then gathered Garden into her arms, he was easy to carry. Serene fussed at her side, mumbling and patting Garden's hand.

"Where do we find this temple?" Sal asked, scanning the street; an angry crowd was approaching, "Garden, ask Fav."

The young couple listened with empathetic eyes, then answered and pointed to the center of the city.

"They say it... is not far," Garden managed to say between haggard breaths.

Twilight came upon them as they forged forward, and they were soon overtaken by a crowd that would not be driven away by the rain. Serene remounted her gillup while her guards kept their path open. Driven with the crowd they entered the courtyard of The Fort; it thronged with an angry mob who were being pushed back from the gates of a castle, while the Fort itself stood as silent witness.

It was shaped with four equal length walls reaching high into the darkening sky. At each corner, a tower stood tall and boasted a long white flag that hung limp in the rain. Steps led up to mammoth sized doors that stood closed to the crowds. It was an old building that had stood watch over its people as the ages passed; Sal wondered what lay within.

They pressed and scrambled through the mob until they at last reached the steps where the crowd thinned out. Serene had lost her cloak and clung to her gillup, drenched and wretched looking. Fav and his wife had managed to keep up with them, Mid gazed at her son worriedly as he cried; but his little voice could not be heard in the cacophony.

In her arms, Garden shivered and looked up weakly at the temple of his people, his breathing was so shallow and slight that Sal could not detect it at all. Behind them, on the far side of the courtyard, screams pierced the noise of the crowd.

Sal turned, almost stumbling on the steps of the temple; a troop of guards had descended on the mob with drawn swords. Serene gasped while her guards looked about for an escape.

"THE DOOR!" Sal called, turning her back and climbing the stairs as quickly as she could, "Open it!"

Ahead of her Fav pushed and pulled on the dark doors. They would not budge. He began to pound and shout pleadingly; there was no answer. He turned back to the screaming crowd; his eyes wide in fear.

"TAKE HIM!" Sal ordered, gesturing for Fav to take Garden; she needed her spear.

Before Fav could take a step, the doors of the temple opened a crack. A pale face looked out at them, bewildered and fearful.

Fav spoke in a rush, gesturing to both Garden and his wife, then to the courtyard beyond. The man in the temple hesitated, indecision playing on his pale features, then he opened the door further and beckoned them in.

They all went in, Garatin peasants, foreign warriors, noble woman and even the gillup. The mammoth door shut behind them, banishing the danger and even the commotion to a distant background noise, like rain on a rooftop. The group stood panting and dripping on the smooth stone floors, their breath, and every little scuffle of gillup hoof echoed in the entrance hallway.

Before them were smaller doors, their black wood identical to the ebony spear shaft the Niben had given Sal. To the right and left, the hallway reached out, seemingly surrounding an inner chamber, vast and richly woven tapestries lined the walls.

The man who had let them enter, stood with three others, their robes marking them as priests, but Sal paid them no attention. She knelt and carefully lay Garden down, Serene was by his side in an instant, cradling his head. "We're here, my friend," the old woman whispered breathlessly.

Garden looked about, wonder lighting his face, "I never thought to see the inside."

Sal wiped away the rain from his wrinkled face; his skin was cold.

Fav and his wife stood before the priests, speaking in muted tones, then the priests held out his arms and Mid handed over her child to be blessed. Sal knelt by Garden, and together with Serene they all watched, the moment feeling surreal and locked in time. This newborn, on his first day in the world, watched by an old man, on his last day.

Catching them all by surprise, the inner doors of the temple opened by themselves, revealing the chamber within. A row of pillars created a final square, and in the center, a raised dais displayed a curious artifact. A vase, beautiful golden figures painted on its sides, and a jewel studded band about its neck. The rim flared out and supported a white silk cloth, stuffed inside the opening. For reasons unknown to Sal, the steps to the dais were covered in parchment ashes while the air twisted with smoke.

Garden gasped, his breath catching in his throat and his body going stiff in Serene's arms. He spoke then, in a strange tongue that had never been recorded, and those listening could never thereafter remember it, but his words were understood by all.

"This day has been awaited, this hour foretold, this child foreknown! Behold and see, hope has come. This child, born this very day, eternity in flesh, the Eloi-man, the warrior returned, the wise king of old, commander of the rising and setting sun, come to reclaim his people."

The priest holding the child stared in awe, while Mid and Fav exchanged knowing looks, but no one spoke, the power in Garden's words demanding recognition.

The inner doors shut once more as though by invisible hands.

Garden breathed heavily and looked up at Salvage and Serene. "The Foretold King was born this day, and the days of the Wise One are now upon us," he murmured once again in the common tongue, a smile touching his face, "Who am I that I should have lived to see this day? I am truly complete now."

Serene and Sal gazed at each other in astonishment, then back up at the child. Sal's attention was shifted back to Garden at Serene's gasp; the old man was gone, a contented smile on his weathered face.

* * * *

Candlelight flickered on one half of the governor's face as he stood by a window high in his castle and watched the darkening streets below; the riots persisted, but they would not last forever. Heroes of the people were cheaply come by, in Endure's experience, they would forget their precious rebel queen in time, and find another. Endure rejected the notion that he had acted rashly concerning the rebel's assassination; he had taken swift action, which was true, but a hesitant man can not run a country.

A soldier, his armor wet and dripping, entered the chamber and brought his fist over his heart.

"Well?" Endure asked, sharply, turning toward him. Nearby, King Radiance waited anxiously for the news.

The soldier caught his breath then spoke, "My lord governor, all of my messengers have returned."

"And!?"

"All of the lords of the court swear on the honor of Tarva that a usurper is not among them. None of them know of a Garatin king rising to power."

Ender tapped his foot, his tension filled bones finding no relief, he looked up at Radiance. Had he orchestrated this to test Tarva's hold on the country?

Radiance returned his gaze evenly, a finger rubbing across his chin the only betrayal of his own frayed nerves, "What now?"

Endure shrugged, "That's the end of it! Those foreigners have come seeking shadows." He watched the Garatin king closely, gaging his reaction for treason.

Radiance turned away, his fingers rubbing together at his side in a nervous tick. "Unless the prophecy is true," he warned.

Endure tilted his head back, waiting to see what Radiance would devise.

"*I* don't believe it is," Radiance clarified, turning back, "But they do." He pointed out the window, "As I warned the foreigners earlier, their quest, should it be made known, would prove disastrous."

"What do you suggest? Wait for those strangers to find their 'Foretold King' and send word back to you? By then it will be too late."

Radiance sized him up, "The Garatin prophecy does not speak of a full-grown man," he reminded shrewdly, "In times of old, it was said the Eloi-man would first come as a child, born to commoners."

Silence stretched between them.

"If word is spread that this prophecy is coming to pass," Radiance warned, "Rebellion will be born with the cries of every newborn boy child."

Endure turned away, his thoughts running down a lonely road; punishment from Tarva would be swift if under his governance they lost control of Garatin. All hope of this prophecy needed to be stamped out before it had a chance to grow.

He turned back to Radiance, "The people are already in need of correction. A message must be sent to remind them of Tarva's unquestionable power."

"I agree," Radiance purred, "a message that will reach every ear, from the lowliest serf to the lords of my own court."

They gazed upon one another, the deed they spoke of sounding less evil with every passing moment. Endure turned on his heel towards his waiting soldier, "Bring this message to Captain Multifarious personally, let none other hear it. '*Send out the assassin army, between sundown tonight and sunrise tomorrow, every Garatin boy under the age of two, born to commoners in Garason, is to be killed.*'"

The soldier's mouth opened slightly, then he clamped it shut and pounded his heart with his fist once more.

"Send word to all the lords in the city, their men are to follow this order among the Garatin servants," Endure added, "There will be no Eloi-man."

★ ★ ★ ★

Salvage slipped through the ebony doors into the night, nothing felt real. The courtyard had been cleared of the mob, and darkness blanketed the city, candlelight flickering from stray windows acted for stars as the sky remained clouded. The rain fell steady now, the thunder having moved off to the east, but the occasional flash of lightning could be seen, illuminating the dark clouds with lurid orange light. The rain fell on Sal's bare head and ran down her back and arms. She did not mind, it helped to ground her, pull her back to reality. Garden's passing left a numbness to all her thoughts, one truth resurfaced again and again though; she had found the Foretold King.

Furthermore, she had helped bring him into the world that very morning! Sweet precious babe, perfect in every way, marked with a destiny too great to fully fathom yet.

Sal breathed deep. How would she convince the others? Serene would help, she could not deny Garden's words, spoken in a tongue that everyone understood, but one no one could explain. What did this mean for Theophany? How could a newborn solve his heart stain? How could the child show him how to pass through the gates of the immortals?

The cry of an infant began in the darkness of the night, soft and terribly familiar it sounded, so much so that Sal did not at first think of it. A woman's scream followed the infant, drawing Sal's attention at last. She glanced behind her at the Fort where Fav and Mid cradled the most precious child in all the lands.

The woman in the night screamed again, her voice pleading, heartbreaking, all the while the infant cried out.

Sal's heart began to race; her visions were coming to pass. The hour was nigh.

The screaming stopped abruptly, at the far end of the courtyard a figure stumbled and fell, sobbing, the woman. After her came a soldier with a drawn blade, he stood over the woman a moment, then fled. Nearby someone came to their window to look out. More screams began in the dark.

Sal's skin crawled and she backed away towards the temple doors, her last vision of a country soaked in blood and a single child's cry remaining, ran through her mind as her heart set a rapid beat. She slipped back into the temple. "Serene- we need to go," she said, keeping the doors open enough to watch the courtyard.

Serene looked up, dazed, "The temple priests are in no rush for us to leave- we should stay with Garden's body...."

Sal looked at her, her heart aching for the woman's sorrow. "We've run out of time. We must keep that child safe." She glanced at Mid, her child- *the* child asleep in her arms.

Another cry in the shadows reached their ears. Serene straightened, her face going taunt, "What's happening?"

"We must get that child to safety!" Sal glanced back out into the night, "The children of the city are being killed- I've seen this in my visions. I have heard the cries."

Serene hesitated a moment, "Close those doors!" she ordered with a point, pushing aside her grief. "Surely no one would dare come into a temple to harm the child."

Mid and Fav looked up at the woman's commanding tone- they had not heard the screams yet. The priests who had momentarily left, returned with a young man in tow who began to gather up Garden's body.

"What are you doing!? Stop that- leave him!" Serene swatted at the young man angrily. The priests spoke to her in calming tones, but their words without Garden to translate were pointless. Mid and Fav began to inch towards the door.

"No!" Sal blocked them- how could she explain!?

Fav took her arm and pointed outside and to the priests, while the priests themselves continued to try and calm the overwrought old woman. Sal guessed what was happening; they did not want them in the temple overnight.

Sal looked around, ransacking her mind for a way to keep the child safe; didn't they know what waited for them in the dark!?

The priests, still speaking, beckoned them along the corridor around the inner room, grateful not to be pushed out the front doors, Sal herded the young couple and Serene along, while Garden's body was carried. Serene's guards were on edge, uncertain what to do.

They reached the end of the corridor to the back of the temple and found a small door letting out into an enclosed courtyard, a horse and wagon waited. The gillup had also been brought there and were standing about, looking strange and foreign in the city surroundings.

"No- we don't *want* to leave!" Serene insisted, but Garden's body was carried out into the rain before she could stop them. "Bring him back!" she shrieked, and her guards moved to obey.

"Wait!" Sal stalled them, "Serene, they won't let us stay and arguing may draw attention to the child."

Serene looked helplessly between Garden's body and the child she now knew to be the Wise One, "What do we do then!?"

"We must get them back to our camp, if you demand a procession to escort you out of the city, we could smuggle them out too!" Sal explained.

Serene huffed, "How do I demand anything when they can't understand me!?" her eyes were torn helplessly to where Garden's body was being loaded onto the cart.

"You'll manage!" Sal turned away to the young couple, they watched, bewildered. Sal prayed they would understand the danger.

The priests again began to urge them out, Sal gave Serene a nod. The old woman huffed again, then began flapping her arms, and spoke in a sharp tone that anyone could understand the meaning of, "I can't just walk through the city- it's dark! Besides, my backside cannot take anymore of those gillup. Surely this rotten city can afford a little hospitality to an old woman! It's not like I won't pay for a decent carriage." she continued in this way and made a show shaking her coin pouch around and glaring until her message was understood.

The priests again tried to soothe her and the young man who drove the cart listened to them for a moment then darted out into the darkness. One hand on Mid to keep her from moving, Sal turned to Serene's guards, "Be watchful, there is death in the shadows this night. We will try to hide among you, if we are stopped- the child's presence *must* be hidden!"

Sal fixed her eyes next on Mid and Fav. "We must be careful," she said, hoping her message of caution was understood. All the while Serene continued her tirade until she was interrupted by a team of horses pulling a carriage into the courtyard, driven by the young man from earlier.

The priests pointed to the carriage, eager to appease Serene, she exchanged a look with Sal, then held her head high and directed her guards to inspect the carriage. "There is room," they reported.

Sal nodded, and ushered the bewildered couple into the carriage, Serene came behind them. The interior of the carriage was small and cramped with four adults and a child especially with Sal's spear- but she would not part with it. She leaned out the door and instructed Serene's guards to ride the gillup and surround the carriage as they went. Serene cast Garden's forlorn body one final, loving look before they rolled out of the temple's enclosed courtyard, the loss of its meager protection left Sal feeling cold.

Nothing could be heard beyond the walls of the carriage except the rain on the roof, but Sal's ears were ringing with cries of the innocent. She closed her eyes and leaned her head into her hand, the profound grief and injustice of the night dragged her into a pit. "They're all dying!" she gasped, feeling physically ill while her past visions played in her mind like a fevered nightmare, their meaning becoming painfully obvious.

"Who are!?" Serene asked, laying a hand on Sal's arm.

"The sons of Garason, slaughtered in their cradles, torn from the arms of their mothers- so many!"

"Why?" Serene breathed, "Who would do this and *why*!?"

Sal forced her eyes open and looked at Fav and Mid, huddled together across from her and Serene, clutching their son, guarding him against the unspoken threat in the night. "Because of him, because of what he will become!"

Serene murmured something to herself while her hand fluttered over her heart uselessly.

Sal closed her eyes again, she felt as though she were adrift in a stormy sea, as wave after wave sent her careening through the waters, helpless. All her visions were coming to pass, the cry of an innocent child, a city drowning in blood, but there was still one thing more; the warrior the wilk warned her of. The baine wilk; the Ancient One. Why would the Ancient

One lead her here of all places? For what purpose were all her visions and warnings if she was helpless in the end? *Was* there a reason?

The carriage was halted, the horses protested loudly while the rain masked what words were spoken in the dark. The voices of Serene's guards grew louder, agitation and a tone of warning reaching those in the carriage.

"Whatever is happening now!?" Serene muttered, but she spoke in fear, her mask of indifference and superiority long since taken from her. Someone pounded on the wall of the carriage, "Soldiers!" a voice shouted in the common tongue, making everyone jump, "they mean to inspect the carriage!"

Serene's eyes flew to Sal, but she had eyes only for the child; she had been led here for a reason.

"Get them out of the city," Sal whispered fiercely to Serene, her mind clearing of pain and narrowing into sharp focus; she was here for a reason.

Serene's guards continued to shout, while the sounds of a fight came ever closer.

"Give him to me," Sal infused her voice with all the confidence and authority she could muster, knowing her tone alone had to convince the frightened mother to hand over her child.

Mid looked at her, eyes wide, fear displayed openly as Sal held out her hands for the boy- he had not even been named yet.

"Trust me," Sal whispered, the shouting drawing nearer.

The child was placed into Sal's arms, into her care. She did not waste a moment. Tucking the child against her chest with one arm she took her spear and kicked open the door. Rain, darkness, and the surprised face of a soldier met her. Serene's guards were engaged in a tense tussle but had been overwhelmed by the city soldiers who had barricaded the road.

Sal ducked and weaved, lashing out with her spear one handed she struck a soldier, her spear head cutting into his chest armor. She drew her spear back rapidly and swung it about, knocking another over his head. Serene's guards gained the upper hand for a moment thanks to Sal's sudden attack, and she raced through them, rain pelting her face.

She slipped in the mud, caught herself with her spear, clutched the child closer and darted into the shadows of an alley, leaving the confused skirmish behind.

The child woke and gave a weak cry, Sal slid in the mud and fell to her knees, her spear rolling into a puddle as she clutched the child with both hands. "Hush!" she fretted, glancing back; no one followed. Looking up and around Sal found she was between two houses, nearby a window with closed shutters drew her attention. A bit of cloth had been stuffed between the shutters to wedge them shut. Reaching up, Sal pushed the shutters open and snatched the cloth; it was big enough for her purposes. With fingers growing numb in the cold rain, she wrapped the cloth about her and the child, securing him close to her chest, muffling his cries.

Scrambling for her spear, Sal rose to her feet and paused; the sounds of the skirmish reached her ears through the rain and drove her forward. She ran, supporting the child against her with one hand and using her spear to keep her balance. The alley led into a deserted, narrow street, keeping her sense of direction, Sal ran towards where she knew the south city gate promised escape. Her booted feet kicked up mud while rain dripped from her eyebrows and blurred her vision.

Skidding around a corner, Sal's feet splashed to a sudden halt, the skin on the back of her neck tingling in warning. A dark figure dropped from the outer wall of a small castle and landed lightly. The rain ran down the front of his tunic, washing away red splatter. His lower face was obscured by a scarf pulled tight, while his dark eyes locked with Sal's, then fell to her precious cargo. The warrior the wilk warned of?

No. This was a child slayer.

He hesitated a moment, bewildered by her presence. Even if he could have understood her, she would not have given him the courtesy of her words. Sal twisted her grip on her ebony spear shaft and in one fluid motion, hurled it forwards.

The child slayer dodged the spear, Sal expected him to, it gave her time to charge. As she drew near, she dropped to her knees and drew her throwing dagger. Skidding through the mud Sal slashed at his legs, he dove forward, only half escaping her blade. Sal scrambled about, staying low to avoid an attack, she braced herself with one hand in the mud, her dagger hilt pressing into her palm.

The child slayer faced her, on one knee, his mask having slipped, he bared his teeth at her in pain as he held a hand to his bleeding calf. She had cut him deeply. Sensing she had time, Sal rose to her feet, and looked down at him in disgust. She found a hatred in her heart; his deeds that night was beyond mercy.

Snarling savagely, he lunged at her, a glittering weapon appearing in his hand.

The constant, now soft falling rain on the tent had long since soaked the fabric and nearly everything inside was wet. The sound of the rainfall on the surrounding area would have had a soothing effect if Theophany and Vigil were merely enjoying each other's company in the solitude of the night, as it was, the ever-constant noise served only as a reminder that time continued to pass at an unforgiving rate. The warriors had made small fires in some of the tents to ward off the numbing cold that settled in with the night, but for the prince and his friend there would be no comfort that night- not for a very long time.

They squatted side by side at the entrance of a tent, the loneliness of their sleeping camp seemed to grow and encompass them like the puddles at their feet. Fortress's departure had left an open wound in the company, one that no one wanted to be the first to tend to, the question of who would be the next to leave hung about the camp like a stray dog, privately acknowledged but openly ignored.

Once everyone had settled in for the dreary night, Vigil had planted himself at the tent entrance, his gaze fixed on the city, glowing faintly in the night. Longing for company, Theoph had silently joined him, but the long minutes stretched out into an hour and still Salvage did not return.

Theoph's muscles began to ache, and he longed to rise, but somehow the action felt as though it would be a betrayal to Vig, so he remained by his side, watching. His thoughts inevitably turned to the events of the day, his fatigued emotions playing themselves out all over again in his memory.

'It is a fool's quest.' He had said to Dyna, it seemed like decades ago, but the words mocked him now. A fool's quest indeed. With apprehension and resignation, Theoph turned his hand over and gently pulled back his sleeve from his wrist; he knew he should have been surprised, but he wasn't. He supposed that's what accepting one's fate felt like.

His infected, rotting wound from the baine wilk had spread past his concealed bandages and now seemed to be reaching for his hand. On a hunch, he pulled back the stiff collar of his leather vest from Jarg. The stench of rotting flesh wafted up to him. He tentatively probed the skin below his collar bone with his fingertips; the wound had spread there too. The heart stain… he thought back to the fateful night in Fisher's Hamlet when he had been led to a secluded hut.

'Some will not believe until they have seen. Others will not see, until they believe.' Voy, the child with the enchanted mirror had said solemnly before delivering the words that changed Theoph's life, '*the mirror reveals the state of your soul; it is plagued by a heart stain. You are the vessel that is broken.'* For the first time since hearing those words, Theoph wondered if his heart had always been stained. He had blamed the child, and cursed the day he left Verlynn Nel, but now, at the end of his fool's quest, he wondered if he had always in fact been stained. Perhaps they had misinterpreted the sea's prophecy about him, perhaps he was never meant to be a 'God Bridge', but rather, furthest from it.

"We'll find a cure," Vigil's sober tone invaded on his introspection. Vig did not take his eyes from the city and spoke with certainty. "I have not stood by my prophesied king all this time only to see him fade away before fulfilling his destiny."

Theoph snorted softly, "You've always had more faith in me than I. Even when my very flesh rots away you do not falter."

"I have faith in the power that predestined you. I have faith in the promise of your future."

Rainfall filled a painful silence between them.

"I am only a man Vig, and a poor one at that."

"Yes."

The single word was hardly loud enough to be heard, but Theoph did hear it, it nestled into his soul, only time would tell if it would wound or heal him.

The rain began to taper off, and a shift in the clouds overhead revealed the moon, large and bright, lighting up the camp in silver hues. A bit of movement from another tent entrance caught Theoph's eye. The Garatin vagabond who had given Fortress directions and then sought shelter from them held out his hand to test the steadiness of the rain. His pale features so much like Garden's, the two men even had the same quietness about them. Theoph absently wondered if all Garatin's were similar.

The vagabond, who had introduced himself as Guild, withdrew his hand and ran it down his chest to dry it. It was a scarred hand, but his movement was smooth- graceful even, not at all like Garden's hesitant and unsure movements. The observation caught Theoph off guard; it triggered a much different comparison in his mind that he did not know what to do with and left him with a feeling of unease in the back of his consciousness.

Theoph's gaze shifted to Vig's hands, hanging out before him, his forearms resting on his knees. Vigil's hands were scarred too, from failed knife throwing tricks with Sal. Theoph opened his mouth, but his words froze when his ears picked up a new sound in the night, the sound of a carriage.

Vig heard it too.

Turning off the road and rumbling over the grassy ground to the edge of the camp came a closed carriage, and riding the trusty gillup, Serene's guards acting as escorts. The sight of them in the now misty rain and silver moonlight seemed to lift a great weight from Theoph's shoulders, but he also realized that Lady Serene still had to be told about their fruitless search and this brought its own burdens.

A stranger with pale skin drove and halted the carriage, he watched nervously as Vig and Theoph approached. Before the guards could do so, the carriage door opened and Lady Serene herself exited with an air of urgency.

"Is Salvage here yet!?" Serene demanded when her sweeping gaze found Vigil.

"Why would she be?" Vig retorted, looking past her to the carriage where the young Garatin couple emerged, strain and fear emanating from every movement they made.

Serene inhaled sharply and wrung her hands, "Something has happened."

Theoph frowned, his earlier unease growing; Garden and the newborn child were also missing.

Vigil realized this at the same time. "Where is Garden?" he asked, a sharp tone creating an edge to his words. "What's happened?"

The young Garatin woman spoke then, her foreign language sounding like nonsense, but her tone of hysteria was unmistakable; she addressed Serene who looked utterly helpless.

Another, calmer voice answered in the Garatin tongue. Looking back Theoph saw the vagabond coming forward, he and the couple exchanged words at a rapid pace before he looked at Theoph and Vig, "Child…?" he said, looking for more words in the common tongue, a strange twist of emotion distracted Theoph from answering.

"Serene- what happened!?" Vig demanded.

"We took Garden to the Garatin temple to- to-" Serene's voice caught on a sudden sob, "He's dead!"

Theoph looked sharply to Vig; a look of disbelief crossed his friends face, followed by a wave of sorrow. "Where is Salvage?" Vig pressed after a moment.

The young couple again spoke, growing more panicked, their eyes turning back to the city.

"Her child-" the vagabond tried again but was silenced sharply by Vig.

"Yes, I know! Serene, where is Salvage and the child!?"

"She took the boy," Serene offered, tears were flowing freely down her face, or it was only the rain, Theoph could not tell.

"Why?" Vig was no longer quiet and spoke above the young couple's growing panic while Serene shrunk back from him. Her guards stepped closer while those in the camp woke and drew near.

"Her visions have come true," Serene flung her hand back to the city, "the city has gone mad, and the soldiers are killing all the babies! It was terrible- they detained and searched our carriage twice!"

Theoph's heartbeat stalled, and his mouth hung open, "Killing the babies?" he questioned, but everyone was speaking now, and he only added to the cacophony of voices.

"She took their boy to save him," Serene added, raising her voice above the others, they all finished whatever it was they were saying and heard Serene's last word. "Sal took the boy to save him," she repeated.

They were silent.

"Where is child?" Guild, the vagabond asked in the silence.

"With my wife," Vig answered, "She'll die before harm comes to him."

Guild hesitated, a heavy frown on his face, then he spoke to the young couple, they remained anxious but spoke no more. Theoph realized then that Dire had silently joined them, if Fortress had not left, Theoph was sure the giant would have added a good deal more noise and confusion to what had just happened.

"I left one of my guards outside the city," Serene explained, trying to regain a bit of calm and failing, "But I don't see how Sal could get past the city gates now- they weren't going to let us out at first! Someone from the palace must have been informed and guessed that I was part of your company- you did get to the palace, didn't you?"

"Indeed, we did, and have much to tell," Dire volunteered when both Vig and Theoph remained silent. "Let us do so next to a fire," he gestured towards one of the tents where the glow of a fire tempted them closer.

The carriage interrupted the moment as the driver pulled away, anxious to leave the camp of foreigners. Serene was handed her staff by her guards, and she gripped it fiercely. Guild spoke to the Garatin couple and herded them towards the tent Dire had shown; it struck Theoph as odd that the man had understood what was spoken. How did a vagabond learn any of the common tongue when the country's own king could not speak it?

"Wait," Serene stalled Dire and Vig from turning away. "There is more that happened." Serene's hand fluttered over her heart nervously.

They were all momentarily distracted when Lady Roam darted from her tent and past her nitora to join them. She clung to Dire and watched them with wide eyes, her unveiled face hiding nothing. Dire tried half-heartedly to send her back.

"Before he…" Serene spoke on, growing distraught again "before Garden-" she couldn't make herself say it again, "He prophesied!" she whispered at last, "we were in the temple and the child was being blessed or something- then Garden began to speak in a language that in all my life I have never heard before, but I understood every word, we *all* did!"

Theoph glanced at the others, trying to decide how to react to the old woman's story; everyone listened- captured by her words, the moonlight shining off the misty rain on their faces.

"He named the child- Fav and Mid's child, the one born in our own camp not one day ago, as the Wise One, the Foretold King, the Prince of the Dawn and Dusk and the warrior we have all been searching for!" Serene caught her breath and waited for everyone to respond.

Theoph felt dizzy, like standing on the edge of a cliff. The events of the day came pressing in like the riots of the city while, the words spoken to him by the Garatin king assaulted him, he could not later have said how the others reacted.

"Believe me I know what you think- I, myself, refuted the notion! How could all those we seek possibly be the same person- a newborn child much less!? But I can not deny the power with which Garden spoke…" Serene faltered and looked around at them, "It is beyond me to fathom- but I know it to be true; the one I have sought my whole life was born yesterday in my *own* camp!"

"That baby was the Prince of the Dawn and Dusk?" Roam asked in awe and confusion, Dire picked her up, the action very much like a father protecting his child in a moment of uncertainty.

"You must believe me," Serene entreated helplessly.

"I do!" Theoph managed, surprising himself. Vigil caught his eye, his own bewilderment mirrored back to him in the warrior's face. "Yet how can this be?" he breathed.

"King Radiance said the governor would not allow anyone to rise to power," Vigil murmured, his brow furrowed deeply. "Our presence proved their prophecy was coming to pass; and now they are slaughtering the children…" the horror of the situation written across his features. "Salvage," he whispered.

"THERE!" Guild called sharply, he had returned from the tent to stand beyond them, furthest from the camp, unnoticed and silent, and now he pointed across the land towards the city. The thudding of hooves reached their ears.

Vigil passed through the others, one of his throwing knives appearing in his hand, Theoph hurried to catch up to him while Serene's guards spread out. But it was the vagabond, Guild who would first meet whoever came.

Over a hillock, stocky and out of place in the silver landscape came a single gillup, bearing two riders, a spear with an ebony shaft was carried by the one in front, but it was the ebony locks of hair flying behind them from the second rider that betrayed the presence of Salvage.

No one spoke, their hopes and fears too vast to speak through as Serene's guard brought the gillup to a halt, the beast pranced nervously and shied away from Guild as he approached ahead of the others.

* * * *

The moon had risen in the west, and so cast all the faces before Salvage in deep shadow; she longed terribly to see them plainly. A man met her and Serene's guard ahead of the others, even in the shadows Sal could make out his pale Garatin skin, he reached up for the child anxiously, as only a father should. With an arm aching in fatigue, Sal surrendered the precious child into his father's waiting arms, then climbed off the gillup.

Vigil and Theoph had now reached her, to their left were Serene and Dire, Lady Roam held in his arms. Sal could tell by their faces that Serene had already shared with them what they had discovered. "We found him," she breathed nonetheless, the wonder of it all like warm sunshine after a lifetime in the dark.

"Your visions," Vig answered, just as breathless, "They have all come to pass."

Sal lifted her hand to her face and touched the cut the warrior in the night had given her before he met his end. His blade had slashed across her cheek, mere inches from blinding her, and cut off the tip of her right ear. It had bled terribly, and her neck and hair were sticky. It did not matter; she had saved the child from her visions at last. "Yes, even the warrior…" even as she spoke it, she realized that she had not shared the details of her last vision with them. Worse still it seemed she had forgotten the warning the baine wilk had given.

'A warrior will come to you in your hour of need,' the wilk had warned, *'Death stalks his steps, but I have claimed him.'*

Death indeed, but how had the wilk claimed the man she had left dead in the street? Sal's eyes were drawn away behind Vig and Theoph to where the child's mother came from a tent, worry and relief on her face, but she was not alone. Her husband, the child's father, was at her side.

To whom, if not him, had Sal surrendered the child to?

A dull roaring in Sal's ear masked what she assumed was a strangled gasp from Serene and Vigil's sharp intake of breath. They and Theoph flinched, horror and disbelief on their faces as they looked past her.

Sal turned- she could not turn fast enough. The Garatin man had stepped back from them, the moon now clearly illuminating his face- a stranger's face. He held the child one handed against himself, tightly, while in his other glittered a wicked dagger, poised to slash at any who came near, or to stab the child held against his heart.

Chapter 20 God Bridge

"Do not come closer"' Wilder warned, his voice in the common tongue sounding harsh and foreign to his own ears, "Hold back your men while the child yet breathes."

The old woman waved frantically at her men who had flinched into action the moment Wilder's dagger was drawn. To fight them all could be the last thing Wilder ever did, right after killing…

The child stirred in his arms, but he did not dare glance down. He did not fear a moment of distraction, rather he feared to look at the newborn, small and helpless. He feared his resolve would not hold.

"Give me the child," the woman with the bleeding face pleaded fiercely, her arms outstretched. Wilder retreated another step, conscious of the uneven ground.

"What are you doing!?" the one called Vig asked, betrayal in his tone, he brandished a throwing knife; Wilder wondered who between the three of them would be the last to die.

"This child cannot be allowed to live," Wilder offered them the courtesy of an explanation, it was all he could do to appease his heavy heart- it was not enough.

"Guild." This time it was the prince, the one whose namesake meant God Bridge. Wilder's fake namesake sounded hollow in his ears, yet to be called by his real namesake would be worse still. Guild was a stranger to him, an assassin, a child slayer. Wilder belonged to Eam and to much grander things; it was Guild who lived this night, perhaps Wilder would never live again.

"Please, return the child to us," the prince raised a hand as though trying to calm a wild animal, "He is more important than you can imagine!" He took a tentative step forward.

Wilder retreated the same distance, his eyes keeping watch of the old woman's men who moved restlessly and alert, waiting for a chance to attack.

"He is the fulfilment of too many prophecies to count- he must live!" the prince entreated, "He is the Foretold King, the Wise One, the reincarnated Prince of the Dawn and Dusk- he is even the fulfilment of *your* people's prophecy! The god bridge- the-" he hesitated, searching for the right word, "The Eloi-man!"

Wilder snorted with bitter scorn, "The Eloi-man is a child's fable. One that will destroy this country; he can not be allowed to live."

"You cannot know that for certain- he could save all the lands for all you know!" The prince challenged. Behind them, what must be the mother and father dared come closer, it tore at Wilder's already wounded heart.

"I have my orders," Wilder whispered, clinging to that last thread, while the price of loyalty felt like an iron anvil hung about his neck. Uninvited, the face of Anifest came to his mind, the way her eyes had widened, and her breath caught when she realized death was nigh.

The child woke in his arms, tiny arms reaching up in jerky uncoordinated movements, his head turning into Wilder's chest. Guild would have to be the one to kill the child, for Wilder knew he did not have the heart to do so. Or perhaps it was that Guild had no heart.

"Your orders are wrong," the prince uttered, authority and certainty grasping Wilder's attention firmly. "And you know it." Theoph had taken another two steps forward.

Wilder found he could not raise his dagger to ward him off, the blade had become too heavy to hold aloft. What had he become?

"Give me the child," the prince said, stepping closer still.

Wilder lowered his dagger completely, his eyes drawn to the child who had grown still once more, resting peacefully in his arm. Rooted to the spot, Wilder found himself handing over the child.

The prince backed away, relief relaxing his intense features, but Wilder had eyes for only the child; no one needed to know of the orders he broke that night. No one.

He stood alone and apart, watching as the child's mother and father reclaimed their child, their tears, and sobs of relief unhidden; they were so young. Wilder felt incredibly old.

★ ★ ★ ★

Mid and Fav clutched their child to themselves, stroking his face and crying over him as they melted to the wet grass. They were safe now. Lady Serene leaned over them to look down at the child, while Dire allowed Roam to see as well. Theophany deliberately turned his back on the would-be assassin to gaze at the child. It didn't matter, all of Serene's guards, the nitora and the Verlyance warriors -who had all woken and gathered by now- created a protective barrier, their unfriendly eyes ever on the lone Garatin man who watched with an unreadable face.

Vigil kept his own eyes on Guild, his throwing knife still handy, although he was not sure it would be much use against this man. He could tell from the way he handled his own weapon that he could just as easily pluck Vig's knife from the air as Vig could himself. How had he been fooled!? How had he not seen this man for what he was?

Breathing deep to release the tension of the night, Salvage stepped close to him and rested her head on his shoulder. Vig put his free hand around her and spared her a glance, she would always be beautiful to him and the sight of the cut across her face enraged him.

"Where is Fortress?" Sal asked suddenly.

"Gone; he felt his Warlord couldn't possibly be here."

"More's the pity, I think, if he had stayed, he would have found something greater still."

Vig could not help but look at her. How was it all their travels, everything they had gone through, had brought them to this?

"In all my visions I've heard him cry," Sal whispered, "The truth seems too obvious now." The moonlight faded as the gap in the clouds closed again.

"It is the governor of the country who wants him dead," Vig shared solemnly.

Sal looked sharply in the direction of Guild and inhaled sharply, her body tensing.

The would-be assassin was gone.

They kept guard all night long, the different warriors and guards gladly taking turns to watch over the child for whom all their toil was for, but they never saw Guild again. The superstitious whispers of 'phantom' were heard more than once through the night.

The child and his parents slept in Serene's tent, her humble invitation coming as something of a surprise to Vig, and he and the others took turns standing close guard. Left alone with his thoughts in the long hours of the night, Vig wrestled with waves of loneliness and sorrow. The end of their quest was far from what he had hoped it would be. It was then that he realized he had long harboured the hope that once they found the Foretold King that Vig could ask him why he had always been denied the presence of the gods. Why he had been shut out. Now it seemed it would always be an unanswered question.

The hour before dawn found Theophany gazing back at his reflection in the mirror shard from Voy. What would become of him? He could not return to his people like this- how could he hold his head high knowing he was only a fool? Everything he ever did would seem foolish after finding the Foretold King.

There was muffled noise from outside his tent and a hush of whispered voices. Theoph sat up straighter, straining his ears.

"Just what's going on here!?" Serene's sharp tone questioned, suddenly loud in the silence. "What do you mean by sneaking about before dawn!?"

Theoph crawled to his tent door and cautiously peered out.

The Garatin couple stood, child in his mother's arms and bundle of belonging in hand, cornered by Lady Serene, Sal and Vig.

"They are leaving," Sal explained calmly, "I have seen it in a vision."

As Theoph watched, others from their company crawled from their tents and gathered in the gray light, including the warriors of Verlyance. Lady Roam's unveiled head poked from her tent, only to withdraw quickly and a few moments later reappear, this time veiled and with Dire.

"Leaving?" someone questioned in vague alarm- nearly the whole company had gathered now.

"None of us can linger here much longer, least of all, them," Sal explained.

Theoph inhaled sharply; he thought he would have more time with the Foretold King! He cast his eyes about his tent in search of his cloak; he could not step out before the others without it. His heart stain had spread beyond his bandages. His warriors would have to be blind not to notice if he stepped out uncovered!

But the cloak was nowhere to be seen! Instead Theoph's eyes snagged on the pouch of jewels he had so faithfully carried. "Wait!" Theoph called sharply and hurried from his tent.

He stood for a moment, trying to ignore the gaze of his friends and warriors alike. Eyes widened and hands covered surprised mouths. His warriors exchanged wordless glances and Vig made a step toward him. Swallowing a lifetime of pride, Theoph met the shocked gaze of his people; now everyone knew the truth. He was no immortal.

Theoph moved forward, feeling breathless, to stand before the young couple. "They can not understand my words," he said loud enough for everyone to hear, "Only my actions."

Theoph knelt, his chest rising and falling heavily as he gazed up at the sleeping child in his mother's arms, just a day old. He imagined how his father would have reacted if he had been there. "I have come across sea and wild lands, over and under mountains to kneel here before the Foretold King," here he paused and forced his mouth to pronounce the name he had heard. "The Eloi-man, to offer an alliance as my father bid me," he bowed his head shamefully. "I see now what a useless thing that is. These treasures of Verlyance might, at least, be of some use." He offered up the jewels.

Mid, the humble, simple mother and her husband Fav accepted the gift, their faces pale as they tried to grasp what was unfolding.

"I am only a man," Theoph said with difficulty, then in his own native tongue, "if Tylus exists, he made a mistake, for I am far from immortal."

His warriors stirred, and Theoph feared to look at them. Taking a deep breath he finished, "My loyalty and life I pledge, such as it, to the Foretold King."

There was a moment of silence, then to his everlasting relief, Theoph saw from the corner of his eye, Vig and Sal lower themselves to kneel in the grass. Then, one by one at first, the warriors of Verlyance did likewise, every single one, following the example of their prince.

Theoph closed his eyes, but the morning still had more wonder to offer.

Dire spoke in the language of his people and in response the nitora called out sharply in unison, then dropped to their knees. Dire knelt and whispered tenderly to Lady Roam. She hesitated, glancing at the babe, then stepped forward, alone, her bare feet padding softly over the trampled grass. Theoph made way for her to stand before the couple and the unexpected Prince of the Dawn and Dusk.

She lifted her veil, her unnaturally pale face shocking next to all the dark ones and her red eyes flashing in the gray dawn light. To Theoph's bewilderment, she lifted a fold of her strange white dress and withdrew a curved dagger, its sheath and handle beautifully crafted. Solemnly she bowed and lifted the dagger up as a gift to the child.

Again, Mid and Fav accepted the gift. Theoph did not know it, but it was the knife that the Niben had expected the Prince of the Dawn and Dusk to accept his perfect sacrifice with.

Bewildered, Theoph risked a glance at Dire and was surprised to find the large Niben man weeping silently with emotions too complex to fathom.

Serene made an indignant sound and waved impatiently at her guards, "You had better kneel too! It seems like the thing to do." She fidgeted awkwardly, "I'm not used to this you know," she explained in a flustered manner. "Fairthin doesn't have kings and such…" straightening out her clothes she stepped forward with all the dignity she could muster. She lowered herself to kneel, "I have waited all my life, dedicated my waking hours in the search of The Wise One. Never did I dare dream I should live to find that which I sought. Then, in the winter years of my life, I discovered that the days of the Wise One had come. Still, I thought surely death would take me, for who am I that I might find myself here." She looked about herself with irony.

"The foolish seek what they do not understand and turn away when they have found it, for that same lack of understanding. Yet the wise read the signs and recognize them when they occur. Surely, I will be accounted among the foolish for not comprehending the events that unfolded beneath my very nose. Yet I shall die a satisfied fool knowing I have knelt in the presence of the Wise One. Please, accept this, a most humble offering; the accounts, stories and prophecies I have amassed that foretell the days of this child."

She held up her most precious book, the one that never left her side through all her days and surrendered it into the hands of peasants that did not understand its true worth.

Mid and Fav were weeping now, and the child woke, his little hands reaching up and out followed by a throaty cry.

When dawn came, the sun shone clear and strong, contrasting the previous day's storm and downpour, the earth was heavy with water and the roads had long since turned to mud. It did not affect Mid and Fav, they set out across the grasslands, southeast, avoiding the roads and cutting through the outer fields of Garason. They carried one of the few Garatin baby boys left living in the land, and from the way they held him, they knew he was far from safe.

Vigil stood on the edge of camp, watching as the young couple faded into the horizon, with him stood Sal and Theoph, the former with tears in her eyes while the latter watched with a long absent peace. Lady Serene, Dire and Lady Roam also stood with them. The old woman held her head high, banishing the vulnerable emotions of earlier while Dire held Roam, perhaps a bit tighter than before.

"Could we not help them more?" Serene asked.

"It would only draw attention to them," Vig answered quietly, "if the governor and king sent one man to watch us, it's likely there'll be more."

Serene grunted but said no more.

"They won't be alone," Sal added softly, her unshed tears glistening in the morning light. "I was shown that they would have a guardian in their travels. The child will live, and one day return to free his people and then all the lands."

"Fairthin will be ready for that day," Serene nodded staunchly, "I shall make sure of that! I will go back and share what I found. I will fill books and tell anyone who will listen. Fairthin will be ready for the return of the Wise One."

They were quiet, after a moment Vig allowed himself a grin, "Speaking of books, how much help do you suppose one written in a foreign tongue will be to that child." He nodded in the direction of the receding couple.

Serene's head whipped around to fix him with rageful indignation, she opened her mouth but could only sputter.

Sal gave Vig a reproachful elbow in the ribs.

"I did wonder about that myself," Dire added, his stone-like expression cracking slightly to betray his own humor.

Serene's face turned a reddish brown in a rare flush and she raised a hand to cover an embarrassed smile. "Shame on you; I could die of mortification!" she muttered, trying to regain her composure. "The book will make them comfortable wherever they settle as long as they sell it to the right person. It is a shame they may well never know the book is about their son though."

Vig continued to smile to himself, knowing full well how much the book meant to Serene and what it meant that she had given it away. His smile faded when he thought of Garden.

Behind them the sound of their camp being packed up drew Serene and Dire away; they would be returning to the west now, as quickly as they could.

"I suppose we may never know for certain what the child grows up to be," Vig murmured, wishing again he could have certainty over such matters the way Sal did.

"*I* am certain," Theophany said, his voice thrumming with excitement, after a moment he turned and faced Vig and Sal, his face was near glowing.

"My father sent me to find a king of war, while I hoped to find a man who could teach me to pass through the gates of the immortals. I guess it is true; I could not see that which I sought with my eyes closed. The baine wilk revealed to me in the tunnels under the mountain that I was a broken man. I think I am remade now." He rolled up his sleeve and pulled back his bandages. His rotting flesh was restored. The heart stain was gone.

Sal reached for his arm to inspect it, while Vig met Theoph's eyes; the prince was at peace.

Mid and Fav rested little as they fled the country of their birth, sneaking past the town of Hirfly in the night. They did not stop till they reached the Corfin forest, even then they were ever on alert, wary of bandits and other dangers. Only when they reached the wild lands on the east of the forest did they breathe freely. From there they traveled north along the Byla river.

Had they only known the danger they brushed so close with every day, they would have heartily thanked their hidden guardian. For Salvage was right. Warding off bandits by night, preparing their path by day was a shadow, a phantom, one who felt he had a debt to repay. The bandits who crossed paths with him never knew another dawn, and word raced through the forest that any who dared to lay a hand on the Garatin couple, would be cursed.

Mid and Fav had realized that they were not alone, for many a night and morning they would discover a four horned deer, or a pair of rabbits skinned and ready to cook. But they never knew where their help came from. When they reached the Quy Marsh, they met a young Garatin man who helped guide them to a band of Marsh folk who welcomed them. The man never shared his namesake though and they never saw him again. Nor did the city of Garason see that man, not for many months, not till he found the courage to return. He carried with him the memory of a lonely country to the east, free of Tarva's control.

★ ★ ★ ★

Sea birds soared overhead, lifted aloft on a tangy salt breeze that buffeted the shoreline and shook the trees. The mid-afternoon sunlight laid visible the oddly comforting sight of Fishers Hamlet, while out in the bay boats bobbed in the sea that would take Theophany and his company home at last. Climbing the rocky ridge, Theoph could see the rest of his company resting on the banks of the river. Some of the Verlyance warriors made their way to the seashore and wet their feet happily, but none seemed to pray; they had given their loyalties to another.

Ahead on the white stone marked path, Vigil paused and saw his warriors as Theoph had done, then he continued to lead the way, Sal took up the rear. None of them spoke, to do so seemed wrong, as though words would only spoil their task. The first time they had taken this path they had nearly lost their way in the dark, but now they could clearly follow it and soon the humble hut they were destined for came into view.

The old woman whom they had mistaken for the Ancient One was squatting beside a fire and deboning a large fish. She looked up as the three travellers approached, her eyes widened, and she jumped up flapping her hands in excitement.

Theoph found himself smiling with Sal and Vig as the old woman greeted them with excited grunting. Her toothless grin revealed that she was also missing a tongue, but this did not hinder her in ushering the three into the hut. There was no one inside and at the wordless insistence of the old woman they sat on the floor, Theoph in the middle.

The old woman left, and a peaceful silence took her place. Nearby a bird lifted his song into the blustery wind. The prince closed his eyes and breathed deep the sea air, his thoughts turning to their return through the mountains, neither as swift nor as uneventful as they had desired, but they had come at last to the sea edge. Theoph opened his eyes at the sound of someone approaching.

The linen door was pulled back and the child Voy beheld them with excited eyes. Voy's dark skin and pale eyes were unchanged, but Theoph detected that Voy had grown a few inches and Theoph wondered suddenly if Voy was a girl or boy- he could not tell.

"The Ancient One told me you would return; but I didn't know when," Voy said, entering and sitting cross legged before them, a childish energy that was missing the first time they met seemed to bubble from the child, shattering the illusion that Voy was otherworldly. Theoph allowed himself a small grin; Voy was like him, bound to their mortality, yet called to something greater.

Voy took a breath and the calmness that marked them as otherworldly returned, "You have found the Foretold King."

"Indeed, it was as you said, I was blinded to what was before me, but now I have seen," Theoph answered humbly.

"Take care that you do not forget, you have been shown many things, none of them were meant as cheap affirmation or finite revelations." Voy spoke sternly but kindly. "The path before you is as treacherous as the one behind and you will still have need of both the Seeker and the Believer."

Theoph waited in the silence that followed, facing his doubts and fears before rising above them at last, "What would the Ancient One have me do?"

"What did the sea stars once promise?" Voy paused looking deep into Theoph's eyes. "One day you will be the king of your people, under your rule Verlyance will unite the islands in a time of peace and prosperity like none other."

Theoph frowned, "I have yet to see the sea god's power at work-why then should the sea's prophecy about me be true?"

"Even the sea must answer to the Ancient One; as all must. Will you?"

Theoph glanced down and gripped his hand, remembering the rotting flesh that had plagued him. "I believed it was my destiny to unbind myself from the way of mortal men and ascend to the gates of the immortals. I Thought that the Foretold King was one who had done such a thing and could teach me." Theoph looked up and met Voy's gaze, "But I am only a man, just as the Foretold King will one day grow to be; bound to our mortality, tasked with being a bridge to the gods for our people." His voice quivered with conviction.

"How close you are to understanding," Voy replied softly, "like the blind comprehending a sunlit sky. Yes, the Foretold King, known also as The Wise One, the Warrior and even the Prince of the Dawn and Dusk, *is* bound to mortal ways, but it was not always so. The Foretold King is the son of the Ancient One, tasked with and freely accepting a path that has led him beyond the gates of the immortals and bound him in human flesh."

Theoph held his breath, thinking over all he had seen, understanding at last.

"Please," said Salvage softly, "Might we know the namesake of the child whom we sought?"

Voy locked eyes with hers, "He will have many names. God Bridge is one translation, Eternity is another."

★ ★ ★ ★

Vigil and the prince began to descend the path, but Salvage hesitated and looked back; the old woman was standing with Voy, her arm around the child's shoulder. Voy held Sal's gaze unblinkingly. Sal turned away, a smile on her lips as she traversed the white stone path, a bird song to accompany her. At the bottom of the hill, Theoph and Vig were waiting for her and together they turned away from the town of Fishers Hamlet and crossed the riverbank to where their company waited. No one had yet to set up tents, by this Sal knew the others had made their decision.

"Well!?" Serene demanded to know. She stood, gripping her staff, the wind blowing her cloak behind her majestically.

"Well, what?" Vig answered aloofly.

Serene pursed her lips and narrowed her eyes, "Did you find whatever it was you were looking for on the ridge?"

"You can climb the white stone path and see for yourself," Vig suggested, grinning at the ire the old woman would doubtfully send his way.

"Yes," Theoph interceded as the others of the company began to gather about. "We did find what we were after, now our path leads directly to Verlynn Nel."

There was a muted sigh of relief and then a cheer from the Verlyance warriors, all of them eager to return home.

Serene smiled sadly, "Alas then, this is where we part. Although I had once thought it would be pleasant to journey with you to your island home, such a journey would be empty without the company of those who are no longer with us."

Although Sal knew that Serene spoke of Garden, Sal could not keep her thoughts from the others who had fallen on their journey. The warriors slain in the mountains, both on their northward trek, and their return home. Rend, claimed by the griffins, his body lost forever. Even Fortress, the thought of him wandering the rest of his life in search of a warrior that he would never find, left Sal with a lump in her throat.

"It is a day of farewells," Dire spoke, his deep voice captivating even the warriors on the outskirts, beside him little Roam stood, veiled and silent like always, "For the path to the Niben Weald lays to the west, and we can not stray from it any longer, though we may wish to." This last part he said looking down at Roam.

Sal swiped away the moisture that blurred her vision; when they had come to the Honorfell Temple, their Niben companions had decided against splitting ways. Instead, they chose to continue the journey along Sentinel's Pass, explaining that they would return to their lands by traveling around the mountains on the south side of them. Even still, knowing that soon they would part did not make the moment when it came any less sorrowful.

"Only fools forbid the words of 'farewell' amongst friends, for they believe the words once spoken can never be taken back," Serene said in her most sagely tone, her head tilted high. "Let us be as the wise and speak farewell just as freely as when once we uttered 'well met', in the hopes we will yet say it again."

Forcing a smile through her sorrow, Sal stepped forward and gently clasped Serene's thin, bony arm, "Farewell, dear friend, may you never walk alone." She spoke the words from her heart, thick with emotion, "And if ever you should find enough grace to forgive me my arrogant and hurtful words in Jarg, do so knowing I will always hold you in highest regard."

Surprisingly, tears sprang to Serene's own eyes, "If there were words that better captured my feelings towards you, my dear, I would speak them now." She leaned forward and brushed a kiss onto Sal's cheek. Fighting to regain her composure, Serene patted her hand and waved her back, blinking her tears away. "As for the likes of the rest of you," she scoured Vig, Theoph and Dire with a sharp gaze before allowing it to soften with a slight smile, "Farewell, and do take care of yourselves."

Theoph bowed low towards her, showing his deep respect, "Our journey would have come to ruin without your wisdom my lady, your namesake will live on in the tales told in Verlyance."

"And in my songs," Vig added mischievously, invoking a chuckle from the warriors gathered and a rueful smile from Serene.

Theoph then turned to Dire, "Verlyance will always be indebted to you and your people for the aid you gave so freely in past months." He turned to Lady Roam and bowed again.

"Let the debt be paid now," Dire spoke, surprising them all. "I speak for all my nitora, for it has laid heavy on our hearts since we found the Prince of the Dawn and Dusk, and the truth therein." He paused, pain like never before seen in his features crossed his face, then he stood even taller and spoke with a tone of finality, "Lady Roam can never return to the Niben Weald, else we admit that she was never offered as a blood sacrifice to the

Prince of the Dawn and Dusk." His words faded and lost their conviction by the last word, choked out with emotion.

No one dared speak, or even move, the dark secret at last being laid bare. Dire turned sharply and knelt before Roam. "Your uncle the king would call it treachery and demand your father and his whole household pay the price," he explained tenderly, holding back a flood of emotion. "The peace your uncle has won in the Weald would be lost and our people would be thrown into war once more. When we discovered that a harmless babe, the fulfillment of prophecies older than the Niben itself is in fact our prince of old, and that even if he could have, he would not have accepted you as a sacrifice, for all your purity…" he bowed his head, "They would not understand."

Sal glanced around at the faces of Dire's warriors, seeing the truth and pain of their leader's words reflected in their eyes.

Dire looked up and hesitantly lifted Roam's veil; she was crying. "I *must* return to our people, and tell them that we succeeded, that the blood sacrifice was accepted. But you… you can not come with me."

A sob escaped from Roam, and she threw herself into Dire's arms. He held her close, then looked up to Theoph, "Will you, in filling your debt, take her with you?"

Theoph hesitated, Sal laid a hand on his arm to reassure him. "Yes, my friend, we will take her," he managed.

Vig caught Sal's tearful eye, she nodded. "She will live under our protection," she promised boldly, "No one but us here will know she is nobility of the Niben. In Verlyance she will only be a child."

Dire nodded and held Roam at arms length. "She will be safe," he then spoke to Roam in their native tongue. She shook her head forcefully and threw herself against him once more.

Then with strength of will, encouraged by more words from Dire, Roam turned her back and slowly crossed over to Vig and Sal. As she did, her nitora stood to attention, grim and silent.

"I vow you all to secrecy," Dire exclaimed. "If her heritage were ever found out on the mainland, her life would be in mortal danger."

Everyone bowed their heads in solemn compliance. Roam reached Sal and Vig, who took her up in his arms, she buried her head into his shoulder and Sal wrapped her arms about her husband and the girl both, her heart aching.

"And you will have good cause to return to the mainland," Serene said suddenly, managing to sound untouched by the emotions on display.

Theoph frowned, "Why is that?"

Serene plucked at her sleeve. "You were sent to make an alliance with someone were you not? Well, seeing as that someone turned out to be the newborn of a peasant, however powerful he will someday be, how would it be if you instead made an alliance with Fairthin? A trading route perhaps?"

Theoph was speechless for a moment, "Are you proposing a treaty?"

"I am. Fairthin as you may be able to guess is quite rich in the way of silver and I understand Verlyance can offer some unique items."

"As can the Niben Weald," Dire joined in.

"Very good!" Serene declared, pretending she was oblivious to the opportunity she had opened for Dire to maintain a thread of contact with Roam, not to mention giving something for Theoph to offer to his father. "I suggest that we send delegates to Fisher's Hamlet a year from now prepared to trade, or… if we so feel inclined, even come ourselves."

Without hesitation Theoph stepped forward and bowed in the Verlyance tradition of closing a deal.

Serene snapped her fingers and one of her guards brought forth parchment and quill, soon the official agreement had been written up in triplet, agreed upon and signed.

The time came to part all too soon, and farewells were indeed said freely, a spear was thanked for yet again, a griffin whistle passed onto Dire, and everyone indulged in more than one embrace; the bonds having been made over their travels refusing to be severed.

* * * *

The clear starry sky reflected on the sea surface so that the horizon was lost in a silky ebony kaleidoscope fit for a dreamscape. Salvage could have drifted in her canoe through that sea forever, but she had a destination; the island of Verlyance came upon her swiftly in the calm waters. Several hours behind her, the prince and the rest of the company followed. Sal and a few other warriors had been sent ahead to prepare the prince's homecoming.

'Tell my father, let him see to whatever details he deems fit for my landing', Theoph had instructed Sal, *'But tell Dynasty… tell her to meet me in the harbor'.*

There was more, Sal had no doubt, Theoph wished to say to his betrothed, but Sal had recommended that he keep his message short, so as to tell Dyna the important things in person.

"Have you ever seen such a beautiful sight?" one of the warriors asked as the palace of Verlynn Nel cut out a shape against the stars.

"Once," Sal admitted. She and the others paddled eagerly towards the harbor, the anticipation of setting foot on their island filling them. The harbor was aglow with stars of its own as fishermen hung lanterns over the water to attract squid into their nets. Sal and the others slipped through unnoted, as much as they wanted to call out to the fishermen, they followed the prince's orders and came home as quietly as they could.

Sal jumped onto a dock, using her ebony spear for balance, then held the boat steady as the others climbed out. "Go to your kin, try not to make a fuss about it though."

'Do not speak to Rend's kin, that burden is mine,' Theoph had said with melancholy.

Sal left the others and made her way through the sleepy streets towards the palace. She was allowed through the gates and front door with little trouble, the warriors on duty smiling broadly when once they saw her and word was sent to the king. But Sal did not wait for the king's reply; she had a message to deliver.

Going to the chambers of Dynasty, Sal waited in the hall as a serving girl woke her mistress. Salvage did not have to wait long; Dyna opened her door, her nightgown billowing about and her eyes wide.

"Salvage!" she exclaimed and threw her arms about the warrior. Sal returned the embrace gladly, tears of joy threatening to spill- Vig would call her silly for crying at such a time.

Dyna pulled back. "Theophany?" she breathed, fear, hope and all manner of emotions swirling about on her face.

"He will be here with the dawn," Sal assured.

Dyna laughed in relief and covered her mouth, "And his mission?"

"It is completed."

The two women embraced again.

The horizon ignited in glorious fire as the sun rose from the eastern sea into a day marked by Prince Theophany's homecoming. The air rang with the song of victory, new verses added to speak of Theophany's quest. It made Vigil wonder what the king expected to hear about the Foretold King- he had yet to hear what Theoph had decided to report.

Beside Vig in the boat, Roam rose tentatively to her feet to better see the crowded harbor. Vig reached out and pulled her back down before she lost her balance and fell into the water. She turned back to look at him in excitement. "What do you think?" Vig asked.

Roam could only nod enthusiastically; her life in Verlyance was going to be drastically different from anything she had yet known.

Looking up, Vig watched Theoph's back as the prince stood in the prow of the boat, one arm outstretched to his people. Beyond them, in the blazing dawn light, the king waited on the longest dock; he looked older, grayer.

Standing up to their waist in the surf, waited the warriors who had gone ahead of them, at their head stood Salvage. The silly woman was wiping away tears. Vig smiled ruefully at her as their gaze intertwined; they had come home.

Sal met the boat and guided it to the dock where the king waited. Roam stood up again and lost her balance. She tumbled into the water with a splash. Vig abandoned his paddle and jumped in after her. Lifting her up above water, the girl sputtered and coughed for a moment then clung to Vig fearfully.

"That's the last time I leave her in *your* care!" Sal scolded with a grin and looked over Roam to be sure she was alright. Together, they waded into shallower waters, the noise and excitement created a cocoon about them, leaving them to enjoy each other's company in a strange privacy. Roam recovered from her fright quickly and squirmed till Vig set her down in the thigh deep surf.

"Look at her, she's fine!" Vig defended and quickly scooped up a spiny sea urchin from the girl's path.

Sal smiled ruefully and pulled him close in an embrace. His gaze lingered briefly on the healed cut across her face and ear; no one would be as beautiful as she. Together they watched as their prince alighted on the dock and was received by the king. Theoph bowed low, displaying the humility that he had found on their return journey. Whatever words were spoken between father and son were rushed for Theoph had eyes only for his betrothed, standing nearby, face beaming in joy. Soon the two lovers were clasped in each others' arms, sharing a long overdue kiss.

Flowers were thrown into the air from the exuberant islanders and adorned onto the homecoming warriors as they each ran to their kin.

Vig was overcome with emotion, his heart feeling swollen like it was too full. Sal leaned against his chest and together they watched as Roam looked about in wonder, her pale face and red eyes taking in every detail.

Vig laughed suddenly, "We have a family!" He looked down at Sal, knowing she had longed for such a thing as much as he.

Everyone's attention was arrested when the water just beyond the bay exploded and a great hooked shell surfaced. There were frightened then astonished cries from the onlookers, Dynasty pulled away from Theoph's kiss and gasped, but the prince and all the others who had journeyed north recognised the creature as the one they had seen in the fog off the mainland, and they smiled in wonder.

"Does that mean we are still smiled upon?" Vig asked, drinking in the awesome creature as its head reached high into the air then rested in the calm sea. Sal did not answer and Vig glanced at her.

She held his gaze steadily and fought to keep her smile from spreading too far, sudden tears glistened in her dark eyes.

"What is it?"

"Something the baine wilk told me."

Vig waited for a moment, "Yes, and?" he pressed with mock impatience.

Sal's smile reached its fullest, "Yes, we *are* smiled upon."

Vig shook his head and laughed at her.

Sal joined in his laughter and pulled his head down to receive her tender kiss.

Vig would never be rid of his longing to hear the voice of a god the way Salvage did, but this he had learned; some must see before they believe. Others must simply trust to faith and believe despite it all.

Vigil held onto Salvage tight.

Epilogue

The dagger was twisted from the bandit's hand, plucked out of thin air by skilled hands and thrown gracefully where it struck a tree trunk high above where it could no longer be used to harm. The bandit tried to wrench his wrist free but was instead flung around to intercept a second bandit attacking the Garatin who dared to travel through the Corfin forest. The two attackers collided and tumbled to the leafy forest floor while their third accomplice stood alone, sword drawn to face the mysterious stranger.

The Garatin calmly removed his cloak, revealing a sword strapped to his own back, but he did not draw it, instead he twisted his cloak into a rope and held it at both ends. In this manner he deflected every deadly sword thrust and then captured the attacker, wrapping the cloak about his head tightly and taking the sword away like he had been simply handed it. He turned casually and faced the other two who had climbed to their feet, he swung the sword a few times to test it, the blade cut through the air with a whistle.

Then he came on the bandits, striking them viciously with the flat of the sword and driving them back until they turned and ran, crashing through the underbrush to escape. The Garatin watched them for a moment then drove the sword into the ground and left it quivering from the force. The bandit he had trapped in his cloak was madly trying to rip it from his face.

The Garatin withdrew a wicked looking blade from a hidden place and calmly held it to the bandit's throat. "Run and pray my blade does not find rest between your shoulders," he whispered then pulled his cloak free. The bandit obeyed. Wilderness watched him go and shook out his cloak; the forest had become overrun with bandits and cutthroats over the years. Tarva had grown lazy.

Swinging his cloak back over his shoulders, Wilder replaced the dagger from where it had come and whistled sharply, two horses, a gray dappled and a dark bay, came trotting through the trees in answer. The horses tossed their heads to communicate their distaste for the interruption of their travels.

Seeing that they were unharmed, Wilder approached a large tree and stood below its leafy boughs. "It's safe to come down now."

High above him a woman's face appeared as she leaned out over the branch she perched on.

Wilder smiled. "You didn't have to climb so far," he teased as the copper hair maiden began her descent.

"I'll remember that for next time," Eam answered, a little breathlessly and paused on the nearest branch to the ground, uncertain how to proceed.

Wilder lifted his arms to her, "I'm hoping there wouldn't be a next time."

She slid off the branch into his arms and smiled ruefully.

"Are you alright?" he asked, knowing she was unharmed, but hating that she had to watch him fight. He was grateful he did not have to kill the bandits.

Eam's smile turned honest, all her past pain and grief still lingering where once there had been bliss, "With you I am."

With hands clasped firmly, they gathered the horses and continued their westward journey, turning their backs forever on the land that had driven them to run.

They were chasing a dream.

The End

★ ★ ★ ★

Namesake Chronicles:

Heart of Stone

Heart of Lead

Heart of Ashes

Heart of Flesh

Author's Note

'Girl's grow quicker than books' is something C.S Lewis said, and well I know it. If you had told the little girl who started scribbling in a notebook about black cloaks and retired assassins that it would be ten years before she would print the final book in that story, I don't think she would have believed you.

Of course, when I started writing the Namesake series, I had no idea where the story would take me. I only ever started with the intent of getting a story out of my head and onto paper. The fact that friends and strangers alike have read that story, is something of a surprise to me! So, thank you.

Many of my readers have pointed out similarities in my books to a much better story found in a much better book, the Bible. I promise this was intentional. I wanted to tell the amazing story of Christ in a way that would make people think about it in a new light. So, if you ever thought that Ree's redemption in Heart of Stone reminded you of the prodigal son, or if Rizon's blindness on the road in Heart of Lead reminded you of Saul, or if the quest of royalty in search of a foretold king sounded suspiciously like three wisemen- then you were right.

However, I fear I failed in portraying in whole, the wonderful, unshakable, never compromising love of Jesus in the character of Eternity. So please, if you haven't already, read the *original* story of Jesus Christ, there was so much that I couldn't do justice to.

With that said, I believe this story has run out of words. That's it. The story that's been cluttering up my head for ten years has been told. A good thing too, I'll need room for another story.

-Rachel M Lang

www.ingramcontent.com/pod-product-compliance
Lightning Source LLC
LaVergne TN
LVHW041102080826
845145LV00007B/1661

* 9 7 8 1 9 9 9 1 4 8 5 1 5 *